KINGDOM COME

The Secret of the Blood Moons

Michael T. Brauner
Larry W. Hawkes

Gleaners Field Press

FORT LAUDERDALE, FLORIDA

Gleaners Field Press
5601 Powerline Road, Suite 205a
Fort Lauderdale, FL 33309
www.gleanersfieldpress.com

Publisher's Note: This is a work of fiction. Names, characters, places, and incidents are a product of the author's imagination. Locales and public names are sometimes used for atmospheric purposes. Any resemblance to actual people, living or dead, or to businesses, companies, events, institutions, or locales is completely coincidental.

Kingdom Come: The Secret of the Blood Moons
Michael T. Brauner, Larry W. Hawkes -- 1st ed.
ISBN 978-0-9960821-1-2

I dedicate this book to my beloved wife, Luciane,
my parents, and my friend and coauthor, Larry W. Hawkes.
Michael T. Brauner, 2014

I dedicate this book to my mother, who has always believed in me, to
my beloved children, Katie and Ethan, to my friend and coauthor,
Michael T. Brauner, and finally, to our friend, study partner and
inspiration for this book, Stephen G. Duame.
Larry W. Hawkes, 2014

"The mind of man plans his way,
But the Lord directs his steps."
Proverbs 16:9

ACKNOWLEDGEMENTS

There are several people to whom we are deeply indebted and without whom this book would not have been created:

Pastor Mark Biltz of El Shaddai Ministries in Tacoma, Washington. Pastor Biltz literally discovered the patterns of the blood moons and created a whole new worldwide understanding of "Signs & Seasons". Thank you, Pastor Biltz, for being so inquisitive and so perceptive.

Pastor Timothy Keller of Redeemer Presbyterian Church in New York City. In one of his sermons. Pastor Keller stated "History begins in the garden and ends in the city." It is such an obvious and beautiful statement, that it helped inspire this book. Pastor Keller's many books can be found online, and particularly a favorite, "The Reason For G-d."

Stephen Duame, our friend and study partner. We have literally spent over a thousand hours with Steve digging into prophecy. Our 10 -12 hour study sessions on Saturdays have become famous among our other friends who show up from time to time. Look for Stephen's first book to be on Amazon soon.

To the rest of the guys at our Saturday Bible study. Joe, Jacob, Harry, Cory and everyone else who shows up from time to time. Your love of the Word, your penetrating questions and your persuasive arguments have never allowed us to relax with what we believe but forced us to always keep digging for truth.

And finally, to our dear friends, and to a great teacher, at the Tuesday night Torah study. No one loves the Word of God more than you. You have made this journey about as enjoyable as it gets. Thank You!

CONTENTS

It isn't so much that the universal language is love, it is that creation itself is the greatest love story ever told. Creation is so elegant, so breathtakingly beautiful, that when He breathed life into us, male and female, it took our breath away. And our sense. Our good sense.

We were made male and female in His image, a divine inheritance, and yet the images we extolled and glorified were so mundane, so depraved, the divine tapestry began to fray at its outer edges and tear at His heart. The rebellion was on!

And so, my fellow rebels, how does this story end? Remember, this is a love story. It not only ends well, but it never ends. History does, however. History ends. And we know the end from the beginning. History begins in the garden. It ends in the city.

And we know something else, my fellow rebels. Love is an adult language. We are children of G-d, to be sure. But His eternal proposition is adult companionship.

In the beginning, Adam and Eve were created as adults. They behaved as children. And our growing pains, which have pained Him so unmercifully, will end gloriously, as the fruit of His mercy. And before our *childhood* ends in the city, history intercedes.

Yes, history intercedes. History is the intersection of man's free will and the divine intention. It is a perilous intersection indeed.

The divine intention is suffused by divine qualities. Divine qualities of mercy, justice, and love are not natural to the flesh. Yet, they echo throughout creation. They await the willing soul. They desire permanent residence. They desire comprehension. They desire a life well lived, an inspired life that has eternal promise.

And when we forsake divine guidance? History may veer. It may even careen. But there is grace. Grace is the divine accommodation. And there is more…

There is the beginning. There are the heavens. The heavens will divide the night and the day. But they will also be for "signs." Signs: the sun, the moon, and the stars. The heavens are for signs. History is an intersection. G-d is saying, "This way, to the righteous!"

CHAPTER ONE

STARS OF THE HEAVEN

"Myself I have sworn", says the Lord,
"because you have done this thing... I will bless you...
I will multiply your descendants as the stars of the heaven..."
Genesis 22:16-17

"If you don't believe in Miracles, it is not practical to exist in Israel."
~ David Ben Gurion, Israel's first Prime Minister

History begins in the garden and ends in the city. In the beginning, the garden was Eden, and then the fall. In the end, the city is Jerusalem, and then eternity. G-d has declared the end from the beginning. Jerusalem, you are the eternal city, a city of destiny. You are not one of the cities of men.

The cities of men, whose glory flashes brilliantly on the plains of history. But, history is a fickle and presumptuous guest. In a moment's time, it scurries from the plains to the horizon, disappearing into the night. How the cities of men once boasted that the stars were arrayed just so, as permanent celestial ushers, guiding humanity to the halls and boulevards of these great metropolises.

But, Jerusalem, you knew their folly. You brooded. And you endured the indignities of the cursed and the grandeur of the blessed. History is your witness.

You have suffered thieves and charlatans and you have been glorified by voices so true history cannot contain them, for they reverberate in the foundations of the world.

You have been defiled by idolatry and abominable sacrifices; and you have been sanctified by the Ark of the Covenant and the Passover Lamb.

You have trembled as stallions and chariots thundered through your streets; and you have been bemused by the wonder of donkeys carrying Kings. And what glorious Kings: David and Solomon. Kings, and Kings of Kings.

Rejoice, Jerusalem. You are the eternal address of "I AM." He has returned his *firstborn* to your embrace. It will not be as in the days of old. Now, they will be with you always. You will see things. You have seen things. But you have never seen the end. Heaven is your witness.

Rejoice, Jerusalem, your sorrows shall pass into the night. Search your memories. At the appointed time, transcendent voices who whispered in your chambers, and your upper chambers, will have universal resound. The great oceans, having been released from the thrall of the moon, will shimmer in exaltation. The Lion of Judah and His celestial armies will stride down the glory roads of heaven and enter through your Eastern Gate. His are not the armies of the night, but the armies of the eternal day. History ends in the city.

But before the end, there were men. And women. There was me. There was her. There was him. There was a boy. There were secrets. Some were shared. Some were not. Some were revealed; even grandly revealed to discerning hearts. I know not how. The boy may know. I am not sure. And so it begins.

It was different then. I was on my way to becoming *David's Mighty Warrior.* The future was at hand. But, the tellers of tales would have to wait. I was a warrior who had survived the sword, and a physicist who, like Galileo, believed that "mathematics is the language with which G-d has written the universe." But a grateful nation had to be grateful in small, hushed ceremonies. Her medals were furtively awarded, and then secreted away in the locked offices of my superiors. Perhaps my death would bring remembrance. I hoped for much more.

Ancient hatreds had come to Jerusalem. And on the third day, it was united again. None of us had been confident of that. Many of us were not even confident of our survival as a state. And if the state could not survive, would the nation?

The odds were long in the run-up to the '67 war. There were two and a half million of us in those days. Less than half of the six million who perished in the Holocaust. Another Holocaust seemed to be in the offing.

The total strength of our forces, the Israel Defense Forces (IDF), was 275,000 troops. We faced a combined Iraqi, Syrian, Jordanian and Egyptian army of 460,000 soldiers. The Arabs also had a qualitative edge. They had four times the amount of combat aircraft, and double the number of tanks.

And there is nothing new under the sun. Over three thousand years ago, by the Lord's beneficence, the children of Israel were bequeathed the land of Canaan. Moses was commanded to send spies to the land of Canaan, and so he did. Moses ordered his spies to see what the land was like, whether the people were few or many, strong or weak.

Moses' spies had bad news for him. He was told that *the people who dwell in the land were strong; the cities were fortified and very large; and that the men were of great stature.*

Three thousand years later, our intelligence services, and the intelligence services of the Americans and Europeans, delivered equally bleak assessments. They told us we were staring at a rout. Gravesites were being prepared at our nation's cemeteries and national parks. Our fear had overwhelmed the miracle that was the State of Israel. Were our people bereft of the spirit of Caleb and Joshua? Our faith had been vindicated by miracle after miracle. Now it was our faithlessness that left us gripped by dread.

So faithless were our ancestors that Moses himself had to intercede for us to convince the G-d of Abraham, Isaac and Jacob that we should not be disinherited.

Faithful men did emerge in the days before the '67 war. One of those faithful men harkened us back to the days of Exodus. Rabbi Menachem Schneerson summoned all Jewish men to remember that G-d brought the children of Israel out of Egypt. It would be as it was in the days of old.

"It shall be as a sign to you on your hand and as a memorial between your eyes, that the Lord's law may be in your mouth; for with a strong hand the Lord has brought you out of Egypt."
Exodus 13:9

"It shall be as a sign on your hand and as frontlets between your eyes, for by strength of hand the Lord brought us out of Egypt."
Exodus 13:16

And so it was that all Jewish men, warriors and civilians alike, were to wear "tefillin" as a sign and remembrance of our Exodus from Egypt. Each tefillin, a small black box with straps, contained scrolls of parchment inscribed with verses from the Torah. We attached one to our head, and one to our arm.

Our spirits were lifted. Our fears were not dashed, but they were at least held at bay. The nation paused to reconsider itself. Should we fixate on the miracle of 1948, or the horrors of the *final solution*? It *was* different this time. We were armed, as in the days of Joshua and David. But would we face our Goliath with the faith of David? G-d said of David that he was "a man after His own heart." So... we would fight for our survival, and hope that G-d would uncover enough "true" hearts among us. We had been in the wilderness, and worse, far too long.

My wife, Shoshana was not completely consoled. She was faithful to G-d, and fearful for her husband.

We had very little to fear in the years leading up to the '67 war. At least Shoshana thought so. As far as the world knew, I was a physics professor at the Hebrew University in Jerusalem. Hebrew University was the fulfillment of a dream of the Zionist movement: a Jewish university in the Land of Israel. The university's first Board of Governors included Albert Einstein and Sigmund Freud. I often told Shoshana that had I been interviewed by Sigmund Freud, I might have found myself teaching at a Bedouin high school in the Negev desert. A man with secrets could unravel quickly in the midst of a withering interrogation by Dr. Freud.

It was a dream come true, and a blessing from G-d. The dream began to take shape when I became a graduate student at Princeton University. Decades earlier, Einstein taught at Princeton. After I received the news of my appointment as professor to Hebrew University, I began to ponder the thrill of devoting my life to completing Einstein's unfinished work on a unified field theory. As I would discover, the unified field theory only recorded the faint echoes of what beat at the heart of the universe. The prophet Joel was right: It is old men who dream dreams; young men see visions.

I met Shoshana when I returned from Princeton. She was a vision of beauty and grace.

My brother Aaron was eager to celebrate my return to Israel. It so happened that I received confirmation of my post at Hebrew University during the week of Passover. That year Passover ended on Friday at sundown, which marked the beginning of Shabbat, the celebration of the Sabbath. I arrived at Ben Gurion airport in Tel Aviv; it was nightfall on Saturday. Aaron insisted that we attend a Mimouna festival. The ride with Aaron gave me an hour to sleep before our entry into Jerusalem.

Before I dozed off, I remember Aaron mentioning that we were going to the home of a Rabbi who taught at Yeshiva University... and something about his daughter.

From the backseat of Aaron's car, through the lens of my sleep-induced memories, I was reliving our days together in the Israel Defense Forces. Although the same age, Aaron and I grew up as brothers.

My mother and father had escaped Germany on October 4, 1938. Their timing was good. The day after, October 5, 1938, all Jewish passports were invalidated. Shortly thereafter, my parents landed in London. But that was not the end of their journey. Early in 1939, they emigrated to the land of Israel. Later in 1939, I was born in Tel Aviv.

Those years among the Zionist pioneers were undoubtedly filled with joy and dread. Arab opposition to the Zionist project became more extreme and violent, especially in the years leading up to the creation of Israel. As the outcome of the war in Europe became clear, there was, however, a palpable feeling of anticipation among the Jewish community in Tel Aviv.

By the time we had celebrated the last day of Hanukkah on December 7, 1945, the joy among our family and friends seemed so buoyant, their voices ricocheted out of our apartment and down the nearby streets. The forced smiles of yesteryear gave way to the broader and broader smiles of a prospective Jewish homeland. It was a good time to be a six year old.

In January of the following year, it was not such a good time to be a six-year-old. The news was grim. My father, who had become world renowned in cancer research, was on his way to an international cancer symposium, which was to be held in Jerusalem. My mother had accompanied him. Their car was viciously attacked. Both my beloved parents died.

They died before the end came for a deranged and soulless enterprise known as the Thousand Year Reich. It was occultist to its core.

And, as I came to understand, its provenance, who lived even at the beginning, was not done.

I was spared because my parents had asked our dear friends, the Weiss family, if I could stay with them until the conference was over. By that time, their son Aaron and I were inseparable. After my parents' death, the Weisses adopted me, and Aaron and I grew up as brothers. Out of respect for my mother and father, the Weisses insisted that I retain the family name.

I am Isaac Singer, and I have had the "gift" of two sets of loving parents. It was a "gift" that Job would understand: *"The Lord gave, and the Lord has taken away; Blessed be the name of the Lord."*

And here I was, sprawled out in the back seat of Aaron's car, dreaming about our days in the Israel Defense Forces. The harsh truth is that, for all of us, there was no such thing as a stint in the IDF.

As our birthdays were not far apart, Aaron and I began our service in the IDF at about the same time. It was a heady experience for eighteen-year-olds. I gravitated to the special forces, while Aaron, who loved anything that could fly, was accepted into the air force.

It turned out there was an actual force behind the gravitational pull that brought me into the special forces. My parents, Benjamin and Leah Singer, had a secret.

Benjamin and Leah Singer had been active in the Haganah. The Haganah, which began in 1920, faithfully defended Jewish settlements from armed attacks until it was dissolved in 1948, after the creation of the State of Israel. My parents were killed during a mission on behalf of Haganah.

Colonel Moshe Stern, whom I later discovered served with my parents in the Haganah, took a particular interest in my military service. After a series of rigorous physical and mental tests, I formally entered Israel's special forces.

Special forces training included extensive time in the classroom. Near the end of my first year, I was told that all financial arrangements had been made so that I could complete my undergraduate and graduate education. At the age of 25, fresh from Princeton, I returned to Israel, now ensconced in the back seat of Aaron's car.

As Aaron crossed into Jerusalem, my eyes flew open. I knew that I would be teaching in Jerusalem. I knew that I would be living in Jerusalem. I didn't know it, but I would be married in Jerusalem. And I had no inkling, but I would meet (him) in Jerusalem.

Over the years, my colleagues in physics would engage in a kind of liturgy that included the oracles of technology: particle accelerators, linear accelerators, super computers, etc. They were searching for the "G-d" particle, or some such thing.

And here I was in Jerusalem. I would learn many things. Oh yes, Jerusalem would teach me the limits of a soulless pursuit of knowledge. Einstein proposed that time occupies a fourth dimension. The fourth dimension is truth. And truth abides in Jerusalem. So do secrets.

I was jostled in the back seat as Aaron suddenly pulled the car over to the nearest curb. He insisted that I get out of the car. Above all, Aaron Weiss was not prone to sudden moves, one way or another. His heart of gold was deeply embedded in a steely countenance.

I asked if something was wrong; a question I had never before had to ask. The unflappable Aaron was all at once reduced to unintelligible, staccato responses. Now...I was worried. I became overwhelmed by fear. Had something happened to my adopted parents? Was Aaron in some kind of trouble?

Through all of Aaron's garbled words, I thought I heard the word Shidduch (dating in orthodox Judaism). I put my hands on Aaron's shoulders to brace him. I told him not to worry if he was adding "Shadchan" to his rather impressive resume. Aaron gathered himself, his usual composure overtaking an unwelcome impostor.

Over the many years in which we bonded as brothers, Aaron often times accentuated a point by placing his right hand just below my left shoulder. And so it was, with his right hand in position, he simply said, "She is beautiful you know." I asked if I could at least know her name. "Shoshana." "Her name is Shoshana." I thought all of that, and all I have is a name. In truth, I was beyond relieved. As a six year old, I learned that the worst can happen.

So Aaron Weiss, intrepid fighter pilot with nerves of steel and reflexes as finely tuned as a Stradivarius violin, was reduced to a being a Shadchan, a matchmaker. I had to restrain myself from uproarious laughter. I came to understand the magnitude of the gift Aaron had given me. G-d balanced the scales. The grief of a six-year-old gave way to unmitigated joy for a lifetime.

Aaron's car finally came to rest in Bayit Vegan, a beautiful neighborhood that sits on the highest point in Jerusalem, in the western part of the city. As I pried myself out of Aaron's smallish car, my thoughts turned to my parents.

Benjamin and Leah Singer offered up their lives as a sacrifice so that this night could be repeated throughout the State of Israel. In many respects, Bayit Vegan had a quality very similar to the shtetls of eastern and central Europe.

It was a place where religious Jews could live out their lives, and their faith, blissfully and peacefully. The shtetls of Europe had disappeared under the boot of the Nazi onslaught.

The Mimouna celebration was in full bloom. The streets of Bayit Vegan were teeming with merrymaking and smiles galore. Minouna came to Israel from North African Jewry. Minouna marked the end of Passover, and it was customary for Moroccan and Algerian families to open their homes for neighbors and guests.

It took me a few steps to gather my composure. As I got my bearings, I turned my gaze to a man and his daughter who appeared to be walking towards us. Aaron quickly turned his head, as if to cough, and with his hand to the side of his face, he whispered, "Rabbi Levy."

Rabbi Levy seemed to acknowledge Aaron, but his eyes were clearly fixated on me. As they approached, I extended my hand and said, "Rabbi Levy, it is an honor to meet you, Sir." I tried not to look at Shoshana and, for a brief moment, it appeared that my greeting caught the Rabbi a little off guard. While at Princeton, I had picked up the American style of greeting, which was too informal, and too familiar, for the Orthodox community. Rabbi Levy quickly composed himself, and offered a firm and polite handshake. "Professor, welcome back to Israel," he said. Before I could speak, the Rabbi introduced me to his daughter. Shoshana offered an awkward smile and said, "Welcome, Professor."

The years in the United States did not serve me well as preparation for shidduch dating. America was self-confident, even brash. She was a country on the move, a superpower, with an appetite to match. I loved America, and its people.

But within the Orthodox community, shidduch dating was a serious undertaking. It would rather quickly lead to marriage, or the couple would decide to move on. It was disciplined. And, at its core, it valued humility and modesty as qualities that both men and women should personify.

Rabbi Levy invited us into his home. Aaron could not have been expected to anticipate my predicament. I took a deep breath. I had to regroup. I remembered that Aaron had mentioned that Rabbi Levy was a professor at Yeshiva University. Thankfully, we found common ground, and I found a safe haven until I could get my wits about me.

Our discussion turned to the Torah. I was more comfortable discussing the word of G-d than my imminent teaching responsibilities at Hebrew University. Reading the Torah was the part of my daily routine that I loved most.

Rabbi Levy and I began discussing what kind of man Moses was that he should be given such awesome responsibilities. We both agreed that it was his humility and faithfulness. In fact, it was said of Moses that he... *"was very humble, more than all men who were on the face of the earth."*

As it turned out, Shoshana's father and I also shared an interest in the prophets. Living in Israel at that time, or at any time since 1948, it was easy to fall into a discussion about the prophetic destiny of Israel, and what Israel's destiny would mean for the world. In the years to come, this would take on unimaginable proportions in my life.

Shoshana and I seemed to have orchestrated our way into a conversation. Throughout the evening we were always aware of where we were in relation to one another. And, step by step, we were finally able to arrange ourselves so that we could talk in relative privacy.

Shoshana seemed to sense that Aaron, our matchmaker, only did half his job. She had a shy quality about her, but she was masterful in showing a genuine interest in me, while filling in the details about her life.

Shoshana and I shared a sense of loss. I lost both parents, and she lost her mother. Her memories of her early childhood were colored by her mother's death. Shoshana was with her father at the synagogue when her mother was struck by a truck in a crosswalk.

Otherwise, she had fond memories of her mother and their life in Morocco. Her father was the Rabbi at a famous synagogue in the city of Fes. The synagogue was the hub of their lives. Less than a year after her mother died, Shoshana and her father immigrated to Israel.

The Book of Proverbs reminds us that "*beauty is passing.*" And so it is. But Aaron was right; Shoshana was a beauty. And her eyes, which were dark, oval and soft, were windows to a soul that was at peace. Some might say she was confident or self-assured. But it was far more than that. Shoshana's peacefulness came from a soul that rested in the palm of G-d's hand. I think I knew that night that Shoshana was my bashert (soul mate).

As the Minouna festival began to take on the subdued tones of a tiring crowd, our conversation turned to our immediate desire to make arrangements to see each other again. My schedule was frenetic and unknowable. So instead of driving ourselves to distraction, we decided to rely on our Shadchan, Aaron Weiss. Smiling, and even giggling like school kids enjoying their first crush, we enlisted the prodigious logistical skills of one Captain Aaron Weiss, Israel Defense Forces.

Aaron was not amused. But he consented. From that moment on, Aaron would be known as the "Flying Shadchan." He was not amused by that either.

Earlier, in getting out of Aaron's car, every joint in my body clanked, screaming for rest. As I left the Levy's apartment, my shoes only touched down on the floorboard of Aaron's car. Aaron looked at me and smiled. "Thank you," I said. I asked if he knew that Shoshana volunteered at Yad Vashem. "No, I didn't," he replied. Aaron sped off to our hotel.

Aaron had the foresight to reserve a room in a small Jerusalem hotel. We both needed the rest. The next day he had to get back to Tel Aviv, and I had an 11:00 a.m. meeting with the President of Hebrew University. Following my meeting with the President, I was to meet with the Dean of Physics, who would be my supervisor and, my mentor, I hoped.

I should have awoken in the pre-dawn hours in an anxious state about my job. Instead, my thoughts turned to Shoshana. I wanted to wake Aaron up so he could tell me it was not a dream. There were many things I thought I knew about her and, while I did not have any burning questions at the moment, I was sure there were facets of her I needed to know more about.

Yad Vashem, the Holocaust memorial. She volunteered at Yad Vashem. I was not bothered in the least that, as an Orthodox woman, Shoshana was volunteering her time. It is true that it was somewhat unusual but, the truth is, it endeared her to me even more.

Yad Vashem... Yad Vashem... Yad Vashem. It is a memorial to vivify memory. In the words of the Prophet Isaiah: *"Even to them I will give in My house... And within My walls a place and a name... Better than that of sons and daughters; I will give them an everlasting name... That shall not be cut off."*

But what is it that we should do... after... memory? We hoped that memory would restrain a fallen world. I never believed that the memory of evil would temper the appetite of evil. All we could hope for is that memory would stir the righteous.

Shoshana volunteered to assist the Holocaust memorial in preserving the memory of 1.5 million children who were murdered in cold blood. Eventually there would be a children's exhibit at the Holocaust memorial. First, all the painstaking preparation had to be done.

My thoughts turned to those children. Their smallish shoes in which they blissfully played children's games; their smallish shoes in which their trembling little bodies walked towards the merciless; the dolls, the prayer books, the eyeglasses and, yes, the diaries. Those children's diaries, bravely recording a child's eye view of what it was like to live inside the Gates of Hell.

The G-d of Abraham, Isaac, and Jacob keeps a diary, too. His memory is long, and unfailing. *"Truly children are a gift from the Lord; the fruit of the womb is a reward."* Our children were vanquished by the forces of perdition. They dwell close by the Father, in our Father's house. And He is the architect of perfect justice.

My pre-dawn musings were overwhelmed by a morning that rushed headlong to greet me. Aaron was up early and had to return to Tel Aviv forthwith. He knew that I would have appreciated a little more of his time to make sense of the whirlwind in which I was thrust in the last hours.

"I'll call you about your next shidduch date with Shoshana. That's the best I can do for now." I am sure that Aaron used the term shidduch to remind me that this was a "marriage dance." As if to emphasize the point, he looked at me with an admonishing eye and said, "I trust you will use the time wisely." At first I thought he was miffed because Shoshana and I had a good laugh at his expense. Even now, Aaron's new nickname, the "Flying Shadchan," brought a smile to my face. But I knew better. After the death of my parents, Aaron felt responsible for me. He wanted to subdue my anguish with as many happy experiences as possible. As if to reassure him, I took a firm grip as we shook hands and said, "Thank you, I'll wait for your call." Aaron was off to Tel Aviv.

There were still almost four hours to kill until my meeting at Hebrew University. I thought better of trundling into the President's office will all my earthly belongings. And I didn't have the money to pay a taxi to chauffeur me from one place to another. It was cheaper, I thought, to stay at the hotel for another night. Besides, I needed more rest.

It's a funny thing about war. It has its own linguistic rules. To describe a war you need a start date, an end date, a winner, a loser, and a proximate cause. If the war is especially protracted, like the Vietnam war, then journalists and others become cranky, and even hostile, about it, and simply want it to end.

Now, if you ask me, my parents died in a war. But that does not fit the template. It was a terrorist or guerilla attack in a low-level conflict. To some, my parents were unfortunate casualties in a "blood feud." In the process, the language becomes so contorted that the fundamental reality of "life on the ground" is indescribable.

In those days, and in all days, any part of Jerusalem in which we lived was fair game. That is not random violence. Nor is it a conflict, or merely a terrorist act. It is a war against every man, woman, child, and institution.

It is war, and even Hebrew University was a target. Five graduates of Hebrew University would receive the Nobel Prize. It would become a leading center of medical and pharmaceutical research, and technological innovation. No matter.

On April 1, 1925 Hebrew University opened its Mount Scopus campus. By the time I arrived, some forty years later, Mount Scopus was under Jordanian control.

With the loss of the Mount Scopus campus, Hebrew University had "improvised" facilities and classrooms in some forty different buildings throughout Jerusalem. My meeting was at their facility in Givat Ram, or so I thought.

As Shoshana was still swirling in my thoughts, I needed to jolt myself to assume the countenance of a physics professor. We could use physics to describe the behavior of objects in the natural world. Physics is incapable of describing the romantic escapades of a would be physics professor. Frankly, I was in a pathetic state. I solved my dilemma like a true physics professor. I began to read my doctoral thesis. It did the trick.

April is a beautiful time of the year in Israel. So I decided to walk the relatively short distance from my hotel to the university. I harkened back to the months it took me to finish my doctoral thesis. Somehow I thought that writing my doctoral thesis would be among the most thrilling times of my life. I was thrilled, but I was thrilled at the end of the process. I dedicated my thesis to my parents. That sustained me throughout the ordeal.

As I found my way to the foyer of the president's office, I was surprised by the informality of the decor. It was a striking contrast to the president's office at Princeton. I came to understand that there was an informality to Israeli society that permeated our institutions. Americans too were informal, but they seemed to tolerate, and even promote, a sense of majesty and gravitas in certain of their institutions, most notably the presidency, including presidents of colleges and universities. Perhaps America never quite completely shed itself of the British influence. And America exuded such a worthy self-confidence that most Americans did not really even entertain the possibility of an existential threat, even when faced with a nuclear armed Soviet Union. Israel's survival was a day-to-day proposition. It was a stark reality that robbed us from the enjoyment of many of the amenities of statehood. Israel had to live to fight another day.

I approached the secretary's desk to alert the president to my arrival. I was 20 minutes early. His secretary looked somewhat familiar to me, and she smiled as if to welcome the return of an old friend. "Isaac, is that you?" she asked. "I'm sorry if I am a little early; could you tell Dr. Bloom that Isaac Singer is here." "Isaac, don't you remember me? I was a friend of your parents in Tel Aviv. My name is Golda Eisen. You and Aaron used to come to my house for cake." I looked at her a second time and then the deluge of memories began. Aaron and I loved to visit the Eisen house because she always had all manner of desserts. We liked the cake best.

"Isaac," she continued, "I was never able to tell you how sorry I was about the death of your parents. I loved your parents, and I loved the visits by you and Aaron." I told her how grateful I was that she should remember my parents.

"Maybe you and your husband would do me the honor joining me for dinner sometime," I asked. "My husband died a few years ago, Isaac. But if you don't mind the company of an old woman, I would cherish any time at all with the son of Benjamin and Leah Singer." "Great," I replied, "it's a date then."

"Mrs. Eisen, I apologize but I would hate to keep Dr. Bloom waiting. Does he know I'm here?"

"Isaac, there has been a slight change in the schedule. Dr. Bloom sends his regrets. He was called away to another meeting. The Department Chairman, Dr. Steiner, will be meeting with you. He is in the president's office now. Please go right in."

Dr. Lev Steiner. I knew the name, and the reputation well. He was brilliant, to say the least. Lev Steiner had been nominated for the Nobel Prize in Physics, not once, but twice... so far. While he hadn't been awarded the Nobel Prize in either instance, the consensus was that it was just a formality. His work in quantum theory was groundbreaking.

As I opened the door, Dr. Steiner leapt from his chair. "Isaac, how wonderful to finally meet you. I'm Lev Steiner." I expected him to be different, somehow. He was fast becoming an icon in physics. His stature didn't necessarily lend itself to portraiture or sculpture. But that would be a problem for some unknown artist to solve in the future.

"Dr. Steiner, it is an honor to meet you. I have admired your work from afar." "Please, Isaac, call me Lev." He asked me if my feet were on the ground yet after the long trip. "Right now, I'm staying at a hotel until I know more about my teaching assignment." I asked him about university housing for professors. "Isaac, we have contacted the hotel where you're staying and secured your room until the end of this week. That will give us time to finalize the details of your assignment." I thought that was unusual. At the very least, I expected a schedule that would take me through the end of the year. This was not what I anticipated, at all. And, how exactly did he know where I was staying?

"Isaac," he continued, "I am sure this seems confusing for you." He must have seen the look on my face. "Isaac, there is another meeting that you'll need to attend this afternoon at 3 o'clock. Here is the address." He handed me a crumpled piece of paper. "The address, Isaac, is a synagogue not too far from your hotel. Take a taxi back to the hotel. Have some lunch. Go to the synagogue on foot. Don't ask anyone for directions; and don't tell anyone you're on your way to a meeting. You're taking a stroll on a beautiful day in Jerusalem. And please, walk at the pace of a sightseer; do not take the shortest route to the synagogue. Golda has a map that will show you alternative routes to your destination."

Meeting Shoshana was a disorienting experience. I was hoping that my new job would provide some semblance of stability. Now I was at the center of a whirling dervish with no prospect for respite. Perhaps this was some sort of perverse attempt at a joke, perpetrated by Aaron in retaliation for his new nickname. Would someone please tell me what is going on?

Golda could see I was bewildered. At least the map she showed me was normal. Jerusalem was still there. My hotel was still there. I was beginning to feel I was nowhere. Golda's reassuring voice was helpful. "Don't worry, Isaac, soon the pieces will fit. Your parents would be so proud," she said. "Oh, and one more thing, Isaac. Please call this number at 8:00 p.m. tonight." She handed me a piece of paper with a phone number written on it. "No sooner or later than 8:00 p.m. Do you understand, Isaac?" All I could say was "Yes." Golda continued, "Identify yourself to whomever answers the phone." Otherwise, don't speak until the other party introduces himself. Here is some money for your cab ride back to the hotel. I hope we will have lunch soon. Now be on your way; your schedule is a little tight."

My schedule is tight. My schedule is tight, and after less than 24 hours in Israel, I was thoroughly baffled. I didn't realize that my job, among other things, would be more difficult to comprehend than quantum mechanics.

The ride back to the hotel was, so far, the best part of the day. Thankfully, the taxi driver did not have any cryptic messages, and our conversation was lighthearted. I jokingly asked him if his taxi company could use any more drivers. What a blessing: to go from point A to point B without detours, and with clear signposts along the way.

I arrived at the hotel with enough time for a relaxing lunch. At this point, I had to trust Golda. She had assured that all was well. And so, rather than fret, I enjoyed my lunch and a brief afternoon nap. As far as I knew, I was still employed as a Hebrew University professor. After my nap, and a quick cold shower to overcome my drowsiness, I ventured out, trusting Golda with every step.

Heeding the advice of Dr. Steiner, I took a leisurely walk to my destination. When I arrived at the synagogue, it appeared to be closed. I knocked. To my surprise, someone immediately opened the door. She didn't bother to introduce herself. All she said was "Follow me."

We walked in single file down a rather long hallway. She opened the door to a nondescript room with two men sitting at a nondescript table. I immediately recognized one of the men sitting at the table. "Do you know who I am?" he asked. "I do. You are Colonel Stern," I replied. "Your memory serves you well, Isaac. I am Colonel Stern, and this is my dear friend, Daniel. Daniel... I have the honor of introducing you to Benjamin and Leah Singer's son, Isaac."

I felt comforted that Colonel Stern mentioned my parents. I thought to myself, how bad could it be if they knew my parents?

Colonel Stern spoke first. "Isaac, Daniel and I both served with your parents in the Haganah. They died as heroes. We are living their dream, Isaac. We have a state for our people."

He continued, "Isaac, how do you suppose the G-d of Abraham, Isaac and Jacob will help us hold off hundreds of millions of people who would like nothing better than to relegate us to a footnote in history? The odds are long, Isaac. Our population is only 2.6 million. And we can't count on 300,000 Arabs in our country to fight for us."

I replied quickly to the Colonel. I was more than just a little irritated by the pessimistic tone of his question.

I answered him this way, "We should have the faith of Abraham, and the heart of David. G-d didn't suffer us this long to see the children of Israel driven from the Land. He will send us miracles. Hasn't He always been faithful to those who are faithful to Him. Indeed, He has been faithful in spite of the faithlessness of His creation. He led us out of Egypt in a pillar of cloud by day, and a pillar of fire by night. He separated us from other creatures by suffusing us with free will and a moral nature. He gave His commandments to Moses and, in doing so, taught us to hone our moral nature to sustain a heavenly gaze. For He is the G-d of heaven."

"Every year, don't we set a place for Elijah at the Passover meal? Are we not told by the prophet Malachi that Elijah will come again to *'turn the hearts of the fathers to the children, and the hearts of the children to their fathers.'*"

"Gentlemen, there is an obsession with the Jewish people that is supernatural. I know it is supernatural because it has a voice that G-d Himself has heard. And that voice has been in the presence of G-d, telling Him that it was going... *'to and fro on the earth, and walking back and forth on it.'* Eventually, G-d will silence that voice. Until then we should, above all, remain faithful."

There was an uncomfortable pause. Daniel finally spoke. "So Isaac, you are as faithful as your parents. Your words bless their memory. We are a tiny country. I only hope you are right." Daniel looked down as his voice trailed off... "I only hope you are right," he said.

Both men seemed to simultaneously come to attention in their chairs. They were coming to the point of this meeting. Colonel Stern began, "Since the founding of our country we have made the development of nuclear weapons a national priority. We must do everything we can to prevent another Holocaust. Fortunately, we have been blessed to have talented scientists."

"Isaac, Dr. Perlman tells me you are probably the most brilliant young physicist he has come across at Princeton. As of now, our nuclear program is advanced. We need you to help us continue to make progress."

Golda was right. It all seemed to be making sense. Nonetheless, I needed them to know that I was frustrated. "Gentlemen, is that what this has been all about? You want me to help defend our country. That's..." Daniel cut me off.

"Isaac, before you give us an answer, you will need a few days to think this through. You learned at a young age that this can be a dangerous life. So, think about it for a few days." Colonel Stern knew that I already had some exposure to the program because of the work I had been doing with Dr. Perlman.

Colonel Stern was looking at me intently now. He was very earnest about what he said next. "Benjamin and Leah Singer were my colleagues, but they were also my dear friends. Think about this carefully, Isaac. Your life will be different than what you thought. And... think about Shoshana. This Thursday is Holocaust Memorial Day. I have it on good authority that for your next shidduch date with Shoshana you will be meeting her at Yad Vashem where she volunteers.

If you are able to help us, come to this place the day after Shabbat at the same time you came today. If you can't help us, there will be no repercussions. You will continue your life as a normal professor at the university. Leave us now, please. Take this on your way out."

I picked up the envelope that Colonel Stern pointed to and walked briskly through the front door. I assumed the envelope contained money, so I secured it in my front pocket before I reached the sidewalk.

I don't know why, but my thoughts turned to Aaron. Perhaps because he had been there almost from my earliest memories. I could safely surmise that Aaron chose what Colonel Stern described as "a life different than what you thought."

I was relieved to know that the life Aaron had chosen didn't change him. Above all, if I were to make a similar choice, I would never want to become cynical, or my heart to become hardened.

My parents gracefully bore the burden of defending our communities. They were not well armed, and they knew our foes were as implacable as they were ruthless. But through a child's eyes, their kindness and their loving hearts always shone through the forbidding haze of a hostile world. It is a popular belief that those who do the work of my parents operate in the shadows. I have always believed it is Evil that casts a long shadow. And when the shadows recede into darkness, the sound you hear is Evil crisscrossing the night.

When I returned to the hotel, I had a message to call Aaron. He wanted to tell me about my next shidduch date, undoubtedly aware that I already knew the basics. I was to meet Shoshana at Yad Vashem on Holocaust Memorial Day. We would then take a short walk to a nearby cafe and have lunch. I liked it. Aaron seemed to have a feel for this shadchan business. If he ever tired of being a young warrior, prowling the skies, defending his homeland, he could parachute to a soft landing as a full-time matchmaker. I felt a little guilty having a good laugh at Aaron's expense. But not that guilty.

Under the circumstances, it was good to laugh, and Aaron wouldn't mind.

Thankfully, I unconsciously put my hand into the pocket of my blazer. I pulled out a piece of paper with a phone number written on it. *What is this?*, I thought. Did Colonel Stern or Daniel slip this in my pocket as I left the meeting?

What could this be? Ah... Golda! Golda gave me this. Her instructions were to call the number at 8:00 p.m., identify myself, and wait for the party at the other end to introduce himself. I would have some dinner, a short nap, and take out a little insurance by asking the hotel staff to make sure I was up by a quarter to eight.

The banging on my door woke me from a very sound sleep. It was the first restful sleep I had since I arrived in Israel. I threw some cold water on my face, and tried to gather my thoughts. I read a short verse from the Book of Daniel and waited for eight o'clock.

As I dialed the number, I felt a certain calm come over me. Take it as it comes, I thought. Could anything really make this day any more unusual than it already was? The phone rang a few times and a somber male voice said, "Hello."

After I identified myself, he simply said, "hold please." Another voice came on the line that was serious, yet familiar and kind. "Isaac, Isaac Singer, is that you?" he asked. "Yes it is. This is Isaac Singer speaking," I said.

"Isaac, this is the Prime Minister. How are you?" I almost dropped the phone. "Isaac, are you there?" I gathered myself enough to blurt out... "Ah, yes Sir." I haltingly added... "This is Isaac Singer, Sir.

The Prime Minister now spoke nostalgically of my mother and father. "Your parents and I were in the Haganah together, Isaac. They were brave, and they were patriots. They spoke of their dream that their son would grow up in a place where he was free to live as a Jew and not be persecuted. And there is something else, Isaac. We learned later that the attack on your parents' car was meant for me. So, I owe Benjamin and Leah Singer my life."

"Isaac, what you are being asked to do is very dangerous. I wanted to personally tell you that you do not have to do this. Nobody will fault you if you decide to live the life of a university professor. If each one of us is indebted to our country, then your debt has been paid in full. Do you understand, Isaac?" "Yes sir, I understand," I replied. The Prime Minister now sounded unburdened, even buoyant. "Good, very good," he said in a confident voice.

Perhaps you and I will meet under different circumstances some-day, and I will have an opportunity to speak to you more about my memories of Abraham and Leah. For now, Isaac, I must say goodbye and good luck." "Thank you, Mr. Prime Minister," was all I could get out by the time he hung up.

There are days in your life that change everything. This was one of those days. It wasn't as if I could simply go out in the middle of a street in Jerusalem and announce to the world that I have just spoken to the Prime of Minister of Israel. Besides, I was far too exhausted, and nobody would believe it anyway. It was all I could do to get my clothes off and put my head on the pillow. I hoped that tomorrow would not bring more surprises.

I woke up thinking I was either a professor in waiting, or some-thing else. It was the something else that puzzled me. I wasn't actually going to be a full-time soldier, although I expected that I would remain active in the special forces, which I liked very much. I could certainly understand how my knowledge of physics could not only help Israel defend itself, but even deter some would be attackers.

To be sure, King David was a warrior, but he also was a writer of psalms, and a skilled musician who was asked to play for King Saul. In contrast to Saul, David was obedient to G-d. After all, it was Da-vid's idea to build a temple, a permanent place where G-d could dwell among His people.

Whatever I decided, I knew that I needed to always have a heart for G-d, like David. *"Truly G-d is good to Israel, To such as are pure in heart... My flesh and my heart fail; But G-d is the strength of my heart and my portion forever."*

I would come to understand just how much the House of David blessed Israel and all the world. The House of David would build a physical temple which could be razed by men. But it would also be the House of David that would create the conditions in our hearts to build a spiritual temple. And... it would be the spiritual temple that would usher in the Kingdom of G-d.

I thought the Prime Minister's call was the crescendo to a few days that had already changed my life. But there was more to come. My life had changed, but I hadn't met (him) yet, and I was not yet aware of the meaning of "wonders in the heavens." I was to come to understand that the lights in the heavens not only illuminated His creation but, as His celestial billboards, were adorned with the signs of things to come. And those signs were invariably tied to the destiny of the Land of Israel, and its people.

The days after the Prime Minister's call were thankfully, days of rest. I had a chance to gain some perspective on the rush of events, and actually gather myself for my next shidduch date with Shoshana. We were to meet on Yom HaShoah.

As was true of so many aspects of life in Israel, Yom HaShoah, Holocaust Memorial Day, led to a debate. Some in Orthodox Judaism wanted the day of remembrance to coincide with the Tenth of Tevet fast, which commemorates the siege of Jerusalem by Nebuchadnezzar II. Others wanted the date of remembrance of Holocaust victims to be on the day of the fast that commemorates the destruction of the First and Second Temples in Jerusalem. The Israeli Knesset chose the 27th day of Nisan, which is the first month in the Jewish calendar. In 1965, the 27th day of Nisan was on April 29th, which happened to be a Thursday. So, for our second shidduch date, I would meet Shoshana at Yad Vashem, Israel's living memorial to the Holocaust, on a Thursday.

The walk to Yad Vashem was not far from my hotel, slightly less in distance than my walk to meet Colonel Stern and Daniel. Except that during this walk, I had a bounce in my step. Whatever anxiety there might be, or should be, associated with shidduch dating, it was completely overshadowed by my "evolving" career options. What a laugh, I thought. The retiring life of a college professor turned into a swashbuckling tale of intrigue and romance. How I wished that was the choice I faced. Yad Vashem kept the names of the victims "alive" for the living, lest with the passage of time we should become complacent. Savagery would never rest. And the days were quickening.

By the time I arrived, most of the formal ceremonies had ended. I was relieved that I had been told to meet a guard at the southwest entrance to the memorial. He seemed relieved to be able to get away for a moment from the throng of people. I was taken to a part of the memorial that appeared to be a work in progress. There were many smaller rooms which circled a large space that was filled with boxes, file cabinets, and storage bins that seemed to reach to the ceiling.

I found Shoshana in one of the many smaller rooms, sitting on an uncomfortable looking work bench, slumped over a desk. She had the intense look of so many researchers I had worked with over the years. I'm sure I wore that look many times. I didn't want to startle her, so I stood quietly while she continued what she was doing. She finally looked up, saw me standing there, and didn't seem flustered at all. As she turned to stand up, a natural smile flashed across her face as she said, "It's good to see you, Isaac. Is this your first time visiting Yad Vashem?" I smiled as I told her that the Weisses, my adopted parents, brought Aaron and me here many times over the years.

I was curious about her work at the memorial. I asked her about it, and she seemed pleased that I did. She straightened up a bit, and her demeanor became serious, with a hint of resignation and sadness. Her speaking voice became slightly muted; it could not have been easy to survey the handiwork of evil on a daily basis.

"Isaac, our work here will lay the foundation for a special Children's Holocaust Memorial, which will honor the million and a half children who were murdered by the Nazis. My work focuses on the Nazi campaign against children with disabilities."

It was strangely reassuring to listen to Shoshana speak as she did about the atrocities perpetrated against the defenseless. She brought a sense of dignity and honor to their memory. Her tenderness belied the homicidal lunatics who seemed to relish the precision with which they murdered the innocent. Those of the "Master Race" were indeed masters of the deep. They emerged from the deepest parts of the depths of hell.

Like everything else they did, the Third Reich covered their blood lust with bloodless decrees and laws. In July of 1933, they established the "Law for the Prevention of Progeny with Hereditary Diseases." It was part of their war on the "unfit." This law called for the sterilization of all persons who suffered from diseases deemed hereditary, including mental illness, learning disabilities, physical deformity, epilepsy, blindness, deafness and severe alcoholism.

After the passage of this law, the Third Reich increased the level of its propaganda campaign against the disabled. It began to portray the disabled as an unworthy burden on society. It labeled those with disabilities as "life unworthy of life" or "useless eaters." A secret operation, code-named T4 and operating from the program's coordinating office in Berlin, began the systematic killing of the mentally and physically disabled who were living in institutions.

In August of 1939, the Reich Ministry of the Interior circulated a decree compelling all physicians, nurses, and midwives to report newborn infants and children under the age of three who showed signs of severe mental or physical disability. At first, only infants and toddlers were incorporated in the effort, but eventually, juveniles up to 17 years of age were also killed. At least 5,000 children with physical and mental disabilities were murdered through starvation or lethal overdose of medication.

There was no way to plumb that depth of evil and ever be the same as when you began the descent. It was the mercy of G-d that kept us upright enough to steady our vision on a heavenly horizon where the 5,000, and all the victims of the soulless, dwelt in the blissful presence of His love and righteousness.

Shoshana and I shared a glance that I recognized as a moment shared by my parents, and the Weisses. We knew what we wanted to do about each other. We wanted to share many such moments in a life together. Perhaps it would be a daily occurrence. Perhaps not. It really didn't matter. It was the recognition that there was a wavelength of life which we both shared. For wont of a better phrase, it was a heavenly wavelength. We wanted to seek His purposes in a life shared according to His design. To be sure, it would be imperfect. It would be bristling with our humanity. And with His love and patience.

As we walked away from Yad Vashem on our way to a nearby cafe, I was unconsciously searching for Shoshana's hand. And she for mine. We found our grip and softly squeezed our hands together. It was not exactly according to plan or tradition. But it bolstered us and, as we continued our walk toward the cafe, we grew more confident of the course we were following.

I knew there was something Shoshana wanted to tell me. I sensed that she felt she had an obligation to tell me, and that it was an important obligation, but that she was not apprehensive about it. In a certain respect, perhaps she felt confident about my response. I liked that. I always liked that about her.

As we sat down, our conversation briefly turned to her work at Yad Vashem. "Isaac, I know that the children who were murdered have a voice in the presence of G-d, and we cannot comprehend the beauty of it... but I hope that I can be their voice. I hope I can help their voices reach across Abraham's bosom and remind us of the living G-d, through whom we can seek perfect justice and mercy." I simply said that I strongly believed that "G-d would use her diligence, and her careful and loving attention to all the details of the children's lives, and horrible deaths, to help us seek Him first in all things, and remember the price of not having Him among us."

Neither one of us seemed to have a big appetite. We ordered salad and fruit, and some iced tea. It was a lovely afternoon in Jerusalem.

Shoshana had a sip of her iced tea, and fixed her eyes on mine as she began to tell me what she felt she had to say. "Isaac, two years ago a physician my father and I both trust, someone who is well respected among his peers, told me that I may not be able to have children. He said it is possible but, at this point, he couldn't be sure it was very probable. There was nothing to do about it, as of now, and that my circumstances wouldn't change in the foreseeable future. I'm sorry, Isaac. Perhaps, I should have told Aaron at the beginning." "Nonsense," I replied. "I don't think the IDF prepared Aaron for such things. He's done rather well up to now. You might have overwhelmed the *Flying Shadchan*." I elicited a smile from her. Thank G-d. In fact, we both smiled. Yet again, it was at Aaron's expense. He was a Shadchan, and then some.

And so, it was my turn now. I said the only thing I would ever say about it. I never wanted her to feel sorry, or sad, for me, for her, or at all. She was a rare and precious gift. Surely G-d had special instructions for such a gift. As I am sure He did, I did my best to divine those instructions.

"Shoshana, why don't we let G-d worry about it. If it's above the rank of one of the IDF's best pilots, and Shadchan, then surely it's something best left in the hands of G-d." We shared a smile about the Shadchan part. Her smile was genuine. There was nothing forced about it. She was at ease. I am sure it was imperfect, but it did seem to put the issue at rest, and us at ease, for a lifetime, and that was a heavenly gift. G-d blessed me by giving me the right words. That was a blessing I thanked Him for every day thereafter.

We were married less than two weeks later. The "Flying Shadchan" was all smiles. If he only knew... if he only knew, I thought. Of course, he never would.

Israelis have always had an uneasy relationship with sublime moments. Geography and demography have not been our cooperative allies in the pursuit of the sublime. It had become the precarious responsibility of the Colonel Moshe Sterns of our world, of the Daniels of our world, of the Prime Ministers of our world, of the Aarons of our world, and, sadly, of the Benjamin and Leah Singers of our world.

Surely, they all had savored sublime moments. Yes, and they all understood the terrible price. Some had paid it already. They provide us a patina of the sublime. We know that is the best we can do for now. It was the reason I would knock on the door leading me to the life that Colonel Stern and Daniel knew all too well. If I could provide a moment, to another, like the moment I shared with my dearest Shoshana, then I would. Not happily, but I would.

The day came for me to meet with Colonel Stern and Daniel again. I don't expect they ever believed that my knock wouldn't come. Men like that are not prone to mistakes of that order of magnitude. They simply can't make such mistakes.

Israel was hanging by a thread. They invested much, and waited a long time for me to knock on that door. It was a door they were careful not to close behind me, but they didn't have to.

I left my hotel to meet with Colonel Stern and Daniel. I thought I should closely observe the instructions of Dr. Steiner. "You're taking a stroll on a beautiful day in Jerusalem," he said. "Walk at the pace of a sightseer." Good advice. I instinctively knew what to do.

The truth is I felt more at home in the special forces than in the physics lab. I knew that the terrain of the physics lab, while not strewn with human butchery and treachery, had numerous cul-de-sacs, trap doors, and false leads. The mysteries of G-d's perfect creation were replete with His instincts and His nature. The battlefield was more suited to the nature and instincts of the human being. Do we not relish and glorify our conquests rather than His name and His purposes?

I did indeed "walk at the pace of a sightseer." And there were sights to see. Colonel Stern was careful that the "sightseer" would have an uneventful stroll to his destination. My special forces training helped me spot Colonel Stern's "minders," who made sure I made it to my destination unmolested. The truth is that the extent of my value was carefully camouflaged throughout my academic career. I was aware of all such activities; frankly, it was a game to me. The game was soon to acquire more serious overtones.

The same woman answered the door. It was as efficient as before, but this time she made eye contact, and her look was expectant, and there was a strange kindness and maternal concern to her demeanor. Days earlier, it might have confused me. Now I appreciated it. In spite of the dangerous world I was entering, she had the look my mother might have had. We all knew the price of sublime moments for the Jewish people in the Jewish state. I remembered my impatience with what I perceived to be a lack of faith by Colonel Stern in our first meeting. I confidently, and somewhat defiantly, told him, "He will send us miracles." I believed that with all my heart. I would learn, however, to be more understanding of the burdens that were born by Colonel Stern, and men and women like him.

Colonel Stern and Daniel greeted me with cordial smiles. They were careful to act with a genuine sense of appreciation for my decision, even though I was confident they were not surprised. I was a little taken aback when Daniel spoke first. "I trust your visit to Yad Vashem went well Isaac. I am comforted that the memory of my father and mother live in the words that G-d spoke to the prophet Isaiah, *'Even to them I will give in My house And within My walls a place and a name Better than that of sons and daughters; I will give them an everlasting name That shall not be cut off.'"*

"I know that before G-d breathed in man's nostrils *the breath of life,* He knew that these words would comfort us. How His creation has pained His heart. Our pain must pale in comparison. Don't you agree, Isaac?"

Whatever I thought I knew about Daniel, it did not prepare me for the nature of his remarks. I guess I didn't think that such a refined and beautiful soul could inhabit the world in which he lived. I was wrong. It was a good lesson. At 25, I didn't know everything.

"I am sorry about your mother and father, Daniel." I struggled for the right words. It was not a familiar predicament for me. "There will be no more need of memorials, I said. I am a scientist, Gentlemen, but I do not put my faith in the mind of man, but in the heart of G-d."

"He kept His promise to Abraham as He said... '*Look now toward heaven, count the stars if you are able to number them.*' And G-d said to Abraham, '*So shall your descendants be.*' Even a physicist can tell you there are 600,000 visible stars. And so it was in the Exodus that '*the children of Israel journeyed (out of Egypt) from Rameses to Succoth, about 600,000 men on foot, besides children.*'"

"But His kingdom has not come to us, yet," I said. We are not alone in the presence of G-d... yet. We are not alone. There is another. We know there is another."

"The sword of perdition lacerated the heavens to quench its blood-lust. It was not 600,000. It was 600,000 x 10. The screams shattered nighttime's window, and with it our glorious vision of coruscating stars. And as each star ingloriously fell to the ground, heaven writhed in anguish."

"But the G-d of Abraham, Isaac, and Jacob preserved a remnant. As in the days of old, we are the *watchman*. As the Psalm says, '*Unless the Lord builds the house, They labor in vain who build it; Unless the Lord guards the city, The watchman stays awake in vain.*' We who are the *watchman* shall not stay awake in vain. The Lord guards the city; the city of Jerusalem is His. I am sure you are right, Daniel, our pain pales in comparison to the pain He feels. He will not suffer such pain forever. I believe that His time draws near."

Colonel Stern smiled, "I see that you and Daniel both share an interest in celestial matters. This is good. You will be working closely together. Oh, and Isaac, the Jordanians may disagree with you about who has the deed to Jerusalem."

Colonel Stern continued, "Isaac, our nuclear program is advanced. We are grateful to the French and, thankfully, the Americans have mostly looked the other way. We are working on delivering these weapons to their targets. We hope that such targeting will not be necessary because of the fear engendered by our mere possession of such weapons. But if our targeting is not credible, then the deterrent is not credible. We are currently working on miniaturization so that we can deliver nuclear warheads by missile. I know that you and Dr. Perlman were working on the details of the necessary modifications to our planes, so that they too could carry these weapons."

"Isaac, you have a gift for the special forces... for our methods. Did you notice anything unusual during your walk to meet Daniel and me? Perhaps, you were able to count the twelve men I had safeguarding your journey?"

"Actually, Colonel, you had thirteen agents, one was a woman."

"Very good, Isaac. I told you he was good, Daniel."

"Daniel will see to your work in the laboratory. I will give you an address where you can stay for the time being. I assume that Rabbi Levy will offer you and Shoshana a second apartment he owns in Bayit Vegan as a wedding gift. It happens to be very nice. It is a good place for us to see to your security. You will spend your time here, in Jerusalem, and Tel Aviv. We have laboratories in both places for the work you will do. I would like you to continue your special forces training. That will also be in Tel Aviv."

Colonel Stern turned to Daniel. Daniel was matter of fact. "If you need to see me, Isaac, notify Golda. Contact her by phone, sparingly. She will have the details about your schedule. There should not be a problem. Your special forces training will serve you well. Good luck, Isaac. You and Shoshana will be in my prayers."

"Thank you," I said. Colonel Stern handed me an envelope. "This has an address and the key for an apartment where you can stay until after your wedding. When the government of Jordan denied Hebrew University access to its Mount Scopus campus, the university rented some spaces from the Custodians of the Holy Land, which is administered by Franciscans. It is in Rehavia, which is about 15 minutes from Bayit Vegan. There is a lab there, and the apartment will be available to you from now on."

"Oh, and, there is one more thing. You will be contacted by Father John Broderick. He is a Franciscan, but he is also an ordained priest. John has been very helpful to us. I believe you and he will have much to talk about. He has an interest in the *heavens*, like you and Daniel. I think you will find his affection for the Land of Israel and the Jewish people remarkable. Yes, remarkable. John has a heart for G-d. I am sure the rabbinate would not approve of me saying so. But there it is, Isaac. Go by and see Golda at 10 a.m. tomorrow morning. Sharp! Good bye, for now."

I showed myself out. I liked it. I liked that I would be seeing Golda much more than I thought. It was probably now out of the question to have lunch together. I hoped she would remember the little Pirushke cakes. Why not the both of us presuming on the President's office at Hebrew University? Surely we could punctuate our work with smiles, and memories of Tel Aviv. As David wrote when he was in the wilderness of Judah: *"Therefore in the shadow of Your wings I will rejoice. My soul follows close behind You."* But Golda and I would be mindful of the harshness of reality, as David wrote in the same Psalm: *"But those who seek my life, to destroy it, Shall go into the lower parts of the earth. They shall fall by the sword; they shall be a portion for jackals."*

At six, I savored the desserts and the joy of Golda Eisen. At six, I learned that there were those who sought my parents' lives. As a man, I still wanted to savor the desserts of Golda Eisen. As a man, I did not want another small boy to know the pain of having your mother and father hunted down as if they were beasts in the wilderness. Golda helped the boy. Now she would help the man help the boy.

I needed to call Aaron. We had spoken briefly after Shoshana and I decided to marry. He and his parents, which were my living family, would make the arrangements for the ceremony. Moroccan Jews had a custom to marry on the fifth day of the week (Wednesday night through Thursday before sunset). We would be married on a Tuesday, the third day of creation, because *"G-d saw it was good"* twice. All other days have a single G-dly "good" attached to them.

I wanted Aaron to give me the name of a Rabbi he would speak to from time to time. I got the impression the Rabbi not only knew Aaron and his family, but also knew the "business" that Aaron and I were in. When I finally reached Aaron, he was more than happy to provide me what I needed. He didn't have a difficult search to get his hands on the Rabbi's contact information. Frankly, he seemed to be expecting my call. I was not surprised.

I got up early Monday morning. I had to meet Golda at 10 a.m. "Sharp," was Colonel Stern's command. I did not want to arrive too early. This was not an interview. It was not a meeting with the President of the University. Golda needed to relay specific information to me. I did not want to put her in a situation where she had to figure out what to do with me in the meantime. I hoped that Golda and I could at some point share some time away from all of this even it had to be in the President's office or some other office at the university. This first morning, the morning to begin the work of sparing other little boys from my fate, was not that time.

I arrived not a minute early, or a minute late. Golda was very pleased. I understood the rules. None of us had the luxury of having the rules explained to us. If the rules had to be explained to you, you might not ever have the opportunity to follow the rules again. Predators don't indulge learning curves for their prey. Daniel was understating the case when he told me that my special forces training would serve me well. G-d had blessed me with the instincts to survive a long war. In the chest of the physics professor beat the heart of a warrior. I was not afraid. Fear was my faithful companion. It sharpened my skills. The predator is surprised by other creatures who stalk the night. I liked surprises.

There was a small room adjacent to the President's office. I noted it on my last visit. As Golda led me to the place where we would meet countless times, she was impressed that I seemed to know where I was going. As she closed the door, she smiled warmly and knowingly. It was similar in some respects to the smile of the woman who greeted me at the synagogue where I met Colonel Stern and Daniel. It was a maternal smile. This time it was the smile of a proud mother. Golda was pleased that I was not just a physics professor.

Golda's instructions were succinct. "Settle in at the apartment in Rehavia. John Broderick, the Franciscan priest, will contact you. He will show you the lab we have set up for you. All will look perfectly normal. Everybody knows that we rent space at the Terra Santa building from the Franciscan Custodians. Your work at the lab will begin after the Shabbat (Saturday) of your wedding week. I will not be attending your wedding, Isaac. I'm sure you understand. I give you a kiss from Benjamin and Leah, and from me. Good luck! You will be contacted when I need to see you next."

And so began my life in service to the Land of Israel. I took heart from the heart of David. *Then all this assembly shall know that the Lord does not save with sword or spear; for the battle is the Lord's, and He will give you into our hands.*

I stayed yet another night at the hotel so I could gradually move my things into the apartment in Rehavia. I was careful to travel at different times, and had the various taxis go to addresses a block or so from my apartment. The apartment itself was spacious and furnished, and then some. This was anything but a Spartan existence.

It was the week before our wedding so, by tradition, Shoshana and I would be out of touch. It was a blessing. I could begin to fill in more details of my work routine. And I wanted to meet with Aaron's

Rabbi confidant. At least that was the way I imagined him. I would soon discover if the description fit. But first, there was the matter of (his) knock.

CHAPTER TWO

THE SEVENTH DAY

"I will display wonders in the sky and on the earth,
Blood, fire and columns of smoke.
The sun will be turned into darkness
And the moon into blood…"
Joel 2:30-31

I settled into the apartment, and waited for Father John Broderick to come knocking. He did, during the second evening I was there. The knock was not hesitant, or the least bit unsure; it was kind and patient. I was not expecting the person who appeared before me as I opened the door.

John Broderick was a bear of a man. He had a shock of hair that looked like it was a frequent victor over a comb or brush. I am sure he didn't give it a second thought. As he held out his hand, he spoke first. "Isaac, please call me John." Colonel Stern was not given to hyperbole, at all. His kind words about John gave me some worry about the polite way to address him. Should I call him Father John, Father Broderick, Friar John, or something else? I was to learn that John belied his stature, and had the gift of putting anyone at ease, quickly. He anticipated my potential dilemma. I appreciated that.

He shook my hand with the kindness and firmness I expected by now. I really wasn't apprehensive about what I believed I had to do.

He knew that. But he also knew that there were questions that needed to be answered. Questions I did not want to have to ask. As we went to sit down, I noticed that John walked with a slight limp. He didn't seem to be in any pain, and it appeared to be something he had lived with for a while. He asked for a small glass of water before we sat down.

"Is Golda well?" he began. "Last time I saw her I ate all of her famous Pirushkes. I haven't seen her since. I hope I didn't wear out my welcome." We enjoyed a short laugh together. He intended to make the rest of our conversation easier. He succeeded. I told John that, although I hadn't mentioned it to Golda, I was waiting for her to invite me for some coffee and dessert. "She will, Isaac. She is very fond of you."

"Isaac, I will come by at 9:30 tomorrow morning. We will take care of a few things." He asked me if I had any glasses. I wasn't sure where he was going. "Isaac, try to look as professorial around here as possible. You know, slightly absent minded, your clothes may never quite match, or fit properly. "I understand," I said.

"Good, I should go now. I'll see you in the morning. I'll see myself out." He winked as he shook my hand. John had secrets too. "Oh... and Isaac, do you have the habit of reading the Torah before you go to bed?" I told him that I did. "Would you take a look at Genesis 1:14 and Exodus 4:22?" "Sure, of course, John," I said. Then he was gone.

I have often wondered why I didn't think that it was the slightest bit odd that I had been asked by a Franciscan priest to read two passages from the Torah. Not the least of it was rather than referring to the Old Testament, he referred to the Torah. That was most assuredly outside the bounds of his training. Perhaps it was a kind and deferential gesture. Or, perhaps not. Perhaps he was kind, and had a providential hand on his shoulder.

Some voices we are meant to hear. It may trouble many, but it doesn't trouble all.

"Before I formed you in the womb I knew you;
Before you were born I sanctified you...
For you shall go to all to whom I send you,
And whatever I command you, you shall speak."
Jeremiah 1:5

The words of the Lord to Jeremiah were, of course, true. There are those it is our destiny to hear from about heavenly matters. And if we are meant to hear a voice, it will not clank on our eardrums. John had a voice I was meant to hear. He was not a prophet. We kill our prophets.

John promptly knocked on the door at 9:30 a.m. I followed John's instructions on wardrobe. Taken together, everything I wore was slightly out of whack. I found some clothes that fit well when I carried a few more pounds and, although I was only mildly nearsighted, I wore a pair of glasses I bought on sale in the States at a store just outside of Princeton. I changed my walk from upright and purposeful with a little swagger to a little hunched over with a crab-like gait. It was an easy transition for a wannabe actor.

As John and I descended the stairs, I could see his smile through the glare of a beautifully sunlit morning in Jerusalem. I was trailing him only slightly, on his right side. I knew the smile was there, albeit well tucked away, because as soon as he opened the door to my apartment, he developed a sly grin that only left his face as we turned to leave.

There was a shyness about John. In a life in which he made all the choices, John would have enjoyed prayer and study, and grand acts of kindness that brought little or no attention to himself. He was a shy man with a supple mind; the kind of mind that enjoyed the irony and comical nature of the daring things, and the dangerous things, we had to do. He found such irony and comedy in the adjustments I made to my wardrobe and manner. All of us had to learn to adapt quickly. It could save our lives. It would save our lives.

John led us to another apartment complex that was less than a block from my apartment. Both buildings had clear markings indicating they were owned and operated by the Custodian of the Holy Land. In the second apartment complex were some of the rooms occupied by Hebrew University.

As John and I got off the elevator on the third floor, the corridors took on the personality of a university administration and academic complex. There were clearly marked administrative offices, classrooms, professors' offices, and a student lounge. John and I entered an unmarked room. It was a laboratory, although probably less equipped than a similar room in the average high school. On the other side of a large, elevated laboratory table, undoubtedly intended for a professor, was a false door. Next to the false door was a real door, extremely well camouflaged. John appeared to be sticking a key into the middle of the wall. A door opened.

As we entered the room, John motioned to me to shut the door. The room was actually an extremely well equipped, and rather large, physics laboratory. It did not have everything I needed, by any means, but it was clear that I could do a substantial amount of my work there.

The room was extensively arrayed with laboratory equipment and work spaces, but there were also rather large executive desks, with comfortable chairs. John pulled an extra chair over to one of the desks, and we sat down.

His first words caught me by surprise. They should not have. "Did you have a chance to read the verses of scripture I mentioned to you, Isaac?" "I did," I said. "It has been awhile since read those particular verses, thoughtfully. In fact, I am not sure whether the verse from Genesis ever really registered with me, even now."

"Isaac, you will go over your specific schedule with Golda on the first Sunday after your wedding. Before we leave, I will give you the key to the front door of this building, and to the door for this room. You won't see much activity on this floor. They are mostly friends of

Daniel. They will, by and large, not have much to do with you, or a colleague, if you are ever working with someone else, here. The university also rents the two floors above us, and those floors are much like what you experienced at Princeton."

"Isaac, I want to explain myself to you. You noticed my leg. You notice everything, Isaac. So, you noticed my leg. It is not the reason I do this, but it will explain many things, especially to someone like you. A few years ago, there was a standoff between the Jordanians and the IDF in a hotly contested border area of Jerusalem. A firefight ensued with both automatic weapons and mortars. The Jordanians were in a building that had women and children in it. A young boy, maybe 6-7 years old, came running out of the building and fell on the sidewalk in front. I was under cover, nearby, in a surprisingly well fortified public restroom in a park. The boy was laying on his side, frozen on the sidewalk. As I ran towards him, there was mortar fire that seemed to be going in the direction of the boy. When I arrived at the boy's side, three mortar rounds landed all around us. Only one exploded. The explosion sounded like a dud; it was almost funny, as if we were in the middle of some cartoon. I wanted to laugh when I heard the sound. I grabbed the boy, and took him to safety. My leg was hit. So, the limp."

"The incident became well known among everyone, especially the Jordanians, who have treated me with deference and respect ever since. The IDF apologized. The mortars should never have been fired. Moshe... ah, Colonel Stern tells me that the odds of all three mortars misfiring, or not firing at all, are well... he said it's never happened before, or since."

"Colonel Stern tells me that you believe that the city of Jerusalem is His. Is that right, Isaac?"

"Yes, it is, I do believe that it is His," I said. I hoped that John would not push too hard. I did not want to talk about secrets yet.

"You are right, Isaac," he said, with more than a little urgency in his voice.

I wanted him to tell me more, so I took out the Torah and the Haftarah. I read from the prophet Jeremiah. *"Behold, the days are coming, says the Lord, that the city shall be built for the Lord from the Tower of Hananel to the Corner Gate. The surveyor's line shall again extend straight forward over the hill Gareb; then it shall turn toward Goath. And the whole valley of the dead bodies and of the ashes, and all the fields as far as the Brook Kidron, to the corner of the Horse Gate toward the east, shall be holy to the Lord. It shall not be plucked up or thrown down anymore forever."*

"Yes, Isaac, I believe Jeremiah's prophecy will be fulfilled. Soon. As you said, Jerusalem is His."

Now I was more than curious. "So, soon is not yet. How soon will this happen?" I asked.

"The next few years, Isaac. In the next few years." John's eyes told me that he really didn't want to discuss this much more. He only said, "Isaac, the feasts that the Lord set were lunar. They were based on the cycles of the moon." He smiled as he reminded me, "Genesis 1:14, Isaac."

"Then G-d said, 'Let there be lights in the firmament of the heavens to divide the day from the night; and let them be for signs and seasons, and for days and years.' Signs and seasons, Isaac. Signs and seasons."

It was one of the verses John asked me to read. "Isaac, take heart. A promise has been made. "Exodus 4:22, Isaac. This was the other verse John asked me to read. *"Then you shall say to Pharaoh, 'Thus says the Lord: "Israel is My son, My firstborn."*

"A promise has been made, Isaac." And he added a verse that I would read later. It was Deuteronomy 7:7-9. *"The Lord did not set His love on you nor choose you because you were more in number than any other people, for you were the least of all peoples; but because the Lord loves you... 'Therefore know that the Lord your G-d, He is G-d, the faithful G-d who keeps covenant and mercy for a thou-*

sand generations with those who love Him and keep His command-ments.'"

Suddenly John took on a serious and worried look. "One more thing before you go, Isaac. I have much contact with the Jordanians. They have been showing more and more interest in what Hebrew University is doing in our facilities. I believe they are beginning to comprehend Israel's growing research and scientific advantage in the region. They have decided it isn't just American aid. Be careful, Isaac. I do not believe the danger is acute, yet. But, be careful. You should leave now. Remember, you are Professor Singer." He smiled, shyly. He didn't need to remind me of my need to stay in character.

I left, with keys in hand. I had finally met *him* in Jerusalem. He walked with an almost imperceptible limp. He was bear of a man... with the heart of a lion. He told me about "signs." He reminded me that G-d told Moses to tell the children of Israel that Moses was sent by "*I AM.*" He did not have to tell me that "*I AM*" is eternal. He told me about tomorrow. So we began a journey together into many to-morrows. Those tomorrows would swallow our triumphs, and our sorrows. After the triumphs, and the sorrows, our hopes would soar. Our faith would abide. His mercy had come. And mercy was the eternal gift of "*I AM.*"

I had to turn my attention to preparing for my marriage. I had asked Aaron for the name of a Rabbi. I did not need to tell Aaron why I needed to talk to this Rabbi. He knew. He knew this business. He probably knew the exact topic. What do I tell Shoshana about what I do? As usual, Aaron was more than a Shadchan.

As he opened the door to his office, Rabbi Chaim Dreyfus exhibit-ed a serious manner. He was a tall and distinguished man with the look of a senior diplomat or an iconic politician. He wasn't the least bit concerned with my comfort, or with developing common ground between us. He got right to the point.

"I have known Rabbi Levy and his daughter Shoshana for many, many years. They are wise about what you and Aaron do. It may be that the accident that killed Shoshana's mother wasn't an accident. I do not know. But I suspect. I am sure your question is what to tell Shoshana, or how do I think she will react. Is that about right, Isaac?"

"Yes, it is. Actually, it is exactly what I want to know."

"Isaac, now I am going to speak to you as a Rabbi, as a man, and as a husband. First and foremost, Isaac, pray to G-d for a peaceful, happy home. If you want a paradise on earth, then pray for a peaceful home."

"If I had to distill it all down to a few 'to dos,' I would tell you the following. Your wife's vitality and happiness will depend on the way you honor her. So, save your criticisms, Isaac. If a woman complains, it is usually because she is being criticized, or because the man is not putting her first in the relationship. Shoshana is very discerning. If she believes that something else is more important to you than she is, the whole relationship will suffer. In short, a real man does not need honor or respect; he gives those things to his wife."

"Shoshana is a normal, but sophisticated woman. Even if you don't tell her anything about what you do, she will figure that you are doing much more than what you are telling her. You don't have to tell her everything. But don't treat her like a child. She is your wife. She will understand if you are not only helping your family to survive, but also Israel. She will always worry. The way to help her is not to say, don't worry. The way that you will have peace at home is to acknowledge that what you do has some risks, but that it is still necessary. It does not take a genius to understand that you are a brilliant young physicist. And in Israel, that is saying something."

"If I were to guess, you and Shoshana will have a wonderful marriage. That does not mean there will not be sadness. You will come to understand that it is G-d who uses those difficult times to make your marriage stronger, if you will turn to Him. Good luck, Isaac. You have my blessing. I am late for dinner with my wife. Wish me luck!"

The experience was not what I was hoping for, but the advice was nearly *perfect pitch* for my circumstances. Aaron made a wise choice. I guess I was hoping that, as I was without a father, he might have been more "fatherly" in his approach. I would settle for advice that would see me through over 40 years of G-d's greatest gift to me: my marriage with Shoshana. There were hard times. None harder than her death, which preceded mine.

The day had come. Aaron had chosen well. Our wedding was being held at the King David Hotel. It was a grand, and poignant Jewish outpost in a part of Jerusalem that became a sort of "no man's land," a potential hotspot among the many disputed territorial claims between Israel and Jordan.

The King David Hotel opened in 1931, so some would say that it was the "grand old man" of Jerusalem Hotels. Hardly. It was the *KING DAVID* Hotel, eponymously named for David, who slew the Philistine, Goliath, and about whom G-d would say, *"a man after My own heart, who will do all My will."*

The King David Hotel was not a relic from the past. It pointed to our future, and our destiny. And that destiny was tied to the destiny of King David's descendants. *"When your days are fulfilled and you rest with your fathers, I will set up your seed after you, who will come from your body, and I will establish his kingdom... And your house and your kingdom shall be established forever before you. Your throne shall be established forever."*

Aaron was my adopted brother, who became my Shadchan (matchmaker) and Shomer (best man). It was triple duty for a man whose love for me knew no bounds. It was mutual. He flawlessly took care all the details that went into a glorious wedding day.

I was nearly brought to tears by many things that day. To see the Weisses, in the splendor of their middle years, was a special delight. My parents were about the same ages as the Weisses. I imagined how proud they would have been. Proud of their son, and proud of Israel. Their son was home, and safe for now.

Shoshana radiated beauty and warmth. If she was nervous, it wasn't at all apparent to me. Neither of us were nervous, in fact. And a rehearsal was not part of our tradition. The cast of characters had to know their lines and "hit their marks." No movie could have ever conveyed the perfect harmony of that day. Even the minor missteps seemed perfect.

Mr. and Mrs. Weiss and Rabbi Levy escorted Shoshana and I to the chuppah (canopy) under which the marriage ceremony would take place. The ring I placed on Shoshana's finger was chosen by Aaron. It was a flawless, plain gold ring, without any other markings or ornamentation. As I put the ring on her finger, I had to gather myself. The tears were making another pass at welling up in my eyes, but as I was slipping the ring on her finger, she ever so slightly touched my forefinger. It steadied me.

I had always looked forward to this part. The glass was now placed on the floor, and I shattered it with my foot. It was to remind us about the sadness of the destruction of the Temple in Jerusalem. We were expressing our commitment to the spiritual and national destiny of the Jewish people. As was said in the Psalm, *"set Jerusalem above my highest joy."*

According to tradition, although it was not strictly in the traditions of Moroccan Jews like Shoshana, we were escorted to a private room (yichud). There, we could share a few of our first moments together as husband and wife, and have a bite to eat. I remembered briefly holding Shoshana's hand as we left Yad Vashem. Now I didn't want to let go.

It was probably against all tradition, and any sane advice to a newlywed, but I chose the yichud room to follow some of Rabbi Dreyfus's advice. I told Shoshana that nothing in the world would ever be as important to me as her. But the Psalm says to *"set Jerusalem above my highest joy."* So I told her that my work would involve helping Israel, and Jerusalem, survive. She only said this, "In my work, I see the consequences for the Jewish people of hoping somebody among us, or among the nations, will defend us. We can only count on G-d. And G-d only has us. Promise me this. Do not be reckless, for my sake... do not do anything... reckless. G-d doesn't ask you to be reckless. Be wise, Isaac. And, be patient with a wife who worries about the safety of her husband. Be wise, my husband."

I was comforted by her words. I was to be even more comforted by her actions throughout all the years. She worried, as promised. But she did not waver.

We joined our guests for a meal, and for a celebration that lasted well into the night. Some of our guests chose to entertain Shoshana and me with rousing demonstrations of juggling and acrobatics. We were thrilled, and all of us were joyously cheering on these incredible performances. I suddenly spotted a lone figure, well across from us, near a canopied doorway that led inside the hotel. He realized that he had caught my eye. He raised his glass. As I turned to grab my glass, he slipped away. I had observed the silhouette of a bear of a man with a white collar. For a man with a slight limp, it was a remarkable exit.

There was supposed to be a seven-day period after the wedding (Sheva Brachot) during which Shoshana and I would be able to celebrate each evening with our family and friends. Seven days became four days, because I had to begin my "job" at Hebrew University. Colonel Stern was right though. As a wedding gift, Shoshana's father, Rabbi Levy, gave us the keys to a beautiful apartment not too far from the apartment he had shared with his daughter. Shoshana was happy. Rabbi Dreyfus would be pleased.

The Americans thought there was a "cloud nine." As Golda greeted me upon my return to the Hebrew University campus in Givat Ram, I was most surely on that "cloud." Something was wrong though. As she led me to our small meeting room, Golda's smile was pained. Daniel was seated near the corner of the room next to a small table. Golda excused herself. As I brought over a chair to sit near Daniel, he stood up and warmly shook my hand. "Congratulations,

Isaac," he said. "May your lives be pleasing to G-d." I smiled, and slightly nodded my head as I sat down.

"Isaac, John was right. The Jordanians, among others, have taken an interest in our scientific talent. It appears that they have too much time on their hands." I wasn't surprised, or concerned. "It was only a matter of time," I said. "Well Isaac, you are probably right. But just to make sure, I met with a few of my counterparts to discourage their inquiries into such matters." I smiled, and chuckled. "Oh," I said. "And how did you discourage them?" "I told them I would hold them personally responsible if any of their curiosities led to a misplaced hair on the head of even one of our scientists, or his family. In other words, Isaac, I would hunt them down, cut their throats, and leave them for the jackals. Stay alert. I don't think you'll have any problems. Consider it a wedding present. I don't want Shoshana to be a widow before her time." And with that, he stood up and left the room.

Golda was still a little rattled as she re-entered the room. I smiled and told her that I was hoping that she would be bringing some Pirushkes to one of our future meetings. She seemed to relax a little. "I promise, Isaac, I will. Do you have your keys?" I looked at her as I said, "Yes," under my breath. "Be careful," she said. And I was off.

Except for that first meeting, I rarely saw Daniel. I saw Colonel Stern more because of my special forces training in Tel Aviv. Golda was always on time with the Pirushkes, and reminiscences from Tel Aviv. My schedule was essentially the same for those first eighteen months. Three days a week in the lab in Jerusalem, and two to three days a week in the lab and/or special forces training in Tel Aviv. I especially liked the weeks when the Tel Aviv part of my job was all special forces training.

Throughout my training, I didn't try to hide my enthusiasm for special forces from Shoshana. I liked Daniel all right. Actually, I liked Daniel very much. But the fact that I saw so little of him gave me a sense that things were going well. Shoshana perceived my satisfaction. She was reassured. That would change.

I was about to turn 27 in December of 1966. As I walked down the hall to the lab in Jerusalem, fully in character, slightly disheveled with black rim glasses that were too large for my face, I saw a familiar figure waiting for me. I hadn't seen John Broderick for some time. We couldn't be certain just how effective Daniel's blunt threats were to his Jordanian counterparts. I am sure that all three men, including Colonel Stern and John, knew that it was best to keep their contact with me at a minimum. And so they did. I missed John. I missed having more time for conversation. I had every reason to believe that our first several contacts would be the norm of our relationship. Daniel's revelation changed that. Frankly, I probably had a rather naive expectation.

John was anxious to get behind the door. We walked through the faux laboratory without speaking, and quickly entered the lab where I had been working for the last eighteen months, sometimes with others, but most of the time, solo.

John's large body seemed to overwhelm a couple of comfortable chairs that he rolled to the center of the lab. December could be quite chilly in Jerusalem. Snow wasn't out of the question. I imagined us in a large guest room that glowed in the warmth of a fireplace. John relaxed.

"Has it been difficult for you these last months, Isaac," he began. "It hasn't at all, John. We have been making incredible progress, and I look forward to the Tel Aviv part of my schedule. My marriage is a blessing from G-d!" "I am sorry I wasn't able to properly offer you and Shoshana my best wishes at your wedding." I interrupted him. "John, you gave me a cherished memory. If I ever need to leave somewhere in a hurry, I will bring you with me as my guide." He smiled nervously.

"Isaac, something is coming. The signs are there. His signs, Isaac. And the signs of men. Men are being driven by something they don't understand, and even if they did, they would happily give over the keys to their hearts, and the keys to their souls. The bargain they have made causes them to mistake their bloodlust for the passion of G-d. It is a bargain made with the abyss. Their hearts go cold, and their souls go dark."

"The Syrians have rapidly increased the pace of their attacks. Syria says it is upset because Israel has created a National Water Carrier to supply it with water from the Jordan River. Jewish children living in the kibbutzim are forced to sleep in bomb shelters, escaping, we pray, the Syrian shelling from the Golan Heights. Syria is continuing their sponsorship of cross-border terrorism, sending saboteurs through Jordan and Lebanon. Just last month, three Israeli soldiers were killed by a mine planted by the PLO's Fatah organization. This year the total number of terrorist attacks has increased to 41, and all against civilian targets."

"John, it appears to me that no one wants war. Isn't this just more of the same?"

"You are right, Isaac, it is more of the same. They will never accept the reality of a Jewish state in the Land of Israel. Never. Period."

"The signs are there, Isaac. You remember... Then G-d said, *'Let there be lights in the firmament of the heavens... and let them be for signs.'* And He also said in the Book of Joel, *'the sun shall be turned into darkness, and the moon into blood.'"*

"You are a brilliant physicist, Isaac. Have you heard of 'blood moons,' or lunar tetrads?"

"No, John, my astronomy is pretty weak."

"Isaac, when there is a lunar eclipse, especially a total lunar eclipse, the moon turns blood red. Very seldom is there a total lunar eclipse. Lunar tetrads are four total lunar eclipses in the course of about a year and a half. A lunar tetrad is rare. It is extremely rare to have four total lunar eclipses which fall on Biblical festivals. As you know, the Biblical Feasts were established by G-d according to the lunar cycles."

"If you go back 500 years, Isaac, there have been two lunar tetrads, each of which happened in about a year and a half, and during which, each of the four full lunar eclipses fell exactly on the days of the Biblical feasts. The appearance of these rare blood moon phenomena were connected to the years, 1492 and 1948. 1492 was the year Columbus discovered America. He was an Italian Jew who was commissioned to seek a place where Jews could live in peace."

"You remember what happened in 1492? The Spanish Inquisition. The Catholic Church persecuted Spanish Jews, confiscating their property and expelling them from the country. And yes, they burned many Jews alive. All because they would not convert to Catholicism. Columbus did find a country where Jews could live peacefully: *The United States of America.*"

"In 1948, the State of Israel was founded. From now on, Israel will survive, and thrive. But what about Jerusalem, Isaac? It is a divided city."

"A *third tetrad* is coming. There will four 'blood moons,' the first on the Feast of Passover, 1967, the second on the Feast of Tabernacles, 1967, the third on the Feast of Passover, 1968, and the fourth on the Feast of Tabernacles, 1968. This is telling us something very important is going to happen in Israel in the period, 1967-1968. Isaac, I believe it may be that Jerusalem will be united. It must happen sooner or later. It could be the next 'blood moon' cycle."

I was silent for a bit, not because I was so stunned by the information or the prediction, but because of the implications for life in Jerusalem during the next year or so. "Jeremiah," I said. "Jeremiah."

"Yes, Isaac, you were right to quote Jeremiah, before. I remember. I wanted to wait before I said anything else about it."

"Well, John, I especially like the end of the verse when Jeremiah refers to Jerusalem, *'It shall not be plucked up or thrown down anymore forever.'*"

"I like that part too, Isaac. I like that part too. Is your work going well here, Isaac? Generally speaking, of course."

"We have made very impressive strides, John. Everyone is extremely gratified."

"Good, Isaac. That is very good." John seemed especially pleased. It wasn't frequent for him at such moments. "Isaac, Israel will need your genius now, more than ever. And, you may have to be a soldier for a time. Prepare Shoshana, won't you please. Prepare Shoshana." "I will, John. I give you my word." "One more detail, Isaac. The Jordanians seem more and more preoccupied as the border incidents increase. I think they have little interest in scientists these days. Do you understand, Isaac?"

"Yes John, I do. Thank you for telling me."

I didn't delay long in keeping my word to John. I waited until the end of Chanukah, which came a bit earlier than the previous year, and until after my birthday. Shoshana and I had just finished dinner. "Shoshana, do you remember my friend, John?" I asked. "Isn't he a priest, or something?" she asked. What a good question, I thought. On second thought, I didn't think priests were in the business of divining the future. He knew far more about the significance of the Biblical Feasts than most Israelis. And, it probably wasn't the norm for priests to describe the Spanish Inquisition in quite the way that he did. So I answered Shoshana in this way. "John is a priest with some unusual insights. He told me the other day that he thought war was coming to Israel. He made me promise I would tell you. So, I am. If he is right, Shoshana, I may be asked to be more than a physicist. We are a small country. We are vastly outnumbered. No one will be overlooked."

"Well, my husband, John may be right. In spite of the words of the politicians, I think that it doesn't look good." Now, she looked into my eyes and spoke from her soul. "Isaac, do you remember what I asked of you?" "Yes," I said. "You asked me not to be reckless." "Will you keep your promise to me, Isaac? Will you not be reckless?" I firmly took her hand, and renewed my promise. "Oh, how I wish sometimes that you were not such a good soldier, Isaac. What are the odds of marrying a physicist who is such a good soldier?" She smiled and, as quickly, the smile was gone. "Be careful, my husband. Please, be careful." "I will," I said. "I promise."

January brought an unusual flurry of meetings with Colonel Stern and Daniel. There was no talk of war, but the pace and the content of the meetings didn't point to a sudden run on ploughshares. There was a sharpening of the swords.

For his part, Daniel's singular focus was the nuclear program. At a mid-January meeting in my Jerusalem lab, Daniel came to point. "Isaac, a weapon needs to be ready that can be delivered by one of our aircraft. I know you know about the modifications to our planes, but will the weapon be ready soon?" "The weapon will be ready. It is crude, but it will be ready," I replied. "You understand, Isaac, this is only going to be used as a last resort. Only if Israel is being overrun. This is not a choice we want to make."

"The Third Reich told us well in advance what they were going to do. And even on the trains to the camps, most of us believed they weren't serious, or something would happen to change things. The President of Egypt has said 'we aim at the destruction of the state of Israel.' He also has said their immediate goal was the 'perfection of Arab military might. The national aim: the eradication of Israel.'"

"Even to a man who has the mind of a non-physicist like me, it sounds like the President of Egypt is not very friendly to the idea of living peaceably with Israel. Wouldn't you agree, Isaac?"

"John doesn't believe there will ever be peace for us. I agree."

"Oh, yes, you believe in this supernatural obsession with us. Is that right, Isaac?"

"It is, Daniel. And I believe in a force greater than that which has kept us alive, and now, has returned us to the Land of our fathers. *This* Land that was promised to Abraham."

"On the souls of my parents, may you be right, Isaac. And for my children. In the meantime, use the mind that G-d gave you to defend our country. We will need it soon, I fear. The closer it comes, the sweeter will be the words of the politicians. Watch for this. Good bye. Good luck." And with that, he was gone.

My work in Tel Aviv took more and more of my time. I was promoted to Segan Rishon, Lieutenant First Class. I became the leader of a small group of commandos who were being trained for urban combat. My work on the weapon was also consuming more of my time. Shoshana was becoming more worried. Rabbi Dreyfus was right. She was no fool. Nor would I ever dream of treating her like one. Nevertheless, I had to keep reminding her that I would keep my promise: I would not be reckless.

In late February, the Syrians announced an ominous change in their military policy. They said they were moving from defensive positions to offensive positions. By mid-March, my colleagues and I were finishing our work on having the first atomic weapon ready for mounting on one of our aircraft.

From the time he first became Prime Minister, David Ben-Gurion was nearly obsessed with realizing a nuclear program which could be used to defend Israel. He was mindful that it was Jewish scientists who had unwittingly, although sometimes wittingly, helped Hitler advance such a program. And both during and after the war, the United States developed "Operation Paperclip" to recruit those same Jewish scientists to work on what became the "Manhattan Project." Ben-Gurion wanted to use our talent to defend ourselves. We were almost there.

By late March, our weapon system would essentially be "operational," within days of an order by high command. We would tinker around the edges, but the work was complete.

IDF was intensifying our commando training. Mornings in Tel Aviv were becoming exhausting. I loved it. After training one morning, I saw Colonel Stern and Daniel approaching my bunk, where I was taking a short nap. I rarely saw Colonel Stern. I never saw Colonel Stern and Daniel together at any of the Tel Aviv facilities where I worked and trained.

Colonel Stern came over to me and asked if I had a chance to shower and change clothes. I had. He asked me to take a ride with Daniel and him. There was little conversation in the car. We had a military driver. Colonel Stern sat in the seat behind the driver. Daniel and I were in the seat behind Colonel Stern. Daniel did turn to me with a reassuring look. I appreciated that.

We entered what appeared to be a military facility, just outside of Tel Aviv. The buildings were nondescript, and the security was tighter than anything I had observed in other such facilities. We pulled up in front of one of the smaller buildings. It was shaped like a cement block, painted in a drab color, with a total absence of any markings that would indicate its purpose or use.

As we went through a door, Colonel Stern walked quickly down a narrow hallway that was lined with security guards who were motionless as we went by them. He opened the door, and we entered a reasonably spacious room with comfortable furniture. The flag of Israel was close by. The flag was unusual. Colonel Stern motioned for us to sit down.

A door opened on the far side of the room. As soon as it opened, Colonel Stern and Daniel flew out of their seats. It didn't take long for me to understand why. Approaching me with his outstretched hand was the Prime Minister of Israel. He smiled in a way that one never saw on television. He was 71, and I do not believe his health was good.

But in the moments before and after he shook my hand, he became young and vibrant, the younger man temporarily putting aside the infirmities of his older counterpart. Maybe it was the gift of a politician. But as he spoke, I thought otherwise.

"It wasn't so long ago that we spoke by phone, Isaac." You are the pride of Benjamin and Leah Singer. And Israel. You have done your work well, young Mr. Singer. Oh, Benjamin and Leah would be so proud. And I miss them so much. Especially, these days. These are hard days. His face changed instantly. He looked at Colonel Stern and, after the Prime Minister gave a short nod of his head towards the door, Colonel Stern walked swiftly to the door, opened it and in walked Aaron.

As we shook hands, Aaron and I were both puzzled. The fact that the Prime Minister grew more serious was of no consolation. What had we done? We all sat down.

The Prime Minister wasted no time. "You are among our best. Isaac and Aaron, you should be very proud." His eyes looked away for a moment. He took a moment for a short soliloquy. "Benjamin and Leah, Israel is proud of your son, and his friend today. Isaac, I am told we would not have a powerful weapon to defend ourselves, except for you. Thank you, again, Isaac. Aaron, you are our best pilot. So Isaac, if we must, your work will be flown to its destination by Aaron Weiss. Aaron and I did not look at one another.

The Prime Minister continued, "I was born in the shtetl of Oratov, in the Ukraine. I did not come this far to see us marched out of the Land at the point of a gun. There will be no march. Only our deaths. I have seen too much death. Too many have died." As he turned his head towards the flag, he seemed disoriented, as if he had lost his train of thought. He hadn't. His eyes stared into mine. "From now on, the tears I shed will be tears of joy. The joy of survival." His youthful vigor returned. "I owe that to Benjamin and Leah, and all my cherished comrades who were taken from us. We will defend ourselves. And as in the days of Abraham and Melchizedek, the righteousness of G-d shall not be stained by the lust of men. We will honor G-d and His righteousness. We do not seek plunder. There is no glory in any of this."

The Prime Minister stood up. At that, we all stood up, led by Colonel Stern. "Aaron and Isaac, good luck my sons. You are the sons of Israel. Good bye, now." He opened the door for himself as he left the room. As we stepped outside, I was blinded by the glare of a bright afternoon sun. It reminded me of how it was when Aaron and I were boys, and we had just seen a matinee on a Sunday afternoon. As boys, we dreamed dreams. Aaron was going to be a fearless pilot, streaking across the skies in all of his glory. I was going to be a physicist, and discover the secrets of the universe. We came close. But not that close. Our boyhood imaginations never quite caught up with our actual lives as men.

We left in separate cars. I went with Daniel, and Aaron left with Colonel Stern. We shook hands as we left. There was nothing to say. It was bewildering, but what was happening was real. If we lived, we could reflect on it as old men. But we had to live. And the job had to be done.

Daniel broke the silence in the car during our ride back. He asked me about the reference the Prime Minister made to Melchizedek. "Who was Melchizedek?" he asked.

I answered this way, "Melchizedek appears in Genesis at the time that G-d helped Abraham prevail over his enemies. He is described as the 'priest of G-d Most High.' In Psalm 110, King David writes about the Messiah's reign in which he sits at the right hand of G-d, and is 'a priest forever according to the order of Melchizedek.' G-d blessed Abraham twice. He made a covenant directly with Abraham, as he did with Noah and Moses. But G-d also blessed Abraham through the high priest, Melchizedek. Melchizedek 'brought out bread and wine...' and said 'Blessed be Abraham of G-d Most High.'"

"G-d delivered the enemies of Abraham into his hands, Daniel. Abraham honored the righteousness of G-d by his righteous behavior towards his conquered enemies. That was the Prime Minister's point: a righteous defense of the Land."

Daniel looked at me with some mixture of scorn, delight and skepticism. "So, you are a part-time physicist and a full-time Torah scholar," he said. He burst out in laughter. It took all the tension out of the past few hours. I laughed too... louder and longer than usual. It would be some time before we would laugh again.

April came to Jerusalem. The sun gods would ring out the last rain from April clouds, and bathe us in the warmth of May. But the G-d of

Abraham, Isaac and Jacob was LORD among the gods. They trembled before him, as did idolaters.

He was clever and subtle in all things. The sun warmed our bodies, as it illuminated the marvel of His creation. But it was the moon that was His divine timepiece. The moon would tell us the days and the seasons of His mo'edim (feasts or appointed times).

It was April, and we would celebrate His first feast according to the moon. In 1967, Passover came so late in April that it extended to the first few days of May. Passover. His first feast. Exodus from Egypt. *"Now the Lord spoke to Moses and Aaron in the land of Egypt, saying, 'This month shall be your beginning of months; it shall be the first month of the year to you. So this day shall be to you a memorial; and you shall keep it as a feast to the Lord throughout your generations. You shall keep it as a feast by an everlasting ordinance.'"*

Passover would begin at sundown, April 24th. It would be the date of the first "Blood Moon." That would mark the beginning of the Lunar Tetrad spoken about by John Broderick. There would be three more "Blood Moons." And G-d said... *"let them be for signs."*

The signs were coming faster now, and they were ominous. On April 7th, Israel finally retaliated for Syria's attacks on Israeli kibbutzim from the Golan Heights. Israeli planes shot down six Syrian fighter planes, MIGS, supplied by the Soviet Union. Colonel Stern told me that Aaron "got at least two." The Soviet Union was providing military and economic assistance to both Syria and Egypt. The Soviets purposely misled Damascus, giving Syria false information that Israel was massing its forces in preparation for an attack. Syria responded with a decision to invoke its defense treaty with Egypt.

The fret in the Land of Israel did not dissuade Shoshana and I from celebrating Passover in a manner that thanked G-d for all His blessings. Most of all we tried to maintain a true "unleavened" spirit of humility and obedience.

I asked Shoshana's father, Rabbi Levy, to read the verse from the prophet Malachi about the return of Elijah.

"Behold, I will send you Elijah the prophet
Before the coming of the great and dreadful day of the Lord.
And he will turn the hearts of the fathers to the children,
And the hearts of the children to their fathers,
Lest I come and strike the earth with a curse."
Malachi 4:5-6

And with that, in keeping with custom, we poured a cup of wine, the "Cup of Elijah," and opened the door of our apartment in anticipation of his return. We recited several verses from the Psalms asking G-d to help us against our persecutors and oppressors. We looked forward to Elijah ushering in the coming of the Messiah.

The bad news in May was as unrelenting as it was in April. Egypt chose May 15, Israel's Independence Day, to begin moving large numbers of troops to the Israeli border. At the same time, Syrian troops were preparing for battle along the Golan Heights. Shortly thereafter, Nasser ordered the UN Emergency Force (UNEF), which had been a buffer between Israeli and Egyptian forces, to withdraw from Sinai. The Secretary-General of the UN, U Thant, acceded to Nasser's request without ever bringing the matter to the UN General Assembly. The Voice of the Arabs radio station responded this way:

"We shall not complain any more to the UN about Israel. The sole method we shall apply against Israel is total war, which will result in the extermination of Zionist existence."

I believed war was imminent, and becoming more so by the day. Tel Aviv was absorbing all my time, now. I saw Colonel Stern, daily. We intensified our urban warfare training. After a long, tiring day of training, Colonel Stern asked to meet with me. It was a private meeting, whose reverberations would blaze through the walls of a smallish room into every nook and cranny of His creation.

"Isaac, if war comes, the Jordanians will try to take all of Jerusalem, if they can. Have you studied the Civil War in America? "Yes, I have, Colonel," I replied. "How did General Lee respond to forces with superior numbers, sometimes overwhelming numbers?" "Surprise and speed, Sir. Lee responded with surprise and speed. Chancellorsville comes to mind. It was brilliant!" Colonel Stern narrowed his eyes to a squint, and looked right through me. "He lost his "right arm" there, General Jackson. I do not intend to lose you, Isaac. What would I say to Shoshana? I want you to develop a plan to take the initiative. How about the Eastern Gate? The Jordanians would never expect us to come at them through the Eastern Gate. Leave now. John is waiting for you at the lab in Jerusalem. 24 hours. You have 24 hours." He didn't usually, but he saluted as he left. I responded in kind, although I was on the move.

John was waiting for me, seated at the exact spot where he was when we last met. My chair was ready. He was relaxed. Some men become calmer in crisis. John was calmer now. He stood and greeted me with a warm handshake. I spoke first. "Colonel Stern wants me to develop a plan to take the initiative on Jordanian positions in Jerusalem. I assume I am here because you can help." My own words banged against my ear drum and fell flat on the floor. I looked at John, apologetically. "I am sorry, John. That was the pressure. Let me start over." He quickly interrupted, "Nonsense," he said. "It's completely understandable, Isaac."

"Isaac, we have had our first 'Blood Moon,' and three more will follow. So let's do what we must. I have sketched out the positions of the Jordanians in Jerusalem, their troop strengths and armaments, and their likely forays in battle. How I got this will be for another day." He handed me two pieces of paper with extensive diagrams and notes. "John, Colonel Stern asked me about the Eastern Gate. He said we might surprise the Jordanians if we came through the Eastern Gate." "You can't do that Isaac. The Eastern Gate is the gate the Messiah will enter through when He comes. It must remain closed until then. We don't have time for an extensive discussion of the verses. You can read Nehemiah 3:29 and Ezekiel 44:1-3 in the Tanakh."

"I understand, John," I said, "I will develop an alternative. And John? I believe that the Messiah has probably entered through that gate once, already." I looked at John for a reaction. I don't know what led me to blurt it out like that. He had to know. He was the one person who had to know. I thought he would understand.

"John, when I was eleven, the Weisses had to leave town with Aaron, and left me to be watched for a weekend by some of their close friends, the Bergers. They were very nice people. They took me to the Immanuel Church in Tel Aviv because they didn't have anywhere else to leave me. They asked the Weisses if it would be alright. They agreed. They just told me to sit quietly until the service was over."

"At one point in the ceremony, I stood with everyone else. I looked at the cross behind the pastor, and I had an experience I cannot describe. I felt there was a light upon me and, somehow I understood that the agony of His death was G-d's mercy and a light to all the world. I noticed that Mrs. Berger was looking at me, strangely. I just smiled, and sat down. She later asked me about it. But I didn't know what to say, so I told her I guess I was a little tired. Maybe I was. But from that day forward, my heart was different."

John didn't look at me with shock or dismay. He only said, "We can talk about this more, later. I know how much it took for you to tell me this, Isaac. I appreciate that, more than I can say. Time is short. You must worry about the lives of your men. About all of our lives. Most of all, about your wife. Do your work well, Isaac. I will pray for G-d's mercy, and His wisdom. We will all need that now. You should go. Change your clothes, Isaac. We need to be especially careful. Go, please."

John was right. I commanded other men. In a certain sense, their lives were my responsibility. When I arrived at our apartment, Shoshana looked more worried than usual. I told the truth. "It is coming.

This thing is coming at the Jewish people again. I love you. I will not ask you not to worry. But I will tell you this. I will not be reckless. There are other husbands with wives who worry. Pray that we will not have brutish hearts during all of this."

May 22 may have been the fateful day that brought us to war. On that day, Egypt closed the Straits of Tiran, which was Israel's only supply route with Asia. The closure of the Straits of Tiran also effectively cut off the flow of oil to Israel from Iran, its main supplier at the time. Israel had been given assurances since 1956 that it would have access to the Straits of Tiran. A virtual guarantee of such access had been made by the United States. Now, all bets were off.

On May 30, King Hussein of Jordan signed a defense pact with Egypt. Nasser then announced: "The armies of Egypt, Jordan, Syria and Lebanon are poised on the borders of Israel... to face the challenge, while standing behind us are the armies of Iraq, Algeria, Kuwait, Sudan and the whole Arab nation. This act will astound the world."

My plan had been accepted by Colonel Stern and his superiors. My men were ready. I broke all protocol and asked Colonel Stern to get a message to Aaron. He was sequestered now, prepared at a moment's notice to be deployed. Colonel Stern reluctantly agreed to my request. I wished Aaron all good luck. He responded in kind. Now I was ready. Shoshana and the rest of Israel were being told that we faced impossible odds. It had an effect on her, but it was the rest of Israel that needed more than just a word of encouragement.

Rabbi Menachem Schneerson was at the ready. He reminded Israel of G-d's promises. He asked that all Jewish men attach "tefillin" to their arms and their heads. Each tefillin contained scrolls of parchment inscribed with verses from the Torah. He said that this would remind us of our Exodus from Egypt. It was the right spiritual medicine. Confidence was much higher because the Rabbi spoke as he did. It was a sign of the miracles to come.

As June approached, there was not a word spoken that was not part of some wartime scenario. It felt as though winter had returned to Jerusalem and Tel Aviv. The words we spoke refused to disappear into the ether, instead they hung in the air, and dimmed the normal brightness of the sky. On June 1, I had to move to a facility in Tel Aviv. Shoshana temporarily moved in with her father.

President Abdur Rahman Aref of Iraq said that "the existence of Israel is an error which must be rectified." On June 4, Iraq joined the military alliance with Egypt, Jordan and Syria. Arab forces were surrounding Israel with 465,000 troops, more than 2,800 tanks, and 800 aircraft.

We had to surprise. On June 5, 1967, we did. The entire Israeli air force launched a surprise attack against the Egyptian, Jordanian, and Syrian air forces. Only 12 planes were left to defend all of Israel. The Egyptian pilots were having breakfast. The Jordanians and the Syrians were similarly caught completely unprepared and, apparently, amazed at the boldness of the strike. One airfield in Iraq was also attacked. By the end of the day, nearly the entire Egyptian and Jordanian air forces had been destroyed. More than half of the Syrian air force had been rendered useless before their planes could even leave the ground. In all, 400 aircraft of the combined Arab air forces had been wiped out. Ninety-four percent of those aircraft were destroyed on the ground. We had the initiative.

I was worried for two reasons. Israel had lost 26 aircraft in the raid. And Jordanian forces were shelling West Jerusalem. Twenty people had already been reported dead in Jerusalem. I made frantic inquiries, with no apologies. Shoshana and Aaron were safe, although I could not speak to either one. Aaron's plane had been hit, though. It was beginning to look like the Prime Minister would not need a weapon of last resort.

We had to move; Jerusalem was under attack. On June 7th, at 8:30 a.m., we did. My plan was to enter into Jerusalem through the Lion's Gate, not the Eastern Gate as some had wanted. The Lion's Gate, like the Eastern Gate, had the advantage of an eastern assault on the city. John's information was nearly flawless. We entered through the Lion's Gate, and coordinated our attack with paratroopers and other special forces. The paratroopers were in process of seizing the high ground the Jordanian forces held at Augusta Victoria Hill. Mount Scopus was also secured. Finally, the Temple Mount and Western Wall were under Israeli control. For some two thousand years, the Temple Mount had been forbidden to the Jewish people. Now, General Rabbi Shlomo Goren, chief chaplain of the IDF, sounded the Shofar at the Western Wall to signify its liberation.

Similar successes began to cascade on other battle fronts, including the Golan Heights, the West Bank, the Sinai Peninsula, and the Gaza Strip. The war had started on June 5, 1967. It was over on June 10, 1967. A six-day war in which Israel had taken control of the Gaza Strip, the Sinai Peninsula, the West Bank, Jerusalem, and the Golan Heights.

All of us were exhausted as we were taken back to Tel Aviv. We were being replaced by fresh troopers who would permanently secure our gains. I entered the Tel Aviv training facility to radiant smiles by Colonel Stern and Daniel. There they were, together for another rare time. "He will send miracles," is all I said. It seemed that they had forgotten our earlier conversation. I continued, "He has been faithful in spite of the faithlessness of His creation."

Daniel spoke through his smile, "We have a surprise for you, ol'faithful one. Colonel Stern pointed me to a small room where we had been holding our planning sessions. I opened the door, and there she was; as we fell into each other arms, relieved and exhausted, tears were gushing down our faces. I put my hands on her shoulders. "No recklessness, my wife. I kept my promise." "And G-d answered my prayer. He has spared your life," she said. With that, a knock came on the door. It was Colonel Stern. "We must get her back to Jerusalem before I am promoted to tourist guide in the Negev. Go now, please." We embraced, and she was off to Jerusalem in the care of a junior officer.

At this point, I cared little about protocol. With tears in my eyes, I thanked Colonel Stern. I wanted to embrace him, but there were limits, even in my state. Daniel came over. "He will send us miracles," he said. He looked at Colonel Stern, and they both looked at me. "We will have to rethink this," is all Daniel said. "We have three more 'Blood Moons' to come," I said. I could tell they knew what I was talking about, but they looked at me as if to say, enough for today. So it was. Daniel said, "Get some sleep, Isaac. We will have a brief meeting in the morning, then you will be free to go back to Jerusalem for a while... *Professor Singer*." I got the message, and then fell fast asleep.

I woke up thinking about Aaron. I needed to know he was alright. I asked Colonel Stern to facilitate a phone call. He did. "Be brief," he said. Aaron was fine. He was relaxed, and still exhilarated by the sheer breadth of events, not to mention our victory. Golan, Sinai, Jerusalem, Gaza... frankly, it was hard to comprehend. I asked about his plane being hit. His smile was beaming through the phone. "Two of my planes were hit," he said. "I took a little shrapnel in the leg. I think some of the pilots of the MIGS were Russian, Isaac. They were tough. Isaac, as the Lord G-d is my witness, I feel at home in the skies. I feel free. You remember, Isaac, our dreams as boys? It feels like that." He asked about Shoshana. "I saw her last night. She has endured this very well," I said. "I will see you soon, Aaron." "That's Shadchan to you, Isaac." We laughed. For a moment we were the boys leaving the Sunday matinee. Those matinees were a welcome escape from the pain I felt as a six-year-old. The pain that men feel was yet to come.

Aaron felt free in the air. He was a soul that deserved that feeling of freedom. His nation had placed heavy burdens on the shoulders of a very young man. There was no choice. He had a gift. His freedom would begin to remove the bondage of fear from a nation under constant threat. In truth, our bondage had been removed by the faith of Abraham. Even as slaves in Egypt, we were free.

There was a stop I needed to make before I returned to my sweetheart, Shoshana. I asked Colonel Stern as to the whereabouts of John Broderick. "Isaac, will your requests of me cease at some point?" I understood that Colonel Stern was tired. These last days could not have been easy. But I thought his comment was a little off. "Colonel," I said, "my nation has made more than a few requests of me. It will make more. I will happily serve, and my wife will persevere." He cut me off. "You are right, Isaac, I apologize. Forgive me. I know where John is. We have checkpoints throughout Jerusalem. I will make all the necessary arrangements for you. I will dispatch a driver, and an escort, to get you to John's location. I am sure he would love to see you. Take your time. When you have finished your meeting with John, the driver and escort will make sure you get safely home." I felt a little ashamed. With a little contrition in my voice, I said, "Thank you, Colonel." Our departing smiles were gracious. I felt relieved.

The war had not been over 24 hours. Not nearly. And yet my trip to see John Broderick went more smoothly than the millions of tourists who would follow me. There was very little traffic. At each checkpoint, the driver dutifully handed a folder piece of paper to an IDF soldier. He would look at it, come to attention, and salute. That was it. I wondered if Grant and Eisenhower were similarly treated. It was a foolish thought. Colonel Stern had made up for our little misunderstanding. The prerogatives of his rank were sure to remove all the rancor from a young Lieutenant First Class. It did.

Colonel Stern had alerted John to my arrival. We pulled up to a small compound in West Jerusalem that appeared to be the permanent residence of the Franciscans. I knocked on the door. An older man, dressed in a brownish "habit" answered. I had taken the time to learn something about Franciscan friars and their dress. Their "habit" had three parts to it: the tunic, the capuche, and the white cord. I particularly like the symbolism of the three knots in the cord. Each knot represented a vow. The three vows were of poverty, chastity and obedience. Not bad, I thought.

John was waiting for me in a beautiful courtyard, which was ablaze with the colors of flowers in perfectly manicured gardens. I recognized the lavender Bellflowers, and I so admired them that John later surprised me with a bouquet that I would deliver to Shoshana.

John and I sat down in the courtyard. I told him that I was troubled. I believed I needed to talk with someone. I believed that I needed to ask for G-d's forgiveness. "John, yesterday and before yesterday, I was a soldier. But my soul belongs to G-d. I am supposed to know the mind of G-d. But during our battle, I lusted for the blood of those who opposed us. It is true that they would have killed me. I am sorry for this. I wish to tell G-d I am sorry. I seek His forgiveness. I seek His mercy. I do not want to feel this way again. There will be future battles." I felt I had said too much. I was silent, at last.

John began. "You speak of the righteousness of G-d. His righteousness and mercy are boundless. Remember that. Pray that He will renew you in His righteousness and mercy. You are right. Battles will come again. They will reveal whether your prayers have been answered. Remember, our renewal, in Him, is according to His timing, not ours. You must seek this. Do not tire. Today, I ask you read from your Siddur (prayer book). Begin with the *Me Chamoecha*. This is the song that your ancestors sang at the Red Sea, 3,500 years ago, thanking G-d for their deliverance. It asks, '*Who is like Thee, O LORD, among the gods?*' This will remind you of the glory and wonder of His works. Also, read the *Geebore Adonai*. This will remind you of the might of G-d. He is the G-d who sustains the living with grace, and resurrects the dead with abundant mercy. Pray for your comrades *and* your enemies who have fallen. Pray for His mercy and grace." With that, John excused himself for several minutes. I believe his words were inspired. They were very wise.

We sat down together, again, in the courtyard. I began. "You were right, John. Jerusalem has been united again. We now have access to the Temple Mount and the Western Wall for the first time in two thousand years." "I fear, Isaac, that there will not be complete control of the Temple Mount. If I'm right, there will be more miracles to come. But yes, Jerusalem is united. I believe this means that the era of the gentiles is over, Isaac. Now, the world will change but again. Oh, how it will change. His will... will be done. But, things will change. It will not all be pleasant. There will be troubles, Isaac."

"Blood Moons, John. Do you mean there will be more Blood Moons?" "Yes, that, Isaac. But there is more. Take heart. We should all take heart. Psalm 19, Isaac."

> *"The heavens declare the glory of G-d;*
> *And the firmament shows His handiwork.*
> *Day unto day utters speech,*
> *And night unto night reveals knowledge."*

"Today is a day to rejoice, and to be comforted, Isaac. Listen to the words of Isaiah:"

> *"Before she was in labor, she gave birth;*
> *Before her pain came, She delivered a male child.*
> *Who has heard such a thing? Who has seen such things?*
> *Shall the earth be made to give birth in one day?*
> *Or shall a nation be born at once?*
> *For as soon as Zion was in labor,*
> *She gave birth to her children.*
> *Shall I bring to the time of birth,*
> *and not cause delivery?" says the Lord.*
> *"Shall I who cause delivery shut up the womb?" says your G-d.*
> *"Rejoice with Jerusalem,*
> *And be glad with her, all you who love her;*

Rejoice for joy with her, all you who mourn for her"...
"As one whom his mother comforts, So I will comfort you;
And you shall be comforted in Jerusalem."

I could see that John growing tired. He too was "battle" weary. I had many questions. "Take these to Shoshana. She has been patient, Isaac. Take these, please, and go. We will talk more." He handed me a bouquet of flowers that were laying on the bench. "Good bye, John. Thank you. Thank you for everything," I said. I left for our apartment.

All these years later and I can still see Shoshana's eyes as I stood in front of her in the doorway of our apartment. How beautiful you were, my love. And, John. Oh, John. You are still a bear of man, with the heart of a lion and, as I was to discover, but what was always all too apparent all along, you have the sensibilities of a lamb.

I stand on the eastern face of the Mount of Olives, looking at the Eastern Gate. I am an old man, now. Old, but not tired. Israel and Jerusalem, they were the first wonders. Most did not know it then. And then more wonders came. And yet more wonders came again. Our cups runneth over.

The door is wide open now. Troubles too. Many troubles. The story is like history: it begins in the garden and ends in the city. It is a story best told by those who have a friend who is a bear of a man, with the heart of a lion, and the sensibilities of a lamb. The friend has a secret. He knows that, in the end, the lion lays down with the lamb.

CHAPTER THREE

A VOICE IN THE WILDERNESS

"The voice of one crying in the wilderness:
Prepare the way of the Lord;
Make straight in the desert a highway for our G-d."
Isaiah 40:3

I had to learn to love G-d more than I hated my enemies. We all did. We longed for the day... the day that the "crooked places" would be made straight.

To love G-d more than we hated our enemies. That was the voice in the wilderness. *"All flesh is grass, And all its loveliness is like the flower of the field. The grass withers, the flower fades, But the Word of our G-d stands forever."*

A voice... a voice anointed by the heavens to tune our ears to the high pitched sounds of high places. The voice, as in all the days of our journey with Him, was loudest in the ears and the mouths of Moses, and all the prophets. So it would always be that some desired to hear loudly the sounds from the highest places, while others would seek the heavenly sounds of salvation at a muffled distance. These were the sounds of the Kingdom of G-d.

Daniel and I agreed that my public persona should be that of a solid, but unexceptional, physics professor. As such, I traveled about as much as you would expect from an unexceptional physics professor. We tried to keep it at no more than twice a year, usually to places that were unlikely to draw the interest of our adversaries. In March of 1977, I decided to travel to America's Midwest.

Holocaust denial was a growing problem. It had many dimensions, and its purveyors were far more sophisticated than anyone was willing to admit. The very first deniers were the Nazis themselves. As the allied victory grew inevitability, Himmler himself ordered a cover-up of the mass murder of human beings. Documents were destroyed, as were crematoria, and other signs of the "Final Solution."

After the war, high-ranking SS officers left Germany and began an effort to rewrite history. They concocted a defense of the German nation by blaming industrialists, bureaucrats and other organizations that were unaffiliated with Hitler and the Third Reich.

Many others happily picked up the gauntlet of Holocaust denial. As always, it was "nourished" by the ancient and desiccated roots of anti-Semitism. These roots have crawled and slithered for millennia, out of the garden, on their bellies, "eating the dust," progeny of a "cursed" and unholy tempter. The tempter knew that in the seed of Abraham, "all the nations of the earth shall be blessed." He lured man, who came from the dust, with all the inherent lies of the dust: the glories of jealousy, greed, power, and hatred. And so, anti-Semitism, a cursed lie of the cursed, brought man back to the dust, devoured his flesh, and damned his soul to the abyss.

Holocaust denial was making its way on to the American college campus. It became more and more popular to couch virulent anti-Semitism with attacks on Zionism. Incredibly, a professor at North-western University published a book in which he claimed that the planned extermination of Jews by the Nazis was a "Zionist inspired myth." I wanted the opportunity to privately offer encouragement to those mounting a public campaign to counter this appalling lie by a university professor.

The Nobel Prize for Physics had yet to be awarded in 1977. When I was visiting abroad, I liked to lecture on the significance of the most recent Nobel Prize in Physics. It was a challenge to explain a particular Nobel prize in dramatic terms. My audiences, who often clapped by tapping a pencil on an armrest, usually responded with uncharacteristic enthusiasm. It was also good that I found it easy to avoid connecting the relevance of any particular discovery to my work in Israel. Thus, for my "talk" at Northwestern, I would be discussing the significance of the 1976 Nobel Prize in Physics, which was awarded for uncovering the existence of a new subatomic particle.

March seemed the best time for me to travel to Northwestern. Passover came early in April that year, and I preferred not to travel in May because of our wedding anniversary. Neither Northwestern campus, Chicago nor Evanston, would have favorable weather conditions, but March was better than January or February.

Northwestern's Evanston, Illinois, campus had a Technological Institute, which incorporated seven engineering departments, and the Departments of Physics and Chemistry. Dr. Lev Steiner, the Physics Department Chairman at Hebrew University, made all the arrangements for my trip, as he had previously been a visiting professor at Northwestern's Technological Institute. It didn't hurt that Lev had been nominated for two Nobel prizes in physics.

As I arrived in Evanston late on a Wednesday afternoon, March 16th, the weather was beginning to cool from a high of about 50 °F. It could have been far worse. One of Lev's colleagues in Northwestern's Physics Department sent a graduate student to pick me at the Chicago's O'Hare Airport, which was only about 20 miles from the campus. I was escorted to a room designated for faculty housing. It seemed to be mostly graduate students. Although I was tired, I needed to finish the notes for my lecture. I had a quick dinner, worked for a few hours, and went to bed.

By the time I roused myself from a sound sleep, it was already afternoon in Jerusalem. I called Shoshana to tell her that all was well.

The political season was beginning to get traction in Israel. Neither Shoshana nor I saw the political "earthquake" that was coming in May. Shoshana was continuing her work preparing for a Children's Holocaust Memorial. She was pleased that part of my trip was to support a concerted effort to oppose Holocaust denial on campus. We both knew it was not nearly enough to just tell the truth. Deniers were impervious to the truth. It was the decent person whom we had to convince that memory was an important defense against the blandishments of evil. Evil was a strategic mastermind, and its appetites never flagged.

Late Thursday morning, I was greeted by the Chairman of the Physics department and his senior colleagues. There were many questions about Lev, especially about when I thought, after several nominations, he would finally be awarded the Nobel Prize for Physics. I am sure they were curious about the nature of his work. Frankly, he knew nothing of my work, and I knew little of his. I was very familiar with his published work on quantum theory. So we delved into Lev's ingenious insights into the quantum theory of light.

I was scheduled to speak at 2:00 p.m. in one of the main lecture halls at Northwestern's Technological Institute. We had a quick lunch in the faculty lounge and headed off to the new library under construction, just east of the Technological Institute. It was impressive, to say the least. There were three stories with 55,000 square feet of library resources for Astronomy, Biology, and the entirety of the Technological Institute Libraries. American universities were the envy of the world for good reason.

As we made our way back to the Technological Institute, a professor in the Electrical Engineering and Computer Science Department stopped me. He asked if he could have a word with me, and promised my other hosts that he would get me to the lecture hall on time. He handed me what he described as a computer science research paper written by one of his undergraduate students. He wanted me to read the paper, and was confident I would share his assessment that it was a brilliant exposition of a key aspect of computer security. I was anxious to get to the lecture hall early. I promised him I would read it.

We did arrive early, but not the usual 30 minutes or so I preferred. My "talks" were better, or at least I thought so, when I had the opportunity to mingle a little with the audience. This routine relaxed me. I did see some familiar faces seated in the first several rows. I took the opportunity to have a few brief conversations, and tried to maintain a relaxed smile. Any nerves would usually disappear the longer I wore the smile.

It was standing room only in the hall. I liked that. Somehow, I thought that I had a better chance with a larger group. I received an enthusiastic introduction, and a very warm welcome from the faculty and students. Now for the risk that I always took. Invariably, I began my speeches with a short comedy skit. Not a joke, but a skit. I figured a joke could easily fall flat. If I did a skit, how could they not admire the effort? After all, according to none other than Father John Broderick, I was a physics professor.

I always loved American comedy. There was no shortage of comedians to watch on television when I was at Princeton. Red Skelton was my favorite. He was often compared to Charlie Chaplin. In fact, he even purchased the Chaplin studios in the early 60's.

Skelton was a master of pantomime. He was also a master of creating lovable, oddball characters. His performance of Gertrude and Heathcliff, two goofy seagulls, not only made me laugh, but whenever I did my version for Shoshana, she wound up in tears from laughing so hard. So I tried it again.

The Northwestern crowd seemed to love it. I could be certain that they had never seen a physics professor do something so out of character. There I was, flapping my arms, wearing a worn out vaudeville hat, sideways, and doing outlandish voices of two eccentric seagulls.

I'm not sure there is a segue to a seminar about the 1976 Nobel Prize in Physics. From Gertrude and Heathcliff to an overhead projector full of mathematical equations written furiously on multiple transparencies. It went over all too well. I was relieved.

I was asked to reserve some time at the end of my talk for questions from the audience. I was impressed with the questions from the students. They came prepared. Seagulls or no seagulls, these student were as serious as any I had ever encountered. But one question stood out from among the others.

I don't know why, but early on in my presentation, I took notice of a young man sitting in the last row of the lecture hall. He was taking notes, constantly hunched over. Rarely did he ever even raise his head. But he did raise his hand. His was the final question. He wasn't at all nervous, but his speech was slow, and deliberate, as if he had trained himself to overcome a stutter.

He asked if entropy was further proof of G-d's existence. Oh yes, the second law of thermodynamics. Entropy, or disorder or chaos, always increases in isolated systems. If the "natural" process favors disorder or chaos, then life is an anomaly. Perhaps life is indeed impossible.

I thought a lot about entropy, particularly because of my faith. I had even developed a mathematical rationale for how to account for maximum entropy, while maintaining the "order" that is essential for life to not only exist, but thrive.

So I began to clean off many of the transparencies because I knew they would fill up quickly with my mathematical "speculations." The faculty reaction was immediate. They began to hurriedly pull out their notebooks, and copy down the mathematical formulae I was spewing out. This was not good. I had to maintain my reputation as an "unexceptional" physics professor. I stopped writing, and turned off the overhead. I complimented the student on an excellent question, and observation. My last words were that in a "world of entropy, life is unnatural, but not unimaginable."

It turned out to be a long afternoon. The Dean of Engineering had a reception, including dinner, in my honor at his house that lasted until about 8:00 p.m. The conversation was unusually lively. Quarks, no. Entropy, not much. It was dominated by two seagulls, Gertrude and Heathcliff, and little else. They wanted a repeat performance, and all the other routines I had in my repertoire. Other professors jumped on the bandwagon and it turned out to be a talent show for nerds, and other misfits of academia. Something must have been in the air that day. That reaction never happened again. I wish it had.

I didn't return to my room quite late enough to call Shoshana. It was still too early in Jerusalem. I would call her in the morning. From my perspective, the difficult part of the trip was over. I felt a profound responsibility to represent Hebrew University well. I did not have a typical assignment there. But when I represented the university abroad, especially in the United States, I wanted there to be a lasting impression. Comedy aside, I think I accomplished my goal for this trip.

I wasn't scheduled to return to Israel until Sunday. On Friday morning, after calling Shoshana, I had Colonel Stern and my duty to the IDF on my mind. Although I was going to be 38 in December, I continued my physical training for special forces duty in the IDF. Northwestern was kind enough to let me train with several of their ROTC units on campus. Most of the trainees were half my age. But special forces is special forces. I think they were surprised that I could more than keep up. I loved being around the young people training that day. They were serious about what they were doing. They were also optimistic, and loved their country. I was most struck, as usual, by their decency and curiosity.

I had a very light lunch so I could continue my physical training in the afternoon. Finally, at about 2:30 p.m., I was satisfied that Colonel Stern got "his pound of flesh." I wanted to shower, take a short nap, and be ready for a Shabbat (Sabbath) celebration at sundown.

I had been invited by Hillel because of my interest to provide support to students, and others, who opposed efforts to minimize, or even deny, the Holocaust. A Northwestern professor had published a book characterizing the Holocaust as "The Hoax of the Twentieth Century." Hillel is a campus organization for Jewish students to learn about their identity and history. It operated on hundreds of American college campuses. The Hillel group at Northwestern had invited me to share a Shabbat (Sabbath) meal with students and professors that I was honored to attend.

I arrived just before sundown at the private home of a professor who volunteered to help Hillel organize student activities. The group was a little larger than I anticipated. I immediately recognized several faces. Sitting in a chair away from most of the crowd was the young man who had asked the question about entropy. As I began my approach to greet him, I felt a tug on the arm of my jacket. It was the computer science professor who had previously handed me the paper to read. He thanked me for coming and wanted to alert me that the author of the paper was the young man in the chair. I was very grateful because I had no opportunity to read even the first word. He whispered in my ear, "His name is David Bass."

As I approached his chair with my hand outstretched, he quickly go to his feet. "David," I said, "what a pleasure to meet you." His firm and confident handshake belied his shy demeanor. "Pro-fes-sor Sin-ger, the ho-nor is mine," he replied. In point of fact, David did not seem the least bit self-conscious about his slower than normal speech pattern. In addition to a confident handshake, he had confident eyes.

"David, I want to apologize, but I haven't had the opportunity to read your paper. You have my word I will read it tomorrow, after sundown. If it is possible, David, maybe you could give me a ride to the airport. My plane leaves Sunday morning, at 11:20."

He wasn't slow to take me up on the offer. "Pro-fes-sor, I... will pi-ck you up at 9:30. Just wri-te down the ad-dress for me be-fore you leave."

"Good, I'll see you then," I said.

Before we were to begin the Shabbat service, I was asked to say a few words to the students and faculty who were present. I had nothing prepared, but I was happy to do it.

There were a lot of smiles after I promised not to do another skit. David was smiling and chuckling. I thanked them profusely for inviting me to share a Shabbat celebration with them.

"My wife volunteers at Yad Vashem, the Holocaust Memorial in Israel. She is documenting the atrocities committed against children because they were declared 'unfit.' One-and-a-half million children perished in the Holocaust. I have seen many of the artifacts, children's possessions really, that are being collected for display at Yad Vashem. To deny the mass murder of 6 million human beings, you either have to be delusional, or be such a coward that you will not say what you really mean: that you regret that the 'Final Solution' was not successful."

"Israel is a miracle. Today, there are about 3 million Jews living in Israel. A de facto war was declared on Israel the moment she was founded. Yet, I assure you that Israel is here to stay."

The service itself was different than what I celebrated with Shoshana. That could be expected. It was a wonderful gift to observe seasoned faculty, and their young "apprentices," worship together.

As we were preparing to leave, I asked if I could read a verse from Jeremiah.

"Behold, the days are coming, says the Lord, when I will make a new covenant with the house of Israel and with the house of Judah... I will put My law in their minds, and write it on their hearts; and I will be their G-d, and they shall be My people. No more shall every man teach his neighbor, and every man his brother, saying, 'Know the Lord,' for they all shall know Me, from the least of them to the greatest of them," says the Lord."

I asked everyone that night to, above all, be faithful. Yes, be faithful to the righteousness of G-d. His gifts far surpass the beauty of creation. I often thought, what is creation without the heart to see it? As the whale breaches the surface of a clear blue ocean, does he fix an admiring eye on his brother whale, who bursts skyward on the canvas of a distant horizon, painted gloriously by the hues of a setting sun?

Does the eagle marvel as his mate floats on wave after imperceptible wave of warmed air that crawls out of the crevasses of the earth?

There is more to G-d than the capacity to appreciate the beauty of His creation. For it is true that we behold beauty because G-d breathed into our nostrils "the breath of life," but justice, the law, charity, and mercy are also gifts conferred on us through the breath of His human endowment. He made short work of creating the tapestry of the universe. Less than a week's time.

He is long suffering. He awaits our spiritual maturity. For He desires the company of righteous men and women.

I made sure I left my address for David. I wanted to get an early start for the airport. One of the professors handed me an envelope. He said, "This is our plan to fight back against Holocaust denial on campus. Please read it, and call me if you have any further suggestions." I told him I would read it tomorrow, after sundown. A plan, I thought. Good. Very good!

David was thoughtful enough to realize that I preferred not to drive, or be driven, on the Sabbath. He drew me a map that would get me back to my room in about 15 minutes by foot. It did! I was asleep in less than that.

I woke up Saturday morning looking forward to my trip back to Israel. I missed Shoshana, and I missed using her nickname. When I was at Princeton, I used to visit a friend of mine who was doing graduate work at Rutgers. It was a short drive on the turnpike, and I shared his love for Italian food. I would call ahead and he would forewarn the restaurant that the "kosher kid," as they used to call me, was on his way. I usually had kosher Caponata and Focaccia Bread. What a treat it was, especially in those days.

The owner of the restaurant always referred to his wife as "my Rosie." They had a great relationship, and somehow the name stuck with me. How "fortunate" Shoshana was that her name meant "rose" in Hebrew. So, "my Rosie," Shoshana, let me use her nickname as much as I liked, if we were alone together. One day, I arrived at our apartment before Shoshana. As I looked out one of windows facing the street, there she was, looking beautiful as she confidently strode towards the stairs. I opened the window and yelled, "hey Rosie," in my best New Jersey Italian accent. She opened the door, and there we were, the only two fools in Jerusalem who could have possibly understood what was so funny. How could you not miss someone who could laugh at something so ludicrous? She was "my Rosie."

Sundown always seemed to come early on the Sabbath. It was the Lord's day. I looked forward to the time when every day belonged to the Lord, as it should. I knew I had a little reading to do. I wanted to make sure that I carefully read David's paper, as well as the plan for countering the hellish lie that the Holocaust was a fabrication.

The plan was a good one, and it involved more than just Hillel. The president of Northwestern not only wrote a letter denouncing the book as an "insult" and an "affront," but he also committed the university to sponsoring a series of four lectures on the Holocaust. For its part, Hillel intended to run an ad in the student newspaper asking students not to register for the professor's spring classes. Not a bad start, at all. I called the professor who had handed me the letter to tell him just that.

David's paper was brilliant, and a fantastical coincidence, although he couldn't possibly have known the extent of the coincidence. I was familiar with the work being done on encryption, which would become central to securely exchanging information over vast computer networks. Eventually, the type of encryption David was writing about would become the dominant method to protecting transactions, worldwide, including between customers and banks, credit card companies and merchants. It also had very important national security applications. We would find out later that the development of this encryption method even occurred during the course of a student's Passover Seder. It would be an interesting ride to the airport.

David arrived promptly at 9:30 a.m. I was on the curb waiting. I planted my suitcase firmly in the back seat, and shook hands with David as I ungracefully plopped down in the front seat. John would have been proud of the awkward professor.

I was surprised that David did not ask me about his paper right away. Perhaps he didn't remember that I had been given a copy. David had the prophet Isaiah on his mind. He began, "Pro-fess-or, the ri-de should on-ly take 30 min-utes. Wha-t did Is-ai-ah mean by a new cov-e-nant with the peo-ple of Is-ra-el?"

"David, I struggle with this, just like everybody else. Now, as in the times of our forefathers, we have to listen to His law, and incorporate the law, and its true meaning, into our hearts. In the course of bringing the law to our hearts, there has always been fleshly resistance. The law is 'filtered' through our human desires. These desires have often overwhelmed our ability to achieve His wish for us: that our joy be derived from seeking His purposes for our lives. Isaiah is speaking of a time when we won't have to learn about His law from a neighbor or a Rabbi, because He will put His law into our minds, and write onto our hearts."

"But, Pro-fess-or, wi-ll this be for fr-ee? "No, David," I said. "I do not think so. Think about your namesake, King David. The House of David was richly blessed by the Lord. *'The Lord has sought for Himself a man after His own heart.'* And David was a man after the Lord's own heart for it was the Lord himself who said to David, *'Whereas it was in your heart to build a temple for My name, you did well in that it was in your heart.'"* I believe the House of David was so blessed because it was *in* David's heart to build a temple for the Lord. David was a man after the heart of the Lord because the Lord did not have to ask David to build a temple. King David had a true heart for G-d. This tells me that G-d will especially bless us if we will take the initiative."

"Bu-t, how wou-ld this be do-ne, Pro-fess-or?" "We will have to be moved to seek G-d with the desire that His law would be written on our hearts," I said. "Our desire will have to be such that He will know that we are prepared to have His law written on our hearts. In a sense, we will be called out of the world so that everyone will hear the sound, a call from the Lord of heaven to seek Him above all else. I think, in short, David, we have to spiritually grow up."

"I m-ust th-ink ab-out this m-ore Pro-fess-or." "David, we don't have much time. Your computer science professor gave me a paper you wrote. I want to tell you that it is exceptional. It may be beyond exceptional, David. You should continue your studies."

"Pro-fes-sor, I ne-ed to s-ay some-th-ing... I wo-uld li-ke to he-lp my coun-try and Is-ra-el." "David, by help, do you mean you would like to help the national security of both countries?" "Ye-s, pro-fess-or." "David, I am only a professor. Do not tell anyone else of this ambition. Let's stay in touch by mail, David. But do not write about this in your letters. Do you understand?" "Ye-s, pro-fess-or." "Now, David, I may know someone you can speak to. I will see."

"Over there, David. Please pull up over there next to the police-man. I need to go through those double doors. Here is my address, David. Write me soon, and tell me the effect of the campaign against that ridiculous book." "Th-ank you, Pro-fess-or, I wi-ll wr-ite." "O-h Pro-fess-or, he-re is a-no-ther co-py of my pa-per." "Thank you, Da-vid."

It was a lot to discuss in a short ride to the airport. David's aspira-tions took me by surprise. He wanted to enter a world I knew all too well. The truth is that, with his talent, eventually that world would have found him. In some respects, it was better that he told me of his peculiar interest. He had a better chance of avoiding some alley ways that led to nowhere, or worse. I didn't mind steering him in the right direction, if that is what he genuinely wanted. There was something about David.

I arrived in Israel and was greeted with a note to see John on Monday evening, if possible. The "if possible" part was not needed. John rarely asked to see me. I would be there.

The laboratory in Jerusalem had become a valuable asset in our research infrastructure. Many improvements were made over the years. To avoid unwanted attention, the improvements had to be accomplished in excruciatingly tiny, incremental, steps. But they were. The lab, with none of the comforts of home, was still our meeting place.

John came through the still "invisible" door of the lab about 30 minutes after me. We were still careful.

The years had been kind to John. John had secrets, to be sure, but I don't think he had a secret to holding off the effects of age. It wouldn't occur to John.

He began by asking about my trip to Northwestern. "John, there is a professor on their campus who has written a book about the Holocaust titled, 'The Hoax of the Twentieth Century.' But the university is fighting back. I was encouraged. The speech went well. I began my speech with a little skit I borrowed from Red Skelton. It went over well." "So, who are you now?", John asked. "Soldier, professor, comedian, and faithful servant of G-d?" "I'll take the faithful servant of G-d part," I responded, "and add faithful husband. I'm not too sure about the others, John." "Oh yes, you are a man of many talents, Isaac. G-d is not given to bestowing so many talents on just one man. He must have a great purpose for you." "Well, John, if He does have a great purpose for me, then I can only say that I am unworthy of this," I replied. "That is why He would choose you, Isaac. Remember what was said about Moses."

He came to the point of his visit. "Isaac, the politics of Israel are so complicated that I never try to speculate. It's ridiculous to even try. Maybe it's just over my head. Something is changing, though. Perhaps the people are just tired. On the other hand, it could be the various scandals. There has been 30 years of dominance by one party. I believe the public thinks that 30 years is long enough." "Is there something in the heavens, John?" I said, with a slight smile on my face. He chuckled. "No, Isaac, nothing like that." "This time the feeling is in my gut. It's not as good as signs from the heavens, but it's not too bad."

"So, John, what do you think this means?" I asked. "This will not be a small shift, Isaac. Let's look for the unexpected. G-d seems to love irony. I think in America they call it a 'curveball.' So, Isaac, I think this election G-d is going to throw us a 'curveball.' We shall see."

"Well, John, I met an interesting young man while I was visiting Northwestern. He wrote a brilliant computer science paper. He was a 'curveball.' He asked me about helping America and Israel in the national security area. I told him I was only a professor, but I may know someone with whom he could take up this interest of his." "Does he remind you of yourself, at all?" John asked. "No, John, he's probably smarter than I am; we spoke about Isaiah and King David on the way to the airport. He listened intently."

"Isaac, you have the heart of a warrior. Fear is your friend. But there are things to be afraid of, Isaac. I know you know this. Daniel and I have discussed this with you. Be careful, Isaac, not for you, but for this young man. It will become more dangerous. Be careful for him. Is this the paper you are talking about, Isaac?" "Yes, John, I put it there to remind myself to speak to Daniel about him." "What is this on the back, Isaac?" "I don't know, John. It looks he was doodling." "May I borrow this, Isaac?" "Sure, John, I have another copy. I wasn't aware that you liked computer science so much. I thought astronomy was more suited to your tastes." "You've come all this way, just to mock me, Isaac. I must say, I missed you. I must go. See you soon, Isaac." "Goodbye, John!"

I decided the world could wait a little longer for David Bass. At least, Daniel's world could. I would wait until after Passover, at the earliest, to discuss David's potential contributions with anyone. Prayer and reflection would be good tonics.

Passover came early in April. I was so looking forward to our Passover meal this year. Aaron was going to be there. I hadn't seen my brother for a while. I knew it had been a very difficult few years for Aaron. His wife had decided on a military career, and she was killed during a training accident. We later found out that she was pregnant at the time of the accident. It broke our hearts. I was hoping that Aaron was recovering the best one could under the circumstances.

On the day of the Passover meal, Aaron called to ask if it would be all right if he arrived a little early. I wished he would arrive early. I wished he would stay at least a week. I wished he lived close by. I wished. Oh, how I wished. I suspected he wanted to come early because he had something to talk to me about.

Shoshana opened the door to our apartment, and there he was, Aaron Weiss. He looked good. Shoshana brought out a little gleam in his eye, and that was encouraging. We embraced. The embrace was a little longer this time. There was much to catch up on.

Aaron sat and had a nice visit with Shoshana. He was a class act. He knew her before I did. And he was very thankful that we were so happy together. He even referred to himself as the flying Shadchan. I thought I wouldn't hear that for a very long while. The laughter was unrestrained. In our neighborhood, it counted for virtual mayhem.

As we started to quiet down, Aaron caught my eye. I knew it was time. I asked Shoshana if she minded if I showed Aaron a few of the additions to our library. We excused ourselves, and Aaron and I sat down at opposite ends of a couch that was against the wall in the library. He got right to the point.

"What did Colonel Stern tell you about my wife's accident, Isaac?" His question hit me like a thud. I briefly looked away towards the window to gather myself. "He told me she died in an accident. That was all he said about the matter." I thought that sounded wrong, as if

Colonel Stern gave it short shrift. He didn't. Aaron didn't seem to mind.

She wasn't killed in an accident, Isaac. Devorah had been visiting her family in a moshav near the border of Lebanon. Terrorists crossed the border at night and entered one of the homes. Devorah fought back and was the first one killed. The rest of her family were held as hostages, and their captors tried to exchange them for Palestinian terrorists in our prisons. The IDF raided the home. Two more family members were killed, and an IDF soldier. All the terrorists were killed.

"Why the cover story, Aaron?" "They didn't want the terrorist groups to have the satisfaction that they killed an IDF soldier, and her unborn child. It would have been a propaganda coup for them. I think that's right, Isaac. But I thought you deserved to know." "And the sponsors of the cell in Lebanon? How about them, Aaron?" "All Daniel told me was they 'cleaned house.' That was enough for me. I asked him about you leading the team. He smiled, and said that the country 'owed us on this one.' That was that."

"Thank you, Aaron, for telling me how Devorah died. You were right, I would have led the team. I don't relish blood, or vengeance. Sometimes things have to be put right. How is Devorah's family?" "She was a righteous woman, from a righteous family. They understand what all of this means. We have to do this, Isaac. If we must bury our dead, it should be in our way, at our appointed time. What that means is that we are living our lives according to our traditions. Freedom, Isaac. We won't be run off the land."

"Devorah has a younger sister that her father would like me to marry. It may be exactly the right thing to do. I am in no hurry." He looked at me with a twinkle in his eye. "I don't have a Shadchan to worry about." We both smiled, and enjoyed a muffled laugh.

Aaron would be just fine. He was our winged sentry. He safeguarded our dreams, and kept our fears from running rampant into the night. He cleared the skies so that our view of the heavens would not

be filled with the dread of lurkers and trespassers. Aaron comprehended the stakes for our nation. Our memorials needed to stand as
monuments to our vigorous defense of our survival, not as rueful reminders that we fell prey to the designs of Evil.

John was right. May did indeed bring seismic changes in Israeli
politics. It also brought tragedy. Fifty-four IDF soldiers were killed
when their helicopter crashed in the Jordan Valley. Aaron knew several of the Israeli Air Force officers killed in the crash. He
volunteered to help comfort the bereaved families. His own experience would probably help console the inconsolable. Shoshana and I
prayed that G-d would give him the right words. It was an assignment
no one could want.

Political shock came to Israel. Thirty years of essentially one party
rule came to an end. It did not bother me that the new Prime Minister
left the Haganah, which was the organization my parents had joined to
defend Jewish communities in the Land of Israel before statehood. He
believed that the British administration during this period had tilted
away from Jewish immigration to the region. That was probably true.
Zionist groups needed to become more aggressive. He became one of
the most "wanted" men in the region. It was even said that he would
disguise himself as a Rabbi. I liked that. It made my absent-minded
professor "disguise" a little more palatable.

John liked the irony. The press hated it. The press had labeled this
new Prime Minister as a "hard liner." They even went so far as to
characterize his resistance to the British as "terrorism." So how could
a "hard-line terrorist," be a peacemaker? They hadn't counted on the
desire of an Egyptian president to reclaim land lost to Israel in a war.

That Egyptian president not only became the first Arab leader to
visit Israel, he gave a speech in the Knesset, the legislature of Israel.
The topic was peace. Peace between… Egypt and Israel. Was this
peace to be the peace that Joseph, son of Jacob, great grandson of
Abraham, had with an earlier pharaoh of Egypt? Or, was it only a
respite?

Shortly after the Israeli elections, I received word that John wanted to meet with me. John was not given to boastfulness. It simply was not part of his nature. Did John really want to discuss how right he was about the Israeli elections? It made no sense.

John knew that I was often in the laboratory on Tuesday afternoons. So when he opened the door to the lab, after his familiar knock, I was not surprised. I quickly got our chairs in order. He looked mildly pensive, which was unusual for John. A bear of a man with a pensive look is an interesting combination. I shook his hand and congratulated him on his political crystal ball. At first, he didn't seem to understand what I meant. Then, he remembered. "Oh yes," he said, "that." It obviously wasn't what he wanted to talk about.

"What is it, John?" Now, I was a bit concerned. "Do you recall that I took a copy of David's paper, Isaac?" "Yes, John, I do. If you are about to hold forth on the brilliance of his thesis, John, then I need to find out more about what you and your brother Franciscans are really up to." John liked that. He smiled, and relaxed a bit.

"I found out something very curious, Isaac. This doodle on the back of the last page. I have a friend who studies ancient languages. His work has always fascinated me. I have learned a fair amount about ancient languages over the many years of our friendship. I thought I recognized something in David's scribbles on the last page of his paper. Look at this, Isaac. You read Hebrew, of course." "Of course I read Hebrew, John. But what you are pointing at doesn't look familiar to me." "According to my friend, this is Paleo-Hebrew, which dates back to the 10th century B.C. Modern Hebrew began in the 5th century B.C., when the Aramaic alphabet was adopted as the writing system for Hebrew."

"Wait a minute, John. You are telling me that a college kid in Illinois is doodling in ancient Hebrew? Do I have that about right, John?" "Actually, Isaac, it's Hebrew from the 7th or 8th century, B.C. And it's probably at least a one million to one probability that David unwittingly scratched out ancient Hebrew." "Was your friend able to translate what David wrote, John?" For some reason I was not anxious to hear John's answer. I had a feeling that the life of a young man in Illinois was about to change.

"This part, Isaac. This part, here." Now I did see more coherence in what looked before to be aimless drawing. "Yes, I see, John. What does it mean?" "It means 'ewe', Isaac. A ewe is a female sheep." I couldn't resist. "I could be wrong, John, but I don't think there are many Jewish sheep farmers these days, do you?" The bear of a man got the closest he ever would to a scowling look on his face. I was appropriately chastened. He moved on.

"Isaac, look also at this part of David's drawing. There isn't a word here, just two letters, S and H. It is likely that they belong together. They are probably part of a word that has an 'sh' in it."

"I am little at a loss, John. What should I do with this information?" "First, Isaac, find out if David is studying ancient Hebrew. There may be a completely reasonable explanation for this. If it can't be explained in that way, then you will need to stay close to David. I should say that we will need to stay close to David." "It means Daniel, is that right, John?" "Yes, find out about his studies first, Isaac. Then we will meet again to discuss the next step. I would recommend that you use the phone. Ask Daniel. Do not tell Daniel about the drawing, just say that David may prove to be an extremely important asset to Israel and the U.S. Do this soon. Is that alright, Isaac?" "Yes, John, I understand."

I contacted Golda and asked her to follow-up with Northwestern University to get David's phone number. I used a secure phone that was located in the room adjacent to the president's office where Daniel and I would often meet.

I felt bad that I hadn't answered several letters from David. They were thoughtful letters, and deserved a reply. Now was my opportunity to make amends. David was very surprised by my phone call. I apologized more than once for not responding to his letters. I kept the conversation on general matters about his courses, and his social life on campus. At the end of the conversation I asked him about whether he studied Hebrew. David only knew a few words in Hebrew. I asked Golda to arrange for John to meet me at the laboratory the next day. I would meet Daniel the following morning.

John arrived earlier than usual. John was never grim, even when the circumstances might have warranted it. John was worried about a young man who couldn't possibly know about everything the world had to offer. The depths of the darkness were even less apparent in the American Midwest. John was right to worry.

John asked about Shoshana. He usually did. His kindness shone through, as usual. "Did you speak with David," he began. "Yes, John, he says he only knows a few words in Hebrew. I have a meeting with Daniel, tomorrow morning." "What will you ask him to do, Isaac?" "I intend to give him a copy of David's paper, and suggest David is someone who could be very valuable to both countries. I will also tell him that David does not strike me as a warrior/scientist, so I will ask him to proceed carefully." "Good, Isaac. Very Good! That's the right way to approach this matter. I worry that David could draw interest from people I would rather not have him know. Do you understand, Isaac?" "I think so, John."

"My brother Franciscans and I haven't seen you recently at our little sanctuary, Isaac. Don't be such a stranger. Alright?" "I promise, I won't be, John." The truth is that I hadn't been to the Franciscan monastery since the end of the '67 war. John's invitation was interesting. It probably meant that I would need as much spiritual strength as I could muster. Fair enough. I hoped they could spare another bouquet of their beautiful flowers. Shoshana would like that.

Daniel was already waiting for me when I arrived at Golda's desk the next morning. I winked at her as I passed by; I was hoping she would understand the "wink code" to mean that, maybe next time, we could have her little cakes and some coffee. I wanted to talk about my parents, and the old days. I had been missing them recently.

The years had been kind to Daniel. He was trim; he looked fit enough to handle any mission that might be assigned to a much younger man. I handed him David's paper, and explained the extraordinary nature of David's hypotheses. I told him of David's interest. He said if the specialists concurred with my opinion of David's work, then he would work with his American counterparts to utilize David's talents. Cryptography was growing in importance to both countries.

I looked Daniel in the eye. "He doesn't know his limits, Daniel. We need his brains not his brawn." "You are fond of this young man, aren't you, Isaac?" "Yes, I am, Daniel." "This is not the business for fondness, Isaac." "Why, Daniel, I thought you were fond of me. Have I been wrong all these years?" "I like your sense of humor, Isaac. That's all. I'll see you." And with that, David Bass began an improbable life, barely hinted at by ancient Hebrew.

Daniel wasted little time. The formal assessment of David's treatise only increased his potential value to both countries. David was contacted and agreed to the plan that had been jointly worked out between Daniel and his counterparts in America. David was to transfer to the University of Illinois. He would continue his education and work for a small software company. Daniel did not want to cut David off from his regular communication with me. But, certain "precautions" had to be taken. He wrote under several pseudonyms. And his letters often had the look of routine inquiries to Hebrew University, mailed from different locations. It was elaborate, but necessary. I welcomed his letters. They were inquisitive, and had an innocent quality about them. That was good for both of us. By necessity, I wrote to him, infrequently.

While he wasn't aware of it, David was fortunate to have the guidance of a man like John Broderick. He was an ordained priest whose ear was tuned to the prophetic voice, but he was not a prophet. He was a man with a supple enough intellect to marvel at, and even comprehend, the elegance of the mind of G-d. G-d's was an elegant mind, bathed in a love for a creature made in His image, never tiring of helping us imagine a future in which His Kingdom would have no end.

My colleagues had a self-aggrandizing tendency to describe their own mathematical representations as "elegant" solutions to a problem. They loved their elegance, but weren't "elegant" enough to plainly tell me from where the winds came when they blew, and where they went when they blew no more. If we emerged from the muck, where was it in the muck that love and mercy, and beauty, resided? Did mercy arrive just after the birds sprouted wings, and just before the rose petal was painted red. Was love crouching in the corner of a primordial cave, ready to enter his heart when man descended from the hilltops to the valley below. And did beauty, shy though it be, burst onto the horizon after the last star was planted in the sky?

The truth is that we do have remarkable faculties. Elegance is a perquisite of G-d. It is of a piece with the heavens, and all of Creation. Shavuot is a holiday celebrating the beginning of the new agricultural season, the Harvest Holiday or the Holiday of First Fruits. It is also a celebration of the giving of the Ten Commandments to Moses at Mount Sinai. We harvest to live. We live according to a moral law to be civilized. Now that is elegant. John would agree.

Was David Bass entering a world in which there was something new under the sun? Peace that is a genuine peace between Israel and her neighbors could be distilled down to one simple question: Would treaties change the obsession? By 1981, an Egyptian president would sign a peace treaty with Israel. His successor honored the peace treaty with Israel and was described by Rabbi Ovadia Yosef as a man of peace who "loves Israel." But there was something else.

The Ikhwan, the Muslim Brotherhood, and their fellow travelers were deeply rooted in Egyptian society, and in the Arab world. And their history, their imagery, and their rhetoric were entwined with the dead soul of Nazism.

The "brothers" were founded in Egypt in 1928 by Sheikh Hassan al-Banna. His dream was to restore the Caliphate, and resume the mighty and final holy war, or jihad, against the non-Muslim world. His first opportunity to launch an international jihad came during the Great Arab Revolt of 1936-1939.

This revolt featured another leader of the Muslim Brotherhood, the Hajj Amin al-Husseini, Grand Mufti (Supreme Muslim religious leader) of Jerusalem. Al-Husseini mobilized his followers to engage in a three-year war against the Jews in the Holy Land. In 1936 the Brotherhood had 800 members. After two years of the Revolt, in 1938, its membership had grown to almost 200,000, with fifty branches in Egypt alone. And by the end of the 1930s, the "brothers" had a half million registered members, in more than 2,000 branches across the Arab world. They also had a growing alliance with Nazi Germany.

Mein Kampf was translated into Arabic as "My Jihad." Nazi cartoons were adapted to portray the Jew as the demonic enemy of Allah. As early as spring 1933, the Grand Mufti Al-Husseini assured the German consul in Jerusalem that "the Muslims inside and outside Holy Land welcome the new regime of Germany and hope for the extension of the fascist, anti-democratic governmental system to other countries." He planned a death camp modeled on Auschwitz to be constructed near Nablus, approximately 30 miles north of Jerusalem. Al-Husseini personally lobbied Hungary, Romania, and Bulgaria to prevent Jews from leaving those countries even though the governments were initially willing to let them go. The Grand Mufti also encouraged Germany to concentrate its efforts on the extermination of European Jewry. As Adolph Eichmann himself recounted: "We have promised him [the Mufti] that no European Jew would enter Palestine anymore."

The president of Egypt who signed the peace treaty with Israel was murdered by associates of the Muslim Brotherhood. They would later take power in Egypt. If there was something new under the sun, it wasn't yet apparent.

There was a growing problem in Lebanon, and David Bass was going to help us with it. Palestinian terrorist groups had been operating in Southern Lebanon since 1968. These groups were the source of cross-border attacks against Israelis. Aaron's wife had been killed in such an attack. In March of 1978, led by an eighteen year old female, a Palestinian group hijacked a bus on the coastal road near Haifa, and then seized a second bus that was headed to Tel Aviv. Bus rides don't usually end in massacres. This one did. Thirty-eight Israeli civilians, including 13 children, were killed and 76 were wounded. Three days later, the "Coastal Road Massacre," as it came to be known, led to a large scale Israeli military operation in Southern Lebanon.

By the end of the operation, the IDF was able to push the Palestinian terrorist groups away from Israel's border. The United Nations created a "peacekeeping" force to pacify Southern Lebanon and help the legitimate government of Lebanon reassert its control there. The UN force was not effective. The crisis simmered over the next three years, and boiled over in 1982.

As a prelude to a wider war, in 1981, Israel struck the Beirut headquarters of the Palestinian terrorists and their positions in South Lebanon, after extremely heavy rocket fire rained down on the towns of Northern Israel. A ceasefire was brokered by the United States.

In June 1982, the ceasefire collapsed. The last straw was a Palestinian terror group's attempted assassination of Israel's ambassador to the United Kingdom. The attack prompted the Lebanon War. It was called Operation Peace for Galilee. IDF forces meant to expel the Palestinian terrorist groups from Lebanon. They also sought to remove Syrian influence over Lebanon. The IDF eventually surrounded the Palestinians and the Syrian army, as both groups became hunkered down, and essentially isolated in Beirut, Lebanon's capital. With little choice, both groups negotiated for safe passage out of Lebanon, protected by international peacekeepers.

In an ominous development, on the fourth day of the war, Syria moved 19 SA-6 surface-to-air missile batteries southwest into Lebanon's Bekaa Valley to protect Palestinian forces there. The SA-6 batteries were Russian-made, and the Syrians believed they would protect Palestinian ground operations from Israeli Air Force attack. Enter David Bass and a small team of sophisticated "safecrackers." They "cracked" the combination to the Russian air defense system.

The Israeli Air Force (IAF) attacked. They used a combination of radar-jamming electronic warfare, radiation-seeking missiles and early unmanned aircraft. The IAF destroyed 17 of the 19 missile batteries, and downed 29 Syrian jets without suffering any losses of it own. Yes, Aaron Weiss, flying Shadchan extraordinaire, was pleased. So was I. I knew something about the unmanned (drone) aircraft.

Eventually, Israel Defense Forces would withdraw from Beirut to southern Lebanon, following an agreement in May of 1983. An Israeli Security Zone was established in southern Lebanon, lasting from 1985-2000, to put Israel's border towns out of range of small arms and mortar fire.

Shoshana had been worried in those years about me being activated for duty in the IDF. Colonel Stern, who had turned down promotions to maintain his "hands on" involvement with the Special Forces, thought better of my return to active duty. "We need technology to be a force multiplier," he said. "Otherwise, we will be overwhelmed by pure numbers." He was right, of course. Shoshana was relieved, of course. It turned out that, according to what a high-ranking member of the Warsaw Pact told a colleague of Aaron's, the Israeli and U. S. technology and tactics were so dominant during the war that it helped change the Soviet mind-set, leading to Glasnost, and ultimately the fall of the Soviet Union.

I missed being a warrior. But I never complained, and I never mentioned it to anybody, not even Aaron, and certainly not Shoshana.

I am sure David was congratulated for his work. And I am just as sure that he allowed himself a sly smile, perhaps even a chuckle, but that was pretty much it. David was not prone to self-satisfaction. Nor could any of us be.

In the years leading up to the Lebanon War, I had been receiving a steady stream of letters from David. They were not quite as frequent as before but, nonetheless, steady. And even more thoughtful. No doubt, David was a young man, by any reckoning. But he seemed to have an innate grasp of the scope of things. His curiosity never waned. But he never mentioned his social life, or any social life to speak of, except for Hillel-related activities. Until Rachel.

David's Rachel caught me a little "off guard." He described his first meeting with Rachel so rapturously that I recoiled a bit. And it wasn't exactly a first meeting. Rachel's visage hit David like a "bolt." But then I remembered something. Even though his advice was perfectly wise, I had wanted more from my meeting with Rabbi Dreyfus. I went to him to discuss how I should best explain my "work" to Shoshana. I had been without a father for most of my life. So I thought Rabbi Dreyfus might "stand in" for a short time and act "fatherly" towards me. He didn't. After a divorce, David's father had little contact with him over the years. Although I was sure it would be imperfect, I decided that I would offer David the fatherly counsel that both of us had lacked.

Rachel literally entered David's life on an August evening. There was a Hillel meeting, and just as the sun was setting, in walked Rachel. The sun's fading radiance caught Rachel's flowing blonde hair, just right. Her porcelain skin and blue eyes probably didn't hurt. Our young genius, in all his computer geekiness, was slayed. He helped "crack" a Russian missile defense system which certainly took weeks, if not months. He was "cracked" in less time than it takes to walk through a door.

The countries of the Middle East did seem united by their desire to see Israel pushed out of the neighborhood. But at least for the time being, internal divisions and shifting alliances benefitted Israel's security. And the picture was never crystal clear.

The Egyptian president who signed a peace treaty with Israel was murdered for his trouble. His successor, and the Egyptian military, supported the treaty, but brutally suppressed their opposition, never allowing the institutions of a civil society to develop, making a transition to democracy far less likely. An Islamic revolution successfully took control of Iran in 1979. But Iran was invaded by Iraq in September, 1980. The war would last eight long years and, in the process, devastate both countries' economies, causing millions of casualties. In the midst of Iraq fighting a war with Iran, Israel destroyed an Iraqi nuclear reactor, which the Iraqis would have undoubtedly used to develop nuclear weapons. And even though the rhetoric of Iran's Islamic Republic was virulently anti-Semitic, Israel supported Iran for a time during the Iran-Iraq war. At the time, Iraq was seen as the greater threat. Israel was also concerned about the rather large number of Jews that remained in Iran. It was all mind numbing. But to us, it was just another day in the neighborhood.

The swirl of events was always distracting, and at times unnerving. But life was meant to be lived. And live we did, with G-d's protection and mercy. I thought that I would rather have Russian SAM missiles glowering at me, than advise David in matters related to Rachel. As it turned out, it wasn't so bad. To be sure, David was, in a manner of speaking, "off the deep end." But he was managing.

There were some challenges. Rachel also came from a less than ideal family background. Her mother and father had an on again, off again, marriage. She was raised as a Presbyterian, because that was the religion of her mother. Her father was Jewish, but he was indifferent to religion, and largely indifferent to his Jewish background. Three months prior to meeting David at the Hillel meeting, Rachel had embarked on a path to convert to Judaism. It wasn't going to be easy for Rachel. It would take at least a year, and to receive final approval, she was going to have to be interviewed by a panel of three Rabbis. So, I did what I always did when David asked for advice about a tough situation. I turned to Shoshana. She never failed me, or David.

Shoshana thought that David should essentially go through the conversion process with Rachel. In that way, she thought that it could become a rock solid foundation of a marriage, if that's what they decided to do. In theory, it sounded great. I had no idea how David would react. I lived long enough in the U.S. to know that most young men his age would not embrace the idea. David did. He loved the idea. It gave him more opportunity to spend time with Rachel. He also wanted a deeper understanding of Judaism. Shoshana was delighted. Our prayers had been answered.

Father John Broderick and I would be seeing more and more of each other in the coming months, and even years ahead. It would be about David, to be sure. But people told John things. Things for which they and their entire family would be killed. Brutally killed. Things for which they would be tortured. Tortured to the point where they begged to be killed.

We all needed to remember that, along with bakers and candlestick makers, there were butchers. Shoshana knew about butchers. In Auschwitz, the majority of children were sent directly to the gas chambers. In the Coastal Road massacre of 1978 in Israel, 13 children were murdered. Their crime was riding a bus. The planners of the attack said they wanted to derail the Israeli-Egyptian peace talks, and damage tourism in Israel. So they sacrificed children in the name of political and economic idolatry. They wanted to trade the blood of children for political and economic goals. It was still child sacrifice. It was as ancient as it was barbaric.

One of the perpetrators of the attack was a young woman, 18 years old, who had studied to be a nurse. One can imagine a young nurse doing the things that young nurses do: offering a comforting word to patients; assisting during surgery; helping with emergency care; cradling newborns in the nursery. Instead, this nurse achieved the rank of lieutenant during a three-month terrorist training course. After the attack, she was hailed as a martyr and national hero. The voice she heard in the wilderness was a howl in the night.

In late February, 1983, John learned of an attack that was planned to stun Jerusalem. It had a new twist on child sacrifice. Five young children, ages 7-9, were each to be driven to popular pizza parlors in Jerusalem. They were to carry a "gift" that was intended for the owner of the pizza parlor whom, they were told, was a family friend. The "gift" was a bomb. As each child entered the crowded pizza parlor, the bomb would be remotely triggered by the driver of the car. The children would not be told what the "gift" really was. Their mothers knew. They approved because their children would be "martyrs."

John's information led us to the drivers, the safe houses, the explosives, and the planners. John's informant was arrested and detained along with the others. The other members of the cell were told that John's informant died during interrogation. He and his family were given safe passage out of the country. The truth is that this particular terrorist cell was small, although extremely capable. We were fortunate, and counted our blessings. Innocent children were spared, at least for now.

It wasn't often that I left for home early. But one afternoon, I decided that I would surprise Shoshana. She liked that kind of surprise. So, I picked up a bouquet of flowers and headed home. Shoshana was on the phone, but flashed her typically beautiful smile, and signaled me she would be off the phone shortly. It seems that a friend who was pregnant with a girl was seeking Shoshana's advice on names. How about Shoshana, I thought, then we could nickname the baby Rosie. Maybe not. Something Shoshana said did catch my attention. Did I hear it right? It couldn't be, I thought.

She was off the phone and into my arms. What a perfect afternoon. She asked me if I felt like going out for pizza. Of course, I hadn't told her about the pizza parlor plot. We settled on Chinese. We were almost out the door when I remembered to ask her about something she said on the phone. "Shoshana, did you say something about a ewe, you know female sheep?" "Yes, I did. My friend Sarah wants to name her baby Rachel. Rachel means ewe in Hebrew. But today, it is used more to mean innocence or purity."

I did hear it right. David's doodle. It never occurred to me. I didn't feel so badly, because it never occurred to John either. I asked Shoshana if she minded me making a phone call before we left. I was lucky that Golda was still at her desk. I asked her to contact John, and ask him to meet me at the laboratory tomorrow afternoon.

After he arrived at the lab, I caught John up on David's love life. I was a little embarrassed, but it had to be done. He listened respectfully. By now John knew that small talk was not my specialty. I delivered the punch line. "John, Rachel means ewe in Hebrew." I asked him if this could be some sort of coincidence. John was looking at me, but was really somewhere else in his thoughts. "No, Isaac, I doubt if this is a coincidence. I have to say, it is possible, but I don't think so." "What are their plans, Isaac? When does she finish the process of conversion?" "Based on David's most recent letter, John, she will be done in May. Their plan is to marry in early June." "Then we will let nature take its course, Isaac. I thought this might be the direction where we were headed with David." I looked at him with a skeptical face. "No, Isaac, I had no idea about David's doodle and Rachel. No idea, at all. But I can't say I'm shocked. Shocked, no."

Before, he left, John asked me if I had written David recently. I hadn't. He thought I should. "Make it the usual, Isaac. No drama, okay?" I understood. "We will just stay close for now, Isaac. It should be interesting." As he left, I thought those would be famous last words: it should be interesting. It was already interesting.

I began to feel genuinely sorry for David and Rachel. Planning for their wedding should have been one of the happiest times of their lives. It became complicated by the times in which we lived. Families seemed to be fracturing. The fault lines shifted, as fault line do. Sometimes it was money, sometimes it was religion, and sometimes, it appeared to be boredom. Lost in all of it, seemed to be any semblance of perspective, or an idea of the sacred. David and Rachel had been caught in the snare of modernity. Rachel's mother wasn't thrilled that Rachel was converting to Judaism, even though Rachel's father was Jewish. Ironically, Rachel's father wasn't enthusiastic about Rachel's conversion either. Rachel's father didn't really want to attend the wedding, and Rachel's mother didn't want to go without Rachel's father. David's father was nowhere to be found. And David's mother seemed to like the idea of the marriage, but was worried about being the only parent at the ceremony. Frankly, my head was spinning. Quantum physics was far easier.

Shoshana and I would have loved to go to David and Rachel's wedding. It just simply was not possible because of the expense, but most of all because of my work. I liked to take a week or so off in early May to celebrate our wedding anniversary. I couldn't very well ask for more time off in June, just a month after my previous vacation. The last option would have been to schedule an official visit to the University of Illinois, similar to the Northwestern trip. Frankly, it would have been a little contrived. It just wasn't right. In this case, our prayers would have to suffice. That was okay.

There was a visit I had been meaning to make. It had been 16 years since I had visited John at the Franciscan monastery. I would honor his invitation. The bear of a man had the heart of a lion. He also had a heart of gold. He was my friend. He was G-d's servant, and my friend. I loved John because he honored the order of things. The fact that he was G-d's servant first, made him a treasured friend. I called John to arrange for a time to visit. He was delighted. I told him to remember to have a bouquet ready for Shoshana. He liked that.

I wasn't sure, but it may have been the same Franciscan friar who answered the door at the monastery 16 years earlier. He was an older man then, but didn't seem to age much in the meantime. John was waiting for me on a bench just outside a small chapel. He looked great! Not too much grey had overtaken his mane of hair. He was a repository for the secrets of many others, including me, but if it took its toll on John, it wasn't apparent.

As we sat down, he offered me a glass of iced tea. I appreciated that. June was almost here, and it was a very warm day. We spent close to an hour talking about the things in our lives that didn't involve life or death, or messages in ancient Hebrew. What a delight.

John asked about David and Rachel. I spared him the tortured details of their family machinations. I simply said there were "family challenges," but Shoshana and I both thought they would have a wonderful marriage. John seem relieved. He asked me if I would join him in the chapel to offer our prayers for David and Rachel. It was a great idea.

Just outside the chapel was a small anteroom. There was a curious and beautiful painting on the wall. I asked John about it. "That, Isaac, was a gift from the Carmelite nuns who live in the monastery on the top of Mt. Carmel. The prophet Elijah is carrying out his challenge to the prophets of Baal. I rather like it, don't you." "It is beautiful. I always liked that challenge, John." "Yes, indeed." John pointed me towards a pew where I could sit. He took his seat a few pews ahead.

After John and I finished our prayers for David and Rachel, we walked through the courtyard, and there, sitting on the bench in the courtyard, just as it they had been 16 years earlier, was a bouquet of flowers. Shoshana would love them no less. "Don't let so much time pass," John said as I left. "I won't John, that's a promise." John thanked me again for coming. It was a great visit. It had been long overdue.

The next thing any of us knew about David and Rachel was that they were on their honeymoon. David apparently got approval to send a postcard. They were honeymooning in Canada. Rachel sent a postcard to Golda from Vancouver. It was a roundabout, but necessary way to get the message to Shoshana and me that everything turned out well. Golda was more than happy to be the intermediary. We had even more to discuss when we got together for coffee and her delicious cakes.

Shoshana and I loved the long days of summer. If there was something I truly did love to do, it was hold Shoshana's hand and walk through the streets of Jerusalem.

I knew all too well the risks that were a part of our life there. But we cherished our long walks on a summer evening, usually punctuated by stops at some of our favorite cafes. On one of the days I arrived home early, Shoshana mentioned that Golda had called and asked if I could stop by and pick up a letter. Hebrew University was a little far for a walk, so we took a taxi to the university, picked up the letter, and, on the return trip, had the driver drop us off about a mile from our apartment. It was a letter from David. We hadn't received any word from David and Rachel since their "honeymoon" postcard. We decided to open the letter over some ice cream and coffee.

It was great news! Rachel was pregnant. We were thrilled for them. David didn't include any other details. But he did catch us up a bit on the wedding. Apparently they had to settle on a Sunday wedding. They would have preferred a Tuesday, which is considered good luck, but it just wasn't possible. By some miracle, all the parents attended, and there were no problems. Even David's father came. They wisely decided to skip the rehearsal, and the rehearsal dinner. Never let the perfect be the enemy of the good. They were wise beyond their years. I made sure that Shoshana heard from me that there were no regrets about our not being blessed with children. She knew that, of course. But she appreciated it just the same.

To begin my week, I decided to drop by Hebrew University to speak to Golda about the prospects for travel in the new year. I knew I wouldn't be visiting any American universities this year, but I thought I would ask about next year. I was hoping to plan for a side trip to see David and Rachel. I even thought that, if we could save enough money, Shoshana could fly on ahead of me to stay with David and Rachel, and I would join them after my stint as a visiting professor. Golda was not encouraging. International travel of that type would probably not happen for the next year. The budget was frozen. If anyone knew it was Golda. Sometimes I thought the Prime Minister called Golda to get his expense account approved, or the odd fighter jet.

I would never ask her age, but 70 something was about right. Those wise eyes had seen so much. Miracles, unspeakable depravity, and everything in between. It was a life well lived. She was steady as a rock in stormy weather, and never lulled into complacency by a long stretch of fair weather. She connected me to the cherished memory of my parents, and my boyhood. And she helped the man protect other boys from the shattering experience of losing their parents, or other staples of their boyhood. Golda was all right.

I had written David and Rachel to congratulate them on the great news that they were expecting a child. He wrote me back to thank me, and indicated a little anxiety about how his life was about to change. Our exchange of letters lapsed for several months, and then, one morning, Golda handed me a letter from David. I smiled, and was curious about how David was handling being an expectant father. The news was not so good.

Apparently, because of some history of Tay Sachs disease in her father's family, the doctors recommended that Rachel have a procedure known as amniocentesis, which could detect any genetic abnormalities in the baby. Thankfully, the doctors found no evidence of Tay Sachs disease, but did find another chromosomal problem. There was almost a third copy of chromosome number 21. It was a sign that the baby had Down syndrome.

This was going to present a challenge for David and Rachel. Children with Down syndrome have some intellectual and physical disabilities that require special love and care. I was not encouraged that David and Rachel were getting some pressure from both families to terminate the pregnancy. It was something to which they were giving little or no consideration. Nonetheless, I believed that they could use all of the loving encouragement we could muster. Shoshana thought that talking to Rachel on a regular basis would be very helpful. It was not easy, but Golda helped to arrange it with Hebrew University, and Daniel.

For my part, I made a commitment to write David more frequently. Shoshana and I both concluded that while the initial news came as a shock, David and Rachel were handling it beautifully. As time passed, though, their families did not seem to want to reconcile themselves to the news. It was not helpful.

David had a plan. David Bass was far shrewder than anybody ever thought. I learned about this quality in David over time. David knew he had leverage. He was brilliant, and he had a knack for cryptography. So, naturally, he had a "sympathetic" ear among Daniel and his colleagues. They knew what they had. David convinced the Americans and the Israelis to let Rachel and him travel to Israel to have the baby. Although it was unusual, he could take a "leave of absence" from his job. He would continue his work in Israel and, after Rachel had the baby, they would return to the States. Daniel and his colleagues made it happen, with a little help from a certain Franciscan priest.

That certain Franciscan priest, John Broderick, agreed to let David and Rachel stay at the same apartment I stayed in just before Shoshana and I were married. David and I would share the laboratory where I worked. Not to be outdone, Colonel Stern would assign a military nurse to stay with Rachel during the day. And of course, when the time came, Rachel would get the best hospital care Israel had to offer. Although our access to David and Rachel would be limited, Shoshana and I would be able to spend some time with them.

The plan was to have David and Rachel fly to Israel in late January, 1984. Thankfully, the pregnancy had been, thus far, uneventful. Rachel was extremely strong. So it was thought that the flight would not be too much. They would first fly to New York, rest for a few days, be seen by a doctor there, and if he approved, fly on to Israel. Once in Israel, she would have about a month or so until delivery. Shoshana and I could not wait.

Daniel was usually not forthcoming about David's ongoing assignments. After the fact, I learned of the success of David's team in deciphering the code that was the key to the Russian air defense system in Syria during the height of Lebanon war. But Daniel arrived at the lab one afternoon with a worried, and puzzled, look on his face. I had seen Daniel worried before, all of us were worried about the armaments arrayed against us before the '67 war. But I had never seen Daniel genuinely puzzled, and somewhat distracted.

He did seem to know what it was he was puzzled or distracted about. They had been monitoring a group that appeared to have tentacles in New York, Vienna, Alexandria, and San Carlos de Bariloche, Argentina. The group's communications weren't overtly anti-Semitic, but they had all of the normal rhetorical affinities for Arab nationalism and the Palestinians. Nonetheless, they seemed to support a "two-state" solution, which implicitly recognized Israel's right to exist.

So I asked Daniel the obvious question. "Why are you so concerned, Daniel? There are hundreds of groups like this around the world. And this one doesn't even seem to be among the worst." "On the surface, I agree, Isaac. Frankly, I don't like the Vienna and San Carlos de Bariloche connection. Something is wrong. Vienna helped "form" and mature Hitler's ideology. San Carlos de Bariloche gave refuge to many Nazis after the war. Two butchers, Mengele and Eichmann, lived there for a time. And then there's this, Isaac. There appears to be a code embedded in their communications. If it is, and we are not sure of this, then it is perhaps the most sophisticated code we have ever encountered. It is at least unusual. I don't like this. Something is wrong, Isaac, something is wrong."

I counted three times that Daniel said "something is wrong." If he said it once, it was enough for me. Daniel was always careful. I had never known him to exaggerate. Through all the wars and crises, his judgment had served us well. He was not paid to be an optimist, or to regard others as generally trustworthy. But he wasn't cynical. I felt a bond with Daniel. Both of us lost our parents to a dark obsession. And both of us believed that ultimately, there was justice.

Before he left, I thanked Daniel for his help in making it possible for David and Rachel to come to Israel for the birth of their child. "We have to be more than 'operatives,'" he said. "If G-d is to honor us, we must demonstrate that we hear and understand what He commands us to do. You do well in this way, Isaac. I guess I like more than just your sense of humor, after all." He left David with quite an assignment. And he left me with something to live up to. I prayed I could.

David and Rachel landed in Israel. Who picked them up? Well, she looked like she could be one of their grandmothers. A "seventyish" grandmother. Golda must have taken some time off from her "duties" as caretaker of the Prime Minister's budget, among others. My guess is that some of Daniel's "friends" were keeping an eye on Golda and her guests as they made their way to their apartment, which was provided, courtesy of the Custodians of the Holy Land, and Father John Broderick. It was a small, and happy family. And soon, there would be a very new addition.

I had not received any word as to how, or if, I should contact David and Rachel. I went to the lab as usual on Thursday, and waited. A knock, followed by quick opening of the door, was a sure sign that John Broderick was on the premises. And indeed he was, with an infectious smile. We both had the David and Rachel bug.

He had just come from David and Rachel's apartment. Rachel had taken a taxi to meet the Ob/Gyn who would be taking care of her while she was in Israel. "How is David?" I asked. "Well, Isaac, I have met a few fathers-to-be over the years. He is about as relaxed as I've ever seen. What a fine young lad. And he thinks the world of you, Isaac. That recommends him, too." John smiled, as if he was pleased he could deliver the compliment. I appreciated it. "Any fallout from the problems with the parents?" I asked. "None, I think he's come to expect it from them. It sounds like they've been a problem since before David and Rachel were married. He has things in good perspective, Isaac."

"Do you have any word about when I might be able to visit them, John?" "I'm sure you already know it is going to be somewhat limited, Isaac. I'll stop by tomorrow, late in the afternoon, and we'll go together to the apartment. David and Rachel will be there. You haven't met Rachel, have you, Isaac?" "Not yet, John. I got a pretty good description from David in his letters. It was enthusiastic." We both smiled. "Yes, I think David forgot I was a priest for a minute, Isaac. It was pretty funny. We hear many things. You can believe that, Isaac." "I'm sure you do, John." "See you tomorrow, Isaac." "See you, John."

The next day, the knock from John came a little bit later than I had anticipated. But come, it did! John said we should wait awhile because Rachel had just gotten back from the doctor. I asked if everything was all right. John said they were just doing some tests, probably duplicating what had been done already, but they wanted to err on the side of caution. It was time.

I felt a little uncomfortable. I had to put on my awkward professor uniform, including glasses, but I thought once I was indoors, the glasses would come off and I would resume being something David would recognize as me. It wasn't that bad, but it seemed that way. I just didn't want David's description of me to come as pure fiction.

David opened the door with a smile that could have filled two apartments. And why not? Rachel was as lovely as she was kind and gentle. "Pro-fess-or, Jo-hn said you mi-ght dre-ss a lit-tle dif-fer-ently." John had given them fair warning. Good for John. I felt much better. "Yes, you see what hanging around John does to a man, David. I'll never be the same." We had a good laugh.

I had been worried about David and Rachel. The challenge of a newborn to a young couple can be a lot to handle. But a newborn with special needs, and an unsupportive family. I could see my worries were misplaced. They were going to be fine. In fact, better than fine.

"Professor, David wanted me to tell you about our name for our son." "Yes, Pro-fes-sor, Ra-chel will say it fas-ter tha-n me." David laughed. They both did. He always had the confidence of someone who could poke fun at himself. David was quite something. They both were.

"Professor, Father John, I am sure you are both familiar with Psalm 89." John and I nodded. "Psalm 89 was written by Ethan the Ezrahite. He is described as one of the wisest men at the time of Solomon, but not wiser than Solomon himself. We want our son to be wise, but to know that, among men, you should always be seeking wisdom, and never believe that you know all wisdom.

It is a beautiful Psalm that speaks of G-d's promise to David. G-d is the G-d that keeps His promises. He will keep His promise to the House of David. And He will keep the promise He made in Jeremiah to make a new covenant with the house of Israel and the house of Judah." David remembered that I had read from Jeremiah. I was touched.

"So we will name our son Ethan, after Ethan the Ezrahite. And there is something else. After speaking with Father John, we will name our son Ethan John, because of Father John's devotion to the Hebraic foundation of his faith. Father John is a man of G-d, who represents a kind of a bridge where we all can stand and see that G-d is the same yesterday, today, and tomorrow."

It was beautifully said. It was inspired. Their son was a gift from G-d. Perhaps G-d changed the wrapping some. But it was divine wrapping just the same. David and Rachel understood that. And they understood that John understood that. Ethan John. Heaven sent. Shoshana will love it.

John spoke. "Thank you, thank you both. I am deeply honored. I will try to live up to the calling of Ethan John Bass. You must be tired, Rachel. We should go!" "Oh, and one more thing. David and Father John, you should both know. The doctor said that I am farther along than we thought. The wait may not be long!"

"That's great news," I said. "Shoshana and I will have to move up our timetable. We wanted to take you somewhere special. We got permission from Daniel. It looks like it will have to be this Sunday. I will call you with the details." "Than-k you, Pro-fes-sor." "Yes, thank you both for coming. We will see you Sunday, Professor."

John and I weren't in a position to speak much after we left the apartment. He had to get back. I could tell, though, that he was genuinely moved by the decision of David and Rachel. Ethan John would be beginning his life with quite a legacy. And it sounded like he couldn't wait to get started.

For a February day, it was not as cool as it might have been. Nonetheless, we made sure we met David and Rachel in the late morning, to take advantage of the warming sun as it moved from the east, high above Jerusalem. Daniel provided the transportation for David and Rachel, and a nurse, just in case. If Rachel was uncomfortable, it wasn't apparent. She was clearly pregnant. But in spite of the fact that she wasn't unusually tall or "big boned," she didn't show as much as many women often do. She wore a constant smile, and didn't need any particular help to move from one place to another.

Nevertheless, we kept the walking to an absolute minimum. I wanted to take David and Rachel to a place where we could see the Eastern Gate of Jerusalem. Shoshana and I hadn't been there in a long while.

I told them the story that, in the '67 war, some of the commandos wanted to enter Jerusalem and assault the Jordanians by blowing open the Eastern Gate. It wasn't done because, according to prophecy, it would be the gate through which the Messiah would enter Jerusalem. There was also something else. In Ezekiel it says that "This gate shall be shut; it shall not be opened, and no man shall enter it." What is interesting is how the gate came to be closed.

It was Suleiman the Magnificent who, after the Turks conquered Jerusalem, sealed the Gate with stones. According to legend, he learned from Jewish rabbis that the Messiah would come through the Eastern Gate as a liberator. So Suleiman ordered the Eastern Gate sealed. He also put a Muslim cemetery in front of the Gate because he believed that no Jewish holy man would defile himself by walking through a Muslim cemetery. David and Rachel agreed with me that it was not Suleiman's intent to help fulfill prophecy. But that is exactly what he did.

We were all staring at the Gate, when Rachel grabbed David's hand and doubled over a little. "Your son has a good kick in him today," she said. Shoshana went to her side, hoping that the pain would soon subside. She let out a nervous laugh when she said, "I think he wants to see the Eastern Gate for himself." The nurse was waiting by the car nearby. I motioned for her to come over. "Do you feel a contraction, Rachel?" she asked. "I think so," Rachel said. She was now feeling a lot of discomfort. The nurse waved the car to drive over to where we were standing. "Let's get to the hospital," she said. And before we had turned around to get in our own car, Rachel was off to the hospital.

By the time Shoshana and I got to the hospital, Rachel was in the delivery room. I'm not sure why, but I called John. He said he would be right over. David was calm, and aglow with anticipation. The nurse came out to tell David that "it was time." "The contractions are coming faster and faster," she said. "The baby is doing fine, David, don't worry." David did not seem worried in the least. I was pacing. Shoshana came by to calm me down a bit. "Remember David," she said. David only smiled, yet again, when I looked his way.

Shoshana greeted John as he arrived. She took his arm and led him over to where David and I were standing. John and Shoshana were both smiling. Everyone was smiling, and I was nervous. I tried to start smiling too. Shoshana filled John in about the sequence of events. He looked at me at said, "Now, the Eastern Gate prophecy has a whole new dimension." John could always make me laugh. David said, "E-than Jo-hn tried to ki-ck the Ga-te do-wn." That even made the nurse laugh.

Although it seemed like it was longer, it was probably about 20 minutes after Rachel went into the delivery room that the doctor came out to see David. The doctor seemed pleased as he was talking to David. I thought that was a good sign. David came over to us, now smiling more broadly than ever. "E-than Jo-hn has ar-rived. Se-ven pound-s, se-ven ounc-es." We all hugged. Shoshana, John, David and me. It was a magnificent moment. Except for David, we all had tears in our eyes. David went in to see Rachel and the baby.

I had to look twice, but there he was. In walked Daniel. On a day of the unexpected, that may have been the most unexpected thing of all. He didn't act that way. He looked at me as if he were in attendance at every birth there was since the hospital opened. I knew better than that. "You're having a bad influence on me, Isaac," he said. Now, Daniel smiled too. I hoped Ethan John could keep this up.

David came out to the waiting room with the doctor. They looked as if everything was under control. The doctor explained that Ethan was moved to the neonatal intensive care unit. He emphasized that it was a precaution only. Ethan was a little premature. Usually newborns with Down syndrome need some pulmonary support. He said Ethan appeared fine. He wanted to start Ethan on some oxygen, anyway, and have him checked out by the pediatric cardiologist.

The doctor mentioned that David got to hold Ethan. I asked David how Rachel was doing. "She's fine," he said. The nurse explained that, if we wanted to, a few of us at a time could go to a little viewing area to see Ethan. Shoshana and I volunteered to go first. The nurse went with us to point out little Ethan. It was a beautiful sight. He was small, and we were beaming. When the nurse came out with us, we noticed Daniel offering David a cigar. I only wished I had a camera. David declined, so Daniel lit up. I thought I had seen it all.

I noticed John out of the corner of my eye go in to see Ethan. He appeared to wearing some vestments I hadn't seen before. David explained that John had asked him if he minded if he offered some blessings for Ethan. David was delighted. Daniel was sitting in a chair enjoying his cigar. What a sight! Shoshana came over to take my hand with a self-satisfied look. "It turned out very well," she said. "What a perfect day, Isaac." I agreed.

John came out of the viewing room with a sort of unusual expression on his face. I noticed the nurse was sitting next to Daniel. As John walked over to say something to the nurse, I walked over next to him. "Thank you for having the other nurse hold Ethan in her arms. It was lovely," he said. The nurse looked at John. She had a bewildered expression on her face. "You mean the doctor, don't you, Father?" "There wouldn't be a nurse in the room, just now." "Oh, I'm sorry, I must have been mistaken," he said. John walked away. I followed. He walked over to Daniel, put his hand on Daniel's shoulder, and said something to him. Daniel hurriedly put down his cigar, and picked up the telephone. I went over to put out the smoldering cigar.

John was standing alone with his hands in his pockets. I looked at his face. His skin was radiant and smooth. He looked twenty years younger. "There WAS a nurse. It wasn't a doctor, was it, John?" He looked passed me. Then he looked up, as if he only noticed just then that I was standing there. Shoshana came over. John seemed interested in what she had to say. "I just had an interesting conversation with David," she said. "He's so overwhelmed with the baby, he forgot to stutter." Shoshana just shrugged her shoulders, and walked away. I looked at John, as he looked at me. "Did you ever notice a baby's cry can sound like a voice in the wilderness, Isaac?" "No, John, I didn't. But, now that you mention it." I walked over to Shoshana to hold her hand. David was still smiling. And now, it suddenly occurred to me, to smile, too.

CHAPTER FOUR

THE TREE OF KNOWLEDGE

"Then the serpent said...
For G-d knows that in the day you eat of it
your eyes will be opened, and you will be like G-d,
knowing good and evil."
Genesis 3:4-5

"Woe to those who call evil good, and good evil;
Who put darkness for light, and light for darkness;
Who put bitter for sweet, and sweet for bitter!
Woe to those who are wise in their own eyes,
And prudent in their own sight"
Isaiah 5:20-21

If someone makes you a promise that you will be like G-d, flee as fast as you can, but flee, without hesitation. Before Ethan John Bass, there was always them. Father John Broderick understood them, far better than I. The plotters and schemers and their dark fathers who crawled out of their holes at night, squinting and salivating in the daylight hours, wolves among sheep. They wouldn't devour us until our fleshly indulgences so mummified our souls that, even the screams of the denizens of perdition, would not dissuade us from opening hell's door. And if they could not entice us to crawl on our bellies like them, they would kill indiscriminately, murdering thousands, or even a thousand thousand, to get to the one. They feared only the light. They feared Him.

The obsession had survived the '67 war to fight another day. I didn't know it then. I didn't even consider then, but it would eventually be filled with fear and trembling. But not yet.

Before the fight, I had received a crucial assignment. But before that I had to consider the miracles of the '67 war. Were they a series of coincidences? After all, it's not as if the Lord, as in the days of Joshua, lengthened the day:

> *"So the sun stood still in the midst of heaven,*
> *and did not hasten to go down for about a whole day.*
> *And there has been no day like that, before it or after it,*
> *that the Lord heeded the voice of a man;*
> *for the Lord fought for Israel."*

In the six days of the '67 war, the sun did not stand still in the midst of heaven. But there were miracles.

Daniel and his colleagues sent a "friend" of theirs to infiltrate the Syrian government. In a gesture designed to show sympathy for the Syrian soldiers, Daniel's "friend" convinced the Syrians to plant trees to shade them while they were preparing to fight the Israelis. Aaron and his fellow pilots used the trees as markers to target the Syrian positions. It sounds ludicrous. Miraculously ludicrous!

Many of the Arabs thought that, during the '67 war, the Israeli Air Force has been helped by foreign agents. The truth is that the IAF pilots had literally memorized every detail about their targets, and had rehearsed their bombing assignments on dummy runways in total secrecy. It is an axiom of war that "no battle plan survives contact with the enemy." Just ask Eisenhower, Grant, Lee, Patton, Jackson and any number of great generals. Except this one did. The IAF relied on precise preparation, and their minds. With a little help from an omniscient friend.

And Daniel and his comrades had even more stunning success. There was either an Israeli intelligence officer or Egyptian informant in every Egyptian airbase and military headquarters. No wonder the IAF pilots attacked the Egyptian airfields when all the Egyptian personnel were having breakfast. They knew in advance exactly when to launch their assault. *"And blessed be G-d Most High, Who has delivered your enemies into your hand."*

But the miracles and the land, and the apparent security they brought with them, did not stop the obsession. The obsession lived on. It would live on until the G-d of Abraham, Isaac, and Jacob finally put a stop to it. And He would have our help.

John Broderick would wisely tell us to maintain a skyward bias with our flitting glances. The flits of our eyes should rest just long enough to comprehend His "signs and seasons." For now, we were in a season of preparation. For war. It was a season in which the insidious effects of weariness could creep into our hearts. If we allowed it, that would be our death knell. We had to maintain a pure heart as an offering to the Lord of hosts. Malachi wrote of this in "The burden of the word of the Lord to Israel." He was not kind to weariness.

And so the seasons could be excruciating. We would wait for the "signs." John advised patience and faithfulness. We would wait, and be faithful.

The ferocity and the persistence of the obsession would prove to be a match for our patience and faithfulness. Some would say we were overmatched. The obsession moved "to and fro on the earth." It inhabited the willing souls of the living, who would begin their long descent to the abyss.

> *"Evil shall slay the wicked, And those*
> *who hate the righteous shall be condemned."*
> *Psalm 34:21*

And the obsession was hard at work in the aftermath of the '67 war. Before "land for peace" became the mantra of those seeking a permanent settlement between Israel and the Palestinians, Israel offered exactly that in the wake of the '67 war. On June 19, 1967, the National Unity Government of Israel voted unanimously to return the Sinai to Egypt and the Golan Heights to Syria, in exchange for peace. The Arab response was as quick as it was unequivocal. The Arab League summit issued a unanimous resolution at its September, 1967 meeting in Khartoum, Sudan. It became known as the "Three No's":

> *"No peace with Israel.*
> *No recognition of Israel.*
> *No negotiations with Israel.*
> *Period."*

After the September Arab League resolution, I was visited by John Broderick, realist and man of G-d, certainly not in that order. John came by the lab to genuinely inquire about how I was doing. He somehow knew Shoshana was fine. I reassured him that I was too. "John, they already have me working so that more miracles can come. I hope G-d answers our prayers before the next war. It will come, won't it John?" I knew the answer to the question. The "Three No's" meant "yes." Yes to more war. "Isaac, they will never accept the existence of a Jewish State in their midst. John had said that to me once before. But this time, my heart sank. I had been through all the anxiety and preparation before the war, then the war itself. I had seen men die, friends and enemies. "What do you mean, John?"

"Isaac, we live in the land of the unreconciled. G-d ordains the order of things. Man cannot. Abraham had two sons, Isaac, your namesake, and Ishmael. Both were honored by G-d as descendants of Abraham. Isaac was given the distinction of being part of the fulfillment of G-d's promise to Abraham that he would establish *'My covenant with him for an everlasting covenant, and with his descendants after him... for in Isaac your seed shall be called.'"*

"Above all, the G-d of Abraham, Isaac and Jacob honors his agreements. The descendants of Isaac live in the Land of Israel. Ishmael, because he, too, was a son of Abraham, was promised by G-d that he would make him a 'great nation.' The 'sons of Ishmael' surround Israel today. What we have, Isaac, is a recipe for eternal conflict. Pride, Isaac, is a deadly sin. So is envy."

"And, Isaac, I have always been curious about other layers of meaning in the Genesis account of Hagar and her son, Ishmael. After she departed from the house of Abraham and Sarah, Hagar ran out of water in the wilderness in Beersheba. She left her son under some shrubs because she couldn't 'bear to watch her child die.' The distance from Hagar to the place she left her son is described as a "bowshots distance." It is the only place in the Bible in which distance is measured using a weapon as a reference. It is also interesting that G-d had to open Hagar's eyes to the presence of the water. She had previously looked away from water, to the death of her son."

My dear friend, John Broderick. He had a gift. He understood about G-d's signs and seasons. We were in a season of preparation. Unbeknownst to us, so were the butchers.

Before another war in the Land, there was Munich. The 1972 Munich Olympics. We loved the illusion of the Olympics as a refuge from politics. Clausewitz said that war is the continuation of politics by other means. So were the Olympics.

Yes, John Broderick understood many things. Signs, seasons, covenants and the divine nature. And human nature. He seemed to know something that no one else could comprehend. This was not a war about the Land. It was a war about *us*.

Munich. We would remember the Munich of 1972 for a long time in Israel. The world seemed to want to forget the Munich of 1972, and the Munich of the 1930's and 40's.

Adolf Hitler referred to Munich as the "Capital of the Movement." Hitler moved to the Bavarian capital from Vienna in 1913. When he returned to Munich after World War I, he joined the German Workers Party and transformed it into one of Bavaria's most influential political parties. Munich became a sort of spiritual heart of Nazism after the Nazis assumed power in Germany in 1933.

It took all of 40 days for Hitler and his psychopathic movement to establish their first concentration camp, not 10 miles from Munich. Munich wasn't the spiritual heart of Nazism. There was no spiritual heart of Nazism. There were only corpses wearing uniforms, cultists, whose inheritance from the Tree of Knowledge was to fancy themselves as lords and princes, masters of the universe whose only distinction was to listen to the lies of an accomplished Tempter.

The Thousand Year Reich, a nightmare that would take the form of a millennial reign by the dead over the kingdoms of the world. The only way they could claim to be alive was to destroy and torture the physical bodies of others. And so, not 10 miles from Munich, they built their first "concentration camp" in Dachau in 1933. There, they were able to "concentrate" on indulging every evil fantasy that knocked on the Gates of Hell. They sought holy artifacts, not holiness.

And the idea of a concentration camp seemed to "focus" the minds of others. Hajj Amin al-Husseini, the Grand Mufti (Supreme Muslim religious leader) of Jerusalem, had planned a death camp modeled on Auschwitz to be constructed near Nablus, approximately 30 miles north of Jerusalem. His homicidal fantasy was not fulfilled. But he had followers. They came to the Munich Olympics in 1972. If a permanent death camp couldn't be built near Jerusalem, they would take their macabre show on the road.

Black September. They were true heirs to the legacy of the Grand Mufti and the human machinery that operated Dachau. Just ask Moshe Weinberg, Yossef Romano, Yossef Gutfruend, David Berger, Yacov Springer, Ze'ev Friedman, Amitzur Shapira, Eliezer Halfin,

Mark Slavin, Andre Spitzer, and Kehat Shorr. They were all murdered. In cold blood. They had two things in common. They were all members of the 1972 Israeli Olympic team. They were all Jewish.

General Dwight David Eisenhower mounted the greatest invasion force in world history. The world had never been witness to such an armada. "Ike" was a laconic farm boy whose mother taught the Bible to the Eisenhower brothers in the original Greek. General Eisenhower had the humility and the political genius to be Supreme Commander of the Allied Forces in Europe. In his capacity as Supreme Commander, he had to maintain a semblance of unity and common purpose among Presidents, Prime Ministers, Kings, Queens, Generals, among whom were statesmen, brilliant strategists, ego maniacs, dilettantes and all manner of what the human family has to offer.

A laconic man needs a voice. Ike had one. Winston Churchill. Churchill sniffed out the evil that was descending on Europe, and the world. He spoke with a moral clarity and force, as if he had been the star pupil with Ike and his brothers in their mother's Bible classes. His wit was priceless. Who else could have said: *"If Hitler invaded hell I would make at least a favorable reference to the devil in the House of Commons."*

And who else would have said: "You ask, What is our policy? I will say; "It is to wage war, by sea, land and air, with all our might and with all the strength that G-d can give us: to wage war against a monstrous tyranny, never surpassed in the dark lamentable catalogue of human crime. That is our policy. You ask, What is our aim? I can answer with one word: Victory—victory at all costs, victory in spite of all terror, victory however long and hard the road may be; for without victory there is no survival."

And so a "monstrous tyranny" suffered an inglorious fate because someone stood in the breach. The breach was a portal into the abyss. There was only darkness. Nazi Germany was physically destroyed. Its physical artifices and its instrumentalities of evil were rendered useless by the onslaught delivered by Ike and the allied forces.

The 1972 Munich Olympics weren't a turning point. They were an exclamation point. The obsession lived on. The breach had not been closed.

We were to learn disturbing facts in the aftermath of the Munich massacre. I was always troubled by the apparent bumbling by the German authorities before, during, and after the Munich massacre. Germany had been warned about a Palestinian terrorist attack at the Games but took no actions to secure the Olympic Village. It was always obvious that the Black September terrorist group had to have help "on the ground" in Germany. They did. They were helped by a Nazi group in Germany to get fake ID's, weapons and access to the Olympic Village. German eventually released all the Munich killers in response to demands made by the hijackers of a Lufthansa jet. And there was more.

The International Olympic Committee (IOC), which sponsors the Olympic Games, had curious, and all too familiar, ideas about who should lead that august organization in 1972. The IOC had chosen a president who was a Nazi sympathizer and anti-Semite. His protégé, who later became the second longest serving president of the IOC, had a secret. He had supported the Nazis, and Spanish dictator Francisco Franco.

Is it any wonder that the IOC turned down Israeli requests for security for their athletes at the 1972 Munich Olympics? Is it any wonder that the massacre of Israeli athletes was not enough for the IOC to cancel, or postpone, the Olympics? As a sports journalist wrote at the time: "It's almost like having a dance at Dachau." Except they weren't just dancing on the graves of the dead. They were nostalgic.

Terrorism achieved far more than to just cow, or intimidate governments and international organizations. It found willing accomplices in academia, government, the media, and business. These accomplices helped the terrorists subtly change the language so that, eventually, their true nature and intentions became virtually invisible. Israeli civilians would become non-combatants in a war of liberation.

It was an attempt to pervert the language to eventually gain acceptance for terrorism as a legitimate political tool. Such a perversion of the language would eventually achieve its goal among the international elites and popular culture. It was the language of a master of deception. It was not new.

"Now the serpent was more cunning
than any beast of the field which the Lord G-d had made....
And he said to the woman, "Has G-d indeed said,
'You shall not eat of every tree of the garden?'"
G-d has said, 'You shall not eat it,
nor shall you touch it, lest you die.'"
Then the serpent said to the woman,"You will not surely die."
Genesis 3:1-4

Yes, it was not new. History begins in the garden. The history of the massacre of Israeli athletes began in the garden. The massacres will end when history ends. History will end in the city. In the city of Jerusalem. And, without miracles, Israel's history could very well have ended in 1973.

There was always the matter of the "Three No's":

"No peace with Israel.
No recognition of Israel.
No negotiations with Israel.
Period."

The "Three No's" were the Arab answer to a land for peace proposal by Israel. The "Three No's" were as sweeping as they were revealing. The West and the international community found (invented really) every conceivable nuance and rationalization to contort the

"Three No's" into a pretzel that gradually became a wedding cake, when it really was what it looked like: a pretzel.

As to an Israeli peace proposal, Israel's political leadership seemed united on at least one point. Withdrawal to the borders before the 1967 war was out of the question. And the language was anything but political.

In 1969, the Foreign Minister of Israel said that "the map will never again be the same as on June 4, 1967," which was the day before the start of the '67 war. He went further, "The June map is for us equivalent to insecurity and danger. I do not exaggerate when I say that it has for us something of a memory of Auschwitz." And he wasn't alone in dramatizing the importance of not going back to the indefensible pre-1967 borders.

Two Prime Ministers of Israel had similar views. One described a proposal for a retreat to the pre-1967 borders as "national suicide for Israel." Another said the pre-1967 borders were so dangerous that it "would be treasonable" for an Israeli leader to accept them. Borders are an outline of the land that a nation inhabits. It seemed unlikely that any peace outline with pre-1967 borders would be possible.

Before the Munich massacre, I was worried. It wasn't that any of us sensed that a spectacular international terrorist attack against Israeli citizens was about to happen. Our worries were local. And I wasn't the only one. John, Daniel, Colonel Stern, Aaron, and, yes, my "Rosie," Shoshana all felt the same thing. After the exhilaration of the Six-Day War in 1967, Israelis seemed discouraged, even disheartened. It is true that peace seemed a distant prospect, at best. Terrorism was increasing. There were new threats from Egypt.

It is also true that Israel had "mood swings." Despair, weariness, ecstasy, calm (very rare), gloom (frequent); they were all present at different points of the Israeli emotional roller coaster. Shoshana liked to say "Gentlemen, we are a Jewish State, for better or for worse." She had a point. And it was understandable to grow a little tired of constantly having to fight for your survival. But we were not only surviving, but thriving. In 1867, after Mark Twain had visited the Holy Land, he said:

"...[a] desolate country whose soil is rich enough, but is given over wholly to weeds-a silent mournful expanse... A desolation is here that not even imagination can grace with the pomp of life and action... We never saw a human being on the whole route... There was hardly a tree or a shrub anywhere. Even the olive and the cactus, those fast friends of the worthless soil, had almost deserted the country."

Now, the desert was abloom. His promise had been kept.

> *"For the Lord will comfort Zion,*
> *He will comfort all her waste places;*
> *He will make her wilderness like Eden,*
> *And her desert like the garden of the Lord."*
> *Isaiah 51:3*

The new president of Egypt sounded familiar themes. Return all the land captured by Israel in the '67 war and there may be peace. It was a nonstarter. He wanted the United States to accept his interpretation of United Nations (UN) Resolution 242, which he said meant total Israel withdrawal from territories captured in 1967. The United States disagreed with the Egyptian president's interpretation of UN Resolution 242. So he pressured the Soviets to pressure the United States. The Soviets appeared more interested in maintaining detente with the United States. So the Egyptians kicked out 20,000 Soviet advisors. In fact, we later learned that this was a ruse by the Egyptians designed to lull Israel and United States into believing that a rift between Egypt and the Soviet Union made war in the region less likely. The ruse worked.

Within days of the Munich massacre, I was visited by Colonel Stern and Daniel. Israel had already bombed ten PLO bases in Syria and Lebanon. Before the mission, Aaron put photos of the murdered Olympians inside his jacket pocket. After each sortie, he would gently pat the pocket with the care of a flight nurse, not an elite aviator. Aaron was Aaron because G-d imbued him with a loving heart that matched his rare talents as a warrior. But there was more to come. Much more. We were armed this time.

Just after the slaughter in Munich, the Prime Minister of Israel had formed Committee X to formulate Israel's response. Colonel Stern and Daniel came to my lab in Jerusalem to talk about part of what we were going to do. Their visit was not a surprise.

Colonel Stern and Daniel stepped confidently into the lab. They weren't prone to swagger or false bravado. They were professionals. All of their training aimed for moments like this. We wished the moments never came. But we knew they would. Colonel Stern spoke first. "The Prime Minister hesitated to embrace our recommendations, Isaac. But the public pressure is just too great." Never before had Colonel Stern or Daniel characterized the internal debate inside the government. Let alone, attribute specific comments or attitudes to the Prime Minister. It just simply was not done. Daniel was unfazed by Colonel Stern's remarks. I always thought his remarks were meant to point to the historic nature of our retribution for the attack on our Olympic athletes. If our response was not overwhelming, even shocking, it would be open season on Israelis on every boulevard and alley way in the world.

And so, Operation Wrath of G-d. The perpetrators and their cohorts would be found, and justice would be done. I have no doubt that our Olympians were defiant to the end. We would see how bravely defiant the terrorists would become.

None of us were young anymore. I knew John loved irony. So did we. We loved John, so we loved irony. The three of us, that is Colonel Stern, Daniel, and I would be involved in a component of Operation Wrath of G-d, Operation Spring of Youth. Spring chickens we weren't. But this operation would require a little guile, and an ability to control the body's adrenaline pump, which I learned comes with age. We were perfect for this mission. And, as I would learn later in our training, there would be "roles of a lifetime," for the frustrated actors among us. They weren't exactly the "roles" warriors would choose. But that was for later. Now, I had to tell Shoshana that I was back in the fight.

When I got home to our apartment, Shoshana was waiting with a smile and a kiss. She seemed like she wanted to tell me something. Whatever it was, she was confident about it. It was almost as if she said to herself, alright so this is the way it's going to be. Whatever "it" was, she was at peace. Most of all, I wanted her to be at peace. She was a gift from G-d. Our life together was complicated. The world had intruded. History had intruded. We prayed that G-d would straighten a path for us through a thicket of gnarled intrusions.

Shoshana had been watching the news. She watched, and she read extensively. And she was wise and perceptive about topical matters. She got right to the point. Shoshana was always direct. Our second shidduch date taught me that nothing was allowed to linger, let alone smolder. "Isaac, after Munich, the public wants something done. They want something big. It probably means that my scientist will need to be a warrior for a while." She smiled, somewhat slyly. I thought to myself. Where are you going with this? Now, I was curious. "Isaac, did you know that one of our Olympians, the wrestling coach, had the courage to hurl himself against the kidnappers as they were moving the hostages from one apartment to another. He knocked one of the terrorists unconscious, and stabbed another with a fruit knife before being shot to death. A fruit knife, Isaac. I only wish some of us had fruit knives in Auschwitz."

"Isaac, this must be answered. We must at least have as much courage as our wrestling coach. I have never said this to you before, Isaac. I may never say it again. Do what you must. I know you will not be reckless. Just, do what you must." I expected something of a serious nature. I am not sure I expected that. "Some men came by my office today. They have something in mind." Now, I had a sly smile on my face. I could see that Shoshana liked it. We both smiled, slyly.

"I suspect our hero, the wrestling coach, will not be disappointed." I wanted to use Shoshana's nickname. Before, it seemed impossible. Now, it seemed about right. I thought, maybe not. My intrepid wife went right for the punchline. "Rosie will do all she can to help you get back in fighting shape. It looks like you could lose a few pounds." We hugged, laughing and weeping at the same time. Before we sat down for dinner, I whispered in her ear. "It may be some weeks before the mission. I will tell you when it is time. I promise I won't be reckless."

The Prime Minister came around to the view held by the intelligence services and the Israeli public. The Germans were responsible for her change of heart. Over a month after the Munich massacre, a Lufthansa jet was hijacked. The terrorist hijackers demanded the release of the Munich killers who had been captured by the German authorities. The Germans capitulated. It was an outrage. The Prime Minister finally had enough. She now fully supported Operation Wrath of G-d, and all of its deadly progeny.

In the aftermath of the Nazi reign of terror, we had been told again and again about the new German sensibilities towards Israel and the Jewish community. Their apparent disregard of the warnings before Munich was bad enough. Then there was their buffoonish handling of the kidnapping itself. The final outrage was the release of the Munich killers. Shoshana was right. We had to "do what we must." We would bring more than a fruit knife.

Terrorism is not a near-death experience. It is death itself. You open Hell's door, and don't look back. Once inside the door, the fruits of death are eternal hunger and thirst. There is no peace. Only victims. Was there some expectation that, before he was locked away in perdition for eternity, Mengele was just a few experiments away from satisfying his blood curdling lusts for human disfigurement and predation? Do we believe that one more scream, one more lifeless child's body, and his appetite would be sated once and for all? The point wasn't just a modest bite from the forbidden fruit. It was death itself.

Eternal separation from G-d. And it isn't just a consuming darkness, pierced only by screams never heard before by human ears. It is oblivion.

We had to be patient. We wouldn't be raining bombs over cities or munitions factories in the manner of World War II. We were after individuals. This was a search for the proverbial "needle in a haystack." Except that the "needles" we were looking for could move. And the "haystack" surrounding those "needles" had deadly layers of security. No, this was more like finding a particular needle among many needles. And the needles had more than just one sharp point. If you weren't careful, by the time you found your prize you would be bleeding out from thousands of razor cuts done with the precision of a surgeon or, even worse, suffering the loss of your limbs from the cuts of a serrated edge usually reserved for pieces of meat. We had to find the needle. Then we had to thread it. With invisible thread. Lethal, invisible thread.

Two Jewish Temples were built with the cedars of Lebanon. It was King David's son, Solomon, who built the First Temple and, who said,

> *"And behold, I propose to build a house for the name*
> *of the Lord my G-d, as the Lord spoke to my father David, saying,*
> *"Your son, whom I will set on your throne in your place,*
> *he shall build the house for My name."*
> *Now therefore, command that they cut down*
> *cedars for me from Lebanon..."*
> *1 Kings 5:5-6*

And...

> *"When Hiram heard the words of Solomon,*
> *that he rejoiced greatly and said, Blessed be the Lord this day,*
> *for He has given David a wise son over this great people!*
> *Then Hiram sent to Solomon, saying:*

I have considered the message which you sent me,
and I will do all you desire concerning the cedar and cypress logs.
My servants shall bring them down from Lebanon to the sea…"
1 Kings 5:7-9

And after the Babylonian captivity, the Second Temple was built.

"…they offered the regular burnt offering,
and those for New Moons and for all the appointed feasts
of the Lord that were consecrated,
and those of everyone who willingly offered
a freewill offering to the Lord.
From the first day of the seventh month
they began to offer burnt offerings to the Lord,
although the foundation of the temple of the Lord had not been laid.
They also gave money to the masons and the carpenters,
and food, drink, and oil to the people of Sidon and Tyre
to bring cedar logs from Lebanon to the sea, to Joppa,
according to the permission which they had
from Cyrus king of Persia."
Ezra 3:5-7

"…But many of the priests and Levites and heads
of the fathers' houses, old men who had seen the first temple,
wept with a loud voice when the foundation of this temple
was laid before their eyes. Yet many shouted aloud for joy,
so that the people could not discern the noise of the shout of joy
from the noise of the weeping of the people,
for the people shouted with a loud shout,
and the sound was heard afar off."
Ezra 3:12-13

Lebanon was no longer the source of cedars to build a dwelling place for the Lord among the G-ds. Its claim to an inheritance of building holy foundations was severed by interlopers, apostates to the Abrahamic tradition who claimed they killed for the Land, but really killed for the oldest and basest of reasons: jealously, pride, envy, all bound up into a virulent anti-Semitism. Like Abel, they could have earned the respect of the Lord, instead they preferred the curse of the Mark of Cain. We found the haystack. And the needles. They were in Lebanon. Beirut, Lebanon.

In those days, Beirut had not yet been destroyed by years of being a shooting gallery, a violent playground in which intense rivalries were settled in the manner of mafia gangs. Palestinian terrorists had been kicked out of Jordan, and saw an opportunity in Lebanon. They took effective control over South Lebanon and West Beirut.

Our intelligence was superb. We not only knew the exact locations of the terrorists, but had the definitive architectural plans of the buildings in which they lived. The terrorists did not live in military compounds. They sought the protection afforded them by living among civilians. It complicated the operation. We had to weave our way through the civilians, past the layer of armed guards, kill the terrorists, and get out of the area before the Lebanese army and police could respond. If we wanted to protect innocent life, we had to thread the needle, and be shot at for our trouble. And the plan involved a form of subterfuge that would not inspire us to say, it was as it was in the "days of old." I don't think so. Perhaps Goliath still would have succumbed to David. Maybe he would have died laughing.

It was February, 1973, and we had what we needed. Now we had to refine our training. Previously, our training was mostly at the special forces facilities in Tel Aviv. In light of the intelligence information, we would shift our training "facilities" to actual apartment buildings in Tel Aviv, and alter them to be virtual identical copies of the terrorist hideouts in West Beirut.

The terrorists lived in West Beirut's "fashionable" neighborhood of Verdun. They were killers who fancied the cachet of the fashionable. They were fashionably fashionable killers who enjoyed quiet upscale cafes, chichi boutiques, and well-manicured, tree-lined boulevards that were just the right width. They luxuriated in its bloodless pomp, notwithstanding the sanguinary messiness of the circumstances that facilitated their serene havens. Like the prophets of Baal, they were demi-gods, whose human sacrifices and perverse lifestyles only hinted at the depth of their fall from grace. They were about to exit this world in a manner suited to their state of nature: gracelessly.

I was looking at Shoshana more closely these days. I hoped she didn't notice. It was homework. We had to become invisible until it was too late for the men we hunted. So, once we on the streets near their apartment buildings in Beirut, we would be everyday tourists. With a twist. Tourists include men and women. And our little band of tourists would have a cadre of very much in love sightseers. Some of us were brunettes, like Shoshana, and some of us were blondes. I was certainly no competition for my wife. So, I decided to go for a blonde wig. But I did look more closely at Shoshana. Her gait. Her sway. The distance of her steps. On and on. Shoshana asked me to "do what you must." Little she did know.

April 9, 1973. It was the week before Passover. It was time to go. Shoshana and I treated it like another day at the office. "Ask Colonel Stern if you can make a short phone call after you get back," was all she said. We sought justice for all the brave souls who were murdered at Munich. We would be bringing more than a fruit knife.

I had called Aaron the day before. I asked him if he still had the family album I liked so much. He knew I was referring to the photos of the Olympians he had taken on his sorties to Lebanon and Syria. He told me he would put them somewhere for safe keeping until I could come by. It meant that he wanted me to call him when I returned from the mission. He wasn't worried. He just wanted to make sure. I got word to John through Golda. I had made a brief stop at the university. I did it out of respect, and love, for both Golda and John. "Call John, and tell him I will see him before Passover, alright Golda." Golda had mastered the routine, long ago. She smiled. "I will be baking your favorite Pirushke cakes," she said. "Come by soon, won't you?" Indeed, I would, if I could.

Our first destination was a naval base in Haifa. There, we boarded an Israeli missile boat, and about 7 hours later we were several miles from the shores of Beirut. Zodiac speedboats, which are fast inflatables with outboard motors, took us the rest of the way in, almost. We shut down the "outboards" on the Zodiacs a few hundred meters from our landing zone and, as the song says, "row, row, rowed our boats" to the beaches.

Daniel was waiting in an unmarked car for my group. Colonel Stern was with another group. Daniel and I made no eye contact, or any acknowledgement that we recognized the other. When we got to the apartment building, he simply said, "you have 10 minutes."

We encountered more Lebanese policemen than we had anticipated. We had the magic formula. It was love potion number 9. We sashayed past the police, hand in hand, as if we were oblivious to the world, and on our way to the rendezvous of a lifetime. The policemen didn't even react. The wigs worked to perfection. We got to the front door of the apartment building. We set an explosion to blow open the door. It did. I knew right where to go. I had practiced it so many times, I may have known the layout better than my own apartment. My target wasn't in his office. He was in his master bedroom. He heard me coming, and slammed the door. I saw his face. It was a face I had been waiting to see. The door to the master bedroom was perforated by blasts from my Uzi. I didn't sashay. I kicked in the door, which by then was in shreds. I finished the job, and left a lifeless body in my wake. The wig too was on the floor, a lifeless calling card. G-d had made provision for cities of refuge. It turned out that Beirut was not one of them.

My comrades took care of the police, and a few guards who were located in the building. Daniel was waiting. We all got in the back seat. I was the last to get in. I could see Daniel glance at me in the rear view mirror. I calmly took my weapon and placed it upright, just above my right knee. I made sure the safety was off. I nodded my head a few times in a self-satisfied manner. Daniel had gotten the message before the Uzi had been balanced on my leg. He was on his way to the Zodiacs before that.

On our approach to the beach, we spotted a Lebanese Army troop carrier patrolling the shoreline. Daniel reclined a little in his seat, he straightened his right arm on the wheel, and placed his left elbow on the base of the driver's side window, with his forearm straight up. He slowed the car. The troop carrier passed us by. I looked to see if I could catch his eye in the rear view mirror. He caught my glance, sped up a little, stopped the car, and we were on the Israeli missile boats, returning to Haifa, in one fell swoop. I don't have any memory of the Zodiac boats, but we were surely on them. The successes of that day did not include walking on water.

Before we even boarded the missile boats we found out what happened. All of our targets were dead, including an operations leader of Black September, the terrorist group responsible for the Munich massacre. As an added bonus, the headquarters of the world's most notorious plane hijacker, was completely destroyed.

We made an impression. The Arab world was shocked, and in mourning. The funerals for the victims of the raid attracted quite a crowd. To say the least. Five-hundred-thousand people crowded into the streets of Beirut.

Operation Spring of Youth had another effect that was a great benefit to Israel, the Jewish people, and, frankly, the world. Terrorist leaders and Arab government now believed that Israel was capable of striking anywhere, anytime. They would think twice, or more, about another operation like Munich, or even terrorist operations in general. Less radical Arab governments began putting pressure on Palestinians to halt attacks against Israeli targets. They did not want the terrorists using passports from their countries in the course of their attacks against Israel.

We made our way back to our base in Tel Aviv from Haifa. Colonel Stern made a point of telling me that he had already contacted Shoshana and Aaron. "She's waiting for you, Isaac. She sounded relieved that you were safe, but it seemed like she was expecting your safe return. She's quite a woman, Isaac. She's quite a woman." Yes, she is, I thought.

We lost two IDF commandos in the Beirut operation. They were good men. They were better than good men. Their families, and their country, could be very proud. They were heroes. Our loss was G-d's gain. But our loss was felt deeply, nonetheless. They paid a price for those sublime moments of which I was so fond. I would happily lay down my life so others could hear the joy of their children play, spend a quiet evening with their wives or husbands, seek our Lord through prayer and supplication, and live a long life full of the hills and valleys that a long life implies.

He had restored us to the Land after the Holocaust. John pointed to His signs, the coincident blood moons of 1949-1950. He had restored Jerusalem to our control. John pointed to His signs, the coincident blood moons of 1967-1968. There were to be more miracles, more blood moons, and more blood. She was a good woman. He was a faithful G-d. She was a gift from Him. He did not want us to be alone.

He was Master of the Universe. A Master of the Universe who was a Master Painter. He did not want us to be alone. And He did not want us to be without signs, without a destination, and without a destiny.

He was Lord among the G-ds. He would have to prove it again. War was coming again. This time, the humiliating loss in the 1967 war had simply "stuck in the craws" of the Arab world. Particularly the Egyptians. It really wasn't about '67. It was our existence. Except this time, they would make it a war between the G-ds.

I knew John would be busy on the Sunday before Passover. But I had promised to see him after I returned, and before Passover began. He was kind enough to come by the lab late on that Sunday afternoon. I wasn't a long lost friend. But I could have been lost to this world. John knew that. He acknowledged it by his smile, which could have stretched across the street, and then some. I was comforted to know that Father John Broderick was praying for me, and my comrades, during the mission. I knew that our Lord heard all of the prayers of His creation. But I still thought, John was a bear of a man, with the heart of a lion, and the sensibilities of a lamb. Maybe those qualities would cause his prayers to echo in G-d's "ears" just a little bit longer. It was silly. But it was human. And I was human.

What a welcome sight John was! He sensed that I was more than happy to see him, and to be safely back in the lab. "That was quite a demonstration in Beirut," he said, with a smile. "Imagine, sightseers come to Beirut. And a half million people fill the streets, after they are already gone. What must have they done? Hmm. Tourists. I thought Beirut loved tourists. Maybe they didn't like such public displays of affection. That's it!! They took offense!" Daniel had no secrets from John. The bear of a man had a bear of a laugh. He too was glad I was alive.

"Rest well, Isaac," he said. "War is coming. The Jordanians don't want it. But it is coming." "You are right, of course, John." "Daniel is worried, Isaac. He knows that the people are weary of war. But they are also strangely overconfident because of the '67 rout. I sense that overconfidence in the people, even the military." "Frankly, John, I sense it as well. It's funny, no one ever says something that you can point to. It's just a feeling I get. Not from Colonel Stern, and not from Daniel. But I do sense it from some of the younger officers, and the political leadership, who are old enough to know better. So, John, He will send us more miracles." "Truthfully, Isaac, they were needed last time. They were needed last week, in fact. Don't misunderstand me, you and the others are the best of the best. But, Isaac, as good as you are, you are not THAT good. Yes, Isaac, more miracles will come. They will have to. You must stay in the Land. They will come against you again and again. But, you must stay in the Land."

"You are alive, Isaac. That is a blessing. I have to get back. I owe my brothers a mass this evening." "Thanks for coming by, John." I said. "You are a blessing to Shoshana and me."

"How is she, Isaac? Will she be ready for another war?" "She is better than ever, John. I think she would prefer I stash my sword away for a while. But she knows the calculus, John. We are on a sliver of land, with a sliver of people."

"Farewell, Isaac. My brothers and I will dedicate our mass to the Land of Israel. And to the warriors who guard Her." "Thank you, John."

On the same day we launched Operation Spring of Youth, an American magazine published an interview with the president of Egypt. He again threatened war with Israel. Just a year earlier, the president of Egypt had said that war with Israel was inevitable, and he was prepared to sacrifice one million soldiers in the showdown with Israel. He was not alone. King Faisal of Saudi Arabia said: "All countries should wage war against the Zionists, who are there to destroy all human organizations and to destroy civilization and the work which good people are trying to do."

Not to be outdone, the Syrian Minister of Defense Mustafa Tlas told the Syrian National Assembly of an example of "supreme valor" by Syrian troops:

"There is the outstanding case of a recruit from Aleppo who murdered 28 Jewish soldiers all by himself, slaughtering them like sheep. All of his comrades in arms witnessed this. He butchered three of them with an ax and decapitated them... He struggled face to face with one of them and throwing down his ax managed to break his neck and devour his flesh in front of his comrades. This is a special case. Need

I single it out to award him the Medal of the Republic. I will grant this medal to any soldier who succeeds in killing 28 Jews, and I will cover him with appreciation and honor his bravery."

Fantasies about cannibalism. The prophets of Baal would have been proud. It would of most certainly put a smile on the faces of the SS. The Syrian president, who plotted along with the Egyptian president, had plans for the '73 war. Grand plans.

The president of Syria wanted the Golan Heights back. It had been lost in the '67 war. He had no interest in negotiations. He believed that only the military option would bring back the territory he wanted. Once he had taken back the Golan Heights by force, then negotiations would begin with Israel. His goal was to force Israel to give up the so-called West Bank, and Gaza. After the '67 war, Syria began a massive military buildup. He believed that with the armaments that came with the buildup, and assistance from Egypt, a decisive victory would be his. In spite of all the evidence, nobody seemed to take the threat seriously. John was right. We would need miracles.

A certain Jewish girl did seem to notice. But, mercifully, she waited until after our wedding anniversary to point out the obvious, and the consequences for our little family. "How could our leaders be so blind," she said. "Isaac, only the foolish would believe they are not coming." Shoshana had never spoken so frankly about our political leadership, or the prospect of war. She was frustrated. She was worried. Not fearful for me, but worried. "You have been training more, Isaac." She looked at me as if she wanted me to tell her that this time I wouldn't have to be a soldier. "We should surprise them, like '67 and Beirut," I said. "But, somehow, I don't think they believe what you and many others can so clearly see. We cannot allow the gains of '67 to be squandered." "Well then, I know you won't be reckless, my husband, but remember, alright?" "My promise was good for a lifetime, Shoshana." That elicited a smile. It was a miserable subject with a perfect ending. We could not be weary.

The Syrian Defense Minister was not just embellishing a story for his audience. He was relating the outlines of a more deep seated, textured and ghoulish fantasy. Shoshana knew where it led. It led to more Holocaust Memorials, if we let it. John was right. We had to stay in the Land. There was safety in the Land. There were miracles.

It was the July after Munich. It was time for the Maccabiah Games, the quadrennial Jewish Olympics that follow the Olympic Games. It was poignant. It was a relief. It was thrilling. And we owed all to a 15-year old boy. Yosef Yekutielli. He never grew weary. A 15-year old who dreamed, and never grew weary. Take heart.

Yosef was Russian-born, but as a teenager grew up in the Land of Israel, before statehood. He learned of the 1912 Olympic Games, and conceived of a Olympics for Jewish athletes from all over the world to be held in the Holy Land. Yosef spent the next ten years working on the details of such an event.

In 1928, Yosef Yekutielli presented his dream to the Jewish National Fund. He proposed the Maccabiah Games, which would be organized to memorialize the 1800th anniversary of the Bar Kochba Rebellion (Jewish revolt against the Romans). Coincidentally, the Maccabi organization was developing ideas to include athletes who were living in the Land in international sporting events. It was thought that this would promote international support for a Jewish National Home.

Yosef's idea was endorsed by all the sport groups in the area of the British Mandate. Final approval for the event was needed by the British High Commissioner. Sir Arthur Wauchope was an admirer of the Zionists, including the burgeoning Jewish sports movement. He approved.

The first Maccabiah Games were held in 1932. It was an overwhelming success. As it was a quadrennial event, the next scheduled Games were to be in 1936. However, because of the rise of Nazism in Europe, the Games were moved up to 1935. As war descended on

Europe, the Games were postponed, indefinitely. The Maccabiah Games were finally reborn in 1950, in the new State of Israel.

The Maccabiah Games survived the Holocaust. They also survived Munich. The Maccabiah Games of 1973 included an Israeli Olympian who had survived both Munich, and the Bergen-Belsen concentration camp. Anne Frank had not survived Bergen-Belsen concentration camp. Neither had 100,000 others. The Olympian also lost his maternal grandmother and grandfather. They died in Auschwitz. When asked about his life he said, "What I can say is that in my life there has never been a dull moment." Never a dull moment. In the camps, and at Munich, there was never a dull moment. And now, as fall was approaching, the soul(less) mates of the camps and Munich were planning the next "dull moment" for the people of Israel.

Beginning in 1972, Egypt had been stockpiling weapons to create an arsenal for war. Christmas had come, courtesy of the Russians. There were MiG-21 jet fighters, SA-2, SA-3, SA-6 and SA-7 antiair-craft missiles, T-55 and T-62, RPG-7 antitank weapons, and the AT-3 Sagger anti-tank guided missile. Our leadership insisted they were Christmas bobbles, ornaments, nothing more.

On September 13, high above the Mediterranean sea, Aaron and his brother pilots found out that those "ornaments" did more than decorate the sky. When was the last time ornaments had lethal intent. Before the fight was over, 13 MiG-21s, so coveted by the Egyptians and the Syrians, were presents from the Russians that should have marked "return to sender." Now they couldn't. They were all broken to pieces and became rather waterlogged at the bottom of their new home, the Mediterranean sea. One of the Israeli pilots got a little wet himself, bobbing and weaving on the ocean surface, thanks to the shots fired by one of the bobbles. He was rescued.

Everything was calm in Israel. But someone was worried. Before the '67 war, Rabbi Menachem Schneerson helped rally a nation full of angst and gloom. Now, we were a nation which had become all too overconfident. In '67, the Rabbi had encouraged all the men to wear tefillin. Tefillin held scrolls of parchment inscribed with verses from the Torah. Now he was encouraging extra Torah learning for children. He was concerned about danger that the Land of Israel was facing. He was encouraging parents to teach their children additional Torah. He cited the verse from Psalms 8:2:

"Out of the mouth of babes and nursing infants
You have ordained strength, Because of Your enemies,
That You may silence the enemy and the avenger."

History will end in the city. Rabbi Schneerson thought that children should come to Jerusalem to pray. They did. Tens of thousands of children. He called for boys under the age of 13, and girls under the age of 12. He wanted them to come to the Western Wall for a special prayer, and to give charity.

They came by private cars, buses, trains and trucks. Everywhere, there were children. In the plaza before the wall and the paths leading to the wall. Every child received two coins. One coin was a gift, with the suggestion that it be given to charity. The other coin was given with the request that it be given to charity. It was a remarkable demonstration of faith, and faithfulness. We needed the prayers. Because we would soon need miracles.

Rabbi Schneerson also seemed to know something else that the military and political leadership would have been wise to heed. Israel devoted extraordinary resources to building what was known as the Bar Lev Line. It was a chain of fortifications built along the eastern coast of the Suez canal. It was described as a "graveyard for Egyptian troops."

Israel apparently didn't learn from the German experience on the western front in World War II. Germany constructed a mazelike network of every conceivable combination of tunnels, chambers, hardened bunkers, and booby-trapped barriers. Germany failed. Israel got the "booby" prize for their efforts. The Bar Lev Line was overrun in less than 2 hours. The Rabbi knew what the experts didn't. The Bar Lev Line "would not be able to prevent them (the Egyptians) from crossing the Suez Canal.

The small commando group under my command had been training to carry out reconnaissance missions in the Sinai. Colonel Stern wanted to deploy us. We had to have "eyes and ears on the ground," he said. He did not expect the Bar Lev Line to hold. It was a perilous mission. It might be impossible if we waited too long. It might be too late.

I was nearly a full-time resident of our training facility in Tel Aviv. We kept waiting for the word to go. We weren't waiting for the weather to break like Eisenhower. Shoshana wanted us to go and get the job done, and come back home all the sooner. John was confident about two things. Israel would prevail, eventually. And, this time, in contrast to '67, our leadership would insist that the attack was not coming, relinquishing both surprise, and the initiative, to a force that was already much larger than ours.

> *"Now the word of the Lord came to me, saying:*
> *"Son of man, you dwell in the midst of a rebellious house,*
> *which has eyes to see but does not see,*
> *and ears to hear but does not hear;*
> *for they are a rebellious house.""*
> *Ezekiel 12:2*

We had eyes to see, but did not see. We had ears to hear, but did not hear. We were still a rebellious house. It was not that we ignored good intelligence. It was not that we refused to hear the words of our foes. But it was that, in spite of miracle after miracle, sign after sign, we still doubted. Our faith lagged. We wanted to be in the Land as a refuge from the inexorable appetites of our enemies. But did we want to belong to Him? His words would ultimately be written on our hearts. Our faithlessness would not lead to captivity this time. For better or for worse, we were back in the Land. He wanted us there. He was longsuffering. He would stand with us. But would our eyes see, and our ears hear?

The Arabs were ready. They wanted a war between the G-ds. They planned to attack in the Islamic holy month of Ramadan. The tenth day of Ramadan was a special day in Islam. It was on the tenth day of Ramadan that Muhammad had his first victorious jihad, conquering Mecca to force conversions to his new religion of Islam at the Battle of Badr in 624 C.E. The Egyptian Chief of Staff Saad el-Shazly thought, how perfect. He code named the attack on Israel: Operation Badr.

Operation Badr was set. King Hussein was worried. He feared a replay of the '67 war, and another major loss of territory for Jordan. King Hussein secretly flew to Tel Aviv on the night September 25 to warn the Israeli Prime Minister that an attack was imminent. In fact, throughout September, Israel received eleven separate warnings of war. And from good sources. The warnings were discounted. The head of Israeli intelligence would later say, "We simply didn't feel them capable [of War]."

So we waited. If you wait long enough, something will give. It did. The tenth day of Ramadan also corresponded to the holiest day in the Jewish calendar. In 1973, Yom Kippur fell on a Saturday, Shabbat. It was October 6th. The Arab commanders were ready to synchronize the start of their invasion. Egyptian War Minister General Ahmed Ismail cabled Syrian Defense Minister Lieutenant General Mustafa Tlas a single word: Badr. Syrian Defense Minister Mustafa Tlas had previously waxed longingly about slaughtering Jewish soldiers "like sheep." Now he and his soldiers would have their chance. The war between the G-ds was on. The Yom Kippur War.

Israel has assumed that its intelligence services would give them 48 hours' notice of an Arab attack. The plan was to execute a preemptive strike. The Americans were pressuring the Israeli government to forego pre-emption. The Israeli Prime Minister was quoted as saying, "if we strike first, we won't get help from anybody."

Israel was on its heels. And then some. There was a reason that a pre-emptive strike was essential. The numbers would never favor Israel. Egypt assaulted Israel's southern border with 70,000 troops. This represented a little less than 10% of Egypt's total troop strength. In the area of the southern border, it was 70,000 Egyptians against about 500 Israelis. The differential in troops and armaments was no better on the Golan Heights. At 2:00 p.m. on the first day, the Syrians crossed the Purple Line, the established ceasefire line of the 1967 war. One-thousand Syrian tanks faced off with 177 Israeli tanks. Five-hundred Syrian tanks came in a second wave. Six-thousand Israeli troops were up against 50,000 Syrians. Israel had 60 artillery pieces versus 1,000 Syrian artillery pieces.

On the second day of the war, Israel's Defense Minister said: "We are in the most critical hour since the day we re-established the new nation. The war is almost lost for us." By the third day of the war, Israel's Prime Minister authorized the activation of nuclear bombs. In a press conference during the Yom Kippur War, the Prime Minister issued a statement: "This people [the people of Israel, the descendants of Jacob], small as it is, surrounded as it is by enemies, has decided to live. And if we have to pay the price for living, we have to pay it. This is not a people that can give in."

It was not as bad as it seemed in the Sinai peninsula. Some of the reports had Egyptian commandos slowing the Israeli counteroffensive against the Egyptian forces. They weren't. They were pretty good, certainly better than we thought, but they were not that effective. My small commando group was supposed to provide early intelligence for a pre-emptive strike. Now we were gathering intelligence, as we could. We had to fight our way through the Egyptian commandos. We were not like the ten spies sent out by Moses. They only reported what they saw. We certainly reported what we saw, but we also reported what we heard, from captured Egyptians.

We had a lot to worry about. Frankly, if we lost the Golan Heights in the north, Israel would not have defensible borders. Before the 1967 war, Syria was using the Golan Heights with virtual impunity to bludgeon Israeli civilian targets with artillery, and launch terrorist operations that not only wantonly killed, but were demoralizing to many communities located near the border. If Syria could recapture the Golan Heights, artillery and terrorism would be the least of our worries.

We needed a miracle on the Golan Heights. It had come before. In 1958, an IDF officer led a company of soldiers into battle with the Syrian Army. The IDF officer had sustained injuries when he was accidentally run over by a tank. Syrian soldiers are trained to shoot (again) any wounded Israeli soldier. When they were about to shoot the IDF officer, the Syrian soldiers suddenly ran away. Later they reported to UN officials that they had seen thousands of angels around the IDF officer, thus they fled. The IDF officer later dedicated himself to the work of the Temple Mount.

It was grim on the Golan Heights. The Syrians had been told by their commanders to take civilian clothes because they would soon be on the streets of Israeli cities, enjoying their plunder. The tank battle on the Golan began with the Syrians mounting a night offensive using their night vision equipment, which the Israelis lacked. They were effective in penetrating Israeli defenses. On the second day, the Syrians came at the Israelis again, and at one point there were only 40 Israeli tanks opposed by 500 Syrian tanks. By the end of the fourth day of battle, seven Israeli tanks were completely encircled by the Syrians. When 13 repaired tanks were sent back into battle by the Israelis, the tank commander ordered his twenty tanks to "move up" against a vastly superior force of at least 150 Syrian tanks. For reasons that are known only to the Syrians, they not only stopped their advance, they retreated.

In the north, on the Golan Heights, it was the turning point of the war. The tank commander was told by the Division Commander, "You have saved the people of Israel." Yes he did. The tank battle itself took place on a plain just above the "Valley of Tears." If the Syrians had gotten past the Israeli tanks, they could have easily gone on to the Israeli cities of Tiberius, Haifa, and even Tel Aviv.

The tank commander received the Medal of Valor, Israel's highest military honor. He was a veteran of the '67 war. In the '67 war, he had been burned over 60% of his body when his tank was hit by enemy fire. After 16 operations, and a year in and out of hospitals, he wanted back into the IDF, and into tanks. The IDF has a rating scale of 1 - 97. He was rated 31. He changed his rating to 97. He was back in the fight, and ready for the Yom Kippur War.

There were many miracles during the tank battles on the Golan Heights. Tanks normally face off at distances of between 2 and 3 thousand meters. At one point, the commander's tank was surrounded by four Syrian tanks at about a distance of 25 meters (about 75 feet). He was able to destroy all four tanks. He went on the radio and announced that he had 41 tanks, hoping that the Syrians were listening. Maybe they were. When he ordered his battered and minuscule tank group to move forward, his men at first refused, believing it was suicide. He cajoled and hectored them to follow him. As he advanced, knowing that his tanks had very little ammunition left, he ordered them to fire on the Syrian positions. At that point, many Syrians got out of their tanks, and ran for cover. Others just retreated in their tanks. But they retreated, nonetheless.

Two Israeli tanks survived the four-day battle. Five-hundred Syrian tanks and armored vehicles became lifeless hulks, memorials to a war between the G-ds. The Israeli tank commander faced his own Goliath. Like David, he believed that G-d would fight with him against insurmountable odds. His faith saved the day. It may have saved Israel.

My commando group was still in the Sinai. On the second day of the war, our combined forces were still trying to get their bearings. We were still reeling a bit. My commando squad was in a kind of "no man's land, about a kilometer from the Israeli front lines, and almost 2 kilometers from an approaching Egyptian column. We were following the movement of the Egyptians when they appeared to run smack into a lone Israeli soldier. I was flabbergasted. How did he get that separated from his unit. I wanted to do something. It was impossible. We couldn't give away our position. We were in a dicey situation as it was. I looked again through my field binoculars. Now he appeared to be leading the Egyptian column to the Israeli lines. I handed my binoculars to one of my men and asked him what he saw. The look on his face told me he saw the same thing I saw. So, we were both crazy. We passed the binoculars down the line. We had all been in the desert too long.

Later, the Israeli soldier explained that he was by himself when the Egyptian commander and his men surrendered to him. The Egyptian commander was asked to explain why he and his men surrendered to a lone Israeli soldier. "One solider? There were thousands of them." The Egyptian commander went on to explain that as they approached the Israeli lines, the "thousands" of soldiers he saw began to disappear. John said there would be miracles. Who was I to argue with a priest.

Our combined forces had absorbed the blow delivered by the Egyptians. Three days after the war began, on October 9th, the front lines in the Sinai had stabilized. We began looking for an opportunity to take the offensive. In the meantime, the Americans delivered a critical tidbit of intelligence to the Southern Command. There was a gap between the Egyptian Second and Third armies. We didn't need much. Stonewall Jackson probably would have driven through the gap and went all the way to Cairo. We just wanted to get over the Suez Canal.

And the American President delivered something else to Israel. A lot of something else. Thanks to his mother. And a certain other interested party. Israel needed military supplies. The Israeli Prime Minister woke the American President at 3:00 a.m., and asked for help. The American President told the Israeli Prime Minister a story from his childhood. His mother would read him Bible stories every night. One night his mother made him promise that if he was ever in a position to help save the Jewish people, he would do it. He then told the Prime Minister that, now, maybe he understood why he became President of the United State. After their conversation, so began the largest military airlift since World War II.

The Egyptian Second and Third armies had been ordered to attack eastward over a broad front. As they attacked, the forces they left behind were insufficient and too dispersed to form an effective defense. We were now in a position to use our superior speed, maneuverability, and tank gunnery.

Egypt's Second and Third armies were armored divisions. They had a combined force of 800 - 1,000 tanks, with artillery support. They were up against over 700 Israeli tanks. The Egyptians believed they could support the armored assault by sending 100 of their commandos to disrupt the Israeli rear. It failed. Sixty of their commandos were killed, and many were taken prisoner. Along with several other commando groups, my team raided an Egyptian signals-intercept site that seriously disrupted Egyptian command and control capability. The Egyptian forces weren't quite deaf, dumb and blind, but they were close.

The Yom Kippur War became a proxy war. The Arabs wanted a war between the G-ds. The Americans and the Soviets made it a proxy war between the superpowers. After Syria collapsed, the Soviets pushed for an armistice. After all, the Soviets regarded Syria as a client-state. The Americans pushed Israel to accept a cease fire. On October 12, Israel agreed. Egypt refused. Egypt wanted a second "crack" at Israeli forces in the Sinai.

Egypt should have accepted the cease fire. They launched into a catastrophe. Their armies and armored support units began going beyond the protections of their anti-missile batteries. They left themselves wide open to Israeli air attack. And they left the canal unguarded. The Israeli Air Force and IDF armor began to rain holy terror on the Egyptian forces. Egypt lost over 250 tanks, and hundreds of soldiers. October 14 was a disaster for Egypt. It was the turning point of the war. On October 15th, Israel crossed the Suez Canal.

From our forward positions near the canal, our commando groups helped shield IDF engineers who were being subjected to withering fire from the Egyptian air force and artillery. The engineers were busily fabricating a bridge to cross the Suez Canal. The bridge was finally completed the afternoon of October 17, and before dawn, two brigades of tanks were across the canal. By October 18, the major part of two divisions of Israeli soldiers had crossed the canal.

The Egyptians wanted out. They had enough. They virtually begged the Soviets to arrange a cease fire at the United Nations. At first, the Egyptians insisted that any cease fire require Israel to withdraw to the lines they held before the war. As their situation deteriorated, Egypt abandoned that position. They made another desperate appeal to the Soviets. On October 22, United Nations Resolution 338 was passed. It called for a cease fire and peace negotiations within twelve hours of its passage.

The superpower confrontation was heating up. The Soviets were alarmed that Israel could and would advance on Cairo. The Soviets issued an ultimatum. The cease fire holds, or the superpowers would be brought to the brink of war. Once on that tenuous precipice, who knows. The Soviets were on the move, militarily, and with their nuclear weapons. The Americans thought they had credible intelligence indicating that the Soviets had "nukes" en route to Egypt. The United States responded. The president ordered a USA DEFCON-3 nuclear alert. It was meant to call the bluff of the Soviet Union.

The United Nations passed two more Resolutions: 339 and 340. This time, the cease fire held. UN observers were in place along the Suez Canal by October 27. Operation Badr had failed.

John knew it well. The children who were summoned to Jerusalem knew it well.

"Thus you shall say to the children of Israel,
I AM has sent me to you."
Exodus 3:14

I AM had delivered us. The war between the G-ds had been settled by the Lord among the G-ds. There is a hymn of praise that is 3,500 years old, but is really about eternity. It was sung by those who were delivered from Egyptian captivity and slavery. The "Me Chamoecha" (Who is like Thee?).

Who is like Thee, O Lord, among the G-ds?
Who is like Thee glorified in holiness?
You are awesome in praise, working wonders O Lord,
who is like Thee, O Lord?

Yes, upon my return to Tel Aviv, I had the "Me Chamoecha" on my mind. So did Colonel Stern, sort of. After I called Shoshana and Aaron, Colonel Stern approached me shaking his head. He told me that one of his commanders was preparing to retreat from the Syrian army in the early days of the war. He suddenly realized that he and his men were trapped in the middle of a minefield. He ordered his men to clear the mines using their bayonets, crawl on the ground and dig 30 inches deep, carefully disengaging the mines. One of the men prayed. Just then, a fierce windstorm came upon them. By the time the windstorm had moved on, it had literally blown off 30 inches of topsoil. Every mine was exposed. The commander and his men quickly made their escape.

Colonel Stern looked at me, and continued to shake his head.

"So I suppose that you and the priest, and maybe Daniel for all I know, are going to tell me of miracles, or some such thing." So I paraphrased: "Who is like Him, O Lord among the G-ds?" "To tell you the truth, Isaac, I'm not sure myself how we survived the first few days. In those hours, I was not thinking about winning, but handing any weapons we had to our people and asking them to defend our cities." "Was it really that bad, Colonel?" Colonel Stern then held out his index and middle fingers. You could have fit the width of sowing thread between them. "We were that close to trying out the handiwork of our physicists," he said. "That close." He put his fingers in front of my eyes for emphasis. I was sure that the memory of those days would stay with the Colonel for a long time. "So you answered your own question, Colonel." He walked away, shaking his head, his hand outstretched, with two fingers indicating an all too uncomfortable closeness to using a device that was supposed to deter. It didn't. And that was the point.

Deterrence would never work. After the war, the Americans issued the following statement:

"Our position is that... the conditions that produced this war were clearly intolerable to the Arab nations and that in the process of negotiations it will be necessary to make substantial concessions. The problem will be to relate the Arab concern for the sovereignty over the territories to the Israeli concern for secure boundaries. We believe that the process of negotiations between the parties is an essential component of this."

History was being stood on its head right before my eyes. It is said that "truth is the first casualty of war."

The statement implicitly legitimized the Arab attack that began the Yom Kippur War. "The conditions that produced this war were clearly intolerable to the Arab nations..." And then the statement accepted the premise that a clever land swap would resolve the conflict, once and for all. "The problem will be to relate the Arab concern for the sovereignty over the territories to the Israeli concern for secure boundaries. We believe that the process of negotiations between the parties is an essential component of this."

Deterrence failed. By the time of the Yom Kippur War, the world believed that Israel had nuclear weapons. And yet, they attacked. Now, land for peace would become the new delusion. If Israel surrendered enough land, peace would follow. Israel's military prowess was never the point. Land was never the point. We were the point. Our very existence was the point.

We had center stage in a righteous G-d's entry into the world. He was the G-d of Abraham, Isaac, and Jacob. Did it mean we had a more righteous nature than other men and women? No. Did it mean human frailties did not befall us like other men and women? No. But it was a blessing in the universe that really counted for something. It also meant that the cursed would pursue our hearts, and tear at our flesh, until we succumbed, or until there was no last trace of us on this earth, or anywhere.

History begins in the garden. It ends in the city. Then, we will have peace.

CHAPTER FIVE

THE END FROM THE BEGINNING

"Remember the former things of old,
For I am G-d, and there is no other;
I am G-d, and there is none like Me,
Declaring the end from the beginning,
And from ancient times things that are not yet done."
Isaiah 46:9-10

We savored those first days and months of Ethan John Bass's life. The doctors counseled David and Rachel that it wouldn't be advisable for Ethan to travel until he was about 3 months old. That was a blessing. We took full advantage of our opportunities to dote on him, and in general make fools of ourselves anytime we were graced by his tiny visage. Even Daniel and John got into the act. It was something to see.

Life had come to Ethan with some immediate challenges. Children born with Down Syndrome often experience cardiac and respiratory difficulties, sometime severe difficulties. The specialists pronounced Ethan apparently free of the cardiac and pulmonary infirmities that might have burdened his health, and his early life. Infirmities. Imperfections. I wonder. Imperfections. Since the foundation of the world, He did not dabble with His creation.

For You formed my inward parts;
You covered me in my mother's womb.
I will praise You, for I am fearfully and wonderfully made;
Marvelous are Your works,
And that my soul knows very well.
My frame was not hidden from You,
When I was made in secret,
And skillfully wrought in the lowest parts of the earth.
Your eyes saw my substance, being yet unformed.
And in Your book they all were written,
The days fashioned for me,
When as yet there were none of them.
Psalm 139:13-16

Ethan was perfect in the sight of G-d. That was good enough for me. It was time for circumcision. It was part of G-d's covenant with Abraham.

"This is My covenant which you shall keep,
between Me and you and your descendants after you:
Every male child among you shall be circumcised..."
Genesis 17:10

Shoshana and I offered our apartment as the site for the circumcision of Ethan John Bass. The doctors said there wouldn't be a problem, but suggested that one of them do the circumcision. As a precaution. It was fine with his parents, and I think that all of us were a little relieved.

Aaron was invited, but couldn't attend. He was on his honeymoon! He finally married his slain wife's sister. It was a long engagement, and an extremely understated wedding. Under the circumstances, it was best. Aaron said that the marriage may be exactly the right thing to do. It was. But too much celebration just didn't seem right. Aaron had a sense of proportion. He honored his wife's memory. Aaron was a man who invariably did what was right. Among his many gifts, that particular gift recommended him as a cherished friend, and brother. He wasn't thrown off by the tragedy that befell him. G-d would bless his faithfulness.

Daniel and Colonel Stern thought better of being seen anywhere near our apartment. An occupational, ah, "concession." A wise concession. What would a circumcision be without a priest? The answer is a normal circumcision. But that "bear of a man" just couldn't be kept away. He took every conceivable precaution. Not the least of which was a disguise that appeared to defrock him of his priestly attributes. To be sure, he knew the craft of our shadowy world. And just for good measure, he had his white collar tucked away in one of his coat pockets. After all, Ethan had John's name as part of his earthly calling card. Father John Broderick had a special blessing for Ethan. And, Ethan had a special blessing that would change everything. *Everything.*

And there we all were. Gathered to honor G-d's covenant with our father, Abraham. Exactly eight days after Ethan came into creation. Ethan had taken it all in and made the only prudent choice, sleep. He was not terribly bothered by a ceremony that had been repeated over many thousands of years. He would have plenty of time to consider the arc of history. Now he wanted to concentrate on the arc of being a new born baby. Eating and sleeping would suit him just fine.

We were ready. Ethan was now in the hands of the *Sandek.* The Sandek holds the baby during the circumcision. The Sandek is usually a grandfather who is being honored by the parents. Ethan's maternal and paternal grandparents were conspicuously absent. So we suggested Shoshana's father, Rabbi Shlomo Levy. David and Rachel loved the idea. It was obvious to all of us that Rabbi Levy loved the idea too. He had Ethan on a pillow on his lap. He looked like he came from "central casting" for Sandeks. Enter the doctor. He was surely going to shake up Ethan's peaceful countenance. He did, but not much. Ethan's beautiful little eyes teared up some. And he made the appropriate face to indicate his dissatisfaction with the interruption of his sleep. But his demonstrations didn't last long. Before long, Ethan was back in dreamland. No worse for the wear.

Shlomo means G-d's peace. As sunset approached, we were all relishing G-d's peace. I hadn't seen the "Sandek" smile that way since our wedding. Shoshana noticed it, too. I saw her look at her father in a way that I had never seen before. She was wistfully delighted. She knew he wouldn't live forever. It was a moment, among moments. She would remember this moment until all her memories were added to paradise.

David was in Israel for the birth of his son, to be sure. But his wits would also help keep us in the Land. Daniel was still worried. It was this "group" that operated out of four cities. Two of the cities spawned a particularly malignant form of the obsession.

Karl Leuger and George Schonerer did not dabble in a new form of hate. They were not particularly clever. They just said publicly what so many in polite society believed, but, at first, would only say, in hushed tones. Those Jews. Someone was listening. He came from a part of central casting whose specialty was "film noir," but his vileness could not be contained by darkness alone. He penned a book that was part memoir, part political ideology, and all maniacal rant. In the book, he claims he learned anti-Semitism from Karl Leuger and George Schonerer. So, Karl Leuger and George Schonerer were present at the creation. The creation of the Nazi Party and its dream of a Thousand Year Reich. It was a dream to turn G-d's creation into an eternal march to death. Karl Leuger and George Schonerer were from Vienna. Vienna, Austria.

After the war, those who used the blunt instruments of war and mutilation to kill tens of millions, turned their twisted souls to survival, and refinement. Survival took an ironic form only evil could savor. A Dutch Carmelite priest, Titus Brandsma, became a martyr after being murdered in the camps for protesting the deportation of Jews. To avoid accountability for his crimes against humanity, SS Captain Walter Kutschmann, who had been a frequent wartime travel companion of fashion designer Coco Chanel, donned the plain robes of a Carmelite monk to complete his escape. Such was the moral nature of the architects of the Thousand Year Reich. They only heard the call of the wild. The savage call. Survival for me, death for thee.

Eva and Juan Peron wanted to become innkeepers for Nazis seeking refuge after the war. They relished the Nazi power and "style" from afar. Hitler's spell had created a cult of personality that could only be satisfied in their lustiest of dreams. They wanted proximity to those who once dominated the world stage. The Perons found a home for some of their friends in a place that had been settled by Germans from Chile. It became an idyllic little hideaway in the Andes, a haven for skiers, tourists, and master killers alike. It was said to have secret celebrations of Hitler's birthday. Secret celebrations aside, these new friends of the Perons hid in plain sight. They hid in a place that eschewed the susurrus whispers of pale pastels for the banshee screams of blood red. San Carlos de Bariloche. San Carlos de Bariloche, Argentina.

For all of the secrecy that surrounded the lab itself, my day to day work at the lab failed to even register on the Richter scale of intrigue. The work was vital. The scale of the work was "game changing." Our survival could depend on it. Our enemies would love to possess it. But John Wayne never starred in a movie about the Manhattan Project. He knew better. It was Iwo Jima. Bataan. D-Day. And he was right. But one afternoon might have changed that a little.

Daniel came to talk about cities. People live in cities. They can find cities on a map. They may have visited the cities. So, it became a day of intrigue. It became a tale of two cities.

Father John Broderick and David Bass arrived early that afternoon. They were fresh from the "Bris" (circumcision) of David's son, and so they were still riding the Ethan Bass wave of bliss. It was nice to see. I tried to maintain that feeling in the lab as long as possible.

I felt sorry for Daniel in some respects. If he requested a meeting, it couldn't be good. It was only a matter of degree. He was the veritable skunk at the garden party. If his information only qualified as "skunk-ish," one took little solace.

Even when he saw three men in the glow of the Ethan Bass life force, he did not change his expression. We all sat down. Daniel got right to the point.

"David, I want you to review this material. We now believe there is a code embedded in these messages. Our preliminary analysis tells us that using our existing methods, we might break the code in ten years. And that means applying nothing special, only brute force. Ten years gentlemen. This is a taunt. It is a deliberate taunt. Vienna, Austria. San Carlos de Bariloche, Argentina. They know we know that Adolph Eichmann spent time in San Carlos de Bariloche before we captured him in Buenos Aires. We also know that San Carlos de Bariloche is still home to Nazi SS. They breathe the same air as free men, good men. They should be at the end of a rope."

"Vienna. Our friends have been making life difficult for the political elite in Austria. Old habits die hard. They are openly appointing, and electing, ex-Nazis to official government positions. Our friends point it out. And they are outraged. Vienna, Austria, gentlemen. Messages are ping ponging between San Carlos de Bariloche, New York, Vienna, and Ismailia, Egypt."

David asked, "What is the Ismailia connection? And what about New York?" They were good questions. All of us knew the answer. I explained. "David, Ismailia, Egypt is where the Muslim Brotherhood was founded in about 1928. The 'brothers,' the Ikhwan, grew exponentially in popularity as their rhetoric began to parallel the Nazi credo about the Jewish problem. Mein Kampf was translated into Arabic as 'My Jihad.' Now, they have begun a process of trying to appear more acceptable to the West." "What do you mean, Professor?" "They are 'westernizing' their dress, and trying to tone down their language. They will never change, David."

"Daniel may have another thought. But, I suspect, David, that the New York connection is because of the United Nations (UN). It will become an ever more pointed spear at the heart of Israel. The Secretary-General of the United Nations from 1972 to 1981 was discovered to be a Nazi intelligence officer for the Wehrmacht. He always claimed to have been injured, and that the injury cut his service short. His fictional narrative included a trip to, where else, Vienna, to attend law school. In truth, he was found by the Americans to have assisted in the smooth operation of a Nazi military organization which committed numerous atrocities. He approved some propaganda leaflets that would have made the Muslim Brotherhood proud."

"In 1975, the UN General Assembly passed a resolution equating Zionism with racism. The vote came exactly 37 years after Kristallnacht, in which the Germans, and to some degree, the Austrians, carried out organized attacks against virtually anything Jewish. They are in Vienna and Ismailia because they never left. They are taking root in San Carlos de Bariloche and New York."

Daniel repeated his haunting analysis. "This is a taunt, gentlemen. This is a taunt, David." John asked the question that needed to be asked. "Daniel, taunt? A taunt is personal. How do we know it's personal?" "I want David to complete his analysis. They embedded this code. But they meant for it to be uncovered. The sophistication of the embedding does not match the sophistication of the code. It is a matter, gentlemen, of judgment. Whatever their assessment of our survival, to this point, they feel secure in treating our existence contemptuously. Of that, I am sure. The cities and the code." Daniel turned to David. "David, why don't you spend the rest of the day with Rachel? Get a fresh start on this tomorrow." David nodded in agreement. "I will see you tomorrow, Professor. Take care, Father John. Daniel." "Good bye, David," said John as David left the laboratory.

John began. "You are worried, Daniel." "Yes, I am, John." "There is something about this code, John." "I can't get the code and the cities out of my mind. It's always been personal, John. Embellish it as you may with ideology. As an ideology, Nazism was a transparent and explosive blend of the personal and the political. They will be more careful this time. The alliances that will emerge will be shocking. No less deadly, but shocking."

"That is a fascinating point you made, Daniel, about this being personal. It has always been personal. It is a spiritual battle. But it is personal."

"So the Lord G-d said to the serpent…
And I will put enmity Between you and the woman,
And between your seed and her Seed;
He shall bruise your head, And you shall bruise His heel."
Genesis 3:14-15

"There is life in the woman and her 'Seed.' There is eternal life in the presence of G-d. In the mind of the cunning, beginning in the garden, death was the antidote to the divine. One easily fell prey to the indulgences that could pass the time once one was in the full embrace of death. Abraham's faith is our path to freedom. Freedom from the curse. Freedom from death."

"Just since the '67 war, miraculous change has occurred. For the first time, millions of Christians are seeking their Hebraic roots. This is only the beginning. Daniel rightly points to shocking alliances. Tens of millions of Christians will come to see the centrality of Israel to the future of all believers in the G-d of Abraham, Isaac and Jacob. They will come 'home' to where they belong. What is left of the West will probably seek an accommodation with Islam. An alliance of convenience may be formed to oppose Israel and its defenders. Shocks will come. And miracles will come. So we stand in the breach. The breach is death's door. G-d will heal the breach. Until then, we stand in the breach on faith."

I wanted John to continue. I felt he wanted to continue. "John, is there a timeline in all of this? Can we understand this in terms of some sort of timeline?"

"If you understand the beginning, Isaac, then you will understand the end. Genesis. The beginning of G-d's creation. There were clues, from the beginning. Many in the Rabbinate believe there is a significant clue in the very *first* verse in the first chapter of Genesis. The Hebrew letter, Aleph, which indicates thousand, is found six times. Hence in the Talmud, we read:

'The world shall last six thousand years, and then it shall be destroyed. This world lasted two thousand years in the law of nature, two thousand years in the law of Moses, and shall last two thousand years in the law of the Messiah.'

"It is fair to say, Isaac, that some look forward to the coming of the Messiah for the first time, and some look forward to the Messiah coming a second time. Both will end the world as it was. And both traditions say that we are living in the era of the Messiah. We lived two thousand years without the law, two thousand years with the law, and the final two thousand years are in the era of the law of the Messiah, as the Talmud states it."

"There is a greater consensus about this than you would imagine. Hippolytus was born in about 170 AD. He became the most important theologian and the most prolific religious writer of the Roman Church in the pre-Constantinian era. Hippolytus taught the 6,000 year "calendar" for humankind. The 6,000 years essentially end, in his theology, when the Messiah returns."

"So, John, we are in the "Messianic era, but what about the blood moons? I know we have experienced rare blood moon 'events' in 1949 and 1967. But what is G-d trying to tell us? And what about future blood moons?" Daniel was listening even more intently now.

"Isaac, we know that G-d uses the heavens for 'signs.'"

Then G-d said, "Let there be lights in the firmament
of the heavens to divide the day from the night;
and let them be for signs and seasons, and for days and years..."
Genesis 1:14

"It is a rare phenomenon to have four total lunar eclipses fall on Biblical festivals. The blood moon, or reddish coloring 'effect' appears during a total lunar eclipse. The lunar disk is not completely dark; it is faintly illuminated with a red light refracted by the earth's atmosphere, which filters out the blue rays."

"We had four total lunar eclipses fall on Biblical festivals beginning in 1949 and 1967. The next time four total lunar eclipses fall on Biblical festivals will begin in 2014. Remember also, Isaac, that the four total lunar eclipses are separated by a solar eclipse, making the event all the more rare. The solar eclipse always occurs after the first two total lunar eclipses. Think of it as a sort of a punctuation mark: Two lunar eclipses, a solar eclipse, and then two more lunar eclipses."

Daniel asked John the question that would permeate our thoughts until 2014. "John, '49 and '67 reestablished Israel, and Israeli control of Jerusalem. What is 2014 about?"

"Daniel, let's review the work of Rabbi Judah Ben Samuel. It will provide further texture to what the blood moons have been telling us. Judah he-Hasis (Judah the Pious) lived and worked from the end of the 12th century until the beginning of the 13th century. His predictions are stunning in their accuracy. He could have not possibly lived long enough to even see the first of his predictions be fulfilled. We must begin with Leviticus, and find the meaning of jubilee according to G-d.

"And you shall consecrate the fiftieth year,
and proclaim liberty throughout all the land
to all its inhabitants. It shall be a Jubilee for you;
and each of you shall return to his possession,

and each of you shall return to his family.
That (fiftieth) year shall be a Jubilee to you;
in it you shall neither sow nor reap
what grows of its own accord,
nor gather the grapes of your untended vine.
For it is the Jubilee; it shall be holy to you;
you shall eat its produce from the field."
Leviticus 25: 10-12

"So, one jubilee is 50 years. Rabbi Ben Samuel predicted that the Ottoman Turks would conquer Jerusalem. They did in 1517. He further predicted that the Ottoman Turks would remain in Jerusalem for eight jubilees (8 jubilees x 50 years per jubilee), or 400 years. In 1917, exactly 400 years after their conquest of Jerusalem, the Ottoman Turks were removed by the Allied forces. Rabbi Ben Samuel further predicted that from 1917, Jerusalem would be a "no-man's land" for one jubilee (50 years). In 1967, exactly one jubilee (50 years) during which the city literally 'belonged' to no nation, Jerusalem became the possession, once again, of Israel."

"Rabbi Ben Samuel's work is astonishing. He said his wisdom came from the prophet Elijah. And he said something else. 2017 will be the end of the Messianic era. As to what will happen in 2014, maybe we should turn to Malachi.

'Behold, I will send you Elijah the prophet
Before the coming of the great and dreadful day of the Lord.
And he will turn The hearts of the fathers to the children,
And the hearts of the children to their fathers,
Lest I come and strike the earth with a curse.'
Malachi 4: 5-6

"There you have it Daniel, Isaac. It would fit the pattern of G-d to send someone to prepare the way. Just as Moses prepared the way for

Joshua to possess the Land. I wait for someone to restore all things. To turn the hearts of the fathers to the children, and the hearts of the children to their fathers."

"Father John, Father John Broderick." Daniel wanted to make sure that John knew the depth of his respect for him. Daniel had a fateful question. "Father, what about the thing that slithered out of the garden? It will try to stop this?" John slumped, as his eyes acquired a sullen, distant gaze as if he was looking through the floor to the abyss. "With all its might," is all he said. Now, we all slumped. John gathered himself, somewhat. "We shall do the only thing there is to do: we will love G-d with all of our hearts, we will do this, no matter what may come." John looked to each of us. I said what came to mind, "Amen." Daniel, likewise, said, "Amen." Our promise would be tested. It was unimaginable, then. Unimaginable. But as John pointed out: History begins in the garden.

There was not a commandment of G-d that David and Rachel did not take to heart.

"Honor your father and your mother,
that your days may be long upon the land
which the Lord your G-d is giving you."
Exodus 20:12

Their days would certainly not be shortened because they did not honor their father and mother. It wasn't easy. And yet, I never heard either one of them utter an untoward word about their parents. Not even a facial expression that betrayed an inner contempt. No, the parents of David and Rachel tried their patience, but their love for G-d won the day. It had to pierce their hearts that anyone could suggest their son was somehow unworthy of the breath G-d breathed into Ethan's tiny nostrils. It was the breath of life. The world and all its wiles had dulled the sensibilities of many to the beauty of His creation. It would not dull the love of David and Rachel for their parents. They would pray, and wait.

David and Rachel had been in regular contact with their parents since Ethan's birth. In a recent phone conversation with his father, David learned of some his relatives that were living in Israel. He had no idea. He was ecstatic. His father was blasé. He did seem to want David to visit them, however. According to the doctors, Ethan was ready. David scheduled the trip for April 12. It was a Thursday. He would return on a Sunday, just before Passover.

David's relatives lived in Ashkelon. It caught my attention. It was close to Gaza. Far too close to Gaza. The obsession lived there. It had been there since the days of Joshua. Joshua did not do what G-d asked. Eventually the land would be for the remnant of the House of Judah. Those would be peaceful days. Halcyon days. These were not.

David and Rachel would travel by bus from Tel Aviv. All the trips in Israel were short. This one was longer than usual. It was about 50 minutes. The bus stopped in Ashdod. Ashdod had also been on the lips of the G-d of Abraham, Isaac, and Jacob. These were the lands of the Philistines. David had slain the champion from the camp of the Philistines. Goliath was gone. There were no more giants. So there were men left who did not have the stature of Goliath. But they were just as lethal.

I needed a reason to join the traveling party of David, Rachel and Ethan. Shoshana was working extra hours to prepare Yad Vashem for Holocaust Memorial Day. Yom HaShoah (Holocaust Memorial Day) was at the end of the month, but no work could be done during Passover. She was busy. Not too busy to understand my sudden interest in travel to Ashkelon. She approved. I asked Daniel to tell David that I would be traveling with them to meet some colleagues in Ashkelon. Indeed, I would. But that wasn't the only reason. I thought better of alarming David or Rachel.

The day came for the bus ride to Ashkelon. David and Rachel couldn't hide their joy as I approached the bus. Why would they? Their joy, and their little "package of joy" was a special gift G-d had given me. Along with John.

John wasn't a prophet. He knew that a prophet could only be chosen from one of the tribes of Israel. John honored his vow to G-d: poverty, chastity and obedience. And so G-d honored John: it was a mission that John carried out with a particular delight. John had received an inspired wisdom. It was a wisdom that could righteously defend against the world's ravenous ways. John was perfect for his charge. He would never surrender to the world's crassness and its crass expedience.

John's obedience led him to the obedient. As it should. As it must. It would make no sense, at all, to the world. The world would never believe, and certainly not comprehend, that the ravenous would give way to the obedient. No wonder. The world was in full rebellion. But G-d's people would not retreat. They were obedient to His call. His call to the Bass family was a particular call. It was a particular call, because it required a particular obedience. It began with David's doodle.

But first, the Bass family had to get to Ashkelon. G-d had entrusted their lives to me. He chose well. It was their joy I understood. The world believed that Ethan was a curse. David and Rachel believed he was a gift from G-d. For David and Rachel, Ethan was an answer to the pain and suffering of the world. Ethan was G-d's joy.

To the ineffable loss I suffered as a small boy, the world offered little or nothing, or worse. Some said my parents were unfortunate casualties in a war with no clear difference between the combatants. Some said my parents' death meant that there could only be a perpetual war of attrition in which both sides fought until there wasn't enough flesh, or treasure, to fight any more. Some said, why fight at all? They suggested withdrawing to some mythical place where there was no fighting at all. It was grim. It was worse than grim. It was finite nothingness.

But how could there be joy in such grievous loss? There was forgiveness. There was mercy. There was understanding G-d's righteousness. There was living a life full of G-d's righteous ways. The Exodus was a kind of call to leave the world and live according to the will of G-d. It wasn't the end of suffering. In fact, it was the beginning of joy. G-d's joy. The world loved thrills. G-d's joy had texture.

David noticed that I was wearing my glasses. I thought it wise. I was armed, of course. Two weapons: one in the middle of my back, one in my sock. With tongue-in-cheek, David told me that I was professor-ish, not exactly the somewhat ungainly professor I was most of the time. That was good enough. It would have to be. Rachel and David parked themselves and Ethan near the rear exit in the back of the bus. It was a good place.

Thirty-six minutes into the trip we got to Ashdod. Up until then, it was the only stop we made. Forty-one souls were riding the bus. There was trouble. Four men were boarding the bus. They looked harried. They didn't appear to be intending a relaxed trip to Ashkelon. I looked at David. He saw the look in my eye. "David, go to the back of the bus. Hurry, now." He followed my instructions without hesitation. The men were still showing their boarding passes to the driver. They hadn't really looked in the direction of the passengers. That was a bad sign. I was standing, as I had been since we got on the bus in Tel Aviv. Rachel looked concerned. I told her to "be calm at all times." I sent David to the back of the bus. It would be easier to protect the boy. And I had to protect the boy.

The boy suddenly awakened. He was alert, and oddly foreboding. They made their move. They brandished their weapons. AK 47's. They were speaking in loud voices. They were inexperienced. The adrenaline was coursing through their veins. If I could stay alive long enough, they would make a mistake. Now was not the time. They were announcing that they were armed with knives and rigged explosives in a suitcase. The suitcase stayed with the men in front. They were the ring leaders. They were also more calm than the two coming to the back of the bus. I did not make eye contact. I told Rachel under my breath to do the same. They were yelling in Arabic. Most of it was the same political diatribe we were used to. They said Allah would bless their deeds. It was another war between the G-ds.

One of the men noticed a pregnant woman sitting next to David. He grabbed her by the hand. He asked the driver to open the back door. The woman was thrown off the bus. He seemed pleased with himself. Not pleased enough. He turned his attention to Rachel and Ethan. He assumed that I was the father. That is what I wanted him to assume. He was yelling in Arabic. Frankly, I was unperturbed. How did I know? The only thought that occurred to me was: why are you yelling? He was standing all of 2 meters from me!

He continued yelling! They were questions to me. He was asking me if I wanted to pay for the sins of all the Jews in Palestine. I understood every word. I maintained a blank stare on my face. No fear. No defiance. Just blank. By now, Rachel was on her knees praying in Hebrew. It unnerved them. The men in front told the men in back to silence her. I noticed out of the corner of my eye that Ethan was following the men's movements very closely. Babies at that age are old enough to follow objects with their eyes. Still, it was unusual.

Suddenly, terror struck both men. They were yelling Abraham in Arabic. *The* Abraham. Now, the yelling made sense. The men in front looked confused. The two men in back screamed at the driver to open the rear door. He did. They ran out of the bus. This was my opportunity. I expected the reaction I got. The remaining hijackers got an extra dose of adrenaline. I told Rachel to stand in front of Ethan. She did better. Her body enveloped him. Good.

The hijackers did what anyone would do. They went to the window to look at their two maniacal colleagues running and screaming through the streets of Ashdod. The woman seated behind me seemed to sense what I was about to do. She leaned left to give me more room. She winked at me for good measure. The two men's weapons were hanging like handbags from their shoulders. They were following the movements of their batty fellow terrorists. They were now too close to each other, entangled gawkers. As I grabbed for the gun at the middle of my back, I yelled in Hebrew for everyone to take cover. Everyone did what they were trained to do. They fell to the floor. It was standing room only. The terrorists now looked in my direction. But terrorism is not a spectator sport. They were stunned. I wouldn't have any more time. I needed to place a bullet in both of their heads. I held my gun with both hands. I didn't need to. It was all over in less than two blinks of an eye, hands down.

I quickly ran to the front of the bus. I wanted to make sure. I asked everyone to remain seated. "Remain calm," I said. Israelis were good about that. Both terrorists had bullet holes in their heads. I got their bodies off the bus. The driver was dazed. I told him and all his passengers to wait until Shin Bet arrived. I could see out the window that they already had. I walked calmly, but at a faster than the usual pace to get to the back of the bus. I motioned for David to come forward. There was disbelief in his eyes. Rachel's eyes too. Ethan was all smiles, clapping as if he wanted an encore. There wouldn't be one. I matter-of-factly asked the driver to open the rear exit. I sternly reminded everyone to wait for Shin Bet. I grabbed Ethan and his stroller to get him off the bus in a hurry.

As I looked at David and Rachel, the passengers on the bus were still applauding David and Rachel were still in a state of shock. Their faces were virtually drained of blood. I put my arms around them and made a huddle. Ethan was in the middle. He was delighted. It was his first trip to a matinee. Except it was nightfall.

I knew what I needed to say to David and Rachel. "Your son is fine. You are both fine. All the terrorists are dead. They can't hurt you or anyone else. Now, I need you to get a hold of yourselves, and do everything I ask." They nodded. They seemed relieved by my words.

I knew the two terrorists who left the bus were dead. I could tell by the look on the faces of the Shin Bet contingent.

I told David and Rachel to stay put for a moment. I approached two Shin Bet officers. They had been waiting for me. I introduced myself. They were about to salute when I stopped them with a forbidding glance, and an imperceptible shake of my head. There was a problem. A monumental problem. This could blow my cover. I told them enough that they got the idea. I got Daniel on the phone. He was already aware of the hijacking. I told him he had 2 minutes to get a car here to take us out of Ashdod. I also told him that the media had arrived. He needed to tell the Defense Minister to make some phone calls.

A nondescript, tan sedan appeared at a curb less than 20 meters from our location. It was motionless. It had a driver and an engine that could get us out of any city street in the world. We only needed a lift to Jerusalem. A determined, steady lift. Nothing fancy. That would be for Beirut.

The driver knew what the "package" was. The rather, smallish, frankly, self-satisfied looking, baby that had only been delivered by the "stork" a short while ago. Why was I beginning to think that the wings of Ethan's "stork" had a heavenly gait?

I got in the front seat but made no eye contact with the driver. He was probably trying to "get the picture." Norman Rockwell and security, me, was the answer. He wouldn't see it that way. He wasn't trained to indulge artistic sensibilities. The security was fine. Who were these civilians in the back seat? And the baby. Please! He was right. If he had an afternoon off, I would try an explanation.

He handed me a satellite phone. I dialed Daniel. "It won't be long now," was all I said. "She knows you'll be home early," was all he said. He said what I called to hear. "David, why don't you spend the day with Rachel and Ethan, tomorrow?" I was speaking to no one in particular. My face was forward. "Good idea, Professor." David was adapting quickly. "John and I will drop by tomorrow afternoon."

"Good, Professor." I'm sure my colleague was now thoroughly confused by the professor reference. An afternoon wouldn't be enough. He was trained to never ask. The mystery man with the sleeping kid and his parents. I could assure him of one thing: he would never see it again, and it didn't have an explanation that fit well in the world in which he operated.

Rachel was still looking a little lost, and her face had only recaptured a fraction of its usual radiance. I turned my head to make eye contact with her. "Rachel, Rachel." The second Rachel got her attention. "Where is your son?" At first, she was slightly stunned by the question. Had she forgotten her son? She looked to her right at a gerry-rigged stroller-car seat, holding a beautiful sight to see, her son sleeping peacefully under the steady hand of his adoring father. She was now more in the present. The face wasn't radiant yet, but Rachel had found her son and her husband in a car.

"Rachel, listen to me," I said. "Your prayers were answered. Your son and your husband are fine. You are fine. You are on your way home." She looked at me, still a little puzzled. "Professor, what happened?" She began to cry. Thankfully. "David, hand Ethan to me, and sit with your wife for a while." He did. Rachel was sobbing. Ethan didn't awaken. It was moving.

The driver and I were trained to do things. We trained for moments. We trained a thousand times. And then, a thousand times more for a moment. The look on the faces of the unwanted bus passengers was not terribly different from their more polished friend in Beirut. They all knew that their time on this earth was about to end. Whatever they dreamed the end would be, it was not the end that came. The families of the '72 Israeli Olympians had only memories. They were blessed, but they would have to live their lives with more empty chairs than just Elijah's. And so we would train. For the next moment.

Now it was time to see my wife. If I could have broken out in song and dance, I would have. The driver didn't stop in front of our apartment. I knew he wouldn't. I knew he would be extremely careful. It was over three hours after sunset. About 10:00 p.m. There wouldn't be a lot of strollers out on a Thursday night. The driver took no chances. He did well. There was a military cemetery not too far from Yad Vashem, farther away was our apartment in Bayit Vegan. There was a small, unfinished driveway, covered by trees. It was perfect. I handed Ethan to David, and made a quick exit. If I was stopped by anyone, my ID would take care of it.

At a reasonable pace, I would be home in less than twenty minutes. I took routes I knew were not frequently used. I was at the stairs of our apartment. I hadn't seen a soul. As I ascended the stairs and looked to my left down the row of apartments, I saw a certain Rabbi, and Sandek, turn toward his door, nodding his head. As I opened the door to our apartment, I saw his daughter. She got to me quickly, and wrapped her arms around my midsection, planting the right side of her face on my chest. She held tightly. The phone rang. She looked like she was expecting it. She answered. All she said was, "the Prime Minister, Isaac." "This is Isaac Singer." "Isaac, you have made the life of an old man busy today." He was 69. I thought the "old man" part was a bit of a stretch. "Your secret is safe, Isaac, do not worry." I was relieved. "I will see you on Yom HaShoah (Holocaust Memorial Day). I have something for you. Benjamin and Leah Singer would be proud. You did us a great service today. Thank you, Isaac. Good bye." These were usually one-way conversations. Good, I thought.

I looked at my wife. She thanked me for Israel with a kiss planted on my left cheek; she thanked me for the lives of all the bus passengers (and a special trio) with a kiss on my right cheek; and the grand finale, the kiss on the lips, was reserved for coming back home to her alive. "Shoshana, did the media report that two of the terrorists voluntarily left the bus?" "Sort of. They said they left the bus because they saw something they thought was threatening. They implied it was a clever trick by Shin Bet." "I don't think Shin Bet has those kind of connections, my love." She looked at me with a smile, wanting to know. "I'll tell you later. It involves a certain Midwestern American girl and her son. Her son did more than he will say. Of course he can't say."

Shoshana knew it was going to be quite a story. She would wait. "Isaac, I prepared a small pot of your favorite tea. It's waiting in the library for you." Shoshana knew my usual routine. There were times I preferred to spend some time in the library, thinking. Sometimes, thinking about nothing. This was such a time. Before going to bed, Shoshana turned to say something else. "I know what you do can't be easy, Isaac. Israel can only survive with men like you. I know that. Of all the men G-d might choose for this, He has never chosen better. You live in the light, but can fight in the dark. Bless you, Isaac."

She didn't have to say anything. She had never said anything like that. Of course, she had a certain bias. But Shoshana was careful with her words. And wise. Her father taught her the Rabbinic ways well. Not in the formal sense. I don't know if Shoshana was right or not. How could I? But it meant something that she said it. It made the day *far* easier. Sometimes I would stay in the library until the early hours of morning. Not tonight. Not necessary. She probably knew that. Yes, Shoshana was that thoughtful.

Once in our library, there was a clear road to thinking about nothing. When I was living in the States, I developed a keen interest in baseball. In many respects, it was a beautiful game, even elegant, when played well. So, I let my thoughts drift to the baseball diamond.

Grass as green as imaginable, and well-manicured, so not a blade seemed out of place. As a highlighter, white lines delineate fair from foul, a ball in play, or not. And how beautiful it was when a ball hit the white line, and evinced a puff of white smoke. That meant grown men racing around a diamond, just as they did when they were small boys. The boys were men now, but they were they were still the boys of summer to the tens of thousands who roared as their heroes circled around the diamond. Fans were not the least bit worried about how exactly their boys of summer circled around a diamond. Baseball wasn't ironic. It was beautiful. It was memory. It was childhood memory writ large.

It was men whose childhood dreams had been encapsulated by the musculature and reflexes akin to gazelles and other beasts. It was a ballet of the wild, tamed by G-d's gifts of memory and consciousness, but not too tame, the genius of G-d was to allocate His gifts in just the right proportions to create thrills that would last a lifetime.

But alas, my temporary escape landed back in reality. Shin Bet. I trained with them. Those boys were good, even incredible. They worked so that we could have some thrilling moments that took us away from our worldly concerns, and closer to the bliss of heaven. Shin Bet. They were our "Unseen Shield." They protected Prime Ministers and other chieftains of the Israeli establishment.

And they protected us. All of Israel. They put a stop to terrorism before it could harm us, and when they couldn't stop it before hand, they stopped it dead in its tracks, before it could make good on its promise to slaughter civilians, or cause the release of jailed terrorists. And part of their promise to us was that they would spy on the spies, who spied on us. Invariably, the spies who spied on us cared not at all about the Lord who commanded Moses to send spies to the land of Canaan, because He was giving this land to the children of Israel. No, the spies who spied on us wanted us out of the Land, altogether.

But we had Shin Bet, our "Unseen Shield," and our unseen shield who sent terrorists running terrified into the night, screaming because they had just seen the visage of Abraham, whom they knew in the recesses of their tortured souls was chosen by the Lord among the G-ds. He was, after all, the G-d of Abraham… Isaac, and Jacob.

Yom HaShoah. The Prime Minister wanted to see me on Holocaust Memorial Day. Golda gave me simple instructions: be at Shoshana's Yad Vashem (Holocaust Memorial) work space (it wasn't really an office) at 4:00 p.m. That was all. As a matter of security, it was ideal. Shin Bet couldn't complain. There was nothing unusual about a Prime Minister of Israel visiting Yad Vashem on Holocaust

Memorial Day. In fact, it was very usual. There was also nothing unusual about me visiting my wife at Yad Vashem. She volunteered there, and it was Holocaust Memorial Day, after all. It would also make it far easier if others wanted to attend. All in all, it was a matter of choreography, taking the right door, rather than the left, and ending up where you needed to be.

The choreography worked to perfection. There we all were right at 4:00 p.m., April 30, 1984. Yes, and the Prime Minister was there, too. The Americans had an expression that fit this Prime Minister. He was a "tough cookie." Yes, he was. His toughness was forged by the diabolical. The Holocaust Memorial where we stood that day included the names of the Prime Minister's parents and his two sisters. His whole family, murdered. When all your family is murdered, in cold blood, for the "crime" of being Jewish, it makes "never again" have a special urgency. He told the story of his father, who having been informed that the extermination of the Jews was imminent, said only that "I have a son in the Land of Israel, and he will exact my revenge on them."

The Prime Minister migrated to the Holy Land in 1935. He joined a Zionist paramilitary group that opposed British control of the Holy Land. He was an outlaw in the Land of Israel before it became the Land of Israel. Hunted by the British, jailed by the British, escaped from British prisons, He eventually had to seek political asylum in France. He returned to Israel after the Israeli Declaration of Independence in 1948.

As a member of Mossad, he had directed Operation Damocles. It seems the then Egyptian President wanted an indigenous rocket program. And the Egyptian President had a peculiar moral calculus. He turned to West German scientists who were previously employed by the Third Reich. Yes, *that* Third Reich. So the Prime Minister, then of Mossad, began a program of letter bombs and abductions targeting the former Nazi scientists. The program was unceremoniously shut down by Israeli government at the time. Operation Damocles was a success, however. All the offending scientists were driven out of Egypt by the end of 1963.

So there I was. And yes, that one "tough cookie" was there also. He was short in stature. But just ask the British and certain mercenary scientists about his stature. To them, he was ten feet tall, and then some. Unlike Goliath, a stealthy and elusive "ten feet."

The Prime Minister brought some guests that I happened to know, and love. Perhaps he understood what their presence meant to me that day. Perhaps not. I prefer to think that he did. The Prime Minister liked to say that as a boy, he dreamed of living in the Land of Israel, and when he finally moved there, he was instantly at home. Inside a man like that beats a heart that encompasses more than just the Land. And so, there to share the short ceremony with me that day was Shoshana; Aaron, my stepbrother; Ariel and Rebecca Weiss, my adopted parents; Father John Broderick; Daniel; Colonel Stern; and Rabbi Shlomo Levy, my father-in-law.

The ceremony had to be brief for security reasons. Except Shoshana and I, everyone there that day had to be separately escorted out so that no one could be connected to anyone else. Once they were all in place, the Prime Minister personally greeted each guest. It was clear to me that he knew Shoshana's father, Rabbi Levy. They were both clever men. But they could not conceal their familiarity. It occurred to me that the death of Shoshana's mother was probably no accident.

The Prime Minister asked me to come forward as the others formed a semi-circle facing us. He said these words: "Your countrymen will never know any of things you have done to keep them in the Land. G-d has seen your work. I believe He sees the same qualities in you, as we do. You are a righteous defender of the Land, Isaac Singer. You honor the memory of Benjamin and Leah Singer. You honor us. I have only to give you Israel's highest military decoration, the Medal of Valor. I know your admiration and love for King David.

And so, to me, and the people in this room, you will be known as one of *David's Mighty Warriors*. Congratulations, Isaac Singer."

There was a brief, and muted, applause. I knew the time was short. I could see it in the faces of the Shin Bet. I tried to keep it short, while making eye contact with everyone in attendance. King David was on my mind. "When he thirsted after a wearying battle, King David longed for a drink of water from the well of Bethlehem. So three of his Mighty Warriors broke through the camp of the Philistines, drew water from the well of Bethlehem, and took it and brought it to King David. He refused to drink it, but poured it out to the Lord, saying that it belonged to the men who went in jeopardy of their lives. I dedicate this medal to all those who have fought with me to make this day possible."

And with that, the Prime Minister shook my hand and was off. The hurried goodbyes included a whisper from my stepmother to "not be such a stranger." She was right of course. One by one they exited, leaving Shoshana and I in the place where our second "date" began. We relished a long embrace. Our Shin Bet custodians were all too happy to oblige this one indulgence. With the medal in Daniel's hands for safe keeping, we too headed for home. It was quite a day.

There were more sacrifices to come. We were in the Land, but our presence there seemed to rouse an uncontrollable primordial outrage that could not be quelled. History had begun in the garden. The trail of our anguish and joy always led back to the garden.

The time had come for the Bass family to leave Israel and return home to Urbana, Illinois. Their time had been eventful, to say the least. From Ethan's birth to a bus ride to Ashkelon, it seemed as though they stirred their surroundings to an incautious flair for the dramatic. All too dramatic, by the reckoning of any young family. But through the tears and the laughter, they were off to begin their life together in the gentle embrace of a charming Midwestern university town. It would be hospitable to any young family, and especially welcoming to the special needs of Ethan.

David's work would never end. The onslaught of plots, diabolical and otherwise, secreted away in codes, and codes within codes, within codes, would span a lifetime. Unless you believed that peace would come. A visit from the tooth fairy would be more likely. Obsessions are not like old soldiers that never die, but just "fade away." Obsessions die hard. They exhaust themselves when the flesh that harbors them is consumed in an inglorious blaze. That was David's reality. It was wave after wave of hate and jealousy, and at its vortex was an obsession that wouldn't give way until it was divinely expunged at the end. We could not know when the end would come. So we survived by our wits, with G-d's sufferance, and His helping hand.

And for a time in Ethan's young life, it seemed as though America, and perhaps the world, had found its moral bearings once again. It had found a voice to remind it again of the inherent rights of man that came from the G-d of Abraham, Isaac and Jacob. It was a reminder that the vertical relationship with G-d could not, and should not, be unhinged by the horizontal relationships among men and women. These wannabe demigods believed that their secular political canons should and would replace, according to them, the "quaint" relationship with G-d.

By the grace of G-d, the years that took up most of the eighties, exposed the spiritual bankruptcy of the Soviet Union. The Soviet's ideological fathers believed the ancient deception that a "new" man could be fashioned by the hands of men. Oh, it had a familiar ring to it. Man could surely be trusted with the knowledge of G-d, to remake himself as his own G-dly attributes would command. There being "nothing new under the sun," this temptation had led to the fall of man, from the beginning:

> *"For G-d knows that in the day you eat of it*
> *your eyes will be opened, and you will be like G-d,*
> *knowing good and evil."*
> *Genesis 3:5*

Hundreds of millions of souls in the twentieth century commended to G-d, by the godless and wanton brutishness of those who wanted nothing more than to "be like G-d." It was every self-absorbed, pathological delusion from the "New Soviet Man" and the "Thousand Year Reich," to the "Long March," and "To Spare You is No Profit, To Destroy You Is No Loss." Every iteration of these G-d-like men, these master minds had only one thing in common: societal ruin, and corpses that piled up so relentlessly they had to find their final resting place in mass graves.

Yes, every nitwit and egomaniac seemed to have a prescription for paradise on earth. The inherent problem was that every such scheme invariably consumed human flesh at such a rate that their "paradise" would be devoid of any human population at all. So by pure exhaustion, or necessity, they introduced "reforms" to survive their own homicidal lunacy.

The story of the eighties became a story of a President and a Pope. One was vastly underestimated, and to the other a question was posed: "How many divisions does the Pope have?" The fateful question to the Pope was asked by the one of the mass-murdering architects of the "New Soviet Man." It turns out that, upon his death, this particular architect was mummified, so his worshipers could go on worshipping him for eternity. In truth, his mummified appearance in death, perfectly captured his state in life. His humanity was in a kind of mummified, deep freeze, for he had long ago lost his soul to a "state of nature." And now a question for the mummified tyrant: Did you believe that you could pile the corpses so high that your mummified body could rest on a throne in the heavens? How high are the outer limits of hell, comrade?

The President and the Pope were quite a team. One had a divine calling. Together, they had a divine mission. It is more accurately characterized as a divine convergence. The two men had a remarkable convergence of ideas related to the Soviet Union, and not only the moral implications of its existence, but the practical means of setting the Soviets on a course to implosion. Resist it. Both men stated the case in clear moral terms. That was the change that marked the beginning of the end for the Soviet empire. It had lost its moral and ideological legitimacy with its own people, not to mention its "subjects," who lived behind the "iron curtain." They were promised a "workers' paradise." The "paradise" devolved in a frequently told joke among Russians: "we pretend to work, you pretend to pay us."

The President and the Pope made their most comprehensive and compelling stand in the Pope's homeland, Poland. The Pope would call his countrymen to resistance by his challenge to "call good and evil by name." In the same year, the President struck a similar chord: "Yes, let us pray for the salvation of all of those who live in that totalitarian darkness–pray they will discover the joy of knowing G-d. But until they do, let us be aware that while they preach the supremacy of the State, declare its omnipotence over individual man, and predict its eventual domination of all peoples on the earth, they (Soviet Union) are the focus of evil in the modern world."

And, during that same time in the United States, something was happening to America's so-called elites. They were deriding the President as "simplistic" and out of touch with their more modern version of America. How dare the President refer to the Bible, G-d and the transcendent meaning of man's existence? America's elites were still in thrall of Marx's materialistic explanation of human nature:

"The nature of individuals thus depends on the material conditions determining their production." It was a shocking departure from American history, and history itself. Could such a "cramped" idea of human nature possibly explain a country like the United States of America. As much as they were moved by the allure of French culture, America's elites seemed to dismiss the most astute insights into American's greatness, as offered by a Frenchman, Alexis de Tocqueville: "Not until I went into the churches of America and heard her pulpits aflame with righteousness did I understand the greatness and

the genius of America. America is good. And if America ever ceases to be good, America will cease to be great."

So what was history's verdict on these "simple" messages of the President and the Pope. The Berlin Wall "fell" in November, 1989. So, the wall fell. The Soviet empire crumbled. Simple was immediately dismissed as "lucky." After all, it was surely going to happen, it was only a matter of time. Funny, while they were scoffing at the "simple," at the same time they were invoking the "naive" label, suggesting that anybody who believed the Soviet Union could be "defeated" was hopelessly "simple AND naive."

They quickly adjusted to avoid the obvious cause and effect explanation that was prove-ably right by the sheer weight of events. Now, it was "inevitable" according to them. Or, it really happened because one of the President's special ambassadors studied satellite intelligence photography with the Pope. America's elites were becoming impervious to actual events, and history. It would get worse.

The President and the Pope, a divine convergence, indeed. A divine convergence implies a divine purpose. The Lord among the G-ds had one. Actually, He had several, including for the children of Israel.

Through the divinely cleansing ablutions of their moral clarity, the President and the Pope exposed the pathetic nature of the Soviets and all their ideological fellow travelers. Behind the utopian rhetoric, stood only brutes and their brutishness. When the brutes lost their nerve, or their hired hands refused to be brutish, they were finished. As it turns out, what they said they knew about human nature was only true insofar as they could "convince" their subjects with the "gentle" assist from the barrel of a gun.

The President and the Pope both understood the radical truth of the creation of human kind in G-d's image. We are, in effect, heirs to the divine family. As such, we possess inherent rights. Life itself is a sacred gift, a physical resonance of divine characteristics. Humans were endowed with the gift of life, not the power, nor even the consideration, to decide who is worthy of the fulfillment of that divine gift.

The divine gift of free will. It was at the heart of our moral nature. We were free to choose right or wrong, good or evil. The sacrifices made to the Lord in Leviticus were "free will" sacrifices. G-d said of King David that he was "a man after My own heart." It was David's idea to build a temple as a permanent dwelling place for the G-d of Abraham, Isaac and Jacob. No wonder he was a man after the heart of G-d. Out of his moral nature came an idea that was pleasing to G-d. But David was not allowed to build the temple that was so pleasing to G-d. He had made some dubious moral choices in the sight of G-d. "You have shed much blood and have made great wars; you shall not build a house for My name, because you have shed much blood on the earth in My sight." The temple would be built by King David's son, Solomon. Still, in the words of C. S. Lewis:

"Because free will, though it makes evil possible, is also the only thing that makes possible any love or goodness or joy worth having. A world of automata, of creatures that worked like machines, would hardly be worth creating. The happiness which G-d designs for His higher creatures is the happiness of being freely, voluntarily united to Him and to each other in an ecstasy of love and delight compared with which the most rapturous love between a man and a woman on this earth is mere milk and water. And for that they've got to be free."

So, a President and a Pope, knocking on the door of a fallen world, reminding their fellow humans that, if they ignored their divine gifts, their connection to divinity would atrophy, resulting in a body count to match unspeakable human suffering, inflicted on a world by whatever the flesh could dream up next.

And there was more. The Pope had to put an end to an unnatural and unholy rift between Judaism and Christianity. It lasted far too long. There was an ugly history to it. Christianity had cut itself off from its roots. It was a branch. It had been grafted in. It had a special gift. But no branch could grow toward heaven without a powerful root to support it. It was Abraham. It was Moses. It was all the prophets. It was Isaiah 61 that was preached in a temple in the New Testament. It was the most quoted book in the New Testament: Deuteronomy. It was all of G-d's patterns and signs. It was Genesis, Exodus, the wilderness, the Land, the holy City, King David, and the son of David. It was Joseph and Jacob (Israel). It was His "firstborn." Yes, it was Israel.

"Since the time of the Apostle Peter, no Roman pontiff had ever spent his childhood in such close contact with Jewish life." He had close friendships with his Jewish neighbors and celebrated the Feasts. He would remember his parish priest preaching that "anti-Semitism is anti-Christian."

As a boy, where it was popular at his high school to form separate Catholic and Jewish soccer teams, the Pope was always ready to play for the Jewish team. Now, he was prepared to do something that would surely reverberate in the great halls of the heavens, and change the arc of human civilization as it lurched towards the millennial kingdom of heaven on earth. Rapprochement would fall short. It was reconciliation that he wanted. In fact, he desired the proper order of things. The G-d of Abraham, Isaac, and Jacob was the master of perfect order. Chaos was introduced by sin.

The order of things. The Pope became a master of relating the personal to the divine order of things. It was memory in service of eternity. Eternity with G-d. He called Auschwitz a place "built on hatred of, and contempt for humanity," and a "place where human dignity was appallingly trampled underfoot." He recalled his friends of childhood who died in Auschwitz's gas chambers. Memory.

He then characterized acts of discrimination and persecution against Jews as "sinful." To the Jewish community of Mainz, German he described Judaism as a "living" legacy that must be understood by Christians. In that speech, he addressed the Jewish community as "the people of G-d and of the Old Covenant, which has never been revoked by G-d." He was not finished. He needed a more precise statement on the order of things. He delivered: "With Judaism, therefore, we have a relationship which we do not have with any other religion. You are our dearly beloved brothers, and in a certain way, it could be said that you are our elder brothers."

After a visit to the Holocaust Memorial in Israel, the Pope left a note at the Western Wall in Jerusalem: "We are deeply saddened by the behavior of those who in the course of history have caused these children of yours to suffer, and asking your forgiveness we wish to commit ourselves to genuine brotherhood with the people of the Covenant." Rabbi Michael Melchior, who hosted the Pope's visit to Israel, said of the Pope's time in Israel: "It was beyond history, beyond memory." Yes it was.

And the President and the Pope had a special gift for Israel. It was quite a legacy. One million strong, or so. The Berlin Wall was the outer limit of a huge cage-like apparatus that kept people in. Human beings were captives. When the Berlin Wall fell, the exodus began. For the Jewish community, it was a large as the Exodus from Egypt. After 1989, and the fall of the Berlin Wall, 1.1 million Russians immigrated to Israel.

The initial reaction in Israeli society to this immigration wave was very positive. A common phrase was used to describe the immigration from the former Soviet Union: "with every immigrant, our strength rises." Full assimilation was not easy. At times, the enthusiasm for such immigration waned. Nonetheless, assimilation occurred on a grand scale. As assimilation accelerated, one out of four staff members in Israeli universities were Russian-speakers. A future Prime Minister would say that the overall effect of immigrants from the former Soviet Union "rescued" the country and should be considered "one of greatest miracles that happened to the state." Another miracle in the Land of miracles. His gift. With a little help from a President and a Pope.

CHAPTER SIX

BLESSED BE THE HUMBLE

"The humble He guides in justice,
And the humble He teaches His way.
All the paths of the Lord are mercy and truth,
To such as keep His covenant and His testimonies."
Psalm 25: 9-10

As the Psalm says, children are a gift from the Lord. Ethan was a gift, then some. Following his young life was a joy of joys. It seemed we marked time with every nuance of change in his development and his abilities. Every letter from Rachel or David was full of the details we coveted. How is Ethan doing? What is he doing?

We learned not to be preoccupied with the conventional expectations of child development. Ethan was full of surprises. He showed remarkable balance, eye-hand coordination, and even strength and a certain agility. His hearing was fine. But, he was not speaking, so he was learning how to communicate with his parents through some combination of sign language, sight and sound recognition, and, there was something else. Prime numbers were a part of David's world of cryptography. As a cryptographer himself, David was showing his son simple examples of prime number sequences. Ethan appeared to be recognizing those sequences. The apple may not have fallen far from the tree. It was unusual.

Ethan was getting older, and so were we. As the 90's approached, so did Golda's eightieth birthday. And except for some hearing loss, she didn't appear to be losing any of her rather acute faculties. And while our friendship went far beyond my boyhood memories, I never tired of her Pirushke cakes. She seemed to love making them as much as I loved eating them. She was always eager to fondly recall her memories of my parents. Over the years, we must have recycled those memories a time, or two. Recycled, or not, her memories of my family, before it was ripped apart, were priceless.

John and Daniel were both worried. They were worried about different things. So, I became doubly worried. John had an instinct he was being watched more closely. He couldn't identify anything specific. Just a feeling. He would be far more cautious now. Perhaps we had become careless. We thought that overconfidence would be something that never crept into our lexicon of "how to operate in the shadows and never be seen." It sounded far easier than it was. We were shadow boxers. Could someone be in the ring with John without us knowing about it. It was perilous for John. And for all of us.

Daniel was still worried about the four cities and the code. Up to now, they were using "brute force" methods common to cryptography to break the code. Essentially, they were trying all possible "keys" until they found the right one. In cryptography, "keys" are used to convert plain text into cipher text, or vice versa during decryption. Discover the "keys," and you could read what no one wanted you to read. It was that simple. Except, it wasn't. Daniel knew there were encrypted messages being swatted around between Vienna, Ismailia, San Carlos de Bariloche and New York. We hadn't broken the code. And watching and listening to their operations revealed virtually nothing. They were far too careful.

Daniel was worried. David had an idea. The "brute force" methods to break the code might never work. Why not use relatively new computing power. Massively parallel computers were a kind of supercomputer. They were a new breakthrough. David believed he could use their unique power to crack the code. Daniel thought, why not? They were in a cul-de-sac. A dangerous cul-de-sac.

David said he would be ready in a few months. At David's request, Daniel sent two of our best computer scientists to help. It would be groundbreaking work. Daniel offered to share all of David's work with the Americans. They were more than happy to cooperate for such a payoff. Daniel wasn't any less worried. But at least he felt we were back in the game again.

I was worried about a country that I grew to admire, and love. Something was happening in America. The President who had teamed with the Pope was gone from the scene. A generation was coming to power that was certainly self-confident. It was a generation that came of age during the 60's in the United States. They were self-confident, and self-righteous. But what was it that they believed exactly? They described themselves as "transitional" figures. A transition to what?

And I wondered about those who had watched while a President of the United States defeated the Soviet empire without firing a shot, and brought a remarkable period of prosperity to his country. I was not so concerned about his bitter opponents, or even his bitter opponents who cleverly masked their bitterness by mouthing some of his rhetoric. I was most worried about those who had a "ringside" seat.

Many spoke with a sense of awe and wonder about what they had seen. That was the problem. They had seen and not heard. They became so awestruck by what they perceived to be style, that the substance of what he was saying was lost on them. Or perhaps, there was a simpler explanation. They just simply disagreed with much of the message. They indulged the country a period of nostalgia, then they were prepared to move on. Again, I ask, move on to what?

Two Presidents, separated by 120 years, invoked powerful references to American exceptionalism. One spoke of America as "the last best hope on earth." One spoke of America as a "shining city on a hill." One freed the slaves. The other freed the captives of the Soviet empire. If their rhetoric was disdained by a new generation of American leaders, what would become of that "last best hope on earth," that "shining city on a hill." I feared the answer. I feared for Israel. I feared for the world.

Daniel alerted me that David was ready. Obviously, there wasn't much I could do except what I had been doing: praying. Praying a lot. David's team had been working for about 10 or 11 weeks. Progress had been slow at first. David had a relentless quality about him. He was so understated in his demeanor, relentless would not be the first attribute you would use to describe David. But, relentless, he was. He didn't personalize progress, or the lack thereof. He just continued to "work the problem," in his words. He loved puzzles. He was unshakable in his belief that every puzzle would eventually succumb. He had been working on this one eight years, and counting.

About a week or so had passed since David started "working the problem." The door opened to the lab about mid-afternoon on a Tuesday. It was a graceful entrance by Daniel. Unusually, graceful. The entrance belied his otherwise infuriated countenance. Daniel was seething. He contained his rage well, but nonetheless, if he ever converted what was inside him to wrath, whole divisions of the enemy might vanish.

Daniel fenced in his rage long enough to clearly explain the source of his inner storm. I soon understood. Daniel had been worried about the cities and the code for the last eight years. It wasn't an obsession, by any means. Perhaps the cities and the code caused him sleepless nights. I doubt it. He was a pro. He was a pro's pro. I vividly recall the manner of his reaction when a Lebanese troop carrier appeared out of nowhere during Operation Spring of Youth. His reaction: He relaxed. There wasn't a moment of hesitation, or trepidation. In spite of what he told me that afternoon in the lab, he never lost his composure. But neither one of us would ever be the same.

Creation itself is resonant of the glory and magnificence of G-d. But, the world intrudes. We marvel, yet we don't. We comprehend at moments which suit us. We listen to the "dark" noises that surround us. We listen intently to the cacophony. Our senses are dulled. Our heart for G-d is dulled. And rage fills the vacuum, where G-d should have been. If only we could sustain basking in His bright light of perfect beauty, perfect love, perfect mercy, and perfect justice. Then, we would understand the equation that is the legacy of our fallen nature. Our free will does make evil possible. Evil is an aberration. Evil is chaos in His ordered creation. But it does exist. And its dark depths match His emblazoned heights. I did not fully understand this that Tuesday afternoon. Neither did Daniel. But we both vowed that our faith would burrow deeper into our beings. It was what He would have us do. It would gird us. We were going to need it.

It wasn't even hours after David had shared his findings, that one of Daniel's operatives was on a private plane back to Israel. It was one of the first methods of cryptography: Personally deliver the message. Moses's spies did not send couriers; one by one, they stood before Moses and told him what they had seen in the land of Canaan.

David and his team did not manage a 100% solution to the code. Thus far, they had achieved about an 65% conversion rate. It was an outstanding start. What they found was stunning. It was a multi-level code. It was like playing three dimensional chess in the dark. They discovered a crucial key to the code. It was the basis of a prime number sequence, which was commonly used in cryptography. It was a word that found purchase in hell itself. It was certainly on the lips of many who, even with their desiccated hearts, wept and wailed as they suffered hell's eternal torment.

Zyklon B. They chose Zyklon B as one of the keys to their complex code. We waited eight years for this revelation, confirming what Daniel apparently already knew. This was personal. How could it be otherwise. Just ask the victims at Auschwitz. Or, what about the victims at Majanek, which was a camp used by the Nazis in service of their grand plan to murder all Jews in Poland. Zyklon B. It was the name of the poison they used in the gas chambers. It was originally a pesticide. They took more care in poisoning the pests than they did human beings.

It WAS personal. They were nostalgic. Daniel was right. They almost certainly meant for us to discover that they were using an encrypted code to communicate. It was a taunt. Here's the code. We're operating in these cities. You'll be dead before you know what we're up to. That was the unencrypted subtext of this diabolical dance. And how did we know they didn't mean for us to "crack" the code. Well, it had to do with a certain priest. It seems John's instincts were keeping him alive.

Cracking a code is like taking sausage and converting it back into its original and discrete ingredients. It is as ridiculous as it is impossible. David's team did the impossible. They found an "original ingredient," part of an actual message sent between Ismailia and Vienna. John was right to suspect that he was being watched more closely. Indeed he was. And the "four cities of the apocalypse" (as I liked to refer to them) were about to plant some information that, if acted upon, would point to John. That was bad enough. They surely wouldn't eliminate John right away. They were after his network, if they could confirm he was what they thought he was.

Daniel had already taken serious countermeasures. John wouldn't alter his basic routine established over the past several months. If he did, it would arouse further suspicion. Of course, any direct contact with Golda, Daniel, or me was out of the question. There was to be a kind of contact between Daniel and John only. That contact was "encrypted." There would be two "layers" of Daniel's best operatives between John and him. And Daniel was going to watch the watchers. John suspected that an Egyptian, who was the newest member of an otherwise all Jordanian team working with the Custodians of the Holy Land, was the eyes and ears of the "four cities of the apocalypse." The Egyptian undoubtedly had help. He probably recruited his own team because he didn't want the Jordanians to know about his activities. Daniel's watchers would watch John, at a very discreet distance.

They would also watch the Egyptian, and follow his trail all the way back to Ismailia, if possible. Before the watching was over, Daniel would pull the mask from the faces of all those that thought our beloved priest stood in the way of their grand designs. In many, many respects, he did. But the beloved priest did not lack for allies.

And so, we waited. We waited for Father John Broderick, a bear of a man, to be on the receiving end of what was effectively, his death warrant, after, that is, he had led them to a broader network. They could play it through several awful permutations. Perhaps they would just publicly expose John and his contacts to the Israeli government. Why not? Internationally embarrass and cow the Custodians of the Holy Land, and the Israeli government. It would be a public relations bonanza for them, and a grievous setback for Israel. Vatican relations. Israeli settlement activity in the so-called "territories." Israeli control over Jerusalem. The books. The articles. The speculations. The intrigue. Israel's very existence would be back on the table. How dare we fight for our lives? How dare we operate in the shadows to defend ourselves.

This was high stakes poker. Frankly, I liked the odds better if the Lord among the G-ds would help a little with our "hand." I wished Rabbi Menachem Schneerson could be enlisted to bring our children to Jerusalem to pray, or urge all of the men of Israel to wear tefillin. I decided I had to take a leap of faith. I wore tefillin throughout this period. Publicly and otherwise. An argument could be made against any such public gesture by an otherwise, slightly daft, professor. I believed that the G-d of Abraham, Isaac and Jacob would honor my intention.

The message came. It was anything but modest or understated. It was bold. It was contemptuously bold. The Egyptian was careful. And clever. He didn't pass the message directly to John. He had ascertained, correctly, the primary source among John's Jordanian colleagues. The Egyptian was after more than just John's Israeli connections. They wanted leverage that they could use against the

Jordanian government. It was a smart move. In relative terms, Israel and Jordan had a peaceful co-existence. The poker players in Vienna, Ismailia, San Carlos de Bariloche, and New York were after a royal flush. They wanted to create an international firestorm against Israel, and compromise Israel's relatively quiescent relationship with Jordan. I felt like handing out tefillin on the street corners of Jerusalem.

The ersatz plot, if that's what it was, hit a little too close to home. The target was Yad Vashem, the Holocaust Memorial. The timing was interesting. They chose the day before Yom HaShoah, Holocaust Memorial Day. They wanted to confirm John's linkages to Israeli intelligence by producing a discernible reaction to the plot by the Israeli government. Heavy security usually surrounded the Holocaust Memorial on Holocaust Memorial Day. The day before, not so much. They were sending five suicide bombers, all women, to various locations inside the Holocaust Memorial.

We had more than enough details to stop the plot well before the plotters entered Jerusalem. We had the make and model of the cars, time schedules, and routes. They made it easy to thwart. John had provided that level of detail before, so there was nothing unusual in the information itself. How brazen were they going to be? That was the question. Would they carry out the plot if we didn't stop them? It wasn't likely. Still, it was a possibility. If they were willing to embrace Zyklon B, would they really pass up an opportunity to strike at the heart of memory, the Holocaust Memorial. It was the grand master of temptations. They loathed such a memorial. It meant they had failed in their primary mission: our extinction.

The final decision was left to a familiar figure. He had honored me in a small ceremony in, of all places, Yad Vashem. The "tough cookie" of a Prime Minister was serving his second stint in that role. He was 76 by the time he had to face this crisis. He wasn't a man to dither. His decision was swift and clear. No reaction by us to this feint. There was a proviso. If they detonated so much as a firecracker, Operation Wrath of G-d would be like child's play. He wasn't a man to make idle threats. Daniel said what the Prime Minister had in mind was to take care of many lingering threats to our security.

March couldn't have made the Prime Minister feel any better about the lethality of suicide bombers. It was a Tuesday afternoon at the Israeli Embassy in Buenos Aires, Argentina. A pickup truck was loaded with explosives. It was driven into the front of the Israeli Embassy. Twenty-nine people were killed, including four Israelis and 25 Argentine civilians, many of them children, and 242 people were wounded. It didn't take long for the Islamic Jihad organization to assume responsibility. They were linked to the "Party of G-d," Hezbollah, and Iran. Hezbollah would characterize Israel as a "cancerous growth," that had to be wiped out. The only comment that emerged from the "four cities of the apocalypse," came from San Carlos de Bariloche, Argentina. They said it was a "sloppy and poorly executed," attack. What they meant was it only killed 4 Israelis.

Argentine leaders claimed they wanted to bring the attackers to justice. They claimed, and they claimed. Years later, they would try to blame Israel for the attack, by putting forth a phony engineering report that said the explosion came from inside the Israeli Embassy. Then, the Argentine government was presented with conclusive evidence that Iran had been involved in the attack on the embassy. Actual phone calls from the Iranian Embassy in Argentina. The Argentine response: they expelled six Iranian diplomats. Oh, Argentina. Eva Peron has "kept her promise." Safe haven for the architects of the Third Reich and their ideas. Architects indeed. It is Jewish buildings that remained unsafe.

I was praying that I would see John again. A best case scenario would be years. Several years. I didn't want to think about a worst case scenario. Daniel said that John was not only holding up, but there was no sign at all that he was feeling the intense pressure that was hanging in the air. John only said "G-d's will be done." He always insisted that Daniel make sure that Shoshana and I knew that "we were in his prayers."

We needed those prayers. I made the decision not to tell Shoshana about the bombing threat to Yad Vashem. I certainly would never use such information to make sure my family was protected. That was out of the question. I had made the decision to be there with her for the several hours when the threat was imminent. I would be part of a monitoring team to identify the would be suicide bombers. I am sure they expected to be intercepted far before they arrived in Jerusalem. Since their whole point was to be captured, they had to have the explosives, and all the accessories, in perfect order. We fully expected that they would carry the charade to its conclusion. As to what exactly that conclusion was, we could not be sure.

I was able to tell Shoshana the latest triumph of Ethan's young life. Not all the details, of course. I just said that he helped his father with his work. He did more than that. David told Daniel's briefer that his son provided a crucial suggestion that helped him, ultimately, to break the code.

David was a patient and loving father who didn't see his son's disabilities, or age for that matter. Rachel marveled at David's forbearance in explaining everything he was doing to Ethan. Apparently, David was showing Ethan his work with streaming XOR ciphers. I knew enough to know that streaming XOR ciphers were used to make encryption codes much more difficult to solve. David was working on an encryption algorithm that he thought would help him find the key to the code. Encryption algorithms can be very complex formula, or a set of steps, to solve a particular problem. David was explaining. Ethan was listening. Ethan looked at David's formula (algorithm), and gestured to his father that he would like to use the keyboard. He did. He typed in a change to a part of David's formula. It worked. David smiled. Ethan smiled. Rachel was dumbfounded. David looked at Rachel and said, "that's my boy." The doctors would say that Ethan had savant-like capabilities associated with autism. It was the one-dimensional world of syndromes and "isms" trying to contain the human spirit.

What led them to Father John Broderick? He stood out in a crowd. True enough. So did a thousand other people. And a priest, at that. What was it? John provided a clue. He believed something was out of place at the hospital where Ethan was born. It was a young nurse. John remembered her because of the glare that burst forth from a crucifix she had hanging from her neck. He had approached her for directions to the maternity ward. Her crucifix caught a hall light at just the right angle, temporarily blinding John with a rush of reflected light. He complimented her on the crucifix. He thought her reaction was awkward, even strange. She seemed embarrassed, even dismissive of his remark. Later, he saw her standing watching us, including Daniel.

Ethan was born at a military hospital. The hospital was also used by Israel's intelligence services. Daniel researched the hospital's personnel. There she was. She was only there for three months. It was an egregious oversight to permit her to work there. When it was discovered, she was gracefully transferred to a hospital in Ramallah.

She was born in Ismailia, Egypt. She later enrolled in the University of Jordan Nursing School. She had outstanding credentials, and by all appearances, was an excellent student. Her father was a veterinarian who was also politically active. Not too active. Just active enough to arrange to become part of the team, which was mostly Jordanian, that worked with the Custodians of the Holy Land. In the scheme of things, it was not a visible, or highly sought after position. It was perfectly suited to El-Masri's purposes. Clever. Very clever.

He represented he and his daughter as Coptic Christians. They weren't. He had ingratiated himself with a Christian who was nominally a part of the Jordanian government, and who cooperated with Israel. He had been a valuable asset. The Egyptian's new Jordanian friend helped his daughter with admission to the University of Jordan's Nursing School. After her graduation, her father asked about placing her at the military hospital in Jerusalem. The Jordanian used his contacts to do so. It was a mistake. She was placed there with a mission. Undoubtedly, the mission wasn't specific. Just wait, and watch. Enter the priest. It was unusual. She followed the trail. Her personnel file indicated that, on several occasions, a camera was found in her possession. No doubt she had a camera to record Ethan's entourage of well-wishers. Dr. Amir El-Masri and his daughter, Reem. Were they to be the nemeses of Father John Broderick? Not if we could help it.

The plotters would "weave their web" just after Passover. Holocaust Memorial Day was the first Thursday after the end of Passover. On Wednesday, the day before, they would have their go at tangling us in the web.

I had the perfect antidote. Aaron and I hadn't shared the joy of a Mimouna festival since the night I met Shoshana. It was quite a tradition, brought to Israel by the Moroccan Jewish community, that included Shoshana and her father, Rabbi Levy. The Mimouna Festival came at the conclusion of Passover. There was food, frolic, and lots of politicians.

Aaron, his wife, and the only parents I had known since age 6, were our guests. What a joy. I also wanted to tell Aaron what Dr. El-Masri and his daughter had planned for Holocaust Memorial. If the worst happened, I didn't want him to be shocked by events. He had a surprise of his own. Daniel and Colonel Stern had recruited volunteers to pose as "tourists" that afternoon at the Holocaust Memorial. At the height of the threat, regular tourists would be seamlessly "guided" to safer locations in and around Yad Vashem. Aaron volunteered. He would be accompanied by his wife. She was serving in the IDF like her, now deceased, sister. I asked Aaron to tell his parents. He already did. Shoshana's father had also been informed. Under the circumstances, I would tell Shoshana after I arrived at Yad Vashem in the early afternoon on Wednesday. I asked Aaron if he was sure he wanted to do this. He said he knew I would be there. He couldn't let me "have all the fun." Fun indeed.

Dr. El-Masri most certainly had the Holocaust Memorial surveilled. He would send his daughter, of course. She would be clad with a crucifix around her neck. Her father probably savored the irony. Daniel went through all the video tapes. There she was. She had the crucifix, and another prop designed to deceive. A baby in a carriage. Photography was prohibited inside the memorial. She wouldn't have been so obvious if photography had been permitted. As it was, they were clever, as usual. The camera was part of the baby carriage.

So, now, based on where she spent her time at the memorial, we thought we knew the locations where the bomb-laden ladies would finally wind up. One of the locations included an area in the Children's Holocaust Memorial, near Shoshana's new office. It wasn't a surprise.

Female suicide bombers were not new to Israel. Sana Mehaidli was only the first. She was 16 in 1985. Sixteen years old! She worked at a video store. It was there that she recorded her last will and testament. A sixteen-year-old who records her last will and testament. She should have been watching videos of the latest pop sensation, or the endless parade of movies about teenage angst. Instead she donned a military style uniform; her young heart was filled with hate, and an ancient and familiar obsession. Her adult handlers thought her young flesh would be just fine splattered all over what was left of the Peugeot she was driving, as well as hell's half acre. She managed to kill two Israeli soldiers in South Lebanon. She became known as the "Bride of the South." Her youth had been "given away" by ghoulish predators, who probably had more regard for the car she was driving than her young life.

The day came. A man like Dr. El-Masri was not going to flinch. If you recruit your own daughter in service of your pathological hatreds, you would surely look forward to the day when you could humiliate the "Zionists," or worse. Long ago, he had deeply inhaled the effluvium of the Muslim Brotherhood, which hung over the Middle East, and all the world. The "Brotherhood's" usual public position was that they would not visit Jerusalem "while it was under Zionist occupation." For this mission, I am sure that El-Masri needed no special dispensation. He was "all in," until his dying breath.

According to their plan, the bombers would arrive at the Holocaust Memorial at about 2:00 p.m. in the afternoon. It was about at the peak hour for visitors to the memorial. Unless told otherwise, I would arrive at about noon, and have some lunch with Shoshana. I would be briefed throughout.

When I arrived at Shoshana's office, looking like the professor she had expected to marry, my wife greeted me with a warm and animated embrace, whispering softly in my ear, "Don't worry. I know why you're here, it will be fine, do what you must." I was relieved.

Just minutes after our lunch, my phone rang. They wasted no time. The cars had been spotted, and were being tracked. They were generally on schedule, perhaps tardy by 10 minutes or so. The cars were moving more slowly than usual. There were five cars, and five women, all in back seats. They brought guests. Five children, two of them infants. It was a family outing to mourn the dead. Not exactly. In spite of the fact that the Muslim Brotherhood had dreamed of building a death camp modeled on Auschwitz during their celebrated collaboration with the Nazis, they now called the Holocaust a "story." So, they told their children they were going to "Fairytale Land." Probably not.

The cars began to enter Jerusalem. They would arrive at Yad Vashem on a staggered schedule. There would probably be 20 to 25 minutes between the arrival of the first car, and the last. They would of course arrive at different locations near the memorial. To do otherwise, would only arouse suspicion. They were contemptuous of us. But they knew we were anything but fools.

Shoshana was calmly doing what she was there to do. The Children's Holocaust Memorial was finally completed in 1986. It was worth the wait. Nothing could adequately memorialize 1.5 million children who were murdered. They died in various states of abject fear and loneliness, sometimes in silent, defiant, resignation.

Many survivors felt a certain alienation or permanent separation from a sovereign G-d whom, they believed, went too far in not interceding in a fallen world, or not suspending His promise of free will to human kind. We could wonder many things. We could wonder why G-d would not permit a man as righteous and humble as Moses, as well as the children of Israel who had escaped Pharaoh, and who were over 20 years of age, to enter the Land; why King David, a man after G-d's own heart, was not allowed to build the Temple, which he (David) had conceived; and, yes, why a sovereign and mighty G-d would bring his "firstborn" back to the Land after nearly two thousand years, a miracle unrivaled in human history, and with miracle after miracle keep them in the Land, but still allow, earlier in the same century, over one million children to perish in the Holocaust. Was there an answer? Probably not an answer that would fall gently and kindly on human ears. And there were still questions.

What exactly was it, we wanted, after all? Did we want some grand bargain with a sovereign G-d? We would exercise some version of the lawless freedom practiced by Adam and Eve in the garden and, in return, a sovereign G-d would save us from ourselves. So, we wanted the freedom to indulge every cockamamie impulse, and just as the death camps were about to get a rush of their first victims, G-d would commission a divine army to stop it. It had the sound of what is in the hearts of many, many human beings. It is a bargain that would mean that, at our best, we would have the equivalent of a child's moral nature.

The blast that tore asunder my parent's flesh did not touch, and could touch, the legacy of their well-developed and G-dly moral foundation, and moral sensibility. Without it, the ghastly thing that happened to a six year old, could have left a man with a primitive, childlike moral arithmetic: vengeance, thoughtless brutality, and a pointless, hopeless life.

Benjamin and Leah Singer sought the Land as a sanctuary from millennia of persecution, and worse. They were not there to settle scores that cried out from countless pogroms and unmarked graves. They knew well the promise that was made to Abraham. And they knew that G-d honored Abraham's righteous restraint in battle. Most of all, G-d honored the faith of Abraham. Abraham's descendants would multiply "as the stars of the heaven." Faith. Faithfulness.

We had it backwards. Our experience informed us that throughout history we had it backwards. We invariably equated freedom with rebelliousness against G-d's righteous path.

"All the paths of the Lord are mercy and truth,
to such as keep His covenant and His testimonies."
Psalm 25:10

But as the "rebels" increased, so would the deterioration of civil society. The rise of the state wasn't too far behind as we desperately turned to despots, demigods, or wannabe social engineers as our saviors. These saviors were only too happy to accrue power unto themselves, assuring us that the idyllic life was a short distance away. It never ended well. Many were quick to tolerate soullessness, if only it would be bloodless. But the blood came. Rivers of blood.

There was no bargain. There was no grand bargain. There was a divine gift. "Mercy and truth," and more. It was our free will wrapped up into a divine equation. Divine equation indeed. Galileo said that G-d wrote the universe with the language of mathematics. There was incomprehensible elegance and beauty, and rules that, without a lifetime of faith and faithful pursuit of His majesty, fell monstrously on the human heart.

I lost my parents. G-d didn't. And their enormous faith wasn't lost on Him. It was shattering to a young boy. But by their faithfulness, I received a divine inheritance. It was a semblance, with all the human limitations in play, of divine proportion and perspective. And, in His mercy, I could forgive. I could learn forgiveness. Forgiveness was mercy, not surrender. It was also life itself. To be alive. I was connected to a righteous G-d by divine threads. Created in His image. It was the true meaning of being human.

His language of mathematics could not be contained by dimensions. But the language of mathematics has certain rules that we can understand. The two sides of an equation are different, but they still are "equal" to one another. It is a form of balance. $1 + 1 = 2$. True enough. Two sides, different, but equal. Balance and symmetry. We suffer the pain of unspeakable loss. We love beyond our understanding and capacity to love. C. S. Lewis was right: Free will does make evil possible. But it also is the "only thing that makes possible any love or goodness or joy worth having."

There were still the 1.5 million children whose memory was being preserved at Yad Vashem. Just seconds before they were in the presence of G-d, they were in a state of terrified, catatonic silence, bringing forth such screams that even the night would seek the comfort of the distant light.

But, if G-d had not entered the world through the Law, and through human beings created in His image, the Holocaust, including the murder of children, would have been the least of it. The call of the wild would have been the irresistible force. We would be savages with the intellect to ramify our savagery to its only logical conclusion: extinction.

Right now, I hoped that Shoshana and I would live to see another day. Shoshana wasn't the least bit interested in the video monitor I was watching in her office. She loved her work. I understood. As 2:00 p.m. approached, we shared a brief glance. She winked at me. I returned the gesture. No matter what happened, we would endure it together. It was as it should be. I reminded her not to leave her office, no matter what. No doubt, she was in the photographs taken the night of Ethan's birth. We didn't want to raise any further suspicion.

El-Masri's first emissary arrived. She was nattily clad, hand in hand with a young boy of about 5 or 6. She walked gracefully, yet purposely, to her destination, the Hall of Names. Each name belonged to a victim of the Holocaust. Six million. She was at the heart of memory. It was a heart whose beat she couldn't hear, or even fathom, through the hate. Did she want to be an accomplice to all this? And the boy, what about him? One could pray that a photograph, or the Pages of Testimony, which document the names and some biographical details of each victim, might faintly etch the beginning of a place where the heart of truth could enter an otherwise forbidding edifice.

One by one they arrived. Reem El-Masri chose to reprise her earlier performance. She came with a baby, a carriage, and all the confidence of someone who thought some hallway conversation with a priest would lead to the unraveling of a network that could be used to humiliate and weaken Israel. Still, she and her cadre of faux tourists had to be surprised. They expected their sworn enemies to "pounce" far earlier.

It was a little after 2:30 p.m. El-Masri's recruits were in place. It was a place they didn't expect to be. El-Masri's daughter was about 40 meters from Shoshana's office. If she decided to exit this world with a flourish, it was a far too close for comfort. It did raise the question, though. They most certainly added explosives to their rather fashionable clothing. It appeared to be just enough. Anything more would have required an unfashionable bulkiness. We also knew that the child Reem El-Masri had in tow was not her own. She and her father lived alone.

I received word that none of the women were acting with the normal effect of visitors to the memorial. Reem El-Masri was no exception. This was their last opportunity to provoke a reaction they believed they could manipulate into a public relations nightmare for Israel. They must have been very confident of their narrative. It probably meant they also believed they could "flip" one or more of John's Jordanian contacts.

The volunteer force of IDF and intelligence personnel were gradually making their way to surrounding the would be bombers. El-Masri's troupe was acting in the self-conscious and nervous manner of amateurs. They were improvising. Their portrayal of amateur behavior was well, amateurish. We had to be extremely careful. It was tempting for one of our "volunteers" to make a friendly and solicitous approach to each of the women. It would have preempted their rather poor performances designed to arouse suspicion.

I was observing Reem El-Masri's feigned bout of fidgeting when I noticed a rather familiar face appear on my monitor. Aaron Weiss. The storied pilot and his wife. It was the first time he had visited the Children's Memorial. He and his wife appeared moved. They were well prepared. They also appeared as normal tourists.

Reem began rummaging through her purse. She pulled out a small, cylindrical metal container. It looked like a detonator. She flipped the top as if it were a cigarette lighter. I watched the monitor. There were no monitors in Beirut or Ashdod. I had to remind myself this wasn't a movie. I began searching for Shoshana's hand. I found it. Our grip was perfect. Of course. Aaron's wife leaned over to coo over the baby that Reem seemed happy to ignore. The baby appeared mesmerized by her surroundings. She was responsive to the overture by Aaron's wife. It was a sweet moment.

Reem was not so sweet. She seemed flustered and perturbed. Not perturbed enough. She sprayed herself with perfume, and dropped the bottle in her purse. She had enough. She turned to leave. She was moving quickly to the exit. Aaron knew where the cameras were. He turned to one, and winked. I looked at Shoshana. Our hands unfurled. She smiled, and shook her head.

Dr. El-Masri was courageous in apparent defeat. He was headed for the airport in Amman, Jordan before his "recruits" had even entered Yad Vashem. He was thinking like the coward he was, and not the mastermind he thought he was all these years since his daughter stumbled into a priest in a hospital hallway. Yes, Dr. El-Masri, Israel would surely let your suicide bombers run amok to conceal our network, and then murder you and the others on the spot. No one in Ismailia, or the other cities, would even notice. He was right to fear for his life. His timing was peculiar.

Aaron and the rest of the "tourists" left the Holocaust Memorial as randomly, and calmly, as any group of tourists. Daniel's "watchers" were still watching when Shoshana and I left under the cover of darkness, well after closing time. Daniel and his team were interested in any other El-Masri operatives who might have been sent ahead of the women for reconnaissance. It wasn't done often. It wasn't done this time either.

Shoshana and I were going to enjoy our walk home. Hand in hand. We would savor the moment. Daniel had a considerate, but untimely, alternative. A car was waiting for us about a one hundred meters into our walk. It was not optional. We were dropped off in a little alley way close to our apartment. Shoshana's father was just entering his apartment as we passed. It was no coincidence. He knew someone in the Prime Minister's office. It was the Prime Minister. He made sure that Rabbi Levy knew about the danger to his daughter. And he made sure that her father knew when the danger had passed.

Hand in hand, we walked through the door of our apartment. Hand in hand, we walked to our couch. Hand in hand, we sat there silently for a while. We finally embraced. I had never apologized to my wife for doing what I could to defend our small country. She would never ask such a thing. But my work put her at risk. That never should have been. When I tried to offer an apology, I was rebuffed. "You have never been reckless, and that is the only thing I ever asked of you," she said. It was probably the right answer. Still, they came too close.

El-Masri was in Ismailia, Egypt trying to explain what went wrong with his infallible scheme. I'm sure that's the way it seemed to him. The women and children he enlisted were all back safely in place, no doubt waiting breathlessly for his next attempt at putting Israel, and Israelis, in jeopardy. They wanted more than to jeopardize.

It was still going to be awhile before I could see John. We needed time. We might have expected a bolder, more daring El-Masri plot to unfold. It was doubtful. More than likely, he would be reigned in for a awhile. Told to watch. Wait for an opportunity. There was probably a hierarchy. Trust was everything in our business. Now, they had questions about him. But he had recruits who could be useful to them. Women. That would be a temptation. But, they had to notice what we noticed. His first inclination: run for the airport.

I wouldn't count the days until I could see John again. "Interminable arithmetic" was a phrase one of my professors at Princeton liked to use. Counting the days until I could see John again was "interminable arithmetic," indeed. My thoughts turned to El-Masri and his gangland harem. Their days were melting away. That was a more ingratiating arithmetic.

Through all the wars, and all the wars that were not called wars, the years had been kind to Daniel, Colonel Stern, and me. By now, Colonel Stern could have achieved a far higher rank. A top slot in the corporation as he liked to say. But the higher you went, the more political it became. Moshe Stern was no politician. He was a leader and a warrior. He was a leader of warriors. Period. He wanted to be the tip of the spear. And that he was. Fearless and daring, with a skeptical and pragmatic nature that helped keep his men alive. He may not have quite equaled Daniel's comprehension of G-d's majesty and prophetic chess game, but his loyalty was something to behold. The priest had to cause some indigestion along the way. But it would be over Moshe Stern's dead body that anything would happen to John.

The relationship that had grown up among us was unusual, to say the least. It would have been far easier to let the natural forces of institutional biases and prerogatives gradually eat away at our extraordinary level of cooperation. Maybe John was the explanation. We all loved John. In a certain sense, John was an outsider. Obviously. But he could explain events to insiders, who were far too "inside," to develop any meaningful perspective. There were too many moving parts. Somehow, John understood the moment. I know not how. People told John things. Secrets. He told me one time that G-d's feasts were divine appointments. Perhaps John's appointment included a divine audience.

Time does impose itself. Daniel and Colonel Stern were looking for successors. There wasn't such an urgency. But there was some urgency. Daniel's candidate was his son, Avner. Colonel Stern's nominee was a junior officer, Dov Lerner. They each made it clear that if John or I had any reservations about the contenders, replacements would be found. Daniel said that he loved his son, but this was about the survival of a people, not loyalty to his son. It would be some time before we were introduced to Dov and Avner, if at all. The incumbents would watch their charges very carefully before beginning a transition. I thought about my first meeting with Colonel Stern and Daniel. I could have been less lecturing, and tempered my righteousness a bit. I liked to think that through my brashness, they sensed that I had a true heart for G-d. I was also a pretty decent physicist and warrior.

Dr. El-Masri told his Jordanian counterparts that he had to return to Egypt for "medical reasons." Something about his heart. He most certainly could blame his failure on us. He had it right this time. He would have a more difficult time with the other elements of the Muslim Brotherhood's perverse rhetoric. I doubt if he would blame his failure on the usual suspects: financiers, media mavens, and the shadowy masters of the American government. How about a young man, his "special" son, several Israeli computer scientists, and some new computing technology. Computer technology aside, it was a modest, improbable foe to a complicated plot, contained in an exponentially more complicated code.

El-Masri and his masters needed a more refined script from which to spew forth their venom. If it became too refined, the venom would disappear, and all that would be left would be a semblance of the truth. In spite of what He described as a "stiff-necked" people, the G-d of Abraham, Isaac, and Jacob kept His promise, and brought His "firstborn" back to the Land. It was the work of the Master of the Universe, not humans who paraded around as demigods. Our survival was in His hands. And He works best in the "humble" and the "contrite." A humble mother and father faithfully loving their son, a son who was reputed to have few of the gifts of the proud. When the divine gift of life was breathed into mother, father, and son, Rachel and David guided their lives, and that of their son, according to the divine intention. With a contrite and humble heart, seek Him. "The humble He guides in justice, and the humble He teaches His way." Psalm 25:9

El-Masri and his cohorts believed it was an all-powerful Jewish cabal thwarting their evil subterfuge. Nothing could dissuade them. There was only stopping them. They would never look in the direction of the humble and guileless. G-d did. They would be His eternal foundation for the world to come.

"I dwell in the high and holy place,
With him who has a contrite and humble spirit,
To revive the spirit of the humble,
And to revive the heart of the contrite ones.
Isaiah 57:15

The Lord among the G-ds found that our memories were short. The Exodus was not a trivial event.

And Moses said to the people, "Do not be afraid.
Stand still, and see the salvation of the Lord,
which He will accomplish for you today. For the
Egyptians whom you see today, you shall see
again no more forever.
Exodus 14:13

An eyewitness account by an Egyptian, Ipuwer, confirms the catastrophe that happened to Egypt: "Plague is throughout the land. Blood is everywhere. The river is blood. Gates, columns, and walls are consumed by fire. Grain has perished on every side. The land is not light."

And the drowning of the Egyptian armed forces in the Red Sea left Egypt open and vulnerable to foreign invasions. The children of Israel saw this and more: forty years in the wilderness sustained by manna from heaven. An endless parade of miracles. And yet, they had not the faith to cross the Jordan and enter the Land. They did not believe that they could overcome the fortified cities and the giants they saw there. They all perished without entering the Land. Only Joshua and Caleb believed in G-d's promise, and only they were allowed to enter. Even a momentary lack of faith by Moses prevented him from crossing into the Land, the land of Canaan, pledged to Abraham centuries before.

Time passed and the children of Israel grew weary. They did not believe what their eyes had seen, and their ears heard. The world had a way of intruding. It hectored, lectured, and threatened. And that was our friends. So, the Israeli people grew weary and agreed to something called the Oslo accords. It had a certain rationality to it. Israeli politicians who agreed to it were reflecting a national mood of sorts. Israel would relinquish land... for peace. There would also be the development of self-government among the Palestinians.

I knew what John would say about "Oslo" and its promises to Israel. Of course, I couldn't ask John just now, but it would be something like: how can an irrational conflict submit to a rational process. The rise of modern secularism would say YES, it is irrational because of religion. Remove religion, and peace will break out. Just ask Stalin, Mao, and since they essentially became cults of personality, why not add Hitler to the list.

And what exactly was the religion that modern secularism had in mind? Was it the Law? The Law given to Moses? Wasn't it the totality of that Law that gave rise to English common law. Weren't the rights they supposedly "cherished," inherent rights of human beings derived by their divine creation. No, it seems that it wasn't religion per se, it was that religion was just a little too confining. The state of nature seems well, so free. Why fear the savage? He could set you free. Indeed.

And was the conflict, at heart, a religious conflict? John would say no. It was sibling rivalry that was perceived to have universal consequences. Well, yes. But, really no. In G-d's economy, inheritance is not salvation, it is inheritance. The first Passover. Exodus. And yet, 40 years or more after Exodus, the children of the Exodus were forbidden to cross into the promised Land. Was their inheritance a curse, or a divine gift? It was a divine gift to those not cursed by a lack of faith.

Enter the sibling rivalry. Two brothers. G-d promised one, Isaac, "an everlasting covenant, and with his descendants after him." G-d promised the other, Ishmael, to "make him a great nation." Ishmael was the first born, but he was not the child of the "promise." G-d honored Ishmael because he was the son of Abraham. But Ishmael and his mother, Hagar, were asked to leave the house of Abraham. And so they did. Hagar, a maidservant of Abraham's wife, Sarah, was Egyptian. She and her son, Ishmael, settled in the Sinai Peninsula. Hagar took a wife for Ishmael from the land of Egypt.

Isaac's son, Jacob, was renamed Israel by G-d. Jacob's twelve sons became the leaders of the twelve tribes of Israel. Ishmael also had twelve sons. They became the Arabic peoples. Both were fathers of nations. Ishmael's descendants belong to the Abrahamic tradition. They belong to the heritage of the G-d of Abraham, Isaac, and Jacob. They belong to the Torah. There they would find their destiny, and freedom. Isaac and Ishmael were brothers. Siblings. Human blood boils. It can only be transcended by the spirit of G-d. Forgiveness. Reconciliation. Love. G-d doesn't change. We must.

For now, David and Rachel decided to homeschool Ethan. It had just become legal in all fifty states in the U.S. Ethan was by no means socially isolated. I had anticipated that the community around the University of Illinois would be welcoming to Ethan. It was. And, although, he didn't speak, he became popular among all the children because he had exceptional athletic ability. David and Rachel would show him videos of various sports, explain the rules, practice with him, and he consistently showed the ability to quickly excel.

When it came time to choose players, Ethan was never the last one selected. His reputation preceded him. He usually became the first one selected. He had speed and strength. But not enough. David and Rachel were never successful in pushing to include Ethan in formal competitions. They didn't push too hard. Everyone had been so kind. If he wanted formal competition, he was welcome to participate in the Special Olympics. No one could imagine anything else. Ethan didn't mind in the least. He dominated the small competitions. But again, David and Rachel didn't push too hard. They did, however, plant a seed. In Israel. They had friends there. But, first, there was another matter that needed the attention of Ethan's friends. There had been an uninvited guest at Ethan's birth.

Dr. Amir El-Masri returned to his work with the Jordanians and the Custodians of the Holy Land. He spent several months in Egypt, and then made his way back to his work. He was waiting. He was waiting for the opportunity to restore his credibility, and the willingness of his masters to let him off their leash. There hadn't been any meaningful chatter among the four city network of the plotters. They were patient. That made them dangerous.

El-Masri had continued his surveillance of John for quite some time after his elaborate masquerade party and its pretense of interest in memory. It then stopped. To be sure, his "cell" was in place. They were lying fallow just now. El-Masri was not being watched by his handlers. That was smart. Just wait. John's Jordanian contacts had become wiser about their dealings with him. They too were waiting.

Routines. We live by routines. Dr. El-Masri had a routine, but it wasn't a precise routine. Still, two or three times a month, he liked to visit Jerusalem. A very old neighborhood in the Old City of Jerusalem. Bab al-Huta. Bab al-Huta was in the Muslim Quarter in Jerusalem. El-Masri frequented a small Egyptian coffee and tea house. They served an Egyptian favorite. A beautiful and tasty favorite. Egyptian Karkady, Hibiscus Tea. It is a gorgeous, ruby-red color. With enough sugar, every sunbird in Jerusalem would want a sip.

It was a warm and comfortable October day in Jerusalem. A perfect day for a stroll. Dr. El-Masri thought so. A taxi dropped him off near Herod's Gate, and his favorite place to enjoy an afternoon sipping Hibiscus Tea, with just enough ice to gather condensation on his tall glass.

He was far more relaxed than a day in April, eighteen months earlier. And why not? He sent his daughter and other young women, strapped with explosives around their shapely bodies, to a place where the names of the murdered can be remembered. G-d almighty knows their names. He knew them before memory. El-Masri's cadre of recruits sported coiffed hair styles, and completed the tableau with beautiful children. Some were infants. Their inherent beauty was lost on those who would use them as props, and worse.

He was steadily quaffing his idyllic looking drink, on an idyllic afternoon, when he received an urgent phone call. The local hospital had just admitted his daughter. It was serious. He should come right away. A taxi would be waiting for him just around corner. Augusta Victoria Hospital was just a short distance. He ran out of the cafe, knocking over his drink. The tea lost its luminescence on the khaki colored floor. As he rounded the corner, he stumbled a bit, his gait became halting. The taxi began pulling away. He yelled for it to stop. It didn't. It slowed to a crawl, but it was still pulling away from him. His gait was feeble. He began to clutch his chest. He could barely cushion his fall. The taxi sped away.

We live by routines. An ambulance took El-Masri to a Augusta Victoria Hospital. His daughter wasn't there. The emergency room staff was overwhelmed as usual. They did what they could. He was dead on arrival. His Egyptian passport alerted the hospital staff to contact the Egyptian Embassy in Tel Aviv. The next day his body was flown to Ismailia, Egypt. His next of kin was nowhere to be found.

Tea time. It was his routine. Jerusalem's old eyes had seen it before. History ends in the city. But not quite... yet.

Daniel had been well prepared. So was his son, Avner. Surely, Dr. Amir El-Masri's corpse was undergoing a thorough autopsy. When all was said and done, the dissection of his lifeless body wouldn't give up the secrets that only Jerusalem knew. Neither would his necrotic flesh betray exactly how he transformed the "breath of life," a divine gift, into one sinister plot after another, serving a much darker, consuming fantasy. Avner would refer often in the coming days and months to Reem El-Masri's "lifeless eyes." No doubt her father worked many years to douse the divine light within her. Reem and the rest of her father's recruits were rendered harmless by Avner and his colleagues. All the members of the cell were now in cells.

The network was dismantled. With a twist. And the twist had more than one ironic turn. As he entered the lab one afternoon, three days removed from the fateful dismantlement, Daniel was relaxed. In all the years, I don't believe he was ever so relaxed. Relaxed, not carefree. None of us could comprehend carefree. Daniel began with a smile. "You will be seeing John soon, Isaac. Dr. El-Masri's body has been flown to Ismailia. Avner has the rest of them." Now, it seemed as though time passed quickly. Some days it did. I didn't want to raise my hopes, only to have them dashed again. "But there is unfinished business, isn't there? There always is, Daniel." "Yes, unfinished business that comes as unexpected gift. The Jordanians will be ecstatic. I am meeting with them later today."

"Isaac, not all of El-Masri's acolytes were devoted. One was co-erced. It was one of the women who was at Yad Vashem. Her brother found her with a crucifix. He asked about it. She told him to mind his own business. He threatened to kill her. She knew he could, and he would. He gave her a way out. Join the El-Masri plot."

"Avner assured her of her safety. She was also worried about her younger brother. She used to read the Bible to him. She asked Avner to get a message to her brother. She wanted her brother to know she was alright, and that she would come and get him at the right time."

"They would both face charges of apostasy. If neither of them would repudiate their beliefs, they would have no future. Death. On-ly, death. I do not think they would repudiate their beliefs, Isaac. She has taken the name, Mary, and her brother has taken the name, John. Mary has confirmed the details of the Yad Vashem operation. She has identified the other women, and the drivers. She never met El-Masri or his network of 'watchers,' who kept track of Father John's move-ments. We have very high confidence that we have all of El-Masri's associates."

"Unfinished business. You are right, Isaac. There is always unfin-ished business. We can thank Mary. But it took a friend of ours to unravel the truth. Mary overheard her brother in a phone conversa-tion. He referred to someone as the 'Falcon.' It was clear by her brother's affect that the 'Falcon' was a very important person. That's all she could tell us. She had nothing else. There was never another reference to whomever it was."

Daniel continued. "I felt comfortable meeting with Father John for the first time since this all began. Avner arranged it. He did well. I went through the details with John. I mentioned Mary's 'Falcon' ref-erence in passing. John said he thought he knew who it was. I was stunned. Five or six months after Dr. El-Masri joined the Jordanian team working with the Custodians of the Holy Land, John was invited to a farm outside Zarqa. Zarqa is about 100 kilometers from Am-man."

"Who invited him, Daniel?" "It was a Jordanian who worked with John. He thought John would like meeting someone whom he represented as a 'devout and knowledgeable Christian.' We are now sure that El-Masri set it up behind the scenes. I am also sure El-Masri knew that John was in Amman for a meeting. His Jordanian contact took him to the farm on a Saturday morning. It was only an hour drive.

The owner of the farm was proud of his nickname, the 'Falcon.' He loved falconry. The farm was a perfect place for his precious hobby. He had an elaborate lunch prepared for John. He said his wife was away. His daughter was the only other family there that day."

"John was underwhelmed. The 'Falcon' engaged him in a discussion of the Bible. Mostly the New Testament. John described his knowledge as 'conversational, pop New Testament.' He said the 'Falcon did not have the spirit within him.' He said you would understand, Isaac." "Yes, I think I do."

"The 'Falcon' did a strange thing, Isaac. He kept going back to the Book of Daniel in the Old Testament. Again and again. Sometimes he would relate it to the New Testament, sometimes not. John thought it was unusual. The Falcon's body language. His facial expressions. John perceived a certain contemptuousness. It made him wonder."

"John asked his host if could use the bathroom. It was inside the house. On his way down a hallway, he noticed a door that was slightly ajar. His curiosity had been piqued by a storyline about a man and his family that just didn't fit. The slightly open door led to the master bedroom. He looked inside the closet. There was a beautiful array of Hijabs. Hijabs are the coverings used by Muslim women. He heard the front door open. He quickly found his way to the bathroom."

"There was something else. He believed the Falcon's daughter wasn't his daughter at all. John observed several looks that would never be cast by a decent man towards his daughter. John assumed she was another wife, or some such thing. Not a daughter.

"John really didn't put it together until the other day. He now believes the Falcon was taunting him with the references to the Book of Daniel. He wanted to unnerve John by telling him in no uncertain terms that they knew about my relationship with him. El-Masri surely showed the Falcon the photographs taken at the hospital during Ethan's birth. They were confident. Disdainful and confident. They didn't count on David and Ethan Bass."

"We checked out John's information. The Falcon is Adnan Hussaini. He has had an excellent relationship with us. John was right about his "daughter." He has no children. Polygamy is legal in Jordan. It is rare, but legal. No matter. He has hidden his second wife from the Jordanians. They undoubtedly believe the same fiction we believed. His first wife is Saudi. Her brother is a high ranking Saudi intelligence officer. We have had dealings with him."

"So, what is it we're talking about here, Daniel?" What we're talking about, Isaac, is a Saudi operation against Jordan. Hussaini was never to betray us, as far as we know. He was well connected with the Jordanian government, including the inner circle, close to the royal family. He has been there for years. It was well done. My compliments to the Saudis."

"So, he went rogue, Daniel?" "Yes, he did. It seems odd to say, but he was recruited by El-Masri. He had good reason to believe El-Masri's scheme would be a huge success. He probably tired of his Jordanian assignment. He knows we're working on a peace treaty with Jordan. The Saudis can't stop it. He became dispirited, bored. His overconfidence led to sloppiness."

"What are we going to tell the Jordanians?" "Just that we became curious because his wife makes a lot of trips to Saudi Arabia, which is true." "When can I see John?" "Soon, Isaac. As soon as this Hussaini business is resolved. It won't be long, now. They will not be happy."

"What about El-Masri's daughter?" "So far, her hate is blinding her to her circumstances. At some point, we will tell her about her

father. It's very sad, Isaac. All that hate. And she is so young."
"What about Mary and her brother, John?" "We will keep an eye on
her brother, just to make sure he is alright. If she asks, we will provide safe passage out of the area. One more thing, Isaac. There is a
problem. We found a recent photo of Ethan in El-Masri's apartment."
"Did you ask Mary about it, Daniel?" "We did. She doesn't know
anything. We showed the photo to Reem. She was indignant. She
wanted to know how we got it. She laughed."

"Avner went back to the hospital to ask hospital staff about Reem.
As a precaution, Ethan had been in the neonatal intensive care unit for
several days. A maternity nurse caught Reem in the unit two or three
times." "Daniel, what on earth was Reem's interest in a newborn?
Maternal curiosity, please." "All the nurse would say is that unusual
things were happening around Ethan. They weren't spooky, or men-
acing. But the nurse wouldn't elaborate. It was something she just
didn't want to discuss." "I must go, Isaac. I shouldn't keep the Jordanians waiting. It won't be long, now, Isaac."

I should have been far more worried about the photo of Ethan
found in El-Masri's apartment. I wasn't. I could only think of seeing
John again. I was also thinking of Mary and her brother.

Now the Lord had said to Abram:
"Get out of your country, From your family
And from your father's house, To a land that I will show you.
I will make you a great nation; I will bless you
And make your name great; And you shall be a blessing.
I will bless those who bless you,
And I will curse him who curses you;
And in you all the families of the earth shall be blessed."
Genesis 12:1-3

As the dragon's tail of obsession swept towards Mary, she heard celestial voices sweetly remind her that the breath of life is a gentle

breeze that wafts from the heavens, and not maniacal pursuits born out of lustful, unquenchable hatreds. She would be counted among the righteous. She and her brother would be blessed, not cursed. A gentle breeze was carrying their names to the Book of Life.

CHAPTER SEVEN

THE FORMER THINGS

"For inquire, please, of the former age,
And consider the things discovered by their fathers;
For we were born yesterday, and know nothing..."
Job 8:8-9

I did not ask Daniel whether he told David and Rachel about the unwanted interest in Ethan. I was sure he didn't. He wouldn't let
anything happen to any of them. And at this point, it wasn't likely
that the danger was very significant. Still, I would have far preferred
to hear that Ethan was off their radar screen.

We were receiving fairly regular updates from Rachel. The safe-
guards became even more rigorous but, nonetheless, the stream of
information was steady. Nothing was more welcome than the adven-
tures of Ethan.

Rachel was continuing her homeschooling of Ethan. She even
took a cue from David. During the time she was doing her own Bible
study, she would also read and explain selected verses to Ethan. Her
explanations were designed for children, but she included more advanced interpretations of the text. He loved it. And he had his
favorites. Was he responding to what he perceived to be her favorites? She didn't think so.

It wasn't that Ethan's favorite verses didn't correspond to hers. They didn't, for the most part. But she was very curious as to why he was so enamored with some particular verses. He loved the passages about Rachel and David, that would be King David, for pretty obvious reasons. Rachel was careful to make some careful, maternal edits. She did not read the account of Rachel's death. She also omitted some of King David's more ungodly exploits.

The history of Hanukkah became one of Ethan's favorites. Of course, the Hanukkah account is not told in the Hebrew Bible, but the Books of the Maccabees. Hanukkah is a celebration of the rededication of the Temple in Jerusalem by Judas Maccabee in 165 BC. In the Temple, the oil was normally burned in the menorah for eight days. There was only a day's worth of oil, but it miraculously lasted for the full eight days. Normally, David and Rachel would follow tradition and light a candle on the menorah for each of the eight days. According to Rachel, during Hanukkah last year, Ethan went to the cupboard, got a small amount of olive oil, and brought out a bowl. David got the hint. He took a ceramic bowl, placed a small amount of olive oil in it, and lit it. It burned for the entire eight days. Rachel accused David of replenishing the oil after everyone was in bed. He insisted he didn't. Ethan was thrilled.

And there were Bible verses that Ethan "asked" Rachel to read on a regular basis. He "asked" because they were on a list she made for him. He pointed to the verses he wanted her to recite. Sometimes he would help find the right chapter and verse in the Bible.

Ethan loved the Genesis account of Jacob's wrestling match with G-d. David decided he would wrestle with Ethan any time they read the verse. Sometime during each evening, Ethan would get a Bible and find Genesis 32: 24-31. He would take it to David, and the wrestling match would ensue. Jacob asked for G-d's blessing, and wouldn't give up until he received it. Ethan too looked forward to the end of his loving scuffle with his father. He would look longingly at David, after which David would say a blessing for his son. Imagine

King David, Elijah the Tishbite and Jezebel as characters in professional wrestling. Somehow, I don't think so.

Ethan's Bible selections also included a dramatic encounter between a man and a whale, and the words of a prophet. He often asked
Rachel to read the story of Jonah to him. Ethan was very fond of a
certain part of Jonah's prayer to G-d:

> *"Yet You have brought up my life from the pit,*
> *O Lord, my G-d. When my soul fainted within me,*
> *I remembered the Lord; And my prayer went up to You,*
> *Into Your holy temple. Those who regard worthless idols*
> *Forsake their own Mercy. But I will sacrifice to You*
> *With the voice of thanksgiving; I will pay what I have vowed.*
> *Salvation is of the Lord."*
> *Jonah 2:6-9*

There was also something about a prophet who liked to say that he
had come from the simple life of a shepherd. Indeed he did. But it
was the Prophet Amos who first used the term "the Day of the Lord."
He spoke of an earthquake 200 years before it was to take place. And
he spoke about something else that Ethan liked Rachel to recite.

> *"Behold, the days are coming," says the Lord G-d,*
> *"That I will send a famine on the land,*
> *Not a famine of bread, Nor a thirst for water,*
> *But of hearing the words of the Lord.*
> *They shall wander from sea to sea, And from north to east;*
> *They shall run to and fro, seeking the word of the Lord,*
> *But shall not find it."*
> *Amos 8: 11-12*

And so it was: the rededication of the Temple; a fish story that
wasn't a fish story at all; a wrestling match with eternal echoes; and a

famine of the "Word." All of interest to a little boy in the American Midwest. Have stranger things happened? A time or two.

Golda Eisen. Eighty-four years on the earth, and still counting. Someday, she would be with G-d in eternity. But, not just yet. She trimmed her hours a bit. She knew secrets I had no idea about. My guess is she remembered every secret she ever knew. She might tell G-d if He ever asked, but He would know not to ask. That was Golda. A truer heart, there never was. Faithful and true. She spoke of Benjamin and Leah Singer as if they had visited just last week. Her Pirushkes tasted as if she had just taken them out of her oven in Tel Aviv, all those years ago.

And one afternoon, on a whim, I stopped by to see Golda for no particular reason. The news I had been waiting for was in her smile. She had seen that "bear of a man." Father John Broderick would meet me at the lab the next afternoon. I was overcome with joy. I was expecting it, yet one can never know. Golda suggested I use the President's private bathroom. It was a good suggestion. I wept uncontrollably. I tried to gather myself. At first, I couldn't. Then I began laughing, remembering the first time I wore my "professor" disguise, with John intentionally lagging behind me by just a few steps. I imagine he struggled to contain a belly laugh or two. It was quite a sight. He would be, too. Our reunion would be jubilant, but now it would have a trace of dignity, absent all my blubbering. I left my blubbering in the private loo of Hebrew University's President. It began with a whim.

The next day arrived, and I knew John would be at the lab at 3:30 p.m. He was usually prompt. I was devoting more and more of my time being the physicist Shoshana thought she was marrying 27 years ago. Israel needed an anti-ballistic missile system. The Arab states were beginning to acquire long range surface-to-surface missiles. It was another life-saving legacy of the President whose strategy led to the collapse of the Soviet Union. He believed it was immoral for western democracies to leave their people defenseless against incoming ballistic missiles. His opponents nicknamed his program "Star Wars" to undermine the seriousness of the threat, and his response. They treated the Strategic Defense Initiative the same way they treated his idea that the Soviet Union could be weakened, and would eventually crumble under the weight of its own incompetence and illegitimacy: with sarcasm and contempt.

In 1986, the United States and Israel signed an agreement to develop a missile defense system. Seven years later, we were now beyond the preliminary testing phase of the program. I was part of the team working on guidance and steering systems for our missile interceptors. In the years to come, we would not only prove that missile defense was technically possible, but our possession of such a capability would be essential to our survival. Another gift from the uncanny prescience of a President, and the American people.

The door to the lab opened as I thought it would: exactly at 3:30 p.m. And there he was. The ordeal didn't seem to age him at all. Perhaps his limp was somewhat more noticeable. But, maybe that was because I hadn't seen him for so long. His hair was as unwieldy as ever. Our embrace was long, and long overdue. A bear of a man with the sensibilities of a lamb. Those sensibilities caused a few tears to flow down his otherwise exuberant face. As usual, he thought of everything. Two handkerchiefs were at the ready. They didn't have much of a mopping up job to do.

"A hospital visit, and we all suffer, Isaac. I could say I wouldn't do it again, but that's not the truth. I would do it again. Who could possibly untangle all the twists and turns of this story. I can't. So, I submit myself to G-d's providence. I am sorry for exposing Shoshana to danger. For that, I am very sorry, Isaac." "I am too, John. But it is my responsibility, not yours. I chose this life. No one chose it for me. You have helped keep me alive all these years, John. That is a fact. Literally, helped keep me alive. And Israel. And, I understand G-d's mysteries far better, and His hand in all this. What a gift, John. What a gift, you are."

"I see that the warrior is very much a physicist these days, right Isaac?" "We need missile defense, John." "Yes, you do. You will need more than missile defense. Is Shoshana well?" "She is. She sends her best, John. She loves that this assignment is keeping me out of the warrior business for now. Her father had a very mild heart attack, John. So, she also is checking on him more these days." "Yes, I heard about Rabbi Levy. Thank G-d, they expect a full recovery."

"Isaac, Daniel told me about the photograph." "You mean the photograph they found at El-Masri's apartment, John?" "We will talk about this more later, Isaac. It concerns me. It concerns me, very much. This group. There is more to this group than inventing clever ways to murder Jews, or embarrass Israel, Isaac. We need to find out what it is they're after." "Do you have any idea what it could be, John?" "What I have Isaac is probably a too fertile imagination. But, I asked Daniel to find the names to go with the cities. I suspect what we're looking for is in San Carlos de Bariloche or Vienna. We need to find the who, so we find the what."

"Isaac, Daniel said as far as he is concerned, our monastery is "open for business." Please come and visit, won't you? And bring Shoshana, our garden still grows, Isaac." "We will visit, John. I promise you that. It will be beyond a pleasure. John, you didn't mention the tefillin." "That's because I didn't want you to take them off on my account." "So, should I leave them on, John?" "Leave them on for a while, Isaac. G-d would appreciate it. Demonstrate your thankfulness for at least a decent interval. You are faithful to G-d, Isaac Singer. And a G-d-send to all of us."

As he walked towards the door, I couldn't resist. "Don't be a stranger, Father John Broderick." The two of us broke out in laughter. We both had our moments at death's door. Better to laugh, than cry. Like a naïf, I wanted to skip home, and dance with anyone who would share some revelry. It was foolish. John was back. We would need him now more than ever.

Watershed moments. They are usually recognized years later, decades later, or too late. You hope the watershed moment swamps the other guy's boat, not yours. Unfortunately, watershed moments for Israel always involved tactics, never strategic goals: 1948, 1967 and 1973. These were the years when conventional "Clausewitzian" war was launched against Israel. In the '67 and '73 wars, conventional Israeli forces were vastly outnumbered by the onslaught. In the '73 war, Israel was nearly overrun. So nearly overrun that the Israeli Defense Minister told his advisers: "This is the end of the Third Temple." In effect, that meant "the end" for Israel. It wasn't. The Third Temple has still not been built. But at long as Israel lives, the dream of a Third Temple lives. The watershed moment? The last time Israel fought an all-out conventional war against its adversaries was in 1973. Good news? Not really. Only the tactics changed. The strategic goal was still the same: remove Israel from the Middle East.

Watershed moments only gradually reveal all their secrets. In warfare, some of their secrets are so insidious that the next watershed moment you experience is the end. My parents, Benjamin and Leah Singer, were killed by terrorism in 1945. Terrorism was nothing new to Israel. Terrorism wasn't a watershed moment in warfare against the Jewish state, it was a familiar method of murder among those who embrace death as a "religious" precept. The Muslim Brotherhood's organizational motto states that "Jihad is our way. Dying in the way of Allah is our highest hope." Whatever its more benign applications in an earlier era, "Jihad" makes it a religious duty to kill in order to establish the primacy of Islam.

Watershed moments in warfare. If it wasn't terrorism against Israel, what was it? Insidiousness. Insidiousness implies a long-term project. Cancer begins with just one cancer cell. It is most lethal when it grows undetected. It insinuates itself. It doesn't announce itself in a blaze of glory. Otherwise, detection, and the end of its scheme to kill to live. Insidiousness. Yes. But first, weaken the host. Use terrorism. Especially, spectacular terrorism. Make sure the blood can be carried away in buckets. The bodies? Perhaps the bodies can't be carried away at all. They are ripped and torn, and minced because of the ferocity of the instrumentalities of Jihad. Weaken the host. Questions begin to arise. How long will this go on? What are we doing over there? Is this really worth it? Can we bear the cost? The questions are posed by a host under assault.

At first, there are no questions. No doubts. No hesitation. The only question is, how hard can we hit back? But then there doesn't appear to be an end in sight. Waterloo. Suicide in a Berlin bunker. Hiroshima, Nagasaki. The Berlin Wall crumbles. Wars end. Even cold wars, in which two superpowers aren't colliding on the battle field. Then there is peace.

Weaken the host. Never stop coming. Then delude. The weary will become delusional. Jihad is not what you believe it is. It is really part and parcel of a religion of peace. Here's our money. We are really your friends. The money flows into colleges and universities. Suddenly, the victimizers become the victims. History is rewritten. Build mosques. Reach out to growing Muslim communities in western nations, especially in Britain and the United States. Insidiousness. Change the narrative. Your troubles will end if you would just get out of the Middle East, and all Muslim countries. Israel is so powerful. We are so weak. Give us a little land, and then there will be peace.

Insidiousness. Why? Conventional warfare didn't work. Enter Plan B. Delegitimize Israel. Isolate Her. Exploit ancient hatreds. Use international organizations, especially the United Nations, as a weapon. Develop curious alliances. The left and Islam. Then what? The real target: The United States. Separate the United States from Israel. Watershed moments. Someone is watching. The G-d of Abraham, Isaac and Jacob.

Saddam Hussein wasn't interested in watershed moments or nuance, period. He had an enormous standing army. He had an enormous debt incurred by a long, pointless, and savage war with Iran, which he started. Oil prices were too low to suit his ambitions, and his sense of entitlement. There were lingering territorial disputes with Kuwait. Voila. He waited all of two years after his war with Iran, and then invaded Kuwait. Twelve hours after his invasion, most of the Kuwaiti resistance folded. Within days, he installed his cousin as Kuwait's governor.

After it had assembled an impressive international coalition, including financial contributions totaling $53 billion, the United States effectively booted Iraqi forces out of Kuwait, and decimated a good portion of Saddam's military, including Saddam's vaunted "Republican Guard." The "Gulf War" was over. Saddam was left in power, but put back in his cage. It wouldn't be the last time the United States would look across a battle field at the face of Saddam Hussein. There were other watershed moments to come.

During the Gulf War, there was angst in Israel. Justifiable angst. Saddam had Scud missiles, and the wanton brutality to use them. He did. They were far less effective than we feared. Still, 74 Israelis died after 39 Scud missiles landed in Tel Aviv and Haifa. Direct hits by the Scuds killed two people, while the rest died because of suffocation or heart attacks. It was a bitter reminder that we needed to accelerate our development of missile defense.

A new front was opened in an old war. A watershed moment. The old war began long before the modern State of Israel. Now, a new front was opened at the doorstep of the greatest military and economic power the world had ever seen. In the nearly two thousand years since the Romans destroyed the Land of Israel, and drove Jews into exile, the Jewish community had never experienced anything like the personal freedom and physical safety available in the United States of America. Old obsessions die hard. This obsession not only never seemed to die, it never seemed to wane. Generation to generation. Atmospheric. Or, something.

The obsession didn't modestly announce itself to the American people. It didn't begin in country fairs, a chance encounter at a shopping mall, or even main street. What could be better than to get

Broadway billing, three miles or so south of Broadway. And, on a stage, no Broadway show could comprehend, let alone contain. It was the theatre of the grandiose, and diabolical. The props included the Statue of Liberty, and towers that made the Tower of Babel pale by comparison.

The conspirators detonated a truck bomb below the North Tower of the World Trade Center in New York City. Their homicidal dream was to knock down the North Tower (Tower One) into the South Tower (Tower Two), bringing both towers down and killing tens of thousands of people. They failed. Six people were killed. They were dismissed as amateurish and incompetent. It became a police matter, not unlike a purse snatching or mugging. Nothing here to see. Move right along. A new American president and his administration were trying to build a new narrative, about America, and him. The specter of international terrorism did not fit the narrative.

Treating the incident like a law enforcement matter had unfortunate and far-reaching consequences. U.S. intelligence agencies were cut off from the evidence collected by the FBI. It was all about grand jury secrecy. In spite of the underwhelming way in which the U.S. administration was handling the investigation, the first World Trade Center conspirators were clear about their intentions. One of the terrorists sent a letter to an American newspaper:

"We declare our responsibility for the explosion on the mentioned building. This action was done in response for the American political, economic and military support to Israel, the state of terrorism, and to the rest of the dictator countries in the region." He later stated that he had hoped to kill 250,000 Americans to show them the exact pain they had caused to the Japanese in the Atomic bombing of Hiroshima and Nagasaki."

The message was simple and familiar: stop supporting Israel and get out of the Middle East. For good measure, the terrorists demonstrated their heartfelt simpatico with the Japanese. How touching. Their declaration was a declaration of war, including its straightforward rationale. Later, as the declaration took on more deadly proportions, the American people would be told about a failure "to connect the dots." If the dots had been connected, it would have spelled "watershed moment." A new war. A wearying war.

The tango. It is an elegant dance that stepped boldly out of the inelegant working class neighborhoods of Buenos Aires, Argentina. It is an exclamation point. The endless dance. No resolution. No resolution is possible. The tango is the incendiary collision of male and female natures. In the natural, their collision has divine and miraculous attributes. They have the power to multiply and sustain life. A divine gift. A divine power. Enter the fall from grace. The divine gives way to the primordial. Trouble. Nonetheless, the tango manages to beautifully and gracefully contain the uncontainable. It is raw Latin sexuality and passion tempered by the cool precision and grace of a Viennese Waltz.

The primordial dance between male and female began with a bite from an apple. It had deadly consequences, to be sure. The curse. The wages of sin is death. But there was still life. Life would be limited; yes it would. But life itself is a gift. There was still hope, and redemption through faith.

The murderers in Buenos Aires still wanted to tango with the Jewish community. The murderers' tango with the Jewish community had none of life's residual, and glorious qualities. It wasn't life at all. It was a tango in the dark, devoid of any of the darkness's romantic allusions. But even murderers know it takes two to tango. The two they had in mind were brothers. Cain and Abel. G-d himself condemned Cain for murdering his brother:

"And He said, "What have you done? The voice of your
brother's blood cries out to Me from the ground. So now you are
cursed from the earth, which has opened its mouth to
receive your brother's blood from your hand."
Genesis 4:10-11

Their first attack was against the Israeli Embassy in Buenos Aires in 1992. From the beginning, it appeared there was no desire among Argentine officials to seriously investigate the matter. The message: benign neglect or encouragement. The result: bombs away! A second bomb was detonated in a Jewish community center in Buenos Aires in 1994. This time, 87 people were killed. It was clear all along that Iran and its murder for hire gang, Hezbollah, were responsible. Years of fitful and sputtering investigations were a telltale sign of Argentine priorities. The windup: a few Iranian diplomats were expelled.

And when we had become all too inured to Argentina's callous disregard for justice for the dead, they managed to demonstrate a contempt for Jewish life, eerily similar to their policy of safe haven for Hitler's band of soulless lunatics. Argentina signed a memorandum of understanding with Iran to form a "truth commission" to investigate the two terrorist bombings. Really? Wouldn't Cain have loved to form a "truth commission" with damnation to investigate his brother's death.

What's worse was the lineup of Iranian officials who approved both terrorist bombings. It included a so-called Supreme Leader, and a former and future President. So, the top officials in the Iranian terrorist enterprise made common cause with the highest levels of the Argentine government. Why? Well, one of the surest of the tried and true inducements: money, drug money. Iran was using drug money to help support the proliferation of Hezbollah throughout South America. Argentine government officials didn't mind being put on the list of payees. It wasn't the last tango, but the latest tango. It was a tango with a decidedly Persian flair. The dance steps followed a trail of lifeless bodies. The trail was clearly marked. It had the Mark of Cain.

In effect, the 90's would bring a daring escalation of the war against Israel. Its perpetrators would invoke cartoonish and ironic language. Big Satan and little Satan: The United States and Israel. The 90's would also unveil what began to be whispered in the caves and back alleys where the terrorists lurked, but also in the fine hotels and garish hideaways of Arab financiers whose pockets were so stuffed with oil money, they spent their days dreaming of the Arabian Nights. They weren't content with re-telling the lavish tales of "Aladdin's Wonderful Lamp," "Ali Baba and the Forty Thieves," and "The Seven Voyages of Sinbad the Sailor."

No, literature fell far short of their ambitions. It was the rebirth of the Caliphate they were after. Its most recent incarnation was the Ottoman Empire, which ended ingloriously as it was incapable of matching the political, military and technological advances of the European states. They saw an opportunity in the rise of a kind of cultural nihilism in the West. If the West was eager to renounce its Judeo-Christian foundations, Islam would happily fill the vacuum. Insidiousness.

Daniel and Colonel Stern agreed with John. Why would Dr. Amir El-Masri have an interest in Ethan Bass? It obviously wasn't El-Masri, but one of his heinous colleagues. We knew that El-Masri's daughter, Reem, was found in the neonatal intensive care unit, where Ethan spent the first few days of his young life. She snapped a photograph. She provided a narrative to go along with the photograph. It was a narrative that interested someone associated with El-Masri. The narrative noted unusual things happening around Ethan. Maybe she embellished the story a bit. Maybe not. Years later, many years later, someone in one of the four cities thought enough of Reem's report to have another photo taken of Ethan. They were watching. Watching for what? Daniel and Colonel Stern weren't going to wait to find out. John sensed danger.

John suspected the answer would be found in Vienna or San Carlos de Bariloche. He believed that someone in one of those cities had an interest in Ethan Bass. But why would they have sent a recent photo of Ethan to El-Masri? Daniel had a plausible explanation. Perhaps they thought their plot to expose John and his network of "friends" would succeed. For a time, they would blackmail John to gather more information about his Israeli connections, and Ethan. They were smart. And ruthless. They believed John could tell them something about Ethan that only a priest could fully appreciate.

It was time for Daniel and Colonel Stern to further test their protégés. Daniel was sending Avner to Vienna. Colonel Stern was sending Dov Lerner to Argentina. Dov was a junior officer in the IDF's special forces. He would join the security detail at the Israeli Embassy in Buenos Aires. Security for the embassy was beefed up after the 1992 bombing. There was a regular rotation. San Carlos de Bariloche is about 1,300 kilometers Southwest from Buenos Aires. Dov was fluent in Spanish, including local dialects. He would make his way to San Carlos de Bariloche. He would blend in as a tourist.

Moments of grace. Grace, the gift from a righteous G-d. G-d's grace. The awe inspiring breadth of G-d's grace. Retribution lasts only four generations, whereas his mercy extends at least two thousand generations. That is the very definition of long-sufferance. Long-sufferance and grace. Grace is His divine accommodation. He awaits the end of our "drift" from Him as the world buffets our human existence.

As a young boy, I had every reason to be consumed in a cauldron of bitterness. It would inevitably lead to an eternal separation from any divine inheritance. But that was not the legacy of Benjamin and Leah Singer. Their righteousness "stored up" enough grace for a time when their son would need it most. Yes, at six years old, I needed G-d's grace. The righteous winds that blew in the sails of my parents' spiritual wings were no longer available to their son. The terrorists made sure of that. I needed G-d's grace. His answer was the Weisses.

Ariel and Rebecca Weiss. Aaron Weiss. Grace. They were G-d's answer to the unthinkable. How does a six-year old begin to comprehend the loss of his parents. No doubt, they asked G-d to look after their boy, just in case. They knew their work could leave me a orphan in the blink of an eye. It did. And now, Shoshana and I were on our way to spend the day with the Weisses. They lived in Tel Aiv, all these years. I spent countless days training at the IDF's Special Forces facility in Tel Aviv. I visited them far too infrequently.

About the time that we entered the IDF, the Weisses moved from the apartment where Aaron and I had grown up. They moved to a Tel Aviv neighborhood known as Azorei Hen. How appropriate. Azorei Hen means "Areas of Grace" in Hebrew. Indeed they were: an area of grace.

My father and Ariel Weiss were colleagues. They both distinguished themselves in the world of cancer research. Dr. Weiss was one of the founders of a cancer research fund that tried to stem the loss of Israeli cancer researchers to foreign universities. It was largely successful. Israel was becoming a center for medical research worldwide. My father would have been proud.

From the very first, I always used the Hebrew word for "papa" to refer to Ariel Weiss. When I returned from the United States, that changed to just the Americanized version, "papa." I liked the way it sounded. And he didn't mind. He may have been the only "papa" in Israel.

Whenever I visited the Weisses, papa often invited me into his library. This day was no different. "Oh, Isaac, I think about Benjamin and Leah so much these days. How proud they would have been of you, and what we've accomplished here. But I miss them so. You know Isaac, your parents loved music. And they loved to dance. And they loved to laugh. We enjoyed those early days. Sometimes, I hear laughter, and I turn, hoping to see their faces. Oh, I miss them."

His love carried me through the worst of it. And it delivered me on the doorstep of G-d's righteous mercy. To know G-d. Now, I could make a small down payment on my debt of gratitude, and lift him, as he had lifted me, all these years. "Papa, they would have no words for your show of kindness to their son. They have only an eternal smile. That smile in heaven, is theirs. The Talmud teaches us that we learn Torah in the womb; but an angel comes and makes us forget all. We emerge from the womb, having taken an oath to be righteous and not wicked. You have taught me the righteous ways of G-d. You are brilliant, papa. But you have the humility to know that human brilliance is a gift. And unless our gifts reflect most brilliantly in heaven, they amount to nothing."

"You are right, of course, Isaac. I hear Benjamin and Leah in your words. They are wise words. Forgive your papa's moment of self-pity." He laughed at his use of my nickname for him. He was pleased. "You know, all of our friends know about this American name you call me, Isaac. They don't really understand. They haven't heard your voice. If they could hear your voice, Isaac, they would understand. Thank you, my son. Thank you for making us so proud. You honor us, and the memory of your parents. We have left our wives alone for too long! Come, we will have coffee before you leave."

The laughter and smiles of that day lasted well past the drive back to our apartment. I was most happy that Shoshana could now better understand the power of what sustained me after the loss of my parents. Memory is recollection. But it is far more than that in the presence of G-d. Even for a physicist, there is a sort of spiritual recollection. That day was spiritual recollection and spiritual revelation. I understood what happened to a six year old. It was a miracle. It was a moment of grace.

As it turned out, the moment of grace granted to a young boy, was revisited upon a grown man. It almost seemed like sacrilege, but as an adult, I had fleeting thoughts there was an infinitesimal blessing to the sudden, and early loss, of my parents. In the natural, mortality is a taste of the curse. It is a unsavory taste, at best. Time and mortality. The years have been kind to my adopted parents... however... There was always a... however. My training as physicist left me bewildered by all the variables. Less than four months after our sojourn to Tel Aviv, Ariel and Rebecca Weiss died, peaceably, less than 24 hours apart. It was a second moment of grace.

I knew that Golda would love to hear about my visit with the Weisses. I recall her telling me that she knew the Weisses years before she knew my parents. No matter. She was overjoyed to hear about my visit to Tel Aviv and, yes, our chat included the ever delicious Pirushkes. Golda had trimmed her hours a bit from the last time we met. She usually was there during the morning, and now only an occasional afternoon. No one would dream of replacing her. It would be far too risky. I am sure that Daniel, or the Prime Minister's office for that matter, would have very different job descriptions for Golda. It raised the question as to whether anybody knew what Golda's job description really was. Whatever it was, it was essential. That we could all agree on.

How could we know what the risks were to Ethan? We didn't know if there was really any risk at all. It was supposition. Whatever Dr. El-Masri actually knew, died with him. It is doubtful that his daughter, Reem, really knew anything at all, beyond what she had heard, and perhaps seen, in the hospital where Ethan was born. Daniel and Colonel Stern dispatched some good men to find out if there was any true danger. The one thing I knew was that John was concerned. That was enough. But, in the absence of having anything specific, the Basses, especially Ethan, had to be left alone to live their lives.

And live, they did. Ethan continued to demonstrate his athletic prowess. He dominated at local Special Olympics competitions. The truth is Ethan could have competed in regular competitions. No one could comprehend the how, exactly. It was an uncomfortable question. Special Olympics was a sort of revolution of the heart and mind. But the revolution didn't extend that far, yet.

If Ethan continued his athletic development, David and I had a plan. It was David's idea, but I would carry the torch in Israel. We would need friends. Friends in high places. Or friends who had friends in high places. I would start with Golda. She would lead into the Prime Minister's office. Good. Then I would seek backing from some of my notable colleagues in Israel's scientific establishment, including Dr. Ariel Weiss. Of course, Colonel Stern, Daniel, and Aaron were all going to be recruited to the cause. I would also enlist Shoshana's father, Rabbi Levy, because he knew at least one former Prime Minster.

David wasn't shy. Neither was I. Neither was Ethan. If Ethan continued to progress in track and field, David and I decided to try to get permission for Ethan to compete in the Maccabiah Games, the Jewish Olympics. They are held in Israel the year following the Olympic Games. There is a category for athletes with disabilities. We wanted permission for Ethan to participate in the regular competition. 2001 was the target year. We had some time. We would need friends.

Dov needed some help. He took a clever route to get it. He went to Golda, first. That would lead him to a reinvigorated Franciscan priest. He asked Golda an interesting question. It was a question that would lead to what John had warned about. History begins in the garden. If the blood moons of 2014 and 2015 were to be "signs" from G-d, then there would be something else. History begins in the garden. Something else would be there too. John said it would try to thwart G-d's purposes with "with all its might."

Dov wanted access to one of the men who had hunted Nazi war criminals on behalf of Israel. He needed to be a specialist in Argentina and, if he had extensive knowledge of the Argentine network that hid Nazi war criminals, then he would surely know about San Carlos de Bariloche. At least, that is what Dov hoped.

It began with a meeting in Strasbourg. The survival of the Reich. Such a meeting could have been held centuries earlier. Another manifestation of the obsession. Strasbourg: In the 14th century, it suffered from the "Black Death," bubonic plague. Every plague needs a cause. A scapegoat is even better. The Jewish community of Strasbourg and, the Jewish community in Europe in general, did not appear to be affected quite so catastrophically by the plague. It may have been that Jews buried their dead much more quickly than Christians, and in separate cemeteries, making their deaths less visible. It may have been that Passover saved a great portion of the Jewish population. In preparation for Passover, every morsel of leavened bread is removed from the home. That would have deprived the carriers of bubonic plague, rats, of food and shelter. The plague peaked in the spring, around the time that Passover would have fallen. No matter. As happened in other European cities, the plague was laid at the doorstep of the Jewish community in Strasbourg. Those who didn't consent to baptism were burned alive in the city's cemetery.

It seems that Strasbourg's rodent infestation lasted well into the 20th century. Time was getting short for the industrialists and bankers who had murdered and plundered their way to riches, courtesy of the Third Reich. Ike's legions on the ground and in the air were getting all too close for comfort. How fitting it would have been for the plunderers to meet at the city's cemetery. But it lacked the swank and fine dining of Strasbourg's Maison Rouge hotel. They needed a plan. First, they required safe havens to park themselves, and their booty. And since they were already condemned, why not plan for the resurrection of the new Reich. Apparently, they loved irony. Their resurrection would only continue their rapid descent. And so, the Black Death was born anew in Strasbourg. It was known as the "Organization Der Ehemaligen SS-Angehörigen," (The Organization of former SS members). It was ODESSA.

The rats found that morphing into an octopus would serve them well. They needed long tentacles to find the safe havens they so desired. Golda had arranged for Dov to meet someone who knew many of the secrets of Odessa. He had helped capture the "chief operating officer" of the "final solution to the Jewish question." Adolph Eichmann was not only captured, but faced a justice system that scrupulously laid out the case against him. He had afforded his millions of victims not a scintilla of justice, or mercy. After his trial, justice was done. He was unmercifully hanged.

For the time being, Daniel and Colonel Stern wanted to still keep their protégés at arm's length from our little network. Yes, the little network who could. It meant that neither John nor I had met Avner or Dov. Given their current assignments, it was a wise precaution. Dov did make an extensive report of his conversation with one of Israel's retired Nazi hunters.

On the basis of Dov's report, Colonel Stern requested that we all meet at the lab in Jerusalem. It was a rare request. Dov knew nothing about John. Because of his interrogation of El-Masri's recruits, Avner only knew that John was a priest, nothing else.

Dov's conversation with an old man revealed a name. It was a name that somewhat haunted an old man because he could never establish that the name really belonged to someone else. In fact, there were two names: father and son. He believed the father had some rather grotesque and perverse professional appetites. He had since died. But his son was still alive. Dov wanted a name so he could begin his research in Carlos de Bariloche with something. There was also something else in the Dov's report. It involved Franciscan priests. Not "our" Franciscan priest but, nonetheless, Franciscan priests. Dov had no idea about "our" Franciscan priest.

Colonel Stern got right to the point. "Gentlemen, we have a name. But we need his real name, if our suspicions turn out to be correct." "Forgive me, Moshe, ah... Colonel, I am getting more sentimental as time goes on. Bless you all. May I say a prayer before we begin?" "Of course, John. I have gotten old and stupid. Please, John, we would be honored." "Thank you, Colonel. Father, bless these men, and bless this country. Shine your light on the darkest corners of our world. May your mercy and justice be with us always. Grant us your peace. Amen."

"And I asked Golda to make us some of her famous Pirushkes. Dig in, please. I am sorry, I got a little head start. Aren't they feeding you at the monastery, John? "No, Daniel, those little wafers are getting thinner all the time." After all we had been through, the banter was beginning to sound normal again. That bear of a man would never let us forget how much we had endured together, and how much we loved each other. These years had been a test of our endurance. There were more tests to come.

"Dov had an interesting talk with someone I have never met." Daniel spoke up. "I have had the honor, Colonel. I think we could make an old man very happy if his information leads to something." "No doubt, Daniel. No doubt." "John, do you know anything about Odessa?" "Yes, I believe, I do. Wasn't Odessa a network organized by the Nazis to enable former SS officers to escape justice." "Yes, and they dreamed of reviving the Reich, too." Now, John got to the point. "Colonel, you said you had a name?" "We have two names, John. A father and a son. The father is dead. But the son lives. Raymoundo Valdes was the father. The son is Lucero Valdes. They both lived in San Carlos de Bariloche since the end of the war. The only records there are claim that the father and son moved to Argentina from Chile. Valdes always insisted that he had a Chilean wife who died, and that his father immigrated to Chile from Italy."

"What are they hiding, Colonel?" "Well, John, our elderly friend believes they are really the Bouhlers. It's funny, but one of the leads we followed on the trail that led to Eichmann was provided by his son, who bragged to a girlfriend about his father's role in the killing of the Jews in Europe. A girlfriend of Ernst Bouhler, the father, swore that he told her that he was an SS officer." "That's all we have, Colonel, a girlfriend?" "No, John, there is one other thing. Have you heard of something called the 'Monastery Route?'" "No, Colonel, I have not." "It was part of the Odessa network. Roman Catholic priests, especially Franciscans, helped move Nazi fugitives from one monastery to the other, until they reached Rome. There was one Franciscan monastery in particular, Via Sicilia in Rome, that was a virtual transit station for Nazis."

A grey pallor took over John's buoyant face. His head drooped, as his eyes stared at the floor. All he could say was, "G-d forgive them.

Those fools, what could they have been thinking?" "Well, John, it may have been misguided Christian charity." "Misguided, Colonel. It's like helping the devil himself." And just as suddenly, John stood tall again, and pounded the table in delight. The bear of a man let loose a guffaw that even startled the unflappable Daniel. He asked for a piece of paper. "Colonel," he said in a loud voice. He lowered his voice when he saw the look of our faces. "Sorry... ah, Colonel, call this number in Rome. Say only this: 'This is about Odessa. John is interested in two travelers: Raymoundo and Lucero Valdes.'"

"The monastery is now closed. The archives were stored at the Vatican." The records should be there. I am sure they saved everything. I did not know that monastery was part of Odessa. The man you speak to will. I cannot give you his name. He will call me." We were all a little stunned. What else was in the realm of possibility for our beloved friend? "Colonel, make the call this evening, about 5:30 p.m. They will have finished their prayers, then. I am anxious for his reply."

"Is G-d's justice knocking at our door, John?" I was wondering aloud if there was more to this than delayed justice. After all, the son could not be held responsible for the crimes of his father. "G-d seeks a just world, Isaac. Yes. But He may have other purposes for the memories of an old man. Dov was wise to contact Golda." "Are you suggesting Golda has contacts that rank above the Prime Minister's office?" "I only know that her Pirushkes are heavenly, Isaac. If we don't finish off this batch, Golda will be disappointed. Please, gentlemen!"

America was the target now. Separate America from Israel. That was the plan. Make America pay for its support of Israel. See how much blood the Americans could tolerate. There were trails of blood. They brought a trail of tears. And the perpetrators appeared to be acting with impunity. Impunity, imagine.

America could be forgiven for wanting to enjoy the fruits of the end of the Cold War. All manner of sacrifices were made during the

Cold War. There were losses to families, and to extended families. Empty chairs, and photographs were unyielding reminders. And to those families for which no bodily remains could be found to bury, there was the Tomb of the Unknown Soldier. It was often said that America paid a price in blood and treasure. Its treasure was its blood.

And all these centuries, G-d's hand had been on America. In the beginning, He breathed life into our nostrils and made us human, with a divine inheritance; He established an everlasting covenant with Israel and the Jewish people; and through the Jewish people He extended His covenant to all the world (the nations); and, yet, the world had never seen a nation like the United States of America.

Father John Broderick told us that major events begin just before the actual years of the blood moons. Prior to the events of 1948 (statehood for Israel and the War of Independence) and 1967 (the Six Day War), we have to go back almost 500 years to find another such episode: four blood moons occurring in back-to-back years, exactly on Biblical feast days. Christopher Columbus's diary begins this way:

"In the same month in which their Majesties (Ferdinand and Isabella) issued the edict that all Jews should be driven out of the kingdom and its territories, in the same month they gave me the order to undertake with sufficient men my expedition of discovery to the Indies."

And so began Columbus's expedition during which he discovered America in 1492. A nation would be founded on the principle of religious liberty.

The President whose rhetoric and resolve ended the Soviet empire explained it well:

"I also believe this blessed land was set apart in a very special way, a country created by men and women who came here not in search of gold, but in search of G-d. They would be free people, living under the law with faith and their Maker and their future."

Foul winds have always swept their way across the plains of human history. Foul winds defile the air, leaving their stench in a musky haze; and they scourge our hearts, leaving those light on faith, faithless and hopeless. Two Presidents. Separated by 120 years. History's foul winds blew strongly across the country they loved so much. They both had the humility to know they needed G-d's helping hand. And they both had the steely resolve to resist the cacophony of contrary and hostile voices. The voice they listened to, the voice they heard, they heard on their knees.

They often found their own voice on the battlefields where the fate of their great country hung in the balance. They both understood the American moment. It was a rare moment of freedom and self-rule. It was obeisance to G-d, not serfdom under men. The King was in heaven, not an earthly castle.

During a great Civil War, one President said it this way:

"It is rather for us to be here dedicated to the great task remaining before us -- that from these honored dead we take increased devotion to that cause for which they gave the last full measure of devotion -- that we here highly resolve that these dead shall not have died in vain -- that this nation, under G-d, shall have a new birth of freedom -- and that government of the people, by the people, for the people, shall not perish from the earth."

And on another great battlefield, far flung from the Civil War battlefield, only in distance, but not in its meaning, the other President said this:

"We're here to mark that day in history when the Allied armies joined in battle to reclaim this continent to liberty. For 4 long years, much of Europe had been under a terrible shadow. Free nations had fallen, Jews cried out in the camps, millions cried out for liberation. Europe was enslaved, and the world prayed for its rescue. Here in Normandy the rescue began..."

"You all knew that some things are worth dying for. One's country is worth dying for, and democracy is worth dying for, because it's the

most deeply honorable form of government ever devised by man. All of you loved liberty."

The President of the 90's seemed to sense a different American moment. He believed that the American moment was his moment to transition to something else. On the beach below the cliffs, where a previous President had honored those who had rescued freedom from the predations of the Third Reich, he fashioned a peace symbol that had been popularized in the counter-cultural protests of the 60's. The boys he honored extended their boyhood well into mid-life, and even into a presidency.

The President of the 90's chose a theme song for his campaign that had been released by a rock group in 1977. The song was "Don't Stop Thinking About Tomorrow." It was thematically seductive because it had the American story half right. America had always invented the future which, in effect, is many tomorrows. So, in a sense, America never stopped thinking about tomorrow. But America's genius was not in its inventions, or its abundance. Abundance and wealth were not both cause and effect. They were the blessings of liberty. There was no limit to what a free people could accomplish. But liberty required far more than thinking about tomorrow. There was something ironic about liberty. Liberty wasn't the freedom to operate in a "state of nature." John Adams said what all the American founders knew and believed:

"Avarice, ambition, revenge and licentiousness would break the strongest cords of our Constitution, as a whale goes through a net. Our Constitution was made only for a moral and religious people. It is wholly inadequate to the government of any other."

And so, it turns out that we can only think justly and clearly about tomorrow, if we remember that yesterday was a divine gift. The President's theme song not only urged us to "Don't Stop Thinking About Tomorrow," but counseled us that "Yesterday is Gone." But the truth is that if yesterday is gone, then our tomorrows will slowly become a series of nightmares.

And even though the Cold War had ended, the other "war" murderously intruded. Until Israel was founded, America was unique in all of world history: it was a safe haven for the Jewish people. And, America helped guarantee Israel's survival. In the demented souls of the obsessed, America became a target. The first attack on the World Trade Center in New York City hugely underperformed their ambitions.

But Persia, now Iran, had embraced the obsession before. According to the Book of Esther, the Persian empire of the 5th century B.C., extended "from India, even unto Ethiopia." Haman, a Persian noble in the 5th century BC, convinced the Persian King, Ahasuerus, that "all the Jews who were throughout the whole kingdom of Ahasuerus" should be destroyed. Eventually, King Ahasuerus was persuaded by Queen Esther to abandon Haman's plan. Haman was hanged.

After its Islamic revolution of 1979, if there were any "voices of Esther" in Iran, they were either silent, or silenced. No, from the beginning of the revolution, the spirit of Haman animated the Iranian leadership. American administrations would persist under the delusion that there were "moderates" in the Iranian government. But actions speak louder than delusions.

America had to be convinced to first, abandon the Middle East, and second, abandon Israel.

In 1996, some United States Air Force personnel were housed at Building #131 in the Khobar Towers in Khobar, Saudi Arabia. A truck bomb containing 20,000 to 30,000 pounds of TNT was exploded adjacent to Building #131. Nineteen U.S. airmen were murdered in the attack. More than 400 Air Force men and women were wounded. The attackers said their goal was to get the United States military to leave the country.

Years after the event, the Director of the FBI, who was responsible for the investigation on the American side of things, made some astonishing disclosures. He made these disclosures in an article he wrote for an American newspaper. First, in terms of the investigation itself, the Director of FBI said it was essential that his agents get the cooperation of the Saudi government to interview suspects. And yet, in order for his agents to get such cooperation he had to get the intervention of a previous American President, because the White House at the time "was unwilling or unable to help the FBI gain access to these critical witnesses."

According to the Director, the FBI was able to unequivocally establish that "the entire operation was planned, funded and coordinated by Iran's security services, the IRGC and MOIS, acting on orders from the highest levels of the regime in Tehran." During the investigation, the White House ordered the FBI "to stop photographing and fingerprinting official Iranian delegations entering the U.S. because it was adversely impacting our "relationship" with Tehran." The FBI had argued that Iran was using these official Iranian delegations "to infiltrate its agents into the U.S."

On the basis of the evidence it developed, "the FBI recommended a criminal indictment that would identify Iran as the sponsor of the Khobar bombing." Unfortunately, the White House "refused to support a prosecution." The President's National Security Advisor described the evidence presented by the FBI as "hearsay." "The prosecution and criminal indictment for these murders had to wait for a new administration." 19 U.S. airmen, murdered in cold blood, still await justice.

And there were more than just Persian plotters behind the assault on the United States. Islam was divided into Sunni and Shiite sects. Iran was home to the Shiites. The Sunni and Shiite factions of Islam were rarely united. In fact, they were literally at each other's throats. They hated one thing more than hated each other: Israel. As John pointed out on more than one occasion, the lust to be the "son of promise" led to a blood lust that cursed the souls of the perpetrators.

"I will bless those who bless you,
And I will curse him who curses you.."

Genesis 12:1-3

The first World Trade Center attack was conducted by a Sunni Muslim terrorist cell. It's ring leader was Omar Abdel Rahman, who became known as the "Blind Sheikh." He and his "cell" were also responsible for the murder of Jewish Defense League (JDL) founder, Meir Kahane; plots to kill the Egyptian president, and a plot to conduct simultaneous bombings of New York City landmarks.

Shiite and Sunni Muslim terrorists especially liked to operate according to a type of Islamic religious decree, or fatwa, which are issued by respected jurists within Islam. James Bond, a fictional character, was apparently issued a "License to Kill." Fatwas were all too non-fictional, and they lacked the attendant glamor of 007. Just ask the 291 persons killed, and 5,000 others who were wounded by the attacks on US Embassies in Kenya and Tanzania in August, 1998.

The justification for the attack on the American Embassies was a fatwa issued in February 23, 1998. The fatwa stated that the United States had been "occupying the lands of Islam in the holiest of places," and that the United States goal is "to serve the Jews' petty state and divert attention from its occupation of Jerusalem and murder of Muslims there." Attack the United States, and separate it from Israel. Isolate Israel. That was the plan. The plan had myriad acolytes within Islam. The February 23 fatwa had several authors. One author, in particular, rather liked such fatwas. It was his "License to Kill." His name was Osama Bin Laden.

The Nazi SS didn't need fatwas. But they loved their alliance with those who issued them. After all, they had a common obsession. The Muslim Brotherhood established Islamic Jihad as a mass movement. The Muslim Brotherhood was to Islamists groups what the Bolshevik Party was to Communism. The "Brotherhood" spawned Al Queda and Hamas. Its obsessed "soul mates" in Shia Islam were Hezbollah and the Mahdi Army, among others.

The special relationship the Nazi SS had with the Muslim Brotherhood was "special" indeed. I knew about the campaign against the Jews by the Grand Mufti of Jerusalem, Haj Muhammad Amin al-Husseini. One of the Grand Mufti's pen pals was a failed chicken farmer whose savagery couldn't have been plucked from whatever he gleaned from animal husbandry. He set up the first concentration camp in Dachau.

His missive to the Grand Mufti was a love letter from inside the gates of hell:

"To the Grand Mufti: The National Socialist movement of Greater Germany has, since its inception, inscribed upon its flag the fight against the world Jewry. It has therefore followed with particular sympathy the struggle of freedom-loving Arabs, especially in Palestine, against Jewish interlopers. In the recognition of this enemy and of the common struggle against it lies the firm foundation of the natural alliance that exists between the National Socialist Greater Germany and the freedom-loving Muslims of the whole world. In this spirit I am sending you on the anniversary of the infamous Balfour declaration my hearty greetings and wishes for the successful pursuit of your struggle until the final victory. Signed: Reichsfuehrer S.S. Heinrich Himmler"

After the war, the Grand Mufti reminisced about one of the denizens of hell he was sure to join:

"Our fundamental condition for cooperating with Germany was a free hand to eradicate every last Jew from Palestine and the Arab world. I asked Hitler for an explicit undertaking to allow us to solve the Jewish problem in a manner befitting our national and racial aspirations and according to the scientific methods innovated by Germany in the handling of its Jews." The answer I got from the Fuehrer was: 'The Jews are yours.'"

The Nazi SS and the Muslim Brotherhood. They weren't finished. Father John called us together for what Golda described as an "urgent meeting." No meeting had ever been described by John Broderick as "urgent." That includes our fateful meeting prior to the '67 war. Gee, at that meeting he had only given me the exact Jordanian positions throughout Jerusalem, and some advice about what Jerusalem gate my commando team could enter, that is if I didn't want to offend G-d himself. As the Lord said to Ezekiel, "This gate shall be shut; it shall not be opened, and no man shall enter by it." But this meeting was "urgent." Yes, it was.

I had never seen a man who was happily pensive. But that's what John was. He was happily pensive. It turns out he was happy he solved a 40 plus year old mystery, sort of. It wasn't really a mystery. It was the strong belief of a former Nazi hunter that he hadn't been able to confirm. John was absorbed by the consequences of what he had found. If evil only complicated our lives, it was bad enough. But evil left a body count. The bodies were lifeless. And many of the bodies had been inhabited by the souls of saints. Life is a gift. Death is a curse.

Unlike our previous meeting, John neither began with a prayer, nor had any of Golda's Pirushke cakes for us to munch on. He simply told us what a friend of his had found after rummaging through some old records at the Vatican. One could imagine the doodles of Pontiffs; or the secrets that the Apostle Peter dared not write down but were recorded anyway by a long forgotten scribe, who had pressed his ear to the door of some inner sanctum. In some respects, the records recorded the mundane. It was no different than the purse snatcher, who after he had snagged his booty, ran with abandon, getting his jollies from outrunning a slightly overweight officer of the law, knowing full well that he was the possessor of a handbag, light on loot. There had to have been a similar self-satisfaction among the SS officers who believed their escape meant they got away with their crimes. Except it wasn't mundane at all.

The SS were lifers. Theirs was an evil in the presence of the beast. It was not present at the creation; it was separation from G-d at the fall. It was not a thief hanging on a cross, comprehending that his claim on righteousness was far short of even the outer reaches of G-d's holiness and virtue. That was a moment of remorse, almost certainly, genuine remorse. It was an act of contrition driven by an understanding, however incomplete, of G-d's sufferance of human creation. It was consciousness in service of a conscience. And it crystallized the meaning of grace, the divine accommodation to the human condition. At some point, humility and remorse would begin the crawl back to a confident, upright stride on the glory road. For a thief, it was the glory road to "paradise."

But there is a point of no return. The eerie sounds of the darkness no longer make the skin crawl, but scintillate a dead soul. Raymoundo Valdes' real name was Ernst Bouhler. There was nothing in the Nazi enterprise that rose to the level of humanity. Neither did it rise to the level of any of the living creatures brought forth by G-d *"according to its kind."* After all, G-d brought forth creatures *"according to its kind,"* and He saw that *"it was good."*

Ernst Bouhler was Dr. Ernst Bouhler, Nazi SS officer. He collaborated with Dr. Joseph Mengele, who upon being accepted in the Nazi party, also applied for membership in the SS. The black hole that was their evil was barely hinted at by Jack the Ripper, or the darkest and most fantastical stories of Edgar Allen Poe. Even Alfred Hitchcock's Psycho, a brief tour through the mind of the criminally insane, writ large on a movie screen, falls far short. If ONLY Bouhler and Mengele had been psychotic.

Bouhler and Mengele were both medical school graduates. Yes, they both had managed to acquire the title of doctor. But only in the sense that their training conferred a certain precision to their activities, which were otherwise devoid of any G-dly resonance. When they engaged in their incomprehensible depravity, they preferred the smooth precision of a scalpel, rather than the serrated edge of a butcher knife.

The Hippocratic writing "Epidemics," commands physicians "to do no harm." Bouhler and Mengele weren't interested in the medicinal, only the homicidal. Their notorious penchant for immaculately clean uniforms and impeccably polished boots covered a blood lust that took them on a murder spree which, just for good measure, included medical experimentation on human beings. They were Frankenstein monsters, thrown together in hell's kitchen, a witches brew of every diabolical fantasy that began ever so improbably, to some, ever so innocently, to others, with a bite from an apple. Death's door was open for business. It was a door that led Bouhler and Mengele to Auschwitz. There, they practiced their "black arts" with less pity than the taxidermist has for the animal he is mounting for the hunter's trophy case.

CHAPTER EIGHT

THE BEGINNING OF WISDOM

"For wisdom is protection just as money is protection,
But the advantage of knowledge is that
wisdom preserves the lives of its possessors."
Ecclesiastes 7:12

"The fear of the Lord is the beginning of knowledge;
Fools despise wisdom and instruction."
Proverbs 1:7

"So John, Raymoundo and Lucero Valdes are really Ernst Bouhler and his son, Friedrich. Is that right?"

"Yes, Colonel, that is right. They took the 'Monastery Route,' you know, ah, part of Odessa, in 1945. Friedrich Bouhler was about five years old at the time. There is no record of Bouhler's wife traveling with them. They apparently went first to Chile. That's all the records show."

"Well, John, I think I can help with the whereabouts of Bouhler's wife. She was listed as a casualty after an allied bombing raid in Munich. She apparently was visiting her sister. This is a great find John. Thank you. Where would we be without you?"

"Where is Dov now, Colonel?" "He is at our Embassy in Buenos Aires, Daniel. I asked him to stay there, until we could resolve this matter of the Bouhlers."

"What about Lucero Valdes? Do we know that there is such a person in San Carlos de Bariloche?"

"We know he was there, Daniel. Dov will have to confirm that he is still there. John, Father John, you look like a man who knows something, but maybe doesn't want to say. Is that right, Father?"

"You are as perceptive as ever, Colonel. Bouhler is there, Colonel. I am sure of it."

"How can you be so sure, John?"

"It's the code that David broke, or at least mostly broke. Zyklon B. They embedded Zyklon B in the code. They started using Zyklon B at Auschwitz. Surely, Ernst Bouhler... and Mengele... both not only knew about, but used Zyklon B. My guess is that Bouhler bragged about it to his son. And his son thought he was being clever by making it a basis for the code."

"But, John, the code wasn't designed to be broken."

"You're right, Colonel, it wasn't. Codes conceal, but this code couldn't conceal a malignant, fetishistic obsession. I have a feeling that Bouhler thought that, someday, the code would be broken. So, he thought, great! The Jews will break the code, but I will have the last laugh."

"John, you are a man of G-d. How is it that you understand evil so well?"

"They know about G-d in the depths of hell too, Colonel. They believe they will overcome Him. I understand that, Colonel. I understand that. Oh, and Colonel, please tell Dov to be careful. I know that sounds ridiculous. Priests normally counsel forgiveness and penance, not worldly caution. But I believe Bouhler is an extremely dangerous, and clever, man. Dov should keep a very low profile. Tell him to spend several weeks putting together the basics about Bouhler. Then, let's reconvene."

"Are you a spymaster now, my dear Father Broderick? Is that what you've become?" We all laughed a little nervously. John's warning about Bouhler was, in some sense, unnecessary, but coming from John, it was chilling.

"Colonel, gentlemen, my value to G-d, and the state of Israel, is not in operations. I hear things, people tell me things, that's all. Forgive me, but this is different. Ernst Bouhler drafted his son in the family business. I have no doubt the Bouhlers had Mengele as a house guest. He did pass through San Carlos de Bariloche, didn't he, Colonel? Mengele, I mean."

"Yes, he did, John, yes, he did."

"Tell Dov to expect a man who is polite to a fault, passive, even obsequious, in his manner. He will have no close friends, only perhaps an occasional female companion. He will be well liked. No one will say a bad word about him. He cleverly hides in plain sight. He suppresses a barbarism, a bestial nature, that is just barely below a benign surface. I suspect he satisfies his dark impulses by lapsing into fantasies about the screams of his potential victims. Up to now, he has probably never killed another human being. Rest assured, G-d has given him over to his own debasement. He is no longer human, in the way that we understand it. He is a beast of the field, more cunning than any other beast. Yes, Colonel, tell Dov to be especially careful."

We were all speechless. My impulse was to break the tension with a witty remark. But I couldn't get my wits about me.

After that sort of monologue, I should have broken out those two goofy seagulls, Gertrude and Heathcliff, who were so popular among my "nerdy" colleagues at Northwestern. Someone had to say something. So, I did. "John, you seem so sure about this?" What else could I say?

"Isaac, I know this is out of character. But, think about it. We should all be aware of what we are dealing with. I can't get it out of my head that he consciously, and for his own amusement, used

Zyklon B as a basis for their code. That adds up to a little more than a couple of kids catching butterflies for their collection."

"Your instincts have never failed us, John. I am sure they won't now. I will scrupulously relate all of your concerns to Dov. You have my word on that."

"Thank you, Colonel."

"I must go, John. I need to contact Dov."

"I have to go too, John. Thank you. G-d bless you." said Daniel.

So, Colonel Stern and Daniel were off. John and I pulled out a couple of comfortable chairs that had been tucked away among the desks. The upholstery on both chairs had frayed a bit over the years. But they were more comfortable than ever. It felt good to sit with John. We did not only meet during troubles. There were times when John came by to "talk about nothing," as he would say. Those were some of the best of times. The trouble would always come. And now I had to ask John about his soliloquy concerning Friedrich Bouhler (Lucero Valdes). I had never heard John speak that way about anyone, or anything. I had the feeling he sensed something from the moment Ethan was born, perhaps from the moment of David's famous doodle in Paleo-Hebrew. And, as usual, he beat me to punch.

"You are trying to figure out whether I have lost my mind. This Bouhler thing. I haven't lost my mind, Isaac. Bouhler is Bouhler."

"I am especially worried, John, because I know in my heart that you are probably right. I just had never heard you speak that way before. What did you mean that G-d had given him over to his own debasement? Is that the way you said it, Father, you know, 'his own debasement?'"

"You're right, Isaac, I was speaking more from the priestly side of things." He smiled. I didn't refer to him as Father, often. We chuckled for a moment. "Yes, Father Broderick, I would like to know about this." Another chuckle, and then John turned serious.

"The G-d of Abraham, Isaac, and Jacob is longsuffering. We cannot possibly comprehend His capacity for love, for forgiveness, for righteousness, and for all the qualities that make life worth living. Isaac, it sounds strange but He makes life, well, livable. G-d will suffer fools and foolishness, but His long-sufferance is not open ended. And I am not really talking about Sodom and Gomorrah. Clearly, Sodom and Gomorrah passed a certain point of no return in G-d's moral reckoning."

"But what about an individual who is left living? And G-d simply walks away? They are turned over to a certain state of nature without grace, and without the ability to reclaim their natural relationship with G-d. After all, we were created in His image. We have an inherent relationship to G-d's divine nature. I would argue, Isaac, that when someone is turned over to his own debasement, that individual is no longer human, in the sense of Creation."

"What is someone in that state, John?"

"They are still alive, Isaac. But they are only separated from the other creatures of the earth because they are not solely driven by instinct. Evil permeates their consciousness, Isaac. Evil drives their being."

"So, that is what you think Bouhler has become?" "Yes, Isaac, like father, like son. He had a choice. And, I believe, he made that choice. When G-d walks away, Bouhler is what is left. Dov must be careful. Bouhler is tickled by the use of pesticides on human beings. Human beings, Isaac. He would kill Dov with no more consideration than swatting a fly. Yes, Isaac, when G-d walks away…"

"So I gave them over
to their own stubborn heart,
To walk in their own counsels."
Psalm 81:12

"The smelter refines in vain,
For the wicked are not drawn off.
People will call them rejected silver,

Because the Lord has rejected them."
Jeremiah 6: 29-30

"And, in Genesis, Isaac, G-d said it very powerfully…"

"My Spirit shall not strive with man forever,
for he is indeed flesh..."
Genesis 6:3

"That was a kind of warning, issued before the flood, but there will be no more floods. It's an ominous warning, Isaac. There is a point of no return."

"I want to study the verses, John. I need to think about this. I have no doubt you are correct. But, to think people like that are walking among us. We know they are, of course. My wife knows better than anybody, I guess."

"How is she, Isaac? She has worked at Yad Vashem, all this time. Remarkable."

"Yes, she is, John. A blessing to me. A blessing to the children who were snuffed out by men like Bouhler."

"We need to find out what Bouhler is up to, Isaac. The sooner, the better." "I have confidence that Dov will have something for us in due time, John. I could see it on Colonel Stern's face. You made quite an impression on him!"

"I have my moments, Isaac. This is a moment I could do without." He was shaking his head as he left the lab that day. The bear of a man suddenly lost a little of his usual vigor.

I forgot to ask John about the knowledge of G-d in the depths of hell. I think I understood that a little better than the limit of G-d's long-sufferance. I would wait until our priest recovered somewhat from having to think about a creature who lived in San Carlos de Bariloche, Argentina. He was worried. I didn't want to mention it, but I think what worried him was that this "creature" had an interest in

Ethan. I was sure he thought that Bouhler was behind any monitoring of Ethan. Bouhler wanted to know about a boy who lived in the Midwest. I thought Ethan was exceptional. I am sure that Rachel and David thought Ethan was exceptional. But we had a certain bias. A normal bias. Friedrich Bouhler was what John said he was. So, I didn't ask John why Bouhler was curious about Ethan. I was afraid of the answer.

Three years into the 90's, the first attack on the World Trade Center had begun the plan to decouple the United States from Israel. The attackers believed they could convince the American public that the costs of supporting Israel were just too high. And, if the United States was turning away from the G-d of Abraham, Isaac and Jacob, not to mention liberty and free enterprise as a basis for its civilization, then it would become a hulking, pitiful ex-superpower adrift, on its way to historical oblivion.

Ultimately, the plan was to destroy any remnant of the Jewish people. But, first things, first.

The first attack against the World Trade Center was an attack on the American homeland. It was not successful. So, the attacks shifted to American military targets abroad, or the closest thing to actual American "soil" abroad, American Embassies. Thus the attack on a housing complex being used as quarters for American military in Saudi Arabia. It became known as the Khobar Towers bombing. Next, the terrorists turned to the American Embassies in Kenya and Tanzania.

Grandiosity characterized the first attack on the World Trade Center. The terrorists took a step back from grandiosity with their attack on a housing complex for American military personnel. It was no less deadly for the families of the American Air Force personnel killed by the thunderous blast at Khobar Towers. Iran, its leadership fully under the spell of Shia Islam's eschatology, was responsible for the murders at Khobar Towers. Not to be outdone, Sunni Islamists carried out the bombings of the American Embassies in Kenya and Tanzania. They were not finished.

Grandiosity that includes homicidal fantasies puts everyone at risk who is on the other side of the maniacal divide. Only a maniac kills in G-d's name. A charismatic maniac is even more pernicious. The next attack was on one of the United States most sophisticated warships.

It was a warship whose technology was far beyond anything that was indigenous to the countries from which the terrorists sprouted. They approached this floating marvel of American ingenuity with deceptive modesty. They were in a small boat more suited to a frolic in some protected bay than a maneuver in the port of Aden in Yemen. The USS Cole was refueling. It was after 11 a.m. in the morning. The occupants of the small craft were intent on committing suicide in service of homicide. Just to make sure, they packed in enough explosives to blow themselves to smithereens. Blowing themselves to kingdom come was not in the offing. They were headed in a darker direction.

The explosion gashed the port side of the Cole. The sailors on board the ship had expected to live out their dreams, sailing the seven seas in service of their country. Now, for some, the wind that was to be in the "sails" would be powering angel's wings instead. They would surely relish the company of angels, but for the time being, they would have been fine in the company of their mates aboard the Cole. The terrorists succeeded, but only in part. They dreamed of homicide and paradise. They murdered 17 brave sailors. Paradise was not their reward.

The assault on the USS Cole actually occurred during the end of the year in which the new millennium was celebrated. But it was really part of a continuum of attacks that began with the first attempt by Islamic terrorists to collapse the World Trade Center. The World Trade Center, Khobar Towers, the US Embassies in Kenya and Tanzania, and the USS Cole. They were battlefields. They were battlefields that weren't regarded as battlefields at all. They were transformed in the imagination of the American administration into crime scenes. As such, crime scenes were thought to require the man with a badge, rather than "The Spy Who Loved Me." To be sure, the muted response from the American President was sometimes couched in tough language. When the tough language languished, and faded, as it always did, the couch assumed, well, a more couch-like pose. It comfortably absorbed the shavings from late-night pizzas, and the whimpering sounds from ingénues whose policy positions weren't the positions de rigueur.

Given their charge, the men and women with a badge performed brilliantly. They adduced evidence with one-way signs pointing to a person of interest, or persons of interest. It would be just enough to raise a posse to lasso an outlaw, drag him into court, and let the jury and judge do the rest. Courtrooms were so neat, and orderly. They were almost sublime. The outlaw's lawyer would counsel him to wear respectful clothes, hoping for a credulous jury susceptible to sartorial blandishments. And if the outlaw would misbehave, he would be dragooned and carted away from the courtroom. If necessary, the court would conduct its business without him. Sublime, indeed.

Along the way, there were exceptional prosecutors who saw that, embedded in the criminal roadmap leading to the Cole and other mass murders, were far more than one-way signs. What they saw was an intricate underworld with real world implications. It was an underworld that was complicated, and a little convoluted, dark, but still intelligible, in the same way disembodied puzzle pieces would eventually render a coherent image, a coherent but gothic image. This underworld was impelled by far more than the usual criminal motives which explained all of the crimes of the century, including the Lindbergh kidnapping, or even the assassination of a charismatic young American President in broad daylight.

The usual criminal motives did not apply because this underworld seemed to take itself out of the world of creation, and beyond.

After G-d's command not to eat from the tree of the knowledge of good and evil, G-d's next command was marriage:

"Therefore a man shall leave his father and mother
and be joined to his wife, and they shall become one flesh."
Genesis 2:24

Marriage was foundational to humanity's place in creation. Looked at from a safe distance, life inside creation was a wondrous and awe inspiring spectacle. That was the intention. The majesty of creation was its inherent gravitational force. It was a mighty tug, planted there by G-d himself, pulling us in His direction. The danger was that if G-d was everywhere, then perhaps He was nowhere. Creation was it. Make of it what you will. Human life, the flesh inside creation would become like all other life. And it would invariably take on the actual characteristics of life inside creation, from close range, the way it is actually lived. It's imperative is survival. Survival is the first rule, and the last. There is no moral architecture.

But His is a saving grace. And marriage was foundational to His moral architecture. Marriage was sanctified because life itself was sanctified. And life would spring from marriage. Life in the natural without G-d is a cauldron. It stews and boils. It lives. That is the most that can be said of it. His plan was not an amorphous architecture leading nowhere. His plan was that we should dwell with Him. Marriage would contain and channel our passions, yes, even our lust. It would mean that we would not be alone to seek the deeper meanings of G-d's intentions: a G-dly quality of righteousness, love, mercy, forgiveness and charity. And that was just the beginning. It would be a long week. Rabbi Judah Ben Samuel said that G-d's "week" would last six thousand years. Thankfully, the end of the week would bring the Sabbath rest.

And for those who killed in G-d's name, there seemed to be only restlessness. That different worldly restlessness made their motives, ah, strange. When courts are asked to administer justice, or pick up the broken pieces of broken lives, the usual motives obtain: jealousy, lust, power, and greed.

What exactly does a courtroom do with lust as an eternal reward? In the imagination of the Islamists, especially suicide bombers, they found support in their sacred texts for carnal rewards in heaven. In fact, there appears to be a hierarchy of heavenly carnal rewards. But what is it that children are actually being taught?

Hamas would become the tip of the spear for the Muslim Brotherhood in Gaza. Beginning in kindergarten, Hamas educates the children in their schools that a martyr is given virgins in paradise. An eleven-year old boy spoke to his class: "I will make my body a bomb that will blast the flesh of Zionists, the sons of pigs and monkeys... I will tear their bodies into little pieces and will cause them more pain than they will ever know." His classmates shouted in response, "Allah Akhbar (G-d is Great)," and his teacher shouted, "May the virgins give you pleasure." A 16-year-old Hamas youth leader in a Gaza refugee camp explained, "Most boys can't stop thinking about the virgins."

Lustful indeed! All those virgins surely transcend ordinary lust. Al Capone's lust led him to syphilitic death. Even Capone's debased mind wouldn't have come up with an equation in which suicide plus homicide equals a carnal reward in heaven. And an eternal carnal reward at that! Under such circumstances, Capone would have become a bible thumping evangelist. Not exactly what the G-d of Abraham, Isaac, and Jacob had in mind.

Jealousy, rivalry, sibling rivalry as Father John characterized it, was closer to the mark. But jealousy of Biblical proportions, literally Biblical proportions, far transcended the jealousy found in civilian courts. This was jealousy that had to be adjudicated in celestial courts. Yet, one party to the conflict would never find satisfaction. The totality of considerations that made Isaac and Jacob (Israel) the children of promise were only known to the mind of G-d. And while the brothers of Isaac and Jacob, Ishmael and Esau, were honored by

G-d in a certain sense, the fact remains that the promise made to Abraham never changed.

The Islamists weren't disinterested in money, or the comforts and gilded playthings that money could buy. Our operation in Beirut took us to neighborhoods with all the finery a terrorist, or anyone else, could possibly want. But nothing could match the priceless accoutrements that decorated the celestial harems promised to suicide bombers and the armies of the Jihad. They included a "dome decorated with pearls, aquamarine, and ruby, as wide as the distance from Al-Jabiyya to Sana'a.'" There isn't enough money in the world to buy that kind of sybaritic indulgence. No, even the gushers of oil money were too paltry to provide sufficient coin of the realm for the realm the Islamists coveted.

The 90's were screaming that America was a target. But America chose a subdued reaction. The terrorists were encouraged by the reaction to their barbarism. They were all too happy to be relegated to the machinery of law enforcement. They were even happier to nonchalantly dodge cruise missiles airmailed to nowhere.

There was more than one reason for the tepid American response. By the time 17 sailors were murdered aboard the USS Cole, many inside the "intelligence community" knew what the American President and his administration would not admit: Islamic terrorism was an international phenomenon. Its ancient hatreds were codified in the 7th century, and its ferocity launched it all the way into modernity. The Islamists weren't adverse to using all the technology that modernity had to offer. Technology was their tool, not the source of the power that drove them. The source of that power lurked in the shadows cast by Abraham. Along with an obsession that began in the garden.

The President in the 90's subscribed to the Oslo delusion. It was a subscription he should have cancelled. He would have found a better match for his natural inclinations on the pages of Cosmo.

Oslo was a delusion, all of apiece. It was a piece of land for peace. As Father John would point out, Oslo was something that the descendants of Ishmael and Esau would just never brook. They couldn't. They were after something no title to land, even all the land, could ever confer. They wanted G-d's imprimatur. They wanted to be the "children of promise." G-d's promise. They wanted to replace their brothers in G-d's eternal trifecta, for He is the G-d of Abraham, Isaac and Jacob.

The President of the 90's famously asked his political guru where he would rank among his peers. It was greatness he desired. But he was a man who was led astray by his desires. And greatness is not the distillation of desire.

True greatness is the coin of a different realm. It isn't minted in the parlors where the bloviations of the self-anointed are peddled as if they have all the nuance and grace of a catspaw gently kissing a cove in an alpine lake. Greatness is not a parlor game. The habitués of the parlors sneer at greatness. They especially sneer at true greatness and then they glare, as if their long condescending stare somehow restores their "natural" superiority.

Man desires greatness. But G-d desires humility. Great men look in the mirror and are skeptical of their worthiness, but never of G-d's grace.

"Whoever Runs After Greatness,
Greatness Flees From Him;
And Whoever Flees From Greatness,
Greatness Runs After Him."
Erub 13b

Kings and Presidents: There have been greats. No greater than David. As a boy, he slew a giant, believing deep in his soul that the scales would be balanced that day, proclaiming to the giant that... "the battle is the Lord's, and He will give you into our hands." After that, David's flesh wavered from time to time, but not his faith, and not his humility. David became an obsession of King Saul. It was an obsession steeped in jealousy and pride. King Saul lost his way, lost the confidence of G-d, and Israel found a King. King David. There is no city of Saul. Only the City of David. Solomon, the son of David, said it well:

> *"The ear that hears the rebukes of life*
> *Will abide among the wise.*
> *He who disdains instruction despises his own soul,*
> *But he who heeds rebuke gets understanding.*
> *The fear of the Lord is the instruction of wisdom,*
> *And before honor is humility."*
> *Proverbs 15:31-33*

And that wasn't all. Abraham and David. Of these two men, one slew giants, but, in the arc of history, both dwarfed a thousand giants stood end to end, or a thousand million giants stood end to end. The promises made to Abraham and David were eternal, and breathtaking. To Abraham it was said:

> *"...And in you all the families*
> *of the earth shall be blessed."*
> *Genesis 12:3*

And to David it was said:

> *"And your house and your kingdom*
> *shall be established forever before you.*
> *Your throne shall be established forever."*
> *2 Samuel 7:16*

Abraham and David, men honored by G-d, and men who honored G-d with remarkable humility before G-d, and men. It was as if the strength of Abraham's faith was like an unbreakable tether, tying every human family to the divine intention. After all, Abraham offered his son, the son of promise, Isaac, as a sacrifice to G-d. A sacrifice that, mercifully, G-d counted as righteous, but did not require.

King David was a warrior. Though his heart did not have the blunt edges of a weapon, but the suppleness of poems belonging to heaven, punctuated by the stars in a nighttime sky. He had a servant's heart, with all the tenderness for G-d as the genteel sway of the lilies of the field, warming themselves in the morning sun.

But in his heart also surged the blood of Judah, for he was of the line of Judah. Judah, one of the twelve tribes of Israel. Jacob, the father of Judah, saw his son clearly, and his son's sons, and their sons, as G-d had given him the sight to see. It was Jacob who said to his son Judah:

"You are a lion's cub...
The scepter will not depart from Judah,
nor the ruler's staff from between his feet,
until he to whom it belongs shall come and
the obedience of the nations shall be his."

This was David's inheritance: gallant and graceful service to G-d. Kings, raised to glory by men, commissioned court jesters and other courtly sycophants to sing songs, and weave epic tales, memorializing their reign for posterity. Judah, the fleshly provenance of Kings, and David, an heir to Judah, was raised by G-d.

"Now therefore,
thus shall you say to My servant David,
Thus says the Lord of hosts:
"I took you from the sheepfold, from following the sheep,
to be ruler over My people, over Israel.
And I have been with you wherever you have gone,

and have cut off all your enemies from before you,
and have made you a great name,
like the name of the great men who are on the earth."
2 Samuel 7: 8-9

King David would sit playing the harp, as if he were in the fields again with the shepherds, praying that his music would drift all the way to heaven, and be pleasing to G-d's ears. He would crouch in the breach, lionhearted, facing every rebel, every enemy of G-d, never for a moment doubting the outcome. David's House would be the House of Kings. They would be Kings who had the heart and the imagination to suffer as G-d suffered, after the fall.

In the natural, although regal among men, they were still accountable to G-d and His righteous ways. Perhaps G-d would suffer fools, but His sufferance did not extend to His appointed King. For his indulgences that offended G-d, David lost a child, and brought a plague upon Israel. But David never faltered in his mastery of a servant's heart for G-d. He asked that others not suffer for his sins. They did suffer, but out of that suffering came a perfect confluence that could only come from He who declared the end from the beginning.

King David ended the suffering of Israel by crafting an altar on the threshing floor of Araunah the Jebusite. It was the place where Solomon would build the house of the Lord. It was also the place where Abraham offered his son, Isaac, as a sacrifice. Abraham knew it as the land of Moriah, Mount Moriah. It became a place that had rested in the imagination of G-d, and came to capture the imagination of men. It became the Temple of the Lord on Mount Moriah. It became the Temple Mount.

So, although separated by 1,000 years, Abraham and David became joined on hallowed ground. It was hallowed by G-d, but paid for by the enduring faithfulness of two men that G-d just couldn't do without. Out of one, Abraham, would come a blessing for "all the families of the earth." Out of the other, David, would come Kings, one of whom would command the "obedience of the nations....to a throne that shall be established forever." And those Kings would defend the righteousness of G-d until only His righteousness remained. And that Kingdom would be without end.

It is unlikely that any American President could ever approach King David's favor with G-d. But there were Presidents whose humility may have captured the notice of G-d. And, in their humility, they sought G-d's counsel, and grace. In a great Civil War, a President arose whose humility was rivaled only by his greatness. A greatness that overshadowed most of his successors. That's not quite the way he was viewed by his detractors, and "friends," at the time though. The criticism often bordered on contempt.

He was described variously as "weak, wishy-washy, namby-pamby, imbecile in matter, disgusting in manner, having made us the laughing stock of the whole world." And if that weren't enough, of all things, it was said that "He is evidently a person of very inferior cast of character, wholly unequal to the crisis." And..."His speeches have fallen like a wet blanket here. They put to flight all notions of greatness."

This was to a man who arguably gave the greatest political speech, not in American history, but human history, period. That is, all 270 words of it. It took several minutes to deliver. It took him about two minutes to perfectly describe the meaning of a war that eventually counted 600,000 dead, strewn over 10,000 battlefields.

And in those 270 words, the President reminded his countrymen that the "ground" of a great battle in that war had been "consecrated" by those who had "struggled" there. It was beautifully said. The President knew intuitively that human blood, the blood of those made in the image of G-d, when spilled, affects G-d and all of His creation. How do we know? After Cain slew Abel it was G-d who said, "The voice of your brother's blood cries out to Me from the ground."

But there is the question of consecration. In the human sense, the President had the perfect grace to say that no one could "add or detract" from what "the brave men" did in that battle. The President also had the well-developed spiritual wits to know that the true moral contours of consecration would be decided by G-d. As he said in another speech:

"Both read the same Bible and pray to the same G-d, and each invokes His aid against the other. It may seem strange that any men should dare to ask a just G-d's assistance in wringing their bread from the sweat of other men's faces, but let us judge not, that we be not judged. The prayers of both could not be answered. That of neither has been answered fully. The Almighty has His own purposes."

And after his re-election, when the great Civil War still raged, his words were comforting and wise, almost prophetically wise, as if he spoke from a national pulpit, rather than as President in his Second Inaugural Address.

"Fondly do we hope - fervently do we pray - that this mighty scourge of war may speedily pass away. Yet, if G-d wills that it continue, until all the wealth piled by the bond-man's two hundred and fifty years of unrequited toil shall be sunk, and until every drop of blood drawn with the lash, shall be paid by another drawn with the sword, as was said three thousand years ago, so still it must be said 'the judgments of the Lord, are true and righteous altogether.'"

It was a war that had to have been deeply galling to most Americans. It was a Civil War. It was American against American. A wrong word, or even an intemperate gesture, from an American President might have unleashed a wave of retribution from which the country would never recover. The country stood at the precipice. Truly great men deliver under those circumstances. And his words were the fruit of his humility, and his faith. He comprehended human suffering. And he understood the limits of humanity to act virtuously, except with the hand of G-d firmly on our shoulder. And so he said after the great war:

"With malice toward none, with charity for all, with firmness in the right as G-d gives us to see the right, let us strive on to finish the work

we are in, to bind up the nation's wounds, to care for him who shall have borne the battle and for his widow and his orphan, to do all which may achieve and cherish a just and lasting peace among ourselves and with all nations."

How closely this American President listened to the counsel of G-d.

*"To the Lord our G-d
belong compassion and forgiveness,
for we have rebelled against Him..."*
Daniel 9

*"You shall say before the Lord your G-d,
I have removed the sacred portion from my house,
and also have given it to the Levite and the alien,
the orphan and the widow, according to all Your commandments
which You have commanded me; I have not transgressed
or forgotten any of Your commandments."*
Deuteronomy 26:13

A hundred and twenty years later, the American people were in the midst of a crisis. America had been fitted with a straightjacket. Somehow the American idea was in question. Containment was the settled policy among the policy elites to halt the spread of Soviet communism. Now, containment was being applied to the American people. Hence, the straightjacket. Suddenly, a free people had to be shackled and contained, otherwise the world, and America, would suffer. The angst was everywhere. Absurd questions began to arise. One of them involved the American presidency itself. Was the world now so complicated, that no one person could manage the presidency?

This "small" idea of America was very appealing to America's foes. Iran was in the throes of an Islamic revolution. It was a revolution whose origins were in the 7th century, but its dark impulses really went back to the beginning. Americans certainly knew about presidents and prime ministers. But Iran was now ruled by an Ayatollah. He was the supreme religious leader, and supreme leader, period. What he actually believed about G-d, creation, heaven, and hell, was pooh-poohed by the Grand Poobahs in the American government, and the American elite. But the Ayatollah knew what he believed. He knew that America was the "Great Satan," and Israel was the "Little Satan." His view of the Jewish state, and Jews in general, bore little difference to the architects of the Thousand Year Reich.

Iranians had been playing chess for over a thousand years. It was a game that came to ancient Iran (Persia) from India. Iran's Ayatollah was ready to make his first move against the "Great Satan." He took Americans hostage. They were the Americans working at the American Embassy in Tehran, Iran. The American hostages in Iran became pawns in a game of public humiliation. The American public got the idea. They revolted. They revolted American style, at the polls. They didn't want to play chess, Persian style, anymore.

The Ayatollah was a grand master chess player who met his match. If you don't like the game, change it. The new American President did. He changed the stakes before he assumed office. Now, the game was poker. The Ayatollah had to decide if the new American President was as resolute as he appeared. Was he bluffing? The Ayatollah didn't like the new game. He returned to chess. He did what many grand masters chess players have done: his move was strategic retreat. He would live to fight another day. He released the hostages just minutes after the new American President took the oath of office.

The American President won the day without firing a shot. How fitting. He was an American original. He had that in common with the American President of the great Civil War. Could you fit two American originals into only one presidency? As the second American original would say, "well, yes," you could. As he would say "well, yes," he would slightly tilt his head, with equal parts sincerity and conviction, and a certain timing and grace that was, well, perfect. Well yes, it was.

Two American originals. Two political masters. Two greats. They were American originals because they were impossible in any other country, at any other time. They were men who understood that the American idea could flourish in small, or frontier, towns. That was the genius of the American idea.

The world had decreed that as boys, these American originals were from such small towns that their fates had been sealed. The world saw them as blended into a landscape that was mottled and untidy, even primitive. According to Hoyle, their lives not only suffered a dearth of stentorian urban acoustics and faux energy, but the orderly orderliness of the urban, and the urbane. As boys, the finely tuned ears of these nascent American originals had deflected the long, ponderous wavelengths of the sounds that had caused so many human generations to swoon; as originals, they had correctly perceived that these were not the sounds of crooners crooning, but beasts baying.

The President of the great Civil War was born to a Kentucky frontier that was short on pretensions but high on American high-mindedness. American high-mindedness was gloriously expressed in its political texts, but on the ground it had a deceptively modest look about it. American high-mindedness never morphed into American high-handedness. Men and women confidently went about their daily lives in a manner that had not been pre-ordained by birthright or title. The old world had been left behind. This was a revolution of the spiritual order of things: kings, a self-anointed political class, and all other would-be intercessors, need not apply. Benjamin Franklin's investigations of lightning were the least of it. This was lightning striking twice in the same place, followed by an earthquake.

"We hold these truths to be self-evident, that all men are created equal, that they are endowed by their Creator with certain unalienable Rights, that among these are Life, Liberty and the pursuit of Happiness. That to secure these rights, Governments are instituted

among Men, deriving their just powers from the consent of the governed..."

It was political revelation. In G-d's economy, it was some distance from Joseph, the Exodus, and the Prophet Daniel. But, G-d finally had something to smile about. He put His hand on America's founders, and they just didn't brush it away. America's founders embraced His divine claim *on* humanity; and the implied attributes of a divine resonance *in* humanity. Life and the exercise of free will itself were divine gifts. Government wasn't a sort of national repository for all of our hopes and dreams, not to mention the moral order of things. Government was loaned power, temporarily loaned power, to protect the unalienable rights of a free people to pursue their own aspirations. No wonder the old world looked contemptuously at America. They bitterly resented a people and a nation that struck at the heart of their comfy political order. And they didn't much appreciate the fact that they just couldn't compete with a free people.

But there was a problem. Some internal contradictions can be reconciled, although with varying degrees of comfort. Life is a gift, and a blessing, but we live in the world, after the fall. That is not a carefree proposition, to say the least. Perhaps we never fully reconcile it. Perhaps we can't. But we inherently understand that it begins our journey back to the divine family. It is our starting point.

America's internal contradiction required an American original. It required a political master who was destined for greatness. Political masters must first master communication in the times in which they live. They communicate to establish a reservoir of trust, to persuade, and to move people to follow their lead.

In the modern sense, pictures are a sort of political shorthand. And why not? If a picture is worth a thousand words, politicians and their "handlers" would prefer a picture or two, a carefully choreographed picture or two, to create the desired narrative. The spoken and written word had to dominate during the great Civil War. It was an era when the transcontinental railroad was high order technology. Argument itself was high drama. Debate was high drama.

As a candidate for the U.S. Senate from Illinois, the President during the great Civil War had been famously involved in a series of debates that drew a crowd of 12,000 on the first day. The topic was slavery. It must have been compelling. On the second day, even more spectators showed up. It wasn't easy, but come they did. They came on foot, on horseback, by horse and buggy, and by train. He lost his bid for the Senate. But in the meantime, there had been widespread coverage of the debate in newspapers across America. He subsequently edited the texts of the debates and had them published in a book. As a result, he was nominated and elected as the 16th President of the United States.

The mothers of these American originals had hearts, supple enough to comprehend the whispers of heavens, and voices true enough, that G-d had taken up residence inside the hearts of their sons. The whispers in heaven traveled in gossamer time: they traveled at the speed of truth; the speed of light, for the sake of illumination, would catch up later. His truth was marching on.

The President during the great Civil War properly noted an irreconcilable internal contradiction of the American idea. It was more than that. It was a deal breaker. He learned it at the knee of his beloved mother in their old Kentucky home. She continually recited Biblical passages to her children, and conveyed a fundamental decency that the President never forgot. He said something about his mother that she was never able to hear because of her early, and untimely death: "G-d bless my mother; all that I am or ever hope to be I owe to her." And so his passion for G-d's righteousness led him to an inescapable conclusion: the American nation could not "endure, permanently, half slave and half free." How could it? American life, as it was lived, was on a collision course with an American article of faith: "all men are created equal."

And so, a monstrous bloodletting ensued. And the trail of blood led to the White House door. Shortly after his reelection, an assassin's bullet ended his Presidency. But not before he saw the Civil War end. The American nation was restored. His faith, and his faith in the American people, were vindicated. His mother would have been proud. She would not have been surprised. There wasn't a poverty of the American idea, and the G-d who blessed it, in the humble log cabin from which her son came. His modesty, and his love of divine virtue, shone through. His service to G-d did not go unnoticed. She would have liked that.

By the time of the great Civil War, the Kentucky frontier, the President's birthplace, had given way to a continental nation. It was "sea to shining sea." It afforded the young nation literal oceans of protection from its potential adversaries. The coasts, east and west, would become connected by a transcontinental railroad and the telegraph. It was a nation that was connected east to west. The west became bound up into the American idea. Yes, it was both a direction and a destination. But somehow, even when populated, even when settled, if you will, the American west and the American idea became fused into an American imagination. It was not an imaginary imagination. It almost seemed that, in the American imagination, reverie became reality. The man from the Kentucky frontier went from hardscrabble and roughhewn to become an American original, a political master, and an American great. He was unfettered by the rules and rulers of the old world, but tempered by the eternal reality of divine righteousness. His all too improbable, even preposterous, personal story became the American story. And so, the American imagination wrote an American story that seemed unstoppable. The nations had never seen anything like it.

As it turns out, the fulfillment of the American story, generation to generation, depends on an American consensus. If you change the American story, you undermine the consensus. Liberty itself comes into question. A hundred and twenty years after the great Civil War, there was a change in America. A growing and potent cadre of Americans broke with the founders. For 80 years, they had challenged a central American idea: limited government. They began an all-out assault on constitutional government. They dismissed the founders as quaint, and outdated. The American miracle wasn't enough. In the simplest terms, they objected to modesty and restraint.

Another aspect of their immodesty was a seeming contempt for their fellow man. They knew better. They should be allowed to have extra constitutional power because America's civil society was full of dimwits and dopes.

It was amusing, but heartbreaking. This self-referential and growing insurgency was taken in by its own pretensions to intellectual and moral superiority, but in reality it was the oldest of tales. They weren't fond of anything that did not reek of the academy, so it was probably useless to point them to the fact that they were heirs to a very old conceit. A very, very, old conceit.

> *"That which has been is what will be,*
> *That which is done is what will be done,*
> *And there is nothing new under the sun."*
> *Ecclesiastes 1:9*

Yes, the attack on the American idea was "nothing new under the sun." It began with Nimrod. His name was interpreted as "he who made all the people rebellious against G-d." Nimrod was described in Genesis as "a mighty hunter before the Lord." His prowess as a hunter was derived from a possession that belonged to creation itself. That possession was the very coats of skin, worn by Adam and Eve, made for them by the G-d of Abraham, Isaac and Jacob. Noah had stowed the coats in the ark. The coats were stolen by Nimrod's grandfather, Ham, and were later given to Nimrod. Nimrod was infatuated with the power of the coats. They made him a successful hunter of beasts, and men. He was the first to make war on other peoples. He didn't bother to mention to his followers that the source of this power was one of history's grandest of heists.

Nimrod traded a modest demonstration of the power of G-d for the glory of men. Of course, the glory of Nimrod was his most compelling delusion. And so, the world's first dictator was loosed on the earth. Like all the dictators to follow him, Nimrod could not tolerate any form of dissent. He became obsessed with Abraham, and the G-d of Abraham.

Nimrod convinced his followers to build a tower that would reach to the heavens. His intention was to strike down the G-d of Abraham. Nimrod's dream was dashed when G-d confused the languages of the earth. Humanity became scattered according to their particular language, no longer able to understand one another. Nimrod's tower became a "Tower of Babel."

Nimrod's fall from grace was compounded by his recruitment of others to his cause. But why follow Nimrod at all? They came under the spell of Nimrod's conceit. Nimrod's conceit was that heaven is province of man, not G-d. Nimrod's conceit was begetting utopia by the hands of men. Nimrod and his followers wanted to glorify man's power and ruler-ship over all the world. He and his followers wanted to "make a name for ourselves, lest we be scattered abroad the face of the whole earth."

Nimrod's followers did not want to "fill the earth," as G-d had commanded them after the flood. That was bad enough, but they failed to comprehend the full extent of their enslavement. To reach heaven, they made bricks, which they baked "thoroughly." They used "brick for stone," and "asphalt for mortar." Nimrod wanted "bricks" to build a tower as a monument to himself, and as a means of dethroning G-d from heaven. But G-d's desire is for stones:

> *"And if you make Me an altar of stone,*
> *you shall not build it of hewn stone;*
> *for if you use your tool on it,*

you have profaned it."
Exodus 20:25

Before the Exodus, the children of Israel were enslaved in Egypt, commanded by Pharaoh to build his country with bricks. Bricks are the implements of slavery. Dictators demand conformity, if not uniformity among their human subjects. G-d desires individuals. In His creation, no two stones are alike.

Nimrod, like all other dictators who came after him, unified his followers by a utopian vision. The twentieth century heirs to Nimrod found their identity in every "ism" known to man, cursing every angel known to heaven. The foundational "isms" were always solipsism and narcissism, which climbed a ladder of benighted adornment to Dante's circles of hell. These rings of hell all had one thing in common: they were really a hybridized circular firing squad and game of Russian roulette, taking historical turns among progressivism, Marxism, socialism, and fascism. It was an all too earthly materialism, replacing G-d and leaving human subjects in His wake.

This infernal merry-go-round of interchangeable and rotating "isms" appeared in a carnival-like atmosphere. It was complete with the "Carny" con man enticing all to "step right up," promising wonders never seen before, once in a lifetime "thrills and chills," ending at the "Fun House," where the joke is on you. The carnival campus invariably included the "House of Horrors," a trump card in what was really a "House of Cards." For the most part, the "isms," and their illusions died in mass graves. The Joker was wild.

Nimrodism was a habit of mind that flourished in the poverty of the spirit. It found its American voice in the progressive era of the twentieth century. It was such a discordant dialect inside the language of the American idea, that it had to disguise itself. And disguise itself it did.

Americans wouldn't just bristle at being transformed into bricks; they would revolt. The progressives had to "massage" the language of politics. The progressive brand of Nimrodism had to slither and in-sinuate itself into the American psyche, cunningly seducing its victims with the poetry of the American idea, but never wavering from the mundane prose of its underlying creed.

The progressive creed burned with the searing idea of what "bricks" could accomplish, if only they would work in unison, build-ing the perfect structure with a pristine edifice that would render heaven, gaga with envy. To assure ratification of the proposed Con-stitution, America's founders were compelled to insert a Bill of Rights, which many believed would provide further protection of the individual from the power of government.

So, during an economic crisis, the Great Depression, the American President, who felt constrained by the constitution, proposed a Second Bill of Rights. It was clever. Nimrod would have been proud. The Second Bill of Rights would, in effect, repeal the First Bill of Rights. Why? Because to implement the Second Bill of Rights, it would have required such a vast expansion of government power that the First Bill of Rights would have been nullified. The Second Bill of Rights never became law. But its language became part of the American political discourse. So, the Second Bill of Rights was passed, piecemeal. Clever, indeed.

Nimrodism was the original liberation theology. It liberated theol-ogy from G-d, and replaced it with the interminable joy of human indulgence. It was human "thrill-ology," inside utopia. with all the tidiness of perfectly sized, and perfectly placed, bricks. And it ended up far more than a stone's throw from G-d Himself. In the spiritual, it was the abyss; in the natural, it was a nightmare.

Americans finally had enough. The nightmare had come home, and abroad. At home, America was an economic basket case. Ameri-ca's economic basket was chock full of booby prizes, leftovers from a left fully bewitched by Nimrodism, and a so-called right that was so confused it was betwixt and between. A political class was emerging that was unprecedented in American history. It was a political class that didn't seem to include the American people. It was a political class, a ruling class really, that began to coalesce after decades of America's dalliances with pretenders and fools who whispered sweet nothings in her ear. It was excruciating to grudgingly concede that America had lost her innocence. But had she lost her mind? Not if he could help it.

He understood her better than she understood herself. And he loved her more than she could ever know. He was impossible without her. And with his help, she would learn to trust herself again. She would embrace old glory, and the former things that would make her great again.. Yes, he was impossible without her. He was an American original.

He loved all of the physical manifestations of the American west: its seamless and yawning open space, with all the contrast and drama that left man awestruck, and G-d with a sly smile on His face; that slyness became all too apparent as vast deserts were dotted by a lurid efflorescence. The bloom may have been off the American rose for a growing secular magisterium, but not in the American west, and not for him. He loved the time he spent on his ranch. He described it as his "open cathedral." How appropriate.

G-d found him as a willing soul who had been forged in the American imagination. Small Midwestern towns saw him through to young manhood, but it wasn't "smallness" that he remembered. He was blessed by a mother who had a name, and a gospel, that was straight out of central casting for American originals. Of the handful of greats who ever occupied the White House, and the even fewer number of American originals who took up residence there, one of them had to have a mother named Nell. And so he did.

In the America professed by American Nimrods, Nell and her family were in dire need of the succor of the cloying tendrils of the welfare state. They were hit hard by an unrelenting economic Depression. Her husband, Jack, was said to have been an alcoholic. But yet, Nell taught her children to dream, and to expect those dreams to come true. She taught them that G-d had a plan for them. And, in spite of all of the hardship, she taught them compassion and generosity. She visited prisoners, poorhouse inmates, and hospital patients. As an Irish American, her husband had known what it was like to suffer discrimination. He felt strongly about it. So strongly that on one occasion when he was out of town selling shoes, he spent the night in his car in the bitter cold of a winter blizzard, rather than stay at the only hotel in town, which refused to serve Jewish customers.

Nell's son had the physical grace of Fred Astaire, but his dance with history stepped far beyond Astaire's beautifully choreographed insouciance. He never spoke autobiographically although, in one of the most remarkable political speeches in American political history, he used a phrase that would come to characterize his presidency: "Rendezvous with Destiny." In the dance with "destiny" that became his presidency, he led, and history followed.

Progressivism was stopped cold, and began to be reversed. It almost seemed as if history was in a sort of suspended animation. For Joshua, G-d stopped the sun in its tracks, and lengthened the day; for the President who loved the west so much, G-d said..."Whoaaaaaaa"... to a history that was galloping away, and in the process trampling on His endowment of unalienable rights, not to mention His blessings, which became the American dream. Nell's boy had grown into a man of elegance and grace, whose words soared after they blazed a path that he, his fellow Americans, and a recalcitrant world would follow.

His words found a home in the mighty, and the modest alike. The mighty always ended at the same intersection: it was the intersection of awe, and just how did he do that? His words and his style found a deeper resonance in the modest. They were modest in manner, but their hearts belonged to the American imagination. He was an American original, but like the American original from the Kentucky frontier, he was also a political master. They both had an uncanny common touch. It was political mastery that defied explanation. It was soigné, Sigma Pi, Semper fi, and Saturday nights at the drive-in. The popcorn was on him.

Progressives reacted to their worst nightmare in typical fashion: contempt, more contempt, and furtive contempt. Why would they do otherwise? Progressives had a monopoly on the culture and all its mouthpieces. Their mouthy echo chambers included film, theatre, lecture halls in academia, and all manner of punditry, including a masquerade party that was known as the nightly news. And oh, did they mouth off: he was an "affable dunce," "simplistic," "lucky," surrounded by crafty "handlers," and all that after he launched his second term with a landslide victory in which he won 49 out of 50 states. The state he lost was his opponent's home state, where the margin of difference was a whopping 0.18%. Not bad. Frankly, it was astonishing.

And what was more astonishing? By the end of his second term, he had translated his preternatural political feats into stunning accomplishments for the American people, and the world. In fact, his political feats were death defying. Like the first American original, an assassin's bullet found its mark. He was close to death, a fact never fully explained to the American people until after his presidency.

Close wasn't close enough for those who were the enemies of freedom, and the enemies of one nation under G-d. But it was close enough for him. The public had no idea. He exhibited a special grace under fire: a grace with a bullet one inch from his heart, after it punctured his lung. He walked on his own power to an emergency room reception area, before he collapsed. On his way to surgery, he didn't miss an opportunity to tell the doctors, "I hope you're all Republicans," and then say to his wife, "Honey, I forgot to duck." His reassuring remarks seemed to cause an entire nation to smile, coast to coast. Along with the smile, his fellow citizens were shaking their heads in a kind of approving disbelief. He had put a bounce in the step of a limping, and dispirited country.

American originals who are political masters leave a legacy. They become American greats. It is an enduring legacy. But Nimrod had planters aplenty in all the generations of man. They planted and planted. In America, Nimrod found his "harvest" in the early part of the twentieth century. Nimrod's American "harvest," progressivism, found devotees among presidents, supreme court justices, and both political parties. The first American original would have been shocked. Less than 40 years after he delivered a political speech for the ages, in which he promised the dead on a great battlefield that they "shall not have died in vain," America elected its first progressive president. The shock: he was from the same political party as the first American original. The problem: what would happen to the promise made on that Civil War battlefield? *"that this nation, under G-d (America), shall have a new birth of freedom — and that government of the people, by the people, for the people, shall not perish from the earth."*

By the time of the second American original, Nimrod's "tares" had deep roots in American life. It made his political mastery over progressives all the more mind-boggling. It's not like they didn't try. They were relentless, vindictive, and what can only be described as desperate, bordering on treasonous.

The second American original became part of an historical pairing that roused the heavens, and gave Nimrod's clansman the willies. It was the President and the Pope. The President and Pope really faced a two-headed monster: One head was the Soviet Union, which had all the grace of Jabba the Hut; and all the mercy of the Grim Reaper, riding abreast with Genghis Khan on one side, and Vlad the Impaler on the other. And it *was* merciless for the living. The living became the dead — 30 million and counting. They were not dead to the G-d of Abraham, Isaac, and Jacob. And they were not really living to the walking dead, who sacrificed them as one of Nimrod's "bricks" to the construction of the "New Soviet Man."

And so, the President and the Pope changed the world for the love of G-d. They refused to succumb to the world's purported "complexities," as propounded by those who had long ago sold their souls so that they could luxuriate in the world's gilded shadows. The "worldly" loved the wiles of world, but not more than they loved being wily, laughing all the way to an earthly bank, whose treasures never found their way to the storehouses of heaven.

The Soviet Union collapsed. But it was part of a two-headed monster. The other head survived. It was attempting to gradually impose itself on the American body politic. The President and Pope were not naive. They understood the Western idea, and America in particular, was being assailed. But it was worse than they knew.

The collapse of the Soviet Union, which the President and the Pope so faithfully engineered, gave up more than just its human bondservants. For a brief time in 1991, the Soviet archives were opened. It revealed a narrative that belonged to spy novels, but became history. It was sordid history.

A President was facing reelection. He had been underestimated by progressives. America was experiencing strong economic growth in the wake of the worst economic crisis since the Great Depression. The President's economic program was becoming "golden" for him in his bid for reelection. The progressives thought there might be another way to stop him.

Progressives always hated the President's moral case against the Soviet Union. They certainly objected because of their own infatuation with moral relativism, the very essence of Nimrod and his legacy. But they also began to realize that the President's rhetoric was not only touching the souls of his fellow Americans, but the souls of hundreds of millions of people worldwide. He was enlisting the moon and the stars, and much of humanity, against the tide of human history: tyranny. His voice was strong and clear, and it was his own voice, but it was also an echo from heaven, and from America's founding. It was first heard by human ears on Mount Sinai, and written down by human hands in the Torah and the Talmud. G-d's breath of life included righteous self-governance.

In preparation for the upcoming presidential contest, the progressives dusted off an old narrative. It was tried, but not true. Because the President loved America's west, they decided to portray his policy toward the Soviet Union as "cowboy diplomacy." The President "shot from the hip;" and he wasn't shooting the outlaws, he *was* the outlaw. He was dangerous, and out of control. And his policy would lead to nuclear war, and the end of planet earth. The "cowboy" narrative had some effect. But the progressives decided they needed some help. A helping hand from the apotheosis of Nimrodism: the Soviet Union.

The progressives went to war. It was war, progressive style. They went to the jungle to find their champion. They called him their "lion." It was a term of endearment. It was their term of endearment that failed the test of history, and probity. Their "lion" went to the Soviet Union "with his tail between his legs." He knew the "cowboy" narrative about a popular American President needed some help. He proposed a collaboration.

The lion sent an emissary to the Soviet Union with a secret message for the Soviet leader. The Soviet leader had undergone the usual "makeover" by an all too progressive western media. He was said to have western tastes and proclivities. The media left out some key details of his biography: he had helped crush the revolts by Hungary and Czechoslovakia against Soviet rule. His resume also included a curious, and infamous, professional calling: Chairman of the KGB. He was regarded as probably the most brilliant Soviet leader since Lenin. And the new Soviet ruler was certainly a match for Lenin's trademark ruthlessness. He almost certainly signed off on the attempted assassination of the Pope in 1981. No matter. The reelection of an American original had to be stopped. The lion of American progressivism promised many things.

The basic premise of the collaboration was simple: the Soviets were asked to help American progressives thwart the reelection of the American President. In return, American progressives would provide the Soviets with immediate and ongoing assistance in their negotiations with the American administration. The lion promised to personally visit Moscow and help the Soviets craft effective propaganda. A KGB officer recorded just how comprehensive the American proposal was. His memo stated:

"The main purpose of the meeting... would be to arm Soviet officials with explanations regarding problems of nuclear disarmament so they may be better prepared and more convincing during appearances in the USA. A direct appeal... to the American people will, without a doubt, attract a great deal of attention and interest in the country. If the proposal is recognized as worthy, then... [the Americans] will bring about suitable steps to have representatives of the largest television companies in the USA contact... [the Soviet leader] for an invitation to Moscow for the interviews... The [Americans] underlined the importance that this initiative should be seen as coming from the American side."

As a former Chairman of the KGB, a spymaster's spymaster, the new Soviet leader could only conclude one thing: this was some sort of trick. No American politician in his right mind could possibly propose such a thing. And, the American President's spymaster, the CIA Director, was known to be a cunning, and worthy, adversary. There is no evidence that the Soviet leader ever even responded to the plan. His ruthlessness aside, he probably never recovered from the shock. He died 8 months later.

I was always envious of American school boys and school girls. They had the opportunity to study American history for years and years, into adulthood. I began my study of American history as a graduate physics student at Princeton University. It was all I could do to catch up. I loved America. Of course, I was all too aware, that without America, every Jew on the face of the earth would have been hunted down, and killed. America was bold and daring, and brave. But there was a G-dly reticence about her. America had no interest in conquest. If anything, she memorialized liberation, and then returned home and went about her business.

And so, as I was to learn, American school boys and school girls had many names on the tips of their tongues. One name was Benedict Arnold. He came to personify a treachery that was deeply offensive to the American sensibility. As a general during the American Revolutionary War, he betrayed the men of the Continental Army, and he betrayed his countrymen, who had endured so much in their quest to break loose from British rule. He began his own perfidious collaboration with the British military. He escaped American justice, but not the unceasing scorn of American history books.

So, the lesson of Benedict Arnold was lost on American progressives. Treason is treason. But even Benedict Arnold may have hesitated to help an American enemy, the Soviet Union, whose systematic tyranny, including mass murder and torture, dwarfed anything ever contemplated by the British empire. And that was the point. Something was happening in America. And before he left office, beloved by a majority of Americans, and credited with bringing America back from the brink, an American original had given America fair warning of the destiny of a country, which loved liberty, but did not love G-d.

He began one of his greatest speeches this way:

"I speak, I think I can say, as one who has seen much, who has loved his country, and who's seen it change in many ways."

And he continued:

"A state is nothing more than a reflection of its citizens; the more decent the citizens, the more decent the state. If you practice a religion, whether you're Catholic, Protestant, Jewish, or guided by some other faith, then your private life will be influenced by a sense of moral obligation, and so, too, will your public life. One affects the other. ... We establish no religion in this country, nor will we ever. We command no worship. We mandate no belief. But we poison our society

when we remove its theological underpinnings. We court corruption when we leave it bereft of belief. All are free to believe or not believe; all are free to practice a faith or not. But those who believe must be free to speak of and act on their belief, to apply moral teaching to public questions...

Without G-d, there is no virtue, because there's no prompting of the conscience. Without G-d, we're mired in the material, that flat world that tells us only what the senses perceive. Without G-d, there is a coarsening of the society."

So many words, and deeds, inextricably bound two American originals, two American greats. One American original began to sense, and feel, what the other American original prophesied over 120 years earlier:

"America will never be destroyed from the outside. If we falter and lose our freedoms, it will be because we destroyed ourselves."

And both American originals found an "identical position," in the same bottom line. In the words of the first American original:

"I have been driven many times upon my knees by the overwhelming conviction that I had nowhere else to go. My own wisdom and that of all about me seemed insufficient for that day."

CHAPTER NINE

THE JOURNEY TO EPHRATH

"Then Jacob kissed Rachel, and
lifted up his voice and wept."
Genesis 29:11

The years were hurtling by as if time itself had become unhinged. In the United States, the 90's blared the ecstatic sounds of wealth creation and stock markets that only seemed to know up, but not down. America was enjoying unprecedented wealth creation, a legacy of the second American original. The American political class was also declaring a "peace dividend." Previously, they had snidely dismissed the possibility of America winning the "cold war" against the Soviets. But an American original interceded with his own paraphrase of a sophisticated strategic plan: "we win, they lose." America won. The peace dividend, which resulted from a revised (and declining) military budget, absent the Soviet threat, essentially paid for the cost of the military buildup during the 1980's.

America and the world were reaping a cornucopia. But you reap what you sow. An American President, an American original, had sowed with liberty. It was political liberty, economic liberty, and a certain individual liberty, which was only fully known by the mind of G-d, who cherished unhewn stones, not identical bricks.

So, why was I so worried? And why did I become more worried as we entered the years of the new millennium. The American political class was dumbstruck by an American original, an American great, whom they regarded as a political master. How dumb could they be? Political masters are a verdict of history. They are made in the crucible of public and elite opinion. And as if that sort of blistering scrutiny is not enough, it is history itself that takes over and renders the final judgment. The first America original became regarded as a political master after he won a great Civil War, ended slavery, and gave his nation a "new birth of freedom," not to mention a new hope for all the world. The second American original assumed the presidency when his country was in unprecedented decline. It was unprecedented because it was so sweeping. America had become an enfeebled superpower, with an enfeebled economy to match. The second American original led his country to defeat the Soviet Union without firing a shot; and supercharged economic growth. Just for good measure, he left the world, and especially Israel, one other gift: he made the twentieth century the American century. It was the work of a political master. In retrospect.

It was predictable that American progressives would be lying in wait, stalking America, waiting for their opportunity to pounce, and resume their quest to gradually rip the American idea to shreds. And so they did. They did not have to wait long. Why? The problem was in the second American original's own backyard. It was his own political party. They simply didn't get the memo. Frankly, they didn't "get him." In all likelihood, it was worse. They didn't actually believe his foundational principles; foundational principles that began with the founders themselves: individual liberty and limited government. And then there was the foundational principle that was the sine qua non of America. It was Latin that had to be translated by a Frenchman: *"if America ever ceases to be good, America will cease to be great."*

I couldn't blame America for wanting to catch its breath in the 90's. The cold war was long and brutal. It had many bridges to cross, and even though the tolls were sometimes "paid in full," they still kept coming. But, the American home is unique in all the world. There was the untold sacrifice and bravery that announced itself with a pensive knock on the door, a door that hadn't been strong enough to contain the brave hearts within.

Now the war against Israel became a war against the United States. It was a war that came far too soon after the end of the cold war. But come it did. This war against the United States began with the first attack on the World Trade Center, and was followed up by attacks against the Khobar Towers in Saudi Arabia; the American embassies in Kenya and Tanzania; and the USS Cole, which was docked in the port of Aden in Yemen. Americans were being murdered in cold blood. The blood ran, and the American administration scurried to brush aside the nexus between individual acts of terror and a clear, and grander, strategic purpose.

In Israel, a thoroughly decent and courageous Prime Minister took a chance on peace based on the "Oslo Accords." It was ill-conceived and ill-fated. But he thought he should try. He was assassinated. The Prime Minister's murder was a deeply offensive act that didn't change the fundamental calculus of the conflict. Five years after the Prime Minister was killed, the so-called peace process took on a special urgency for an American president, who was desperate for a foreign policy achievement to burnish his place in history before he left office. It came to nothing. Oslo was "land for peace." Oh, they wanted the land, to be sure. For an abattoir.

It was time that San Carlos de Bariloche give up something of its secret life. It was an unregenerate secret life that shunned the beauty of a place that was baptized in a heavenly incandescence. The generations who lived there after the war should have anointed its earthly spires, calling out G-d's name from mountaintop to mountaintop. Instead they summoned prowlers and slinkers who had cast the shadows of death, and reveled in commanding others to walk in those dark valleys. It was past time to fear no evil. And we didn't.

Colonel Stern had dispatched Dov Lerner to tease at least one secret out of San Carlos de Bariloche. We knew that Raymoundo and Lucero Valdes were really Ernst and Friedrich Bouhler. They were father and son. They lived for a time in San Carlos de Bariloche. I was sure that "around town" they were known as Raymoundo and Lucero Valdes. But I was also sure that, among many residents of that idyllic little village, they were esteemed guests, caretakers of the Reich. San Carlos de Bariloche may have reminded Ernst Bouhler and his fellow miscreant, Joseph Mengele, of the German Bavarian Alps. Ernst Bouhler was dead. But we needed to confirm that his son, Friedrich, was alive, and living in the village of the damned. If he was there, John was sure that it was Friedrich who designed the code with Zyklon B as a key.

Dov's report came later than we had anticipated. It was worth the wait. Although, at first, it didn't seem so. After reviewing the report with Dov by phone, Colonel Stern left a single copy locked in a desk drawer in the physics lab. John, Daniel, and I each reviewed Dov's report, which was available to us throughout the week. We agreed not to share our findings until we met on Sunday. John spent at least as many hours reviewing Dov's report as Daniel and I, combined. Sunday came. John looked as glum as I had ever seen him.

And there was something else about that meeting. It was Colonel Stern. In all those years, Shoshana's prayers had been heard by the G-d of Abraham, Isaac, and Jacob. He heard her prayers, and put His holy and merciful hand on my shoulder to face those, who like Pharaoh, were driven by hearts so hard it wasn't holiness they were after, but our blood first, and then our skins. They hunted us down as if we were animals. Colonel Stern had grown weary of their maniacal persistence. G-d's hand had given me the calm and the resolve to do what had to be done. I never had a moment of indecision, or the slightest buckle in my knees. But after Colonel Stern's first words that Sunday morning, I almost had to be peeled off the floor.

"We have all had a chance to review Dov's report. His report is replete with details, but it is up to us to complete the analysis. He did as well as anyone could have done. Before we begin our discussion, I am going to usurp a little time usually given over to our dear friend, Father John Broderick. Is that alright Father? This was probably a time you might offer a prayer before our meeting. I am not so good at prayers, Father, but I will have a little help from the Psalmist." John was already distracted. The request by Colonel Stern caught him by surprise, too. He spoke haltingly, as if he really didn't know what to say. "Sure, Colonel... ah... sure, please... ah... go ahead." John knew that he appeared off-kilter, even confused. He was embarrassed. G-d wasn't going to have any of John's glum confusion. The bear of a man came out of hibernation. His eyes went from dull grey to cerulean blue. His presence became such that it reminded me of the force of his silhouette long ago, shouting as it did across the grounds of the King David Hotel, a wedding gift from a dear friend, and dear man, who never wanted a secret life, but was obedient to G-d in all things.

Unconsciously, perhaps John overcompensated. His voice acquired a booming resonance. "Please go ahead, Colonel." I felt relieved, if not a little overwhelmed, by John's sudden recovery. Colonel Stern's words meant that he had found G-d's peace.

"I have not sought G-d's comfort enough during these years. I was foolish and proud. G-d is wise, and finds willing hearts among the humble. My friends, the Psalm 120 says:

"In my distress I cried to the Lord, And He heard me. Deliver my soul, O Lord, from lying lips And from a deceitful tongue... My soul has dwelt too long With one who hates peace. I am for peace; But when I speak, they are for war."

"No, I am not getting old and tired. My eyes now see what was obvious all along. We have help. It is the kind of help that this small country depends on for its survival. And we have the help of younger men too. They are brave to stand against these impossible odds. So now, they need our wisdom to help them survive. As G-d gives us that wisdom."

I didn't know what to say. Neither did John. The corner of Daniel's mouth was cracking a smile. Only Daniel and Colonel Stern would ever know the conversations that led to the Colonel invoking the words of the Psalmist. It was another miracle in the land of miracles.

"Isaac, are you going to break your silence? We have ways to make you talk, you know." Colonel Stern caught us off guard, and this time Daniel was as bewildered as John and I. G-d was adding a sense of humor to the Colonel's personality. Moshe Stern started to laugh. We joined in. It continued until it suddenly donned on us why we there. Oh, this was an unpleasant business.

"Who wants to start?" Colonel Stern looked in my direction. Some things hadn't changed. I was being volunteered. "I agree, Colonel, that Dov's report is superb. All we know for sure is that Lucero Valdes is alive and living in San Carlos de Bariloche. That is no small thing. Friedrich Bouhler lives. He maintains a very discreet distance from this organization that takes positions on many aspects of Middle Eastern politics. They have an unremarkable point of view regarding a two-state solution. They do tilt towards the Palestinian side of things. But there is nothing in their publications that is overtly anti-Semitic. In fact, it would be difficult to point to anything about them that is anti-Semitic."

"This organization, 'The Peace in the Land Institute.' The woman who runs the Institute is obviously a friend of Bouhler. But Dov was only able to document their association one time. One time! Bouhler is careful. Extremely careful. But the photograph doesn't lie. Bouhler runs a magic shop. I believe that's where we will find the real Friedrich Bouhler."

Daniel went next. "Isaac is right. The magic shop will give us the answers we want. The SS would be proud. It is a clever cover. It seems harmless enough, doesn't it? He does birthday parties for children, mostly. He sends clowns and magicians to entertain and amuse. It has made him popular, even well-respected, in the community. The area's hotels recommend Bouhler to tourists who are celebrating birthdays, or anniversaries. He covers his tracks, this Bouhler. Dov has done his job well. He is worthy of you in every respect, Colonel. Now our investigation has a foundation that can lead us to the answers we seek. We cannot send Dov back to San Carlos de Bariloche to find those answers. He has spent too much time there as it is. We should wait for a few months. Then we should send someone else to San Carlos de Bariloche to finish the job."

"That won't be necessary." John's voice filled the room again. "It may be that Bouhler is careful, even extremely careful, as Isaac has said. Frankly, Bouhler is careless." The Colonel quickly cut John off. If Bouhler was careless, Dov should have been able to do far more than to confirm that Friedrich Bouhler was living in San Carlos de Bariloche as Lucero Valdes. "I see no evidence in Dov's report that Bouhler is careless, John." The Colonel was being protective of his protégé. He was right to be. Dov's report was as good as I'd ever seen.

"I am implying nothing about the quality of Dov's work, Colonel. What he did was flawless. Now it is time to do our work. It is we who have the experience to comprehend Friedrich Bouhler. That is what I meant to say. I won't argue the point about Bouhler's carelessness. Bouhler is driven by a bestiality that is uncontainable. It is an unspeakable depravity."

"Nazism is not well understood. The answers are there, gentlemen. Many scholars still believe Hitler was a kind of a Christian. They probably believe this because Hitler advocated 'positive Christianity.' Positive Christianity is not Christianity at all. What Hitler had in mind was restoring old pagan Nordic values, and substituting the spirit of the hero for that of the Crucifixion. The Reich was a means of erasing Christianity from Germany, and replacing it with a neo-pagan religion based on pre-Christian Germanic legends."

I was confused. And by the looks on the faces of Daniel and Colonel Stern, I wasn't the only one. "John, I am not following what this has to do with Bouhler." "Be patient, Isaac. Please." The look in John's eyes asked for latitude. He shouldn't have had to ask at all. I was a little ashamed. "I apologize, John, continue."

"So, what exactly was Nazism? We want to sanitize it by calling it insanity. It wasn't insanity. It had a mind, but it was a movement whose members had lost the soul that G-d had given them. They made a free will decision. They replaced their divine inheritance with the occult. Hitler was at the center of this cultist infatuation. He was regarded as a psychic medium in contact with powerful forces that would eventually create an omnipotent Aryan nation. Many saw Hitler as the 'Dark Messiah.'"

"Himmler, Bormann, and Hess were members of what was known as the Vril Society. Vril occultists promoted Aryan power through evoking the spirits of the dead, human sacrifice and bringing forth mysterious energies (or Vril) through sexual orgies. This obsession with the occult and Satanism dated back to 19th century Germany. There was a fascination with eastern mysticism and 'prophets' of occult religions. One so-called 'prophet' believed that Europeans descended from a race of angel-like creatures known as Aryans. They claimed that the Aryans had used mysterious psychic forces to build the pyramids, Atlantis and a network of cities beneath Antarctica."

I was still confused. But, nonetheless, we were all riveted.

"Their goal was a Thousand Year Reich. They wanted to build a national religion based on Aryan mythology. Himmler had elaborate plans. Under the auspices of the SS, Himmler set up an occult research bureau known as Ahnenerbe. Ahnenerbe was instructed to prove German racial superiority by linking them to the mythical race of ancient Aryans. They believed in the power of holy artifacts. They set out to find those artifacts to harness that power. Ahnenerbe also undertook huge expeditions to search for supposed ancient Aryan cities in the Himalayas, the Middle East, and Bolivia. The Ahnenerbe employed astrologers. One such astrologer, Karl Krafft, quickly rose to prominence after correctly predicting the 1939 Munich assassination attempt against Hitler. Hitler believed that the astrological forecast and his survival was proof that the occult G-ds supported his 'Final Solution.'"

"And that wasn't all. Himmler named himself the 'Black Jesuit.' He developed plans for pagan temples to be built across Germany after the war. These pagan temples would replace churches. And on every altar there would be a copy of Hitler's 'Mein Kampf.' Himmler planned for a new religious city centered around Wewelsburg Castle. It was to be an occult Vatican dedicated to all things evil. Colleges would educate Germany's future leaders in the occult, such as psychic medium-ship, hypnosis and divination."

John wasn't done yet. Far from it. "Take a look at these," he said. He motioned us to come over to one of the lab tables where he was laying out photographs. "Dov must have taken hundreds of photos inside Bouhler's shop. He must have sensed something. Dov took snapshots of the walls and Bouhler's display tables from many different angles. Now, look at these two photographs. Bouhler has two kinds of nondescript abstract-looking reliefs hanging at about equidistant points from the far corner of his shop. Now, look at this." John was pointing to another photo. "Do you see the object on the table. It is about a quarter of the size of a Rubik's cube." John suddenly pulled what appeared to be a replica of the object from his pants pocket. John began rotating the cube. "You see, it's translucent. except for one side. It allows light in, but it is only transparent on this one side, here! There are mirrors on the inside of the cube."

"I had my brothers at the monastery help me with a little experiment. We tried, as best we could, to place copies of the reliefs on corner walls, in their exact relative position, according to the photograph Dov had taken. Then we placed a replica of the cube on a table at about the same distance it was from the reliefs in Bouhler's shop. If you rotate the cube so that the mirrors pick up both reliefs, you get this. This is the image that appears on the transparent side of the cube."

"What is it, John?" None of us had any idea. "It is an occult symbol that the Nazis believed brought them power. Look at the photograph. Bouhler placed the cube in something that cleverly looks like a little doll's house. He surrounded it with figurines. The doll's house, if that's what it is, sits on a small stand on the table. My guess is that Bouhler opened the back of the doll's house so he could see the cube at all times."

"How did you know, John?" "It was the photographs of the reliefs, Isaac. I thought I recognized something about them. But the images seemed a little distorted. So I took them to a friend of mine who is an expert in the occult. He said this sort of trick is often done by occultists. The cube predates the Nazis. Hiding in plain sight. There is no doubt that Bouhler learned this little deception from his father."

"This is further confirmation of Bouhler's identity, but it doesn't quite explain everything. We may never know the identity of this group's ringleader. It probably doesn't matter. We do know they used El-Masri against us. For Bouhler, this was never about El-Masri and our humiliation."

John's last remark caught Daniel's attention. "What do you mean, John? Are you saying that El-Masri was some kind of sideshow?"

"In a certain sense, yes, Daniel. Oh, Bouhler would have loved the vicarious thrill of killing a few of us, blackmailing me, and humiliating Israel. But that wasn't the main attraction for him."

"What then, John?"

"I apologize, but we need to go back to history. Please indulge me for a moment. Hitler and his men believed there was power in human sacrifice. They were taken in by this Vril Society cult. In the 1920's, hundreds of children disappeared in Munich. The children were murdered to call forth Vril energy. These children were subjected to a barbarism that later found its way to the concentration camps."

"Dov's report is exceptional for its detail. And there is a detail that requires our immediate attention. Bouhler's magic shop has become a kind of "miracles central." He collects stories about miracles involving children. The internet has made his craze far easier. It looks benign, doesn't it? He has a rather nice little cubby hole in his shop where his patrons can read about miracles in the lives of children. I am sure he encourages tourists and others to send him such stories from all over the world."

Daniel and Colonel Stern looked like they understood what all this meant. "I had no idea it would lead to this, John. This is about Ethan. It was always about Ethan, wasn't it?"

"Yes it was, Isaac."

Daniel looked a little perplexed. "John, if he wanted to carry out child sacrifice, why would he care if the children were involved in miracles. And it seems to me that Bouhler doesn't need to cast an international net."

"You are exactly right, Daniel. Bouhler is interested in more than just child sacrifice. He wants to sacrifice particular children."

"What kind of children, John?"

"First, it will be male children. He collects stories about boys and girls, but it is the boys he wants. Take a look at this photograph. It is a small drawing hanging in Bouhler's shop. It is a black and white sketch of a castle with four moons in the backdrop. They appear to be New Moons, but it really doesn't matter. The castle bears a striking resemblance to Wewelsburg Castle. Remember what I said about Wewelsburg Castle. Himmler planned for a new religious city centered around Wewelsburg Castle.

"They see the blood moons coming, gentlemen. They know that these are signs from the G-d of Abraham, Isaac, and Jacob. They know what the blood moons in 1492, 1948, and 1967 meant to the Jewish people, and to the whole world. They fear that G-d will anoint a voice to speak to the world. It is a voice that they detest. They will try to stop it. From their point of view, they must stop it. That's what the Holocaust was all about. Whether they were conscious of it, or not, and I believe they were, their plan was to thwart G-d by killing all the Jews on the face of the earth."

"Is Ethan in any immediate danger, John?" "Probably not, Daniel. But they are watching. If they suspect that any of the young boys they are monitoring are part of G-d's plan, they will not hesitate." I looked at Daniel. "Daniel, you still look a little puzzled."

"John, would I be correct in saying that you have left out some details that shaped your conclusions?"

"Yes, Daniel, but it is not intentional. This is enough for now."

"I agree, John. Colonel, I think we should go. We need to get some rest."

"Yes, we do, Daniel. Good bye, Isaac. Thank you, Father. We won't be needing to send anyone else to San Carlos de Bariloche, just now."

"John, I think I will be going as well."

"I need to get back too, Isaac."

"Are you sure about your conclusions, John?"

"We don't have the luxury of perfect knowledge, or perfect insight, in this business. You know that, Isaac, of course, you know that. I will be the happiest man alive if I am proven wrong."

"But, you don't think you're wrong, do you, John?"

"I fear not, Isaac. Give Shoshana my best."

The plan all along was to make it possible for Ethan to compete in the 2001 Maccabiah Games. It was a determined and relentless push by all of us. Rabbi Levy, Golda, and even Colonel Stern took up the cause. We had wanted Ethan to be able to compete in the regular games. There was never going to be a problem for Ethan to participate in the Paralympics. But we wanted to achieve the impossible. And we had finally come to an inspired compromise. We had reached an agreement with the Maccabiah Games organizing committee.

Ethan would be able to compete in the regular games. The other athletes were completely supportive of the idea. The caveat was that Ethan would only get to compete in the trials. We were thrilled, as was a certain family in Illinois.

San Carlos de Bariloche changed all of that. The stories about Ethan would have made their way to Bouhler. And that would have exacerbated an already grave, and growing, risk to Ethan's life. Things hadn't changed much since the 1935 when the games were held despite official opposition by the British Mandatory government in the Holy Land. Bouhler's father and his pack of pathological wolves were on the loose in Germany. One hundred and thirty four Jews defied an order from Nazi Germany not to attend the games. The 134 Jews bravely refused to fly the German flag during opening ceremonies. The 1935 Maccabiah Games became known as the "Aliyah Olympics" because many of the athletes chose to remain and settle in Israel. Now, the same deranged obsession that shrouded the 1935 Maccabiah Games jeopardized Ethan.

David may have suspected otherwise, but there was another reason to cancel Ethan's trip to Israel. It was Intifada. Intifada was certainly a way to understand another manifestation of the obsession with the Jewish people. But the Intifada also became a microcosm of an international order returning to form. These were not the "former things" that belonged to the G-d of Abraham, Isaac, and Jacob. As more and more years separated the world from the horrors of the Holocaust, the world became short on memory. It longed for its worldly arithmetic. It added up to a return to callousness and indifference. At its best, it added up to wishful thinking and the fanciful.

Intifada means "shaking off." There was also an "intra-fada." And a cruel and deadly charade. The first Intifada began with a murder in Gaza. Gaza was first mentioned in Genesis, and was known to Joshua as the land where some of the Anakim remained. On December 6, 1987, an Israeli was stabbed to death while shopping in Gaza. Subsequently, a traffic accident killed four residents of the Jabalaya refugee camp in Gaza. Of course they were linked. Well, of course, they weren't linked at all. The rumor mill created the fiction that the four deaths in the Jabalaya refugee camp were in retaliation for the murder of the Israeli shopper. Violence ensued. It was widespread. Gaza, the West Bank, and Jerusalem were engulfed. Then, more rumors. It was said that Palestinian youths wounded by Israeli soldiers were taken to an army hospital in Tel Aviv and "finished off." Then, more rumors. There was a claim that Israeli troops poisoned a Palestinian water supply in Khan Yunis.

The first Intifada finally ended in 1993. Six years of violence, a form of warfare against Israel that didn't require large standing armies and fancy technology. During the first four years alone, there were 3,600 Molotov cocktail attacks, 100 hand grenade attacks, and 600 assaults with firearms and explosives. And then there was the "intrafada." "Intrafada" was murder and disfigurement in the name of punishing those who were deemed to be collaborating with Israel. Putative collaborators were stabbed, hacked with axes, shot, clubbed and burned with acid.

The second Intifada, which bedeviled the 2001 Maccabiah Games, marked an escalation of the unconventional war against Israel. At the end of his second four-year term, the American President hosted the Israeli Prime Minister and the Palestinian leader at Camp David, the presidential retreat named for President Eisenhower's grandson. The president hoped that it would be the culmination of the Oslo process. The Oslo formulation was land for peace. No agreement was reached.

It was said that the second Intifada began with a visit to the Temple Mount by the leader of the Likud political party in Israel. His visit to the Temple Mount was done with the knowledge, and approval, of the Palestinian leadership. He went to the Temple Mount during normal visiting hours. Nonetheless, a visit was morphed into a provocation, which became a pretext. The result was the second Intifida, which began the next day. This time the violence was ratcheted up. It was a cocktail of violence that went far beyond Molotov's incendiary brew.

It was suicide attacks, mass murder shooting sprees, car bombs, and the indiscriminate use of rockets and mortars. Four years later, the second Intifada finally fizzled out.

Intifada was an exposition. It put on display the new strategy against Israel. It exposed the United Nations for what it was: at the very least, the UN was anti-Israel; in fact, the UN was almost certainly, anti-Semitic. And Europe began to gradually lose its sense of responsibility, and shame, related to the Holocaust. In the new war against Israel, strong European support for the Jewish state would be the first of many casualties.

Much of the world wanted to wish us away. But by G-d's grace, it wasn't all the world, for there were those otherworldly souls who reminded us just why we had been called out of the world in the first place, beginning with Egypt. It was a call they heard too. It became an urgent call to uncover the truth of San Carlos de Bariloche, to first resist it, and then defeat it. So, John called us back together. He wanted to be briefed on just how we were going to keep Ethan safe. And there was something else too. John knew just how wise Daniel was in these matters. Daniel didn't dispute John's conclusions. But he had delicately pointed out that John needed to buck up his narrative about the true nature of Friedrich Bouhler's intentions.

But first, there was the sadness. In a dramatic breech of protocol that only hinted at our gratitude, Daniel lovingly hung a photograph on the north wall of the lab. The photograph was in a modest frame. It was perfect. It perfectly framed a life in service to others, but belied a holy boldness in service to G-d. None of us wanted to say anything. We preferred the silence of the broken hearted. I had written something of a personal nature, but I knew the others would recognize it in their own recollections. I used a thumb tack and suspended my words from the photograph, frame and all. I couldn't say everything I wanted to say:

"It is in learning to forgive, as He forgives us, that we keep closest only the sweetest of memories, and see, as G-d has given us the sight

to see... righteousness, justice, mercy and love, which light the way to heaven's door. And her door was always open. As a boy, it was a door that G-d opened for me on earth, so that I might be touched by a gentleness and a kindness that knew heaven, but also knew that on earth, hell's fire was close at hand. And it was hell's fire, which steeled her heavenly soul in an earthly countenance, helping the boy I was, and the man I became, to hold dear an all too earthly sentiment (never forget) with the only heavenly recourse possible (always forgive)."

John, Daniel, and Moshe Stern each took a turn in reading my last missive to a dear friend. Golda Eisen died shortly after she had taken a bad fall. She did not suffer.

We did not begin our meeting until sometime later that afternoon. Each of us had retreated to different, and we hoped remote, parts of the lab. John finally gave himself a slow, and ungainly lift out of his chair. His sadness allowed his age to temporarily overwhelm him. He softly called each of us by name, and we gradually formed a semicircle around him. He eased us into the meeting as only John could do. He reassured us that one of his Franciscan brothers would endeavor to make us some Pirushke cakes. Just then, I caught a glimpse of her photograph. She was admonishing me and the others to get on with it. And so we did.

"Daniel, do you think you could spare Avner for a little trip to San Carlos de Bariloche around Yom Kippur."

"I am sure I could, John, what did you have in mind?"

"What I have in mind, Daniel, is a demonstration of what he is, this man, Freidrich Bouhler. That is, Daniel, if you can really call Freidrich Bouhler a man." "This sounds like you're looking for confirmation, John." "Well, Isaac, I believe I owe everyone in this room a certainty beyond any reasonable doubt. We have already cancelled Ethan's trip to Israel to compete in the Maccabiah Games. I am sure Daniel is increasing security around Ethan. If I'm wrong about Bouhler, this is one of the great wild goose chases in all of Israel's history. There are not unlimited resources in this country. We need to be sure. I need to be sure!"

"What does this have to do with Yom Kippur, John? It is the holiest day in Judaism." I had never heard Colonel Stern speak that way. He was reciting Psalms, and now this. It was touching. It is not something I would have predicted after that first meeting regarding a future I had no idea about. But, after all, he did suffer through my bout with self-righteousness. It is not that I said anything wrong at that fateful meeting, it wasn't wrong; it's just I could have been a little more graceful in the way I said it.

Thankfully, John's previous profile of Bouhler prepared us for what he said next. "According to the Talmud, Ha-Satan always hoped to be especially active during the ten days of penitence between Rosh Hashanah and Yom Kippur. Those are the days when Israelites seek forgiveness of their sins. The sounding of the ram's horn (Shofar) on Rosh Hashanah confounds Ha-Satan, and on Yom Kippur Ha-Satan is powerless to oppose Israel's plea for forgiveness. The letters of Ha-Satan (the Satan) have the numerical value of three hundred and sixty-four, indicating that on three hundred and sixty-four days of the year he has power to oppose, but on the Day of Atonement he has not that power."

"So, what I propose is simple. Yom Kippur is the day that Freidrich Bouhler feels abandoned, and vulnerable. As the creature he is, he will try to compensate. This year, Yom Kippur falls on a Thursday. Rest assured, Bouhler's shop will be open for business. He would never close his shop on a Jewish holiday, no matter what. But he will seek the reassurance of an object that calls upon Vril energy, while Ha-Satan is out of the world. Avner should look for a ring on Bouhler's right index finger, or perhaps something around Bouhler's neck. Avner must get a photograph of the ring or pendant. Bouhler will make sure it is in plain sight. This is dangerous, Daniel. It is extremely dangerous. If Bouhler discovers Avner's true intentions, he will try to have him killed. Bouhler has friends. They may not be apparent, but they are there. And we certainly don't want Bouhler to go underground, which he will if he suspects anything at all."

"You are sure about this, John?" "What if you are right about everything else, but Bouhler forgets to wear something that day." "He won't forget, Daniel. Of that, I am sure. Bouhler's father and Mengele were known for their rigid adherence to all manner of protocol, including timeliness. Bouhler won't forget. Tell Avner to be careful. Please, tell Avner to be careful."

"Avner will be careful, John. He will do his job well. If Bouhler is wearing what you suggest, you will have your photograph."

"Isaac, you look worried."

"I am, Daniel. What are we doing about security for Ethan?" "We have rented the house just behind David and Rachel. Friends of ours, a married couple, now live there. They will set up discreet monitoring of the house and grounds. Did you know that David and Rachel have built a detached bedroom for Ethan in their backyard?" "No, I didn't know that, Daniel. Is that wise?" "In fact, it is probably better because Ethan's bedroom is closer to the house we rent. Ethan has a workspace attached to the bedroom. He has become quite proficient in computer repair, which he does for many of the synagogues and yeshivas in the area. We will keep him safe, Isaac."

"But for now, we need to make a visit to Bouhler on Yom Kippur. I suppose, John, you wouldn't recommend that Avner wear a kippah?" That brought a needed smile to all of our faces. "No, I don't think so, Daniel. But because it is the Day of Atonement, how about if Avner dons the vestments I wear to hear confessions. Do you suppose Bouhler would be so confused, he would run screaming out of the shop?" We all managed another glimpse of her photograph before we left. We ended the meeting the way she would have wanted it. She used to say, "there is danger in hesitation, Isaac. We can't hesitate, because our enemies never hesitate." And she never hesitated to love us, with that same kind of urgency. It was a love that helped carry us through the worst of it.

Sixteen days prior to Yom Kippur that year, was the second day of infamy in American history. The attack on Pearl Harbor was the first. The second was the attack on the World Trade Center in New York City. America and the world were shocked. It was shocking. It was shocking that such a thing could succeed. The operation could have unraveled in a thousand different ways. But it didn't. The operation did more than just collapse a symbol of American power. Nearly 3,000 human beings were murdered, including citizens of more than 90 countries worldwide.

In the Middle East, Iran and its stooges in Hezbollah quickly circulated the false rumors that 4,000 Jews did not show up for work at the World Trade Center because they had been warned by Israeli intelligence to stay away. Not that Iran or Hezbollah cared about the truth, but the 4,000 figure appeared to come from a report that Israel's Foreign Ministry in Jerusalem had received information that over 4,000 Israelis were believed to have been in the vicinities surrounding the World Trade Center and the Pentagon at the time of the attacks.

Americans were also shocked to see the post-9/11 celebrations in the Palestinian territories. They were celebrating the attack on "Big Satan" (America) because it supported "Little Satan" (Israel). It was perceived as a stunning success in the campaign to isolate Israel. That was always the end game. Israel would never be made to disappear from the Middle East as long as it enjoyed American political, economic and military support. The idea was to make the cost of American support for Israel unbearable. Turn America inward from an all too complicated and violent world. At the same time, begin to undermine support for Israel among American elites, including on college campuses.

At first, it was the plotters, their supporters, and their cheerleaders who were shocked. American power was unleashed. America spoke with a clarity worthy of the president who collapsed the Soviet Union. Libya was so cowed it voluntarily gave up all the pieces to its nuclear program. Terrorist training camps and hideaways throughout the world were dismantled. In Afghanistan, which was identified as the safe haven for the terrorist network primarily responsible for 9/11, the terrorists came under a barrage of firepower. It was a firepower that they hadn't anticipated, and frankly, couldn't imagine in their wildest dreams. It was an impressive and effective start. It wouldn't last.

The campaign to woo American elites had begun long before the events of September 11, 2001. The campaign to undermine support for Israel had its own twin towers. It was money and progressivism.

America's appetite for oil provided barrels of money for Saudi Arabia, the largest oil producer in the Middle East, to pursue a campaign to weaken American support for Israel.

Saudi oil and money became such a force in the American body politic that what the Saudis actually believed, what they taught their children, and what they promoted abroad including in America never seemed to register on the American political Richter scale. Even after 9/11, in which most of the hijackers were Saudi, including the reputed driving force behind the operation, the Saudi-American relationship was largely undisturbed. All of this was true despite the authentic Saudi underbelly: Wahhabism.

Wahhabism has been Saudi Arabia's dominant faith for more than two centuries. Wahhabism requires a literal interpretation of the Koran. The American founders knew that freedom and self-governance could only be sustained by a moral and religious people. It would be what future Americans actually believed that would shape the unique American experiment in self-governance. So, how could it be irrelevant what the Saudis actually believed, practiced, and used petrodollars to spread around the world, including in the United States.

Saudi school books for children and adolescents are textbook examples of a society that does not seek a peaceful co-existence with western society, especially the United States and Israel.

From an 8th grade Saudi textbook there is this: *"The Apes are the people of the Sabbath, the Jews; the Swine are the infidels of the communion of Jesus, the Christians."* And, Saudi twelfth-graders are subjected to this:

"Jihad for the sake of Allah is the only path to liberating Palestine. Only through jihad did the Muslims conquer Jerusalem, and only through jihad did the Crusaders leave Palestine. Likewise, only through jihad will the Jews leave Palestine."

"The only point of departure in our handling of the issue of Palestine [should be] absolute faith in Islam and in the fact that all rulings related to this issue must be derived from [Islam]."

American's founders had a special relationship to the First Amendment of the United States Constitution. Fifteen years prior to the First Amendment's ratification, the founders made this promise to one other: *"And for the support of this declaration, with a firm reliance on the protection of Divine Providence, we mutually pledge to each other our Lives, our Fortunes, and our sacred Honor."* That promise was made in the Declaration of Independence. Their lives and fortunes were certainly at stake. But it was their "sacred Honor" that they cared most about.

It never would have occurred to America's founders to suspend the First Amendment rights of American citizens abroad, particularly on American soil. As a matter of international law, an American embassy, or consulate, abroad *is* American soil. And yet, Americans in Saudi Arabia, even Americans standing on American sovereign territory such as an embassy or consulate, seemed to be at the mercy of Saudi law. In the 1990's, while American embassies and consulates had previously provided some space for non-Muslim religious activity, as it was known, it became strongly discouraged. American citizens who expressed interest in religious services were sent to the British consulate. In Jeddah, Saudi Arabia American citizens were occasionally beaten and tortured for as little as possessing a photograph with a Star of David in the background or singing Christmas carols.

The U.S. mission in Saudi Arabia had a protocol with the Saudi Ministry of Foreign Affairs to the effect that no American diplomats thought to be Jewish by the State Department would be permanently stationed in the kingdom of Saudi Arabia.

And then there was this: In 1990-91, when over half a million American forces were stationed in Saudi Arabia to defend the kingdom, the Pentagon agreed not to assign non-Muslim military chaplains to minister to the troops. The President of the United States at the time agreed to eat his Thanksgiving meal on a ship off the Saudi coast for fear of offending the Saudis with a prayer before eating. The American troops did not celebrate Christmas services that year, but attended what came to be known as "C-word morale services" held in unmarked tents or mess halls.

In the 1980's, an American President, an American original, was ridiculed because he unequivocally and proudly espoused American values. The ridicule came from all directions. It came from a permanent Washington establishment, in which his own party was now comfortably ensconced, and it came from progressivism, which put down its deepest roots in America's democrat party, but found plenty of fertile ground in America's republican party as well. The Washington establishment had a marginal interest in the American Constitution, as long as it didn't interfere too much with its material comfort, but progressives wanted to replace the American Constitution altogether. Period.

Based on American values, the President defined a strategic goal during the 1980's: victory over the Soviet Union. It was a strategic goal with an elaborate strategic plan, including kicking the legs out from under the Soviet economy. Oil was a critical source of revenue for the Soviet Union. The Soviets were therefore extremely vulnerable to falling oil prices in the world market. The American administration persuaded Saudi Arabia to increase the world supply of oil. Oil prices tumbled. It was a blow, among many blows, that led to the Soviet implosion. It was clarity and purpose. It was unabashed and unafraid. It was the American idea explained to Americans, and to the world. It was fearless. It had been replaced by mush. And the Saudis knew it.

Following the apparent success of the 9/11 cataclysm, Daniel's "four cities of the apocalypse" were strangely silent. Their phony front group, The Peace in the Land Institute. issued the usual internationalist pablum, expressing "concern for the fate of the peace process, and the ongoing cycle of violence that would just claim more victims." But there were no encoded messages. None. Whether Bouhler was gamboling his way to work that day, clicking his heels to some diabolical beat, we will never know. But there he was, just as John said he would be, sixteen days after September 11th, in his shop, and open for business. As Avner approached the counter in front, Bouhler turned to face him. He was pleasant enough, but just slightly wary of a face he didn't recognize. Avner smiled, complimented Bouhler on his charming magic shop, and pointed to an item in the display case that had caught his eye. He asked Bouhler if he could see it. Bouhler grabbed it with his right hand, and placed it on top of the counter. Bouhler put both hands on the counter, palms down. He was leaning forward, ever so slightly. There was a ring on his right index finger. It appeared to be sterling silver, with a flat, wider, and slightly thicker bezel on top of the hoop. Avner got the shot. Before he left, Avner mentioned how terrible the attacks were in New York City. Bouhler only shrugged his shoulders, smiling sheepishly.

Actually, Avner managed six shots of the ring. It was more than enough. The photos were developed, then magnified so that John could clearly see the engraving on the bevel. And there was an engraving! The ring was sterling silver, and bore a remarkable resemblance to the rings issued to the Afrikakorps. The Afrikakorps was formed upon Hitler's personal orders on January 11, 1941. They were commanded by none other than Erwin Rommel. As it turned out, Bouhler's brother was a tank commander in Rommel's Afrikakorps. He died in the Libyan campaign. One of his personal effects made it back to his brother, Ernst Bouhler. It was a ring he gave to his son, Freidrich. Either father or son changed the engraving on the ring. It was an engraving that was known to Vril cultists and their fellow lunatics in the Nazi command. John wasn't surprised. Neither was I.

Hitler's Reich had an alliance with Hajj Amin al-Husseini, Grand Mufti and Supreme Muslim religious leader of Jerusalem. It was not a natural alliance. The Nazis believed in Aryan supremacy, and the Thousand Year Reich. Hajj Amin al-Husseini believed in the inevitability of Islamic ascendancy, first in the Middle East, then the world. Their hatred, and their alliance, was cemented in the crematoria of the Final Solution. Bouhler and his friends could only look with wonder at Saudi Wahhabism. Saudi Wahhabism was thwarting American strategic interests, insinuating itself in American culture, and galvanizing a global jihad with its own version of the Final Solution: the elimination of the State of Israel.

Even after 9/11, when American success in Afghanistan was so dependent on Pakistani support, Saudi money poured into Pakistani schools, radicalizing Pakistani students with the Wahhabist creed. And the Taliban, which had allowed the 9/11 masterminds to virtually operate as an independent state within Afghanistan, copied Wahhabi religious practices. Could all the American power in the world overcome the power of indigenous culture? In Japan, it did. Japan was devastated, thoroughly defeated, and demoralized. The old order was largely swept away, and replaced with a modern constitution, American style. In the culture war with Islam, where the war against radical Islam would actually be won or lost, encouraging the education of young girls in Afghanistan is, in relative terms, a pinprick.

And then there is the city. History ends in the city. But first, history happens to the city. Saudi Wahhabism wanted the city's history, and the city, for itself. Saudi Wahhabism was the tip of the Islamic spear that wanted the conquest of Jerusalem.

But why Jerusalem? Jerusalem appears in the Jewish Bible 669 times and Zion, which usually means Jerusalem and sometimes the

Land of Israel, 154 times, or 823 times in all. In contrast, the column-ist Moshe Kohn notes, Jerusalem and Zion appear as frequently in the Qur'an "as they do in the Hindu Bhagavad-Gita, the Taoist Tao-Te Ching, the Buddhist Dhamapada and the Zoroastrian Zend Avesta"—which is to say, *not once.*

Jerusalem became a holy city to Judaism over three thousand years ago. Jerusalem is the only capital of a Jewish state. Jews pray facing Jerusalem and the Temple Mount. When Muslims pray in Jerusalem, they are turning toward the city of Mecca in Saudi Arabia, with their backs to the Dome of the Rock and the Temple Mount. A mayor of Jerusalem said it well: Jerusalem represents "the purest expression of all that Jews prayed for, dreamed of, cried for, and died for in the two thousand years since the destruction of the Second Temple."

So, why Jerusalem? Deep in the recesses of their being, they un-derstand why we are there, and Who it is that is the irresistible force in these matters. In the '73 war, in a battle that may have saved Israel, why did the Syrians suddenly retreat, folding in the face of a belea-guered Israeli tank group whose only ammunition was the faith of its fearless commander. Seven million people on a sliver of land, holding off hundreds of millions, perhaps a billion, of people, who are mari-nated in hatefulness, and hate our very existence. These are not the odds of an Alamo or Bastogne. These are no odds at all. It is faith, not odds, that sustains. It is Abraham.

> *"Look now toward heaven, and count the stars*
> *if you are able to number them. And He said to him,*
> *So shall your descendants be.*
> *And he believed in the Lord,*
> *and He accounted it to him for righteousness."*
> *Genesis 15:5-6*

Abraham believed. If only the Wahhabists would believe. If only they would look to the heavens. There is reconciliation in faith. The unreconciled wander earthly plains, coveting what their eyes see, instead of what their hearts desire. Why Jerusalem? Because *we* are there.

> *Since the day that I brought My people out of the land of Egypt,*
> *I have chosen no city from any tribe of Israel in which*
> *to build a house, that My name might be there,*
> *nor did I choose any man to be a ruler over My people Israel.*
> *Yet I have chosen Jerusalem, that My name may be there,*
> *and I have chosen David to be over My people Israel.'*
> *2 Chronicles 6: 5-6*

When G-d puts His name on a city, true hearts everywhere feel the divine tug. David knew the risks. Rachel suspected as much. But a boy had become a young man, and he wanted to fulfill his heart's desire. The Maccabiah Games debacle was deeply disappointing to us all. It was years of persuading, followed by disappointment, more persuading, cautious optimism, and ups and downs that made roller coaster rides seem tame by comparison. Then, a breakthrough. Then, anticipation. Then, Bouhler. Our hearts broke for Ethan. David and Rachel said they would have rather endured another bus ride to Ashkelon than have to tell their son the news. When it finally came time, they cried, but Ethan was there to reassure them that it was G-d's will.

In the aftermath of the Bouhler revelations, and the Maccabiah Games disappointment, my reaction never changed: I seethed. Quietly, discreetly, but nonetheless, I seethed. And to my great surprise, I wasn't alone. One by one, I found the identical reaction. First, Shoshana, then John, then Daniel, and then Colonel Stern, whose colorful language on the matter was priceless, and cathartic. On a visit to Tel Aviv, I found my brother Aaron had a similar state of mind. With one inspiring difference: he was defiant. The ace pilot also aced the Colonel Stern colorful language as catharsis test. But he did something else. He planted a seed.

Quietly seething is no way to live. It is a step better than acceding to the holding pen that was the ghettoization of Jews by Nazi Germany, but it wasn't defiance. I began to test the waters for a plan of prudent defiance. It was faith, and faithfulness. It was faith in G-d's protection, and faithfulness to a young man who was a miracle of love, and a marvel of courage. As an infant, he was witness to a brazen act of terrorism aboard a bus, with no more concern than if he was with his mother in the park, trundling along with a sign on the stroller that was only for the carefree: "baby on board." The foul incident on the bus was an indication that life wasn't going to be a carefree proposition. Bouhler was the exclamation point. But cowering in a corner, even seething in a corner, was living life in a crouch. The State of Israel was G-d's counterpoint to Bouhler's exclamation point. Life was to be lived with a holy boldness. G-d's intention for holy boldness included a soul of wit, and all the lionhearted reticence that only the humble could master. The brave and the humble wanted to come to Israel. His name was Ethan Bass.

Defiance needed a plan. The first part of the plan was to maintain surveillance of Bouhler. And Daniel did. But it was far too risky to rely solely on Avner and Dov. So Daniel enlisted some of his best, and most experienced, friends. It wasn't bad duty. Just go to San Carlos de Bariloche for a few days. Monitor Bouhler from afar. There would be no need to browse around his magic shop. Just note any peculiarities in his routine, and take special note of any company he kept.

Daniel was receiving regular reports on Bouhler. But something was missing. He needed Avner to go back to Bouhler's shop. It was Bouhler's cubby hole of miracles. There were names there. There were names that belonged to human beings who Bouhler and his squad of goons may have been watching. Ultimately, Daniel wanted to know if any of these "innocents" had suffered any harm, or worse.

Avner wasn't sent back to Bouhler's shop until several more Yom Kippurs had passed. Even if by some off chance Bouhler recognized

Avner, it is unlikely his visit would arouse any untoward suspicion. No doubt, many tourists dropped by Bouhler's place more than once over the years.

Avner's trip back to San Carlos de Bariloche went off without a hitch. The cubby hole was still there, and so was Bouhler's interest in stories about children and miracles. Bouhler was as polite as ever. Avner leisurely roamed around the shop, ducked into the cubby hole, photographed anything and everything, and even bought a "souvenir" before he left. The ring was gone from Bouhler's right index finger. It wasn't Yom Kippur. Everything was right again with the world according to Freidrich Bouhler.

Our analysis of the articles Avner photographed began immediately. As usual, John's guidance was crucial. He said to look for young men who would be about the same age as Ethan. At first, it seemed as though the articles disclosed fewer names than we had anticipated. There were twelve, in all. One name was missing. That name was Ethan Bass. Ethan's birth was a miracle, of sorts, but it certainly didn't make the local press as such. No, the information about Ethan came from Reem El-Masri, and found its way in a report made by her father to a group with at least one man that Dr. Amir El-Masri had no idea about. So, with Ethan's name added to the list, the total came to thirteen young men who were potentially being surveilled by Bouhler. John's reaction was understated, but certain. "That was about right," he said. "In Wewelsburg Castle, there was a sunken circular altar, and from there you could see thirteen lanterns flickering on the curved walls. Thirteen is a number that has significance to men like Bouhler." For the first time, I felt sorry for John. He was a man of G-d, and yet he carried the terrible burden of understanding how evil crawled and scratched its way into G-d's creation. It couldn't have been easy.

We began planning for Ethan's first trip to Israel since his birth. My memory wasn't perfect anymore, but I could not recall a time when Aaron had visited the lab. Now, he joined the usual suspects at the lab on a regular basis. We were honored to have him. Frankly, we needed his help. And what a gift! It was like old times again, harkening back to the days when Aaron and I first joined the IDF. We had become even closer since the deaths of "Papa" and Rebecca Weiss. We had also become wiser. We cherished every moment together. Each time he walked into the lab, it seemed as though we couldn't stop smiling. But the smiles were always wiped away. Bouhler was lurking in the shadows.

Shoshana couldn't wait. She couldn't wait to see David and Rachel. And she especially couldn't wait to see Ethan. She had collected every letter, every anecdote, and every newspaper article about Ethan. She collected the anecdotes about Ethan in a small diary. Ethan had sweetly sent us Bible verses over the years to commemorate special occasions. He never missed our anniversary, or our birthdays. He always added his own special touch to the Bible verses. Shoshana referred to them as Ethan-taries. They were remarkable. So was he. He was a treasure. And so was my wife. The details of Ethan's life became a memorial to the details of young lives that never came to be because of a maniacal rampage. In Shoshana's obedience to G-d, her work at the Holocaust Memorial, and her careful, loving biography of Ethan's life, became a kind of testimony for the voices who were silenced on earth, but had the ear of G-d in heaven. Yes, she was quite something. She was my Rosie.

Our Ethan Bass planning sessions began as bi-monthly meetings at the lab. We could continue meeting at bi-monthly intervals until about three months before Ethan's arrival in Israel. At the three month mark, we would meet on a weekly basis. We already had a tentative date for his visit, so our meeting timeline was basically set. We met on Thursday afternoons. Aaron and his wife now also had an apartment in Jerusalem. It was in a Jerusalem neighborhood where a lot of retired IDF officers lived. Aaron wasn't retired yet; he still taught some classes to IAF pilots in Tel Aviv. So, at least twice a month, I could rely on Aaron spending four days in Jerusalem. I loved it. So did Shoshana. He was our Flying Shadchan.

Daniel was rarely late, but this Thursday afternoon he was. He usually started off the meeting with updates about Bouhler. Daniel had previously briefed us on the well-being of the other young men who were probably being watched by Bouhler's network. And, thankfully, all the young men were well. There had been a few broken bones along the way, and other minor accidents, but nothing life threatening. It wasn't practical to provide the other young men the same level of the security available to Ethan. But they were being monitored. And that would have to be good enough for now.

Daniel began with meeting with an announcement that caught us all by surprise. The four cities of the apocalypse had broken their silence. They had sent an encoded message. "Were David and his team able to come up with anything?" I asked. "Only a fragment, actually only a word, Isaac. And David has only 20 percent confidence in the word. Bouhler's group has modified the code somewhat. David and his team are working on it. But, it's going to be tough." "What is the word, Daniel?" "Well, John, David thinks it's Franciscan. He thinks the word is Franciscan." John wasn't fazed. I was.

"Why don't you let me take a plane to San Carlos de Bariloche, Daniel? I will take care of this once..."

John cut me off. "That would be a mistake, Isaac. I appreciate your sentiment. I do. But you know that would be a mistake."

Aaron was next to admonish me, gentle though it was. "He's right, Isaac. Besides, I would be the one to go. I could use a vacation."

Aaron smiled. John didn't. "This changes nothing, Daniel. And I will change nothing about my routine. Those days have passed. I have been a reliable servant to G-d. If my service is over, then so be it. Daniel, have your men watch me. Not to assure my security, but just in case I have become of interest to them again. If they have an interest in me, Daniel, then I have no doubt you will find this out, and when you do, you will know how to handle it. Is that alright, Daniel? I mean, you are the expert in this matters, is that alright?"

"You are far too modest, Father Broderick. I like it. We have become even bolder in our old age. Yes, I like it very much."

"John, I have a feeling you don't believe you have become a target. Would I be right, Father?"

"Why, Aaron, now I know why you are the Flying Shadchan. It is that sixth sense of yours." Aaron had a hearty laugh. I joined in. I couldn't help myself. "Yes, Aaron, you are as perceptive as ever."

"I'm not following this, John. What does Aaron mean?" "Moshe, Colonel Stern, Aaron means that they probably don't want to kill me, just yet. That's not the meaning of this." "I think you're right about that, John. But what is their interest?" "Why now?"

"Aaron, in Bouhler's world, a man like me is the object of a special loathing, and to some extent, fear. He sees this as a chess match. It's him and me. If he kills me, it's game over. He wants to know what I know. And we need to know more about this group of his."

"Is Ethan a pawn in this chess game, John?"

"No, Isaac, Ethan will checkmate the lot of them. They can't play on his level, Isaac."

"I have no idea what you're talking about, John. But, if I asked, you wouldn't tell me, would you?" "No, Isaac, I am afraid not."

Daniel chimed in. "So it's settled then. The chess game is on. And so is Ethan's visit. Does everyone agree?" We did, without hesitation. We were all strangely confident. That bear of a man could have that effect on people.

In Illinois, the security for the Bass family became tighter. But not so tight, that their lives significantly changed. Ethan still competed in track and field. Except it was extremely irregular, by design. He often entered competitions at the very last possible moment. Sometimes he depended on someone dropping out an event, so he could slip in. He trained at different indoor gyms in the area, and he often trained at off hours, under lock and key, and always under the watchful eye of a modest security detail. Under the circumstances, David and Rachel had a relatively normal family life. They went to restaurants, museums, ball games, synagogue and to the homes of their friends.

The Bass family was looking forward to their trip to Israel. On our end, we were trying to make sure that we could accommodate their proposed itinerary. Ethan had asked if he could visit the Western Wall at the foot of the western side of the Temple Mount. That wasn't going to present a problem. Ethan also requested something else. There was a residential facility in Jerusalem for children and adolescents with disabilities. Many of the young residents had Down syndrome like Ethan. It wasn't a permanent care facility. Families stayed in nearby hotels, while their children received specialized social, educational and vocational training. It was a 3 - 4 week program, and it had a great reputation. Ethan didn't want to stay there, just visit several hours during the course of a few days.

Ethan was still unable to speak. But he could type, and the computer could do the talking. He wanted to share the Bible with the other students. It meant a lot to Ethan. The request didn't surprise us. It was Ethan being Ethan. So, we added it to Bass itinerary.

Our meetings were weekly now, as Ethan's visit was only a few weeks away. My brother Aaron was in rare form. "John, I see you're still here. It is a chess match, isn't it? There are no chess matches like this in the skies, John. Only pieces of planes falling to the ground!" John could only shake his head. He smiled. He seemed to love the banter. It was different for us, Aaron's banter that is. It was also exactly what we needed.

"Alright then, I think we have it, gentlemen. David and company will be arriving during the week of Hanukkah. They will arrive on Wednesday, December 20th, and leave on Tuesday, December 26th. We agreed that it would be best to split the family up. Ethan will be staying with Aaron and Shayna Weiss. Rachel will be staying with Isaac and Shoshana. And David will be staying at a small military facility which is cordoned off from the street. Isaac, your apartment has both an entrance and exit that is off the street. Is that right?" "Yes, it is." "And the same thing for your apartment, Aaron?" "Yes, that's right." "Good, very good."

"I have given each of you a copy of the itinerary. Does anyone see a problem with it?"

"No, Daniel, I don't. So, Ethan will have a chance to visit Rabbi Levy at his apartment. Is that right?"

"Yes, Isaac, it is." "How is Shlomo these days?"

"Shoshana and I haven't seen her father this excited since Ethan's bris. He is doing very well." Daniel's use of Rabbi Levy's first name reminded me that Shoshana's father had a life that neither one of us really knew about. It was a life that included at least one Prime Minister: the "tough cookie." They were both tough cookies.

"Is there anything else?" Daniel asked. We looked around at each other. I looked at Golda's picture on the wall. "Oh, John, one more thing. I almost forgot." Daniel said. "You know that Ethan wants you to go with him to the Western Wall?"

"Really, when would that be, Daniel?"

"Hmm, that's funny. I just realized something." said Daniel. "He wanted to go on the 22nd. That is on a Friday. It will be best to go at dusk. There will be a special Shabbat celebration as well. I would ask Colonel Stern, and you Aaron, if you could recruit 25 to 30 IDF officers to provide additional security that evening?"

"So this will be a reprise of the Holocaust Memorial scenario, Daniel?"

"I thought that worked rather well, didn't you Aaron?"

"It did. Shayna and I weren't blown to bits by Reem El-Masri. I especially liked that part!"

"We'll have your recruits, Daniel, even if we have to volunteer them."

"Thank you, Moshe. Are we set, then?" Daniel repeated the question as he made eye contact with each of us. We all nodded, one by one.

Security for the Bass family in the U.S. never detected any surveillance of Ethan. But it was there. Avner found a photo of Ethan in El-Masri's apartment. It wasn't a baby photo. But the photo was taken well before the current level of security for Ethan. After El-Masri's death, they would be far more careful. It probably just became a monitoring operation. Confirm the Bass family is there. Nothing more.

Nonetheless, we took no chances. It wasn't a "suitcases in the car and everybody to the airport operation." David and Rachel packed a few things for themselves and Ethan. David left a few small suitcases at the base of the fence near Ethan's bedroom. The suitcases were picked up that night, as were the Basses at a pre-determined location the next morning. They were taken to the airport. Their car was driven back to their garage, and could be seen leaving their home from time to time. Ethan Bass was on his way to Israel on a private plane. The pilot was a protégé of Daniel and a certain Flying Shadchan. That meant he was one of the best.

I opened the door to our apartment and there they were: Shoshana and Rachel looking at Shoshana's collection of the life of Ethan Bass. Rachel must have been stunned. Shoshana was a professional. There were tears all around. It appeared to me that Shoshana and Rachel got a little head start in the tear department. The years had been especially kind to Rachel. She was as beautiful as ever. David Bass did well. Why wasn't I surprised?

I knew that Rachel didn't know all the details about the nature of the threat to Ethan. For that matter, neither did David. But she knew enough. And I wanted to make sure she felt comfortable asking me any questions. Some questions I couldn't, or wouldn't answer. Rachel knew that. She asked me the one question I dreaded. It was a question that a mother would ask first. How long? How long would this go on? I told her the truth. I didn't know for sure. But I thought everything was pointing to the blood moons. John hadn't told me everything either. Rachel seemed to understand. It wasn't the happiest of answers. It meant all this wasn't going to end in in the next several weeks.

Rachel's next question took me by complete surprise. She asked about the bus trip to Ashkelon. Rachel was very sketchy on the details. I knew she was in a state of shock after the events on the bus. The shock must have affected her recall. Obviously, Daniel and Shin Bet reviewed the bus incident with me after the fact. That sort of review is excruciating in detail. Every nuance is recorded and analyzed. That's why our training became the best in the world. But I hadn't even thought about it since then. And Shoshana never asked me about any of it. Shoshana and I were always happy G-d brought me back alive. That was enough. But, I really didn't mind going through the details of the bus attack with Rachel and Shoshana. I thought maybe it would make Rachel more confident about Ethan's security.

Rachel didn't remember praying. She didn't remember her son's composure. And she also didn't remember the shots I fired that ended the threat. Rachel wanted me to explain how she and Ethan got off the bus. She did remember one thing. She remembered the driver of the car that got us out of Ashdod. She remembered seeing his face in the rear view mirror. She described him rather well. Daniel would have been impressed. I could see that Shoshana, too, was curious, even fascinated by it all. But she wisely moved the conversation on to other, less sensational events. Shoshana asked Rachel about Ethan's many successes in track and field. It was a welcome relief. I could have listened to Rachel talk about Ethan for hours.

The next day I had a pressing assignment at the lab. Israel had completely withdrawn from Gaza. It was a mistake. A flurry of rocket attacks from Gaza was targeting cities in the south of Israel. It would get far worse in the future. We needed a better defense against the rockets.

John knew I was in the lab. Thankfully, he came by. Of course he wanted to know all about Rachel. "She wanted to know about the threat to Ethan, John. You know... how long all of this is going to last." "What did you tell her, Isaac?" "I told Rachel the truth, John. I told her that I don't have all the answers. But, I did say this was all pointing to the blood moons." "Yes, Isaac, that is about right. We can't know for sure, but I think you said the right thing to Rachel." "This will end, won't it, John?" John paused for a moment. "Isaac, it is a little complicated. In the sovereign will of G-d, there will be an end to all of this. But we live in the natural, Isaac. We make our free will choices, and ask G-d for his guidance. Through all of it, the faithful hearts will be revealed. In the meantime, there is Bouhler. And yes, at some point, Bouhler's day will be done. But as to all the days that will be necessary to count the true hearts for G-d? That, we cannot answer. I do know this. Your faith will sustain you, Isaac. G-d can always count on you." "Well, John, I appreciate that more than you know. I do know that my faith will not falter. I sometimes tire of all of this though." "Isaac, it is life as G-d has given us to live it. I will see you tomorrow at the Western Wall. At the Western Wall, surrounding the Temple Mount and His Temple. G-d decided that He would dwell among humans, Isaac. It is inexplicable to some. Let us try to be worthy."

On Friday, I did not get home as early as I had wanted. So, Shoshana and I were rushing to get to the Western Wall. We hadn't seen David and Ethan yet. Fortunately, the Western Wall was less than twenty minutes from our apartment in Bayit Vegan. Daniel sent a car for us. The car's driver wasn't *the* driver... who Rachel remembered so well, but he was a driver who got us to the Western Wall on time, with something to spare. I expected no less.

Unlike visiting the Temple Mount, where visiting hours were restricted, the Western Wall was open 24 hours a day, all year around. Shabbat services on Friday evening could be especially crowded. As we began approaching the Wall, Shoshana and I spotted Ethan immediately. We began running towards him. I let go of Shoshana's hand so she could greet Ethan first. She shrieked a bit before enveloping him in an embrace. David and I embraced for a long time. I remembered him as a young man in the back of a lecture hall asking marvelous questions. The questions kept coming over the years. My embrace of Ethan included tears steaming down my face. Ethan sensed the pain I felt for his current predicament. He began to comfort me. We had both kept our wits about us when we faced terrorist on a bus together. Now, one of us had kept their wits, and it wasn't me.

There wasn't a lot of time. Colonel Stern and Daniel were at opposite ends of a shallow semicircle surrounding Ethan. The recruiting had gone well. The semicircle was wider and deeper than just 30 or so IDF officers. I estimated 60, including Aaron and his wife. I noticed Aaron at the rear of the phalanx. He was watching. Strolling and watching carefully. If there was any danger out there, my brother would sense it.

Ethan knew about the time, too. He knew it was his time to do what he came to do. He was wearing his prayer shawl. He grabbed Father John's hand. John looked like he expected it. They made their reverential approach to the Western Wall. John stood to the side as Ethan did what so many had throughout the centuries. He inserted his petition to G-d into the cracks of the Wall. Then Ethan did something quite unusual. He handed a petition to John, too. John put it in his pocket. Ethan put his hand on the Wall for a moment. Then, he stepped back and began to pray. I tightly held Shoshana's hand, and our grip became even tighter as we watched Ethan praying. We were fighting back the tears. I glanced to my left and saw David and Rachel embracing, with their heads turned to watch Ethan.

It was time to go. Daniel signaled me with a glance. I also began to notice that Shin Bet were stationed all over the Prayer Plaza, and beyond. John put his arm around Ethan's shoulders as they began to leave. Ethan put his arm around John's back. Daniel's recruits formed their own circular cordon around John and Ethan. It was masterfully done. The choreography was perfect. So was Daniel's exit. Even I had trouble keeping up. Before I knew it, someone tugged on my arm. He was moving with the speed and stealth that I once had, all those years ago in Beirut. Before we had time to think about what we just witnessed, Shoshana and I had been dropped off at a discrete distance from our apartment. The driver said nothing as we got out of the car. It was about a ten minute walk to our apartment. It was just a few minutes after sunset. I noticed a razor thin sliver of the moon in the sky, not that far above the horizon. There were clouds all around, but the moonlight seemed brighter than usual. We were finally home. Rabbi Levy was waiting for us. It was Shabbat. I couldn't wait to thank a merciful G-d.

Rabbi Levy would stay with us until Sunday, when we were to all meet again at his apartment. He was about 86 years old now, as best as we could tell. Shoshana wasn't sure either. Her father wasn't a man who let you get very close. He carried burdens, and secrets. One was just exactly how Shoshana's mother died. Actually, it wasn't so much how she died, but the circumstances surrounding her death. He would never discuss it. And we knew not to bring up her name. I was sure that the death of Shoshana's mother was no accident. I knew men like Rabbi Levy. Perhaps I was a man like Shlomo Levy. There were some secrets that just could never be told. Still, he was brilliant and kind. We could talk for hours. Just never about his days in Morocco. Those days were safely locked away.

Sunday came, and Rabbi Levy wanted to get home and get everything ready for Ethan's arrival. Years earlier, he had had a minor heart attack. But he looked better than ever. The very mention of Ethan's name brought a rare smile to his face. As he left our apartment, I could see his housekeeper of many years waiting for him at the bottom of the steps. I wasn't sure, but I didn't think she was in an enviable position. She was loyal, though. And you could see how much she cared for him. He depended on her far more than he would ever admit. I especially didn't envy her this particular morning. Ethan was coming. Nothing would ever be just right. Everything would be redone, and reconsidered. He would be behind her all the way, doing things over, and doing them over again. I liked to imagine her smiling as he fussed and fretted. Shoshana was standing by my side as we turned to go back into our apartment. I looked at Shoshana. "G-d help her." She knew exactly what I was talking about. All she said was, "You aren't kidding." We couldn't help but laugh.

We were all to meet at Rabbi Levy's that afternoon. It was a staggered arrival schedule. I asked to be last so that everyone would be there by the time of our arrival. We opened the door to smiles and louder than usual voices. It was almost raucous. As I expected, Ethan was sitting next to Rabbi Levy. In the cosmology of the Talmud, G-d is located in the seventh heaven. If there was a seventh heaven on earth, then Shlomo Levy had found it. Ethan had brought his laptop so he could communicate. The voice activation software was working well. Ethan quickly typed a message which I heard loud and clear: "Did you say hello to the Sandek?" We immediately shook hands. I left the Sandek alone to be in the bliss of Ethan's company. Shoshana couldn't have been happier for her father. It must have reminded her of the days in Morocco before her mother was killed.

John wasn't quite in seventh heaven, but he was close. The bear of a man was in good voice and, for him, rare form. He was teasing David about his penchant for Paleo-Hebraic doodling. "I may be a priest, David, but I am wise to the ways of the world. You were trying to impress Rachel, weren't you? You know, David, if you would like to confess..." John's voice trailed off; he burst into laughter. I hadn't heard John laugh like that in a long time. Just as I put my hand on John's shoulder to ask him a question, I heard a phone ring. I glanced over and Daniel had a phone in his hand. Daniel put his phone away and zoomed past all of us towards the door. "Moshe, Aaron, you're with me. David and Rachel, get Ethan, let's go!" I looked out the door. There were two SUV's already waiting. Aaron's wife, Shayla, stayed behind. I knew what to do. We had planned for this scenario.

I told Shayla and John to immediately leave by the rear exit of Rabbi Levy's apartment. There would be two cars waiting, one for

each of them. John knew where to go. We were next. I took Shoshana by the hand and told Rabbi Levy to follow us out the rear exit to
our apartment. We quickly went inside. Shoshana's father was moving well, to say the least. He knew the drill. Once inside, I told
Shoshana to close the blinds and curtains. We would stay in the library for a while, and wait for a phone call. Seventh heaven had been
intruded upon.

The Americans had a phrase for a man like Shlomo Levy. He was
a cool customer. Frankly, so was his daughter. Why bring a world
full of fraught to a library? We had a very pleasant conversation.
Anxiousness and worry were always at the ready. We relied on faith.
The phone rang. Daniel was brief. I'll see you at the lab tomorrow.
Same time. Ethan is on his way back to America. Thank you. Click.
I asked Shoshana to go over to her father's apartment and collect a
few things. "The Sandek will be staying with us, tonight," I said.
Rabbi Levy and Shoshana smiled. I knew by the sound of Daniel's
voice that whatever the danger was, it was contained. That was good.
But something had gone very wrong.

I became so absorbed in what I was doing, that I had forgotten
about our meeting. John was the first to walk through the door. I
asked him if he could have a seat while I tied up a few loose ends.
The bear of a man looked spry. Good, I thought. I hoped that he
would look as spry when he was about to leave. In 30 minutes or so,
we were all sitting down, waiting for Daniel's explanation.

Daniel did not start slowly. "A bomb went off at the facility Ethan
visited. You know, the special care facility for kids with disabilities.
No one was harmed. The bomb was a virtual dud. A loud dud. John,
it was like the mortars that didn't go off in that incident with the
young boy." John nodded. "They must have thought Ethan was staying there. He was asked to sign his name in the guest registry before
he entered the facility. By mistake, he signed the wrong registry. He
signed his name next to a room number on the residential registry.

The bomb was planted nearby that room. Had it not been a dud, it would have killed at least 30 to 40 children."

I looked at Daniel. "How...?" He cut me off. "Ethan said he had done research about the facility on the internet. He was cautioned about making any reference to the trip in any of his work on his personal computer. He didn't. But he made a mistake. None of us thought to warn him about not using the internet to do research about the trip. His computer has already been taken by our people for analysis. We should have confirmation later today." "So they were watching the facility, then?" "Yes, John, they were. Ethan went into the facility by the front entrance. He left by a rear exit, so they thought he was staying there. The residential registry confirmed it."

"John, this ends now! We will pick up Bouhler and bring him to Israel for interrogation." "Where is Ethan going to stay?" "We already had a contingency plan in place, John. Ethan and his parents will be staying at a military base for the time being. They will be living in a residential community for officers only. It is perfect. It has been used for this kind of thing before. They'll never find them there. David and Rachel can live a relatively normal life. It won't have to be forever. We'll wait until we are absolutely sure the danger has passed."

I was relieved. I wouldn't say John was as reassured. "My guess is that Bouhler is gone, Daniel. You should also check on the well-being of the other young man." "You may be right about Bouhler. Do you have an idea where he might go, John?" "I do, Daniel. But let's follow your plan first. If it doesn't go quite the way you anticipated, then let's discuss other options. Is that alright?" "Very well then, John. The Bass family is safe. That is a great place to start." John wasn't as spry now. But he wasn't beaten either. He had friends in high places.

Ethan was returning to an America in which her gallant sons and daughters in battle fatigues became emblematic of a nation growing weary of sending her best to hostile lands. Those hostile lands ap-

330 · MICHAEL T. BRAUNER / LARRY W. HAWKES

peared altogether impervious to brave and charitable hearts, whose bright and shining chivalry just wasn't enough in the lands of a dark legacy. And the hostile lands had come home. In the land of the free and the home of the brave, there was hostility to all of the above.

The American President had an endearing humility, and trustworthy mien. In the first months and years after the 9/11 atrocities, he daringly mobilized his nation and made the terrorists and their supporters prone to scurry, that is, if they hadn't already assumed a prone position. It was an impressive beginning that did not last. The progressives were certainly doing their part to undermine and destroy a presidency. They wanted at least part of the murder/suicide pact in which they were engaged. It was killing off a presidency, and the suicide of the American nation.

For his part, the American President stumbled, lost his way, and cleared the path for an undoing, progressive style. It began with "small ball." The president was known to tell his aides he didn't want to play "small ball." Who could blame him? He and his party claimed the mantle of the second American original, an American great. Whatever the second American original actually did, it wasn't "small ball." The question was: what exactly was the opposite of "small ball."

The American Republic was not a small idea. It was an inspired idea of self-governance and liberty.

But it was also what one of the founders said it was: it was "made only for a moral and religious people." Under benighted auspices, the American nation would flourish. But there was an inherent modesty about it. It wasn't smallness, in fact it was grand, but it was modest. It was self-restraint, and a constitutional system of restraining influences on competing branches of government.

The second American original grandly explained the modesty inherent in the American idea. And then he grandly explained its staggering accomplishments. Government responsibility to the civil society was modest but essential: security for the individual and the nation, and the establishment of the rule of law. It is stunning to realize that the first president in American history rode horseback, in the manner of King David, nearly 3,000 years earlier. Not that much had changed. By the time of the first American original, 70 years later, technology was changing everything, at breakneck speed. The American idea was taking hold.

And there was something else about the American Republic. A government of the people, by the people, and for the people could not sustain long wars, and serial foreign entanglements. If war was necessary, there was a kind of furtive "tick-tock" ticking in the American body politic. Had his generals not achieved momentous and timely victories on the battlefield, the first American original would have lost reelection. The great Civil War had lasted over 4 long years. Enough was enough.

Presidents took note. It took about the same amount of time for America and the allies to defeat Imperial Japan and Nazi Germany. And presidents had to learn the lesson anew. The Korean war followed too closely to the end of World War II. The American people said enough, and they elected a war hero to get them out of it, with honor. The long Vietnam war was the scourge of several presidencies.

As it turned out, "small ball" took on the grandiose appearance of impossible projects to change hearts, and rebuild civil society, in both Afghanistan and Iraq. There was a phrase that was used to characterize the United Nations peacekeeping mission in the Somali Civil War: "mission creep." It came to be applied to military missions that seemed to lose their way on the road to victory. Afghanistan and Iraq bore a creepy resemblance to missions, off course.

The American Constitution played "small ball" with the government appetite to spend. It wasn't the sort of "small ball" that the president had in mind. Defending the nation aside, so-called "domestic" spending dramatically increased to accommodate his plans to federalize education reform, not to mention prescription drug coverage for senior citizens. It was part of a pattern of either acceding to, or actually believing in, an unconstitutional federal role in everything from soup to nuts. It was justified by "political realities," and a mantra that went something like this: we're not as bad as the other guys. Perhaps it would win the hour, but it would lose the day. If the political answer to the other guy's philosophy of governance is me too, except not quite so much, then what is a citizen to do? Well, most citizens wouldn't want a copy but, rather, the real deal. They would prefer soup to nuts... over mush.

The American culture had changed. Truth was the first casualty. Especially, His truth. George Orwell explained it all too well: "The further a society drifts from truth the more it will hate those who speak it." The "drift" became a deluge, followed by an inundation. The flood of deception that came swamped the White House. There was a new American president. For a man who was all too cool, his clothing was all too antique. Familiar, very familiar, but still antique.

His notorious ascendancy began with his campaign. He hired Hollywood myth makers who decorated his outdoor political convention with Greek columns. It was a stage more suited to a petty tyrant like King George III, who had been summarily dismissed by American colonists who were serious about G-d and G-d-given rights. In an earlier America, that kind of stagecraft would have been met by a guffaw so loud it would have reverberated through the Rocky Mountains. But at least half of America had become so unserious it swooned, followed closely by America's fortunes as a light to all the world. That light was now a searchlight, assuming its natural perch in the heavens, scouring the earth for a divine vector among a growing array of human weathervanes, which twisted and twirled with every mundane flash on a dim horizon. It dazzled men, but heaven was underwhelmed.

America's grandness had been grandly captured on Mount Rushmore. But America was now in the whirlwind of a 60's rush, a progressive rush that turned their inheritance, from a Mountain, to a mole hill. The Greek columns were about right. But it was Greek mythology that had written at least part of the story: it was Narcissus. The President's speeches were so laced with me(s) and I(s), they were either preparation for his singing debut in vaudeville, or practice for a spelling bee, hoping the first word would be Mississippi or, more to the point, insufferable.

And then there was the President's signature achievement. It was his signature, but the handwriting on the wall had a certain derivative quality. Stripped of all its pomposity and grandiosity, his affected penmanship succumbed to an obtuse, dystopian hieroglyphics. If history had been merciful, these unimaginative scratching's would have been lost to subterranean caves. But, in fact, they had come to see the light of day all too many times. We knew they were subterranean because their authors had a different title in mind: their only true desire was to be master of the world. Yes, they wanted the world, and they wanted it now. Progressivism had a vice grip on America. Nimrod would have been proud.

In fact, Nimrod would have been especially proud. The President was. He was a man prone to making declarations. He plainly crowed about *"The Road We've Traveled."* It wasn't so much a road, as a roadmap. It had been written by progressives earlier in the century. So, it was a road that had been traveled before. Yes, the President was a traveling man, who wouldn't dream of traveling from the west. He hailed from a lineage of bricklayers who fancied the grandiose, not the grand. When the modest built the grand by the sweat of their brow, his only response was: *"You didn't build that."*

Life was becoming more and more difficult for Israel, and impossible for the Bass family. The "Road We've Traveled" became a clear road for the Muslim Brotherhood and Wahhabism. The Muslim Brotherhood had never renounced their profound and endearing associations with Nazism. Now, the Muslim Brotherhood was meeting with the President in the oval office. It was an oval office that had shimmered proudly, and had grieved mightily, in the sacrifice of so many Americans who finally stopped the rise of Nazism's cold dead hand in Europe. No matter. And now the President's administration was encouraging fundraising in the United States to support scholarships to attend virulent Wahhabi Sharia centers in Saudi Arabia. And why were 30,000 American school children essentially receiving a Wahhabist education? Weren't the 9/11 hijackers and terrorists products of a Wahhabist education? It was troubling.

It became impossible for the Bass family to continue to live in the protected environment of an American military base. It was safer for them to finally move to Israel, once and for all. Daniel made the arrangements. Rachel would come first, and begin making sure their new home had some furniture. Ethan had to have a very minor heart procedure before he could travel. David would stay with Ethan. Shoshana was thrilled beyond belief. Rachel would be staying with us until the apartment for the Bass family was ready.

Daniel preferred Rachel stay put in our apartment unless he had made the necessary arrangements. Shoshana asked Daniel if she could leave Rachel alone, and venture out to visit John at the monastery. She hadn't seen John since his stroke, and it was going to be a slow recovery, even for a bear of a man. Daniel consented, probably reluctantly, but he knew how much it would mean to John. Shoshana was delighted.

Shoshana walked to the Holocaust Memorial, and took a taxi from there. My Rosie was clever in all things. His brothers at the monastery prepared a private room where John could continue his recovery. They had done so at John's request. The last thing Father John Broderick would ever want to be is a burden to others. He barely tolerated his brothers checking on him from time to time. They brought him his meals, and he kibitzed as best he could, but the stroke was serious, leaving him with some paralysis, and severe stiffness on the left side of his body. His speech was noticeably slower, and slightly slurred. The doctors weren't predicting anything like a full recovery. But John was. He wouldn't even consider the alternatives. The bear of a man had a bear of a will.

John was ready for Shoshana's visit. She walked through the door, and there he was with a computer and voice activation software. Shoshana lovingly kissed a face that was noticeably gaunt, but his shock of hair was at the ready, and Shoshana made a point of using her fingers to put any stray strand in place. A few tears welled in their eyes, but nothing a well-placed dab from Shoshana's handkerchief wouldn't handle. "I'll let you use that thing, if you promise that you will speak to me at least once before I leave." "I promise," he said, in a soft, gravelly voice. He smiled puckishly, and Shoshana loved it. "That won't count, Father John Broderick. You won't be getting off that easy today." He typed his reply. He must have been practicing. He qualified as a digital maestro, albeit a digital maestro with only a right index finger in hand. "Oh, Rosie, you just won't give an old priest a break." I had warned Shoshana that I shared our secret with John. She didn't mind. And she especially didn't mind his sense of humor. All of John was in there somewhere, she thought. And if he's still in there, it is only a matter of time before he comes out.

"John, when is your next doctor's visit?" "He comes here, Shoshana. He may the last doctor in the world to make house calls. My guess is that it is Daniel's doing, but he would never say, and I would never ask." "I wouldn't say this is a house, John. It is far more than that. Wouldn't you agree?" "It is a house for people who love and seek G-d, Shoshana. In that respect, it is much like the house of Isaac and Shoshana Singer. Or the House of David and Rachel Bass." "No wonder my father respects you so much, John. You have the heart of a Rabbi." "Thank you, my dear Shoshana. I do try." He winked with his right eye, and managed a muted laugh. John Broderick's wry sense of humor was fully intact. "It is easy to understand why Isaac loves you, John." "Shoshana, Isaac has a true heart for G-d, and he is a skilled warrior. King David possessed those qualities too." "May I tell him you said so, John?" "Of course, you may. Just now, I don't remember if I have said that to Isaac. If I didn't, I should have.

"Is Ethan well?" "Yes, John, very well. He will be here soon." Shoshana's phone began ringing. They were both distracted by a loud slamming of John's door. "I'm so sorry, John, I forgot to turn my phone off." Shoshana looked at her phone. It was Daniel. "Why would Daniel be calling me?" "Hello. Yes, he is. "John, Daniel wants to know if there is a brother here by the name of Arias?" "Why yes there is, Shoshana." Shoshana hurriedly got off the phone. "Father, this is very important. Daniel believes that Arias is not who he claims to be." "Shoshana!" John's voice was raspy, but about as loud as he could make it. He signaled Shoshana to listen. "Father Arias has been bringing by my dinner for the last week. He must have been listening at the door. Shoshana, please go out the door and find the first brother you see. Tell him that I am looking for Father Arias. Go quickly!"

Shoshana left John's room. She was gone for about 10 minutes, but it seemed far longer to John. "Father Arias is gone, John. He was seen leaving by the front gate. He said he needed to run a brief errand, and asked another brother to bring by your dinner." He didn't seem flustered at all. "Call Daniel, Shoshana, please." Shoshana's conversation with Daniel was brief. "Avner will be coming here to search Father Arias's room, John. In the meantime, Daniel wants me to stay here until Avner arrives. Oh, John, Daniel wanted me to ask you if there was anything else he should know about Arias?" "Let me see, Shoshana. I save my typed responses during conversations. "Here is something. Hmm, that's strange. It seems that yesterday I told Father Arias that Ethan would be visiting me today. I meant to say you, Shoshana, but I guess I had Ethan on my mind. He must have heard you say that Ethan would be here soon." "When is this going to end, John? There must be an end to all this." "Ethan will be fine, Shoshana. Please do not worry."

There was a knock on John's door. It was Avner, and he had John's dinner tray. He was holding the dinner tray like the best waiter in a Tel Aviv restaurant. A swanky Tel Aviv restaurant. "Would you care to see a wine menu, Father?" "I only indulge in sacramental wine, Avner." Avner couldn't contain himself. He would have laughed louder but he knew it would make it more difficult on John. John's smile was an awkward half smile, but it was a half-smile that could have filled the whole room. "Father John, if you don't mind, I'd like to visit your beautiful garden in the courtyard for a while." "Please do, Shoshana, the flowers will love your company."

"How are you feeling, John?" "It's a hindrance I could do without, Avner. But what is my suffering compared to the glory of G-d? I don't take it personally, Avner." "No wonder my father would go to the ends of the earth for you, Father John Broderick. What faith, oh my, what faith." "Avner, what about this Arias business?" "David Bass, John, David Bass. He had a hunch. Do you remember David's speculation about the fragment in the coded message?" "How could I forget? David thought it was 'Franciscan.' It hit home, Avner." "Yes, I imagine it did, Father. "As you know, John, that fragment never recurred. Until now. In the last several months, there it was again. At first, we thought they were just curious about you. They may have picked up word of your stroke through someone on the periphery of the Custodians of the Holy Land. But David thought it might be more than that. John, if you are right about what men like Bouhler think about men like you then, for them, you are the key. David believed they needed to get someone close enough to know what you were up to. If they could do that, then they would know what to do about Ethan."

"The first fragment was probably the beginning of their plan. It would take years to groom someone, and years more to get them inside the monastery. They knew that. How long has Arias been here, John?" "He arrived about 6 weeks ago from Venezuela, which would fit David's timeline perfectly, Avner. His name is Joaquin Arias.

He never shared much about his background, only that he wanted to come to Israel and study Judaic influences on the early church. He said his plan was to study for a year, and then ask for an assignment to a parish in his hometown in Venezuela." "Avner, how did you discover Arias's connection to Bouhler?" "We began monitoring all calls coming in and out of the monastery, John. Arias was using a satellite phone. It is a sophisticated bit of technology, with some encryption. But it's nothing we couldn't handle. We picked up a short communication last night, and another one today." "I assume he was calling Vienna, Avner?" "Yes, he was, John." "Was it Bouhler? Was it Bouhler he was talking to?" "I doubt it, don't you, John? Bouhler is far too careful for that." "Of course, you're right Avner. But I had to ask."

"Avner, if you'll excuse me, my doctor wants me to do these infernal exercises. He wanted to send over someone to help me with my rehabilitation. You know, some specialist. But I have all the help I need." John looked skyward." "Yes you do, Father John." "So, Avner, what is your plan now?" "Well, John I know my men already found the satellite phone in Arias's room. I doubt they found much else of value to us. Bouhler will deploy some of his minions to watch to see if Ethan visits the monastery. They will be well concealed. So will we. We need one, John. That's all. Just one. Now, we need to leave before Arias returns. We will slip out, just as we slipped in." "What about Shoshana, Avner?" "Isaac won't be returning from Tel Aviv until very late tonight, John. I prefer Shoshana wait here for a while. I'll tell her to call us for a ride home a little after sundown. It won't be long now." "Avner, Rachel is at Isaac's apartment." "Yes, I know. They aren't interested in Rachel, or Isaac's apartment, John. They believe Ethan's coming to visit you today." "You need to get going, Avner. I am sorry I kept you so long. Can you imagine, all of this a few days before Passover?" "Yes, Passover, John... they'd love to slaughter us all like lambs, wouldn't they?"

Avner and his men faded into the night. Shoshana was standing near the front entrance to the monastery. She was at the ready, but she was mostly thinking about what was out there: grotesque centaurs who were seduced by the clarity of their nocturnal vision, which was completely predatory: it fed their flesh, but lost their souls to the cover of darkness. It was their predatory instincts that she hoped to use against them.

As Shoshana expected, a taxi appeared just outside the front gate. A woman, riding shotgun, paid the driver, and hurriedly made her way to the taxi's rear door on the passenger side. She deftly opened the door, and extended her winter coat to cover the other rider as he ducked down. Shoshana opened the gate; they were inside before the taxi driver could reconnoiter, and continue to his next fare.

There was little time for pleasantries. "Ari, I am sorry for this. You'll understand later. Please follow Brother Stephen to the chapel. Wait there for about an hour." Shoshana handed Ari Peretz a scrap of paper. "Call this number. Use my name. Tell the man on the phone that you need a ride home. Let me see your face in the light, Ari. Oh, Ari, you look like a teenage Isaac Singer. You will make someone very happy. Go now, quickly. Give my love to your parents!"

"Shoshana, I brought the clothes." "Good, very good. They will do. They will have to do. Where did you park your car?" "Six or seven blocks east of here, just as you suggested, Shoshana." "Perfectly done! There is a rarely used exit on the east side of the monastery. I doubt Arias knows about it. Brother Stephen has the key. Just walk at a normal pace to your car. If you are followed, go back to the apartment. If not, I will see you in about ten or fifteen minutes. Does that sound about right?" "Closer to fifteen, I think, Shoshana." "That's fine. I'll be ready!"

Both women briskly followed Brother Stephen, whose embrace of obedience and guilelessness momentarily gave way to a more worldly service. Shoshana had a stop to make. She knocked on John's door. She hesitated, and then approached John's bed. She was becalmed by all the years. They were so many years. Years that had glacially moved by, depositing the fruit of a life well lived, a holy life, on her heart that was now so heavy with sweet memories. There was nothing frail about John Broderick, she thought. Half paralyzed, he was still a bear of a man. His hair was always unruly, but never untidy. He was shy, but was never susceptible to the cacophony; the voice he heard shot across the ages, and pierced the willing heart. It was the voice that spoke creation into existence, and loved in such pure, unrequited magnificence, that even its faintest echoes etched a calling card on the human heart.

John was propped up in his bed, carefully reading and rereading the pages of a book. The stroke had affected the vision in his left eye. It was probably ill-advised, but he was wearing an eye patch over the left eye, training his right eye to do all the work. He removed the eye patch as Shoshana leaned over to kiss him on the cheek. John began typing. "What's in the bag, Shoshana?" "Just some clothes, John. I'll be leaving soon. I just wanted to stop by to say goodnight." "Did you call Daniel for a ride?" "Thankfully, I didn't have to. Did you finish your exercises, John?" "Yes, and had you come by a few minutes later, I probably would have been sleeping. I still tire too easily. But I never tire of seeing you and Isaac, Shoshana." "You are our dear, Father John Broderick. We love you. What would we ever do without you? And what would Israel do without you?" "I suspect that G-d would find someone else. As He must, Shoshana. His will be done." "Yes, Father, His will be done." "I'll leave you now. I know you're tired. Oh, John, I have something for Isaac. I'd like to leave it here in the drawer. Do you mind?" "Not at all, Shoshana, please."

"Shoshana, I already asked you about the bag, If I asked you about the note to Isaac, and how exactly you are getting home, you wouldn't answer, would you?" "I can't just now, Father. Not, just now, please." "Then I will ask you to be careful, Shoshana. This business we share with your father; it's a dangerous business." "You are too wise for the world, John Broderick. That is why the world fears you, and one of the many reasons why we love you. I'll see you soon, Father." Shoshana was approaching the door, but waited for John to type his response. "You are in the palm of G-d's hand, Shoshana, Bless you."

There wasn't much time. Shoshana quickly changed, and handed a bag full of clothes to Brother Stephen for safekeeping. He took the bag, averting his eyes. Still, he couldn't help but notice that Shoshana had tucked her hair under a cap. Brother Stephen was an American, like John. For all the world, it looked like Shoshana was wearing a baseball hat. She thanked Brother Stephen, and made a mad dash for the front gate. The wait seemed interminable. Suddenly, she felt silly standing there. Maybe she should change back into her other clothes, and get rid of that ridiculously looking baseball hat! In fact, her timing was impeccable, as usual. A car pulled up in front of the gate. Now, there was no going back.

Shoshana was in no particular hurry to get to the car door. It was after dark. The street was not well lit. The driver had carefully placed the car in the shadows. As Shoshana reached to open the car door, she noticed someone on the sidewalk about 10 meters from the front gate. Just as he entered the light, she sat down and closed the door. "It's Arias," she said. Shoshana quickly and firmly put her left hand on the driver's shoulder. "Don't speed. Nice and easy. Track him in your rear view mirror. What is he doing?" "He is running to the front gate. He went inside." All Shoshana said was, "Good!"

"I'll get better at this. I'm just a little nervous, Shoshana." "You're doing great! We'll have time to talk, soon. But now, we need to leave an impression. Take a left here, please! Do you see that taxi up ahead?" "Yes." "Pull up behind it. Keep the car running. Please, give me your cell phone." "But, Shoshana!" "Don't worry. I'll be right back." Shoshana signaled to the driver to wait a moment more. She crouched near the passenger door. "Daniel, is that you?" "Shoshana, where are you?" "Daniel, I will call you later. Everything is under control. Have your men ready." Shoshana opened the rear passenger door. She handed the driver a wad of bills, He peeled away. Shoshana was back in her seat, deciding on the next move. "Isaac calls this Van Gogh chess," she said.

"I programmed the GPS. It will guide us. Isaac and I have taken this trip many, many times. He never takes the same route twice. We'll go through the territories on an Israeli highway."

"What about our cell phones, Shoshana?" "The taxi driver is an old friend. He'll drive the coastal roads. He'll give a wide berth to Tel Aviv. He knows about roads that aren't even on the map. It will frustrate Daniel and his men. But they will follow him. The cell phones will be their guide." "What about Arias?" "He did his job well. No doubt, they are on the road looking for us. We will change cars at a small Samaritan village in Nablus. Isaac has a friend there."

"Avner, I want to ride with you and your men."

"Father, we can handle this. I would rather you didn't."

"Am I so old that I cannot even be part of the chase anymore, my son? After all, Shoshana did call me."

"You know better than anyone how dangerous these men are, Father. But, she called you once, she will call you again. She hopes to lay a trap. We will need a good shot. You used to be able to shoot the eye out of a needle at 100 meters."

"I think my age has taken that down to 75 meters, my son." "That's good enough. Ride with me, Father!"

"Avner, where are they now?" "Do you really think they are in the car, father?" "No, Avner, I don't. Shoshana is Shlomo Levy's daughter. She is also Isaac Singer's wife. She would never make such a silly mistake with a cell phone. But she wants us to go north, Avner. She will call us again, when the time is right. Where is the car now?" "It's just passing Tel Aviv. He is very good, this driver Shoshana recruited." "I have no doubt he is a friend of Isaac. I'm sure he is a professional, Avner." "Do you have any idea where they are going, father?" "Isaac likes to drive. I know he and Shoshana took many trips over the years. But he never really said where he was going.

Sometimes they would go to Tel Aviv to visit his step parents. Shoshana is going somewhere familiar to her. She believes that will keep her safe. I pray she is right."

"It was risky to bring a young man like Ari into this, Shoshana."

"It was. G-d forgive me, it was. But, I wouldn't have tried it if I thought he was in any serious danger. In this country, we live on the edge. On the other side is extinction. That is no justification…" Shoshana's voice began to fade into tears. She was sobbing. "How have you done it, all these years? There just seems no end to it."

"Shoshana, I have wondered the same thing about your work. The children, Shoshana. All those children, murdered. How, Shoshana? How?"

"Even in death, they are our life. Their lives testify to G-d's love. Their deaths remind us of the fall. There is no bottom to the fall. They murder our children. But they can't condemn them. They are the condemned. And Israel lives. Israel is a miracle they despise. Israel is a shadow of things to come. Yes, what I do, I do in service to memory. G-d knew every child at the foundation of the world. He saw every tiny hand in the womb. In every tiny hand is the hand of G-d. I try my best to honor that. Oh, I should have never jeopardized Ari. May G-d forgive me!"

"Don't be so hard on yourself, Shoshana. This is an impossible situation. Ari is home safely, by now. Someday, he may even regale you father with stories of how he was part of a secret plot, complete with a Franciscan Monastery, costume changes, and cars speeding away into the night."

"It doesn't sound so bad, when you put that way. I love this road. It is known as the 'Way of the Patriarchs.' Can you imagine, it was frequently travelled by Abraham, Isaac and Jacob. I bet you have a special interest in Jacob. You have no idea why I would say that, do you Rachel?" Rachel began to smile for the first time since they left Jerusalem. "Yes, Shoshana, it seems that Jacob had a special love for Rachel. But I was always sort of partial to Leah. She suffered the trials of the world, but still honored the righteous ways of G-d. And Shoshana, she was the mother of Judah." "Yes, Rachel, she was the mother of kings." "But, Shoshana, I know Rachel is a blessed name. Joseph was her son. He suffered the rejection of his brothers, and imprisonment by Pharaoh. But in time, G-d raised him up and he brought the known world under his control. Pharaoh was so grateful he gave the children of Israel the best land in Egypt, the land of Goshen. We will see whether the modern day Pharaohs are so wise." "I seriously doubt that, Rachel." "So do I... so do I."

"Slow down a bit, Rachel, we are near the exit for Nablus." "Why are we going there, Shoshana? Isn't it dangerous for us?" "Don't worry, if we are stopped by Israeli police, I will show them a document Isaac gave me. They won't bother us. The Palestinian police aren't usually around here much. But we need to stop to change license plates. We need the "yellow" plates after we get past Jenin, farther north. We will also change cars."

"Here, Rachel, take this exit! Go slowly, just follow the GPS. This is tricky. It's that road!! Yes, that's right. Now, slower please... right here! Good! He left the garage open. Pull all the way in. Rachel, don't say anything. Just get into the car next to us. When I get in, pull out of the garage. Please, give me the keys." They exited the car. A man appeared at the door. Shoshana took off her baseball hat, and quickly made sure her hair fell on the back of her shoulders and neck. She confidently tossed the keys to a smallish, dour looking man. He caught the keys with his left hand, and waited for Rachel to drive out of the garage. By the time the car was on the street, the garage door was closed.

"You wear my son's clothes well, Shoshana." "I keep wondering what Isaac would think. My father told me that during the raid on Beirut many of our men wore women's clothes. And wigs too, can you imagine? I always tried to picture Isaac in a wig. I never could figure out how to ask him." "He wore a blonde wig, Shoshana. David said Isaac didn't want to compete with his wife. All that danger, and

Isaac thought about what he might look like next to his wife. Is he coming home from Tel Aviv, tonight?" "Probably not... it's about, you know, this Iran thing." "I don't think the Israeli pilots will be wearing wigs, Shoshana." "I don't know, maybe the wigs would startle Iranian radar." "It worked in Beirut, Rachel."

"Isaac, if you want, you can stay at my house tonight. My wife would love to see you. You are a favorite of hers." "Why, Colonel... Moshe, I don't know what to say. This is the first time you have invited me to stay overnight at your house. Is something wrong, Colonel?" "No Isaac, and I am ashamed this is the first time. There should have been many times before this. I could have used your company. It is wise company, Isaac. I used to think you were sentimental. But I was foolish. Will you accept an invitation from a repentant old man?" "There is a phrase they use in America, Colonel. 'Rain check.' May I take a rain check on your invitation? I was looking forward to staying in the barracks with some of the younger officers. They are good men, Colonel. Brave men. But even brave men need reassurance. They see what we see, Moshe. They see the world coming against Israel." "Of course, Isaac. Aviva and I will take this rain check for now."

"You sound a little discouraged, Isaac. I take it the meeting on Iran didn't go so well." "Their words tell us their intentions, Colonel. That is the lesson of history. And I worry about a western world that is asleep. They only seem to awake in their hatred of Israel. Yes, I guess you could say I am a little discouraged." "I seem to remember a young man... oh, how brash he was... he lectured a senior officer, and a man who knows the world like few others. And, you know what, Isaac. We needed to hear what you said. Every syllable... even the syllables with the accent on the self-righteous. You were right then, Isaac. Take your words to those young officers. Tell them to believe in miracles, Isaac. Tell them that the miracles will come again. Tell them about the Land, Isaac. Most of all, tell them about the righteous and holy G-d of Abraham, Isaac, and Jacob. Tell them to defend this place, Isaac. Tell them to serve the world, and defend this place!"

"I guess I have days when the boy is not so much the father of the man, Moshe. The boy is still there. It's just that he gets a bit weary, from time to time." "Isaac, that boy spoke like a man. I had the privilege of listening to him through all the wars, all of our trials. Do you remember Isaac, how skeptical I was about the miracles in the '73 war? They were right before my eyes, and yet, I did not see." "I see Colonel, but I worry. I do worry." "It is good to prepare, Isaac, but do not worry. The first blood moon will be here in a few days. We may not see it in Israel, but it will be in the sky. It means He is there, Isaac. He said the lights in the heavens would divide the day from the night. And Isaac, even before the lights in the heavens were to mark the days and the years, they would be for signs and seasons. Signs, Isaac! And seasons, not the seasons followed by the farmers and shepherds, but the seasons that are His appointed times. His appointed times: the feasts. Passover, Isaac. The first and third blood moons are on Passover. In the Passover season there was anguish, then freedom. He will free the righteous of the world, Isaac. But there will be anguish. Like Pharaoh, the cold-hearted will resist. They will insist on the abyss, where their cold hearts find comfort in the darkness."

"You were always my senior officer, Colonel Stern." "Even now, Isaac?" "Especially now, Colonel. Those young officers may get more than they bargained for, Moshe." "I think not, Isaac. This is a small country. Who doesn't know about Isaac Singer, brilliant physicist, and may I say, Isaac, brilliant special forces officer. There are many tales that are told about you, Isaac." "Yes, Colonel, some of them are even true." "You were always able to make me laugh, Isaac. Of course, I made sure you never knew that. I do know this, Isaac. The true stories about you are all anybody ever needs. They are the stories of the son of Benjamin and Leah Singer. They were my friends. They died as heroes. And their son has lived a hero's life." "I have tried to live a life that is worthy in the sight of G-d. I pray that my wife, especially my wife, but also my friends and my parents would understand my life in that way." "We do, Isaac, I assure you, we do." "Before I leave, Colonel Stern, there is just one more thing. There is something I should have done much more, but I didn't. Forgive me."

Both men held their salute longer than usual. Colonel Stern was especially touched by the gesture. As he turned to walk away, Moshe Stern could be heard saying, "Oh, Benjamin and Leah, you did well with this boy of yours. You did very well."

"Rachel, I still don't quite know sometimes how you and David take your next breath." "Fortunately, Shoshana, G-d doesn't allow us to consider every breath. But when the fear takes hold, and it does, I hear myself breathing, and it sounds like an animal on the run in the night. It's not a sound that I wish on anyone. But you're right, Shoshana, David and I have despaired for our son's safety. But he has saved us." "What do you mean, Rachel?" "Ethan always senses our moods, Shoshana. He comforts us. He understands the danger, but he has no fear. None."

"My son loves the stories of Jacob. He has his feet firmly planted on 'Jacob's ladder.' No wonder he insisted on going to the Temple Mount." "Yes, Rachel, Jacob rested his head on a stone on Mount Moriah, the Temple Mount. His father, Isaac, was taken there by his father, Abraham, as a sacrifice to G-d. As Jacob's head rested on the stone, he dreamed of a ladder that was set up on earth, and its top reached to heaven. The angels of G-d were ascending and descending on the ladder. 'Jacob's ladder.' It is the destiny of all those of faith. Our faith is the power, and the word of G-d is the bridge." "The angels have carried my son to a place of peace. He is resolute. Nothing will deter him. That is our strength, Shoshana. It is G-d's solace to us. It is how we take our next breath."

"He seems to have stopped, Father." "Where is he now, Avner?" "Zikhron, it looks like he stopped in Zikhron." "Interesting. I am sure Shoshana asked him to stop there. That is probably his last stop. She will contact him, and tell him to go back to Jerusalem." "Why would she do that?" "We are supposed to take over from there, Avner. She will be calling to tell us where she is going." "The car is stopped just up ahead, father." "Good, pull up behind him. I'm sure he is expecting us. He won't be startled." "Something is wrong, Avner, Be careful!" Avner was looking ahead as he tapped softly on the taxi window with the slightly bent fingers on his right hand. There was no reply. He opened the driver's door and, for a moment, his right hand disappeared inside the taxi. He motioned to some of his men to surround the car. Their guns were drawn. He looked at this gun as he walked determinedly back to the car where his father, Daniel, was sitting. He opened the car door and sat with his gun in his lap. "He's dead, father. He has a bullet hole in his head. Small caliber."

Daniel's phone rang. It was Shoshana. "Daniel, are you near the taxi? I can't seem to get a hold of the driver." "He is dead, Shoshana." There was silence. Daniel waited, but he couldn't wait any longer. "Shoshana, the ruse worked. They took your bait. Let us finish this now. Tell us where you are going! The silence continued. "Shoshana! Shoshana! These men know where you are going. The driver knew, didn't he, Shoshana. Shoshana!" Finally, Daniel heard a soft, but unintimidated voice. "Yes, I never specifically told him, but he knew, Daniel. He knew because he knew where Isaac and I liked to go. Tell your men to meet us at Mt. Carmel." "Go back to Jerusalem, Shoshana. There's no need to continue this." "We'll be fine, Daniel. Take care of the threat to Ethan. You'll find us in the monastery. Good luck."

"Avner, we're going to Mt. Carmel. Let's go. They have a head start. Call Haifa and tell them to send a team to clean this mess up. We'll need six more men to meet us at Carmel." "Are you expecting an army, father?" "I would face them alone, Avner. I'm not sure if I have the faith of David. I pray I do not have a vengeful heart. But I have a son to think about." "Is Shoshana going back to Jerusalem?" "No, I asked her to go back, but I knew what the answer would be.

She's determined to stand in the breach, Avner. For Ethan, and for all those children whose memory she has kept alive. I have heard you have driven your way out of some tight spots. Get us there as fast as you can, Avner!"

"I'll drive now, Rachel. Put all of that beautiful blonde hair under your son's hat." Shoshana was fighting back the tears. "Rachel, they killed the driver. If you want to go back to Jerusalem, just say so." "Where is Daniel, Shoshana?" "He's on his way to Mt. Carmel." "Is that where we're going Shoshana, Mt. Carmel?" "Yes, it is. Isaac and I have been going there for years. I called ahead to the monastery. I told Daniel to meet us there." "I've never been to Mt. Carmel, Shoshana. Let's go, shall we?" "You have the calm of your son, Rachel. He's thousands of miles away, but you have the calm of your son." "Yes, I do, Shoshana. Yes, I do."

"Why Mt. Carmel, Shoshana?" "It started with a painting Isaac saw outside a little chapel where John lives. It was a painting of Mt. Carmel. The first time Isaac and I visited there, we fell in love with the place. Do you remember the evening we went to the Western Wall with Ethan, Rachel?" "Yes, of course, I do." "There was just a sliver of a moon that night. But the light from that moon lit up Mt. Carmel as if it was day. You have to listen to heaven, Rachel. It is a beautiful place. King Solomon compared the beauty of his bride to Mt. Carmel."

"Isaac loves to visit before it gets too hot, and pick a rakefes to put in my hair. It is a gorgeous flower. I think you call it a cyclamen in English. It is said of the rakefes that it bows his head to the ground, waiting humbly for the Messiah. When Messiah comes, then the rakefes will proudly lift its head upward. So, we are going to Mt. Carmel, Rachel. Besides, they usually make Isaac and I a delicious soup. And I am getting a little hungry. How about you, Rachel?" "I haven't thought much about food, but now that you mention it. Is that thunder I hear in the distance, Shoshana?" "Yes, it is. That's funny. I know it rained very hard here this morning. But it was supposed to be clear this evening." "There it is again, Shoshana. The thunder, I mean." "We'll be there soon, I need to call Daniel."

"Daniel, is that you. Are you close?" "Yes, we'll be there in a few minutes How about you?" "We're almost there. We'll enter on the south side. There is a road leading to the monastery. I'll cut our headlights and park the car in a little stand of trees. Rachel and I will go on foot to the monastery. We'll see you there." Just then, lightning shed its bright light on an otherwise dark road. There was a car well up ahead with its headlights off. As it turned on its lights, Shoshana was temporarily blinded. She saw the road to the monastery. She turned quickly and sped up the gentle slope of Mt. Carmel. Now two cars, maybe more, were following her.

"Get ready, Rachel." The lights behind her weren't making much headway. Shoshana was 30 meters short of her turnoff. She shut the lights, as the car careened before it came to a standstill near a laurel tree. "Run for it, Rachel." Shoshana took Rachel's hand and began running for the monastery. The morning rains had stirred up a muddy stew. It became a slog, a slow-motion frenzy for the safety of the monastery. There was a quick flash of lightning. The thunder boomed. It muffled the rat-a-tat-tat of gunfire. The lightning again followed. It seared the scene. It was a petrified forest of a tableau.

CHAPTER TEN

THE STARS OF ITS MORNING

"May the stars of its morning be dark;
May it look for light, but have none,
And not see the dawning of the day;
Because it did not shut up the doors of my mother's womb,
Nor hide sorrow from my eyes. Why did I not die at birth?
Why did I not perish when I came from the womb?"
Job 3:9-11

Stillness after the crescendo wasn't bliss. Daniel knew that. The stillness was deafening to a heart that ached because of what his refined instincts told him. Daniel had learned that stillness had a language. The language was silence. It was the language of funereal reverence.

On their approach to the south road, Avner and his men were witness to the chase, the blaze, and now this. Daniel advised his son to park the cars just past the entrance to the south road. Avner didn't quite understand. Daniel understood that his son was a taut spring that had to be unwound. He gently placed his left hand on Avner's forearm. "Wait for me, please." The other men followed Avner's lead. They were alert, and watchful; their guns were drawn. Daniel slowly removed himself from the car. He walked a few meters ahead, and stopped, to make sure they knew to follow his pace. Daniel seamlessly leaned over, bent slightly at the knees, his eyes always looking forward as he tied his left shoe. He stood erect and adjusted his pants and, using his index fingers in a semi-circular motion around his waist, made sure his shirt was tightly tucked in. Avner marveled at his father's condition. He was trim, and surprisingly agile for his age. Avner knew there was one more thing for this father to do. His father didn't disappoint. He swept his left hand, palms open, over his hair. Daniel's hair was closely cropped but, nonetheless, it had to be done.

Avner was convinced the familiar routine was over, and began to move forward. Not quite, not yet. There was one more thing. Something, Avner never saw his father do before. Daniel removed a handkerchief from his pocket. Avner was now at a closer distance to observe. The near full moon wasn't visible, but there was just enough starlight. There was a tear zigzagging down his father's left cheek. Daniel mopped up his face, and carefully folded the handkerchief and put it back in his pants pocket. Avner put away his gun. His men did likewise. Daniel began walking.

Daniel motioned for his son to walk at his side. He signaled Avner to tell his men to give them some distance. Avner's men began to lag behind. Daniel approached Shoshana's car, and used a pocket flashlight to look inside. He knew it would be empty. It was a formality, and a necessary interlude. Just as Daniel pointed the flashlight to the ground in front of the car, he paused. He put his left arm in front of Avner's path. He pushed Avner back a step or two. Avner's men halted their slow advance. They too took a step back, perhaps two steps back. Daniel looked at this son, and pointed his finger at his ear. What was that noise? What was it? Daniel recalled his grandmother's old tea pot. The sound wasn't the high pitched whistle of her tea pot at full boil. This sound droned a bit, just as her tea pot did a minute or two before the whistle. But, there was more than one. It was a droning chorus of grandma's tea pots, with a sizzle.

Daniel used a left hand to caution his son and the others to stay put. He made about a half step forward. The starlight became slightly brighter. He caught a glimpse of an evanescent sparkle. It moved, then it disappeared. Daniel took his flashlight and shined it towards the moving sparkle. He saw what he needed to see. The years with Father John Broderick had served him well. He pointed to his flashlight. Avner knew what to do. One of the men brought forward a light more suited to the Broadway theatre. It illuminated what Daniel expected. There were more than he had anticipated. Each incinerated grave marker had a serpentine headstone. It was a live serpentine headstone. They were each perched on a pile of ash. Daniel drew his gun. He motioned the others to step forward and do the same. He approached the first, and aimed his gun. Its eyes seemed oddly focused on him; they were almost knowing eyes, but G-d made those eyes to see a kaleidoscope of images. The question is: which image to strike? It didn't slither. But it did lurch. The bullet left a lifeless belly in the dust. One less tea pot for the chorus. The remaining chorus was quickly silenced. Avner gasped at what his father did next. Daniel violently crushed every serpent's head with his heel. The men were stunned by his ferocity. Then Daniel said, *"enmity between the seed of the woman and you."*

"And I will put enmity Between you and the woman,
And between your seed and her Seed;
He shall crush your head, And you shall bruise His heel."
Genesis 3:15

Daniel managed a furtive smile. He restored orderliness to his shirt and pants. He didn't bother with his shoes. He wanted it over with. Oh, those grim next steps. Daniel took out his flashlight. Avner let him go alone for now. The mud was no longer a quagmire. It had been baked, and glazed. He came upon Shoshana and Rachel. They were face down, but their bodies were untouched by the lightning. Daniel knelt next to Shoshana's body. He straightened her hair, and turned her head so he could see her face. He did the same to Rachel. Rachel's hair seemed to radiate every light in the sky. Daniel had seen too much death. But he had never seen such serene beauty among the dead.

He was still kneeling, tidying up their clothes when Avner approached. Daniel looked at his son with tears streaming down his face. "They always dressed so beautifully, Avner. It was the least I could do. Did you call our friends, Avner? I don't want to involve the police in this." "They'll be here soon, father." "Please bring me some sheets from the monastery. I don't want to leave them like this." "We already took care of that. Here they are." "Thank you. Avner, wait for me in the car. I shouldn't be long."

Daniel thought how appropriate it was for their bodies to be wrapped in the white linen from the monastery. This linen has heard our urgent prayers, he thought. He lovingly wrapped their bodies in the linen. They wouldn't have to wait long, the men who Avner called were standing nearby. "You're not done with me yet", he said. "And I will never be done with you. Save me a place on the cloud with the old spies." Daniel laughed through a few tears.

Just before he turned to walk away, a light from the monastery shone brightly in his eyes. He shielded his eyes and looked down at where the bodies of Shoshana and Rachel laid and noticed something he hadn't seen before. There was something that looked like writing that appeared in the ground above Rachel's head. He asked the men to give him a few more moments. He took out the flashlight and knelt down to look more closely. There was something written in the ground. She had written the name of her son, Ethan, before she died. Rachel's own journey to Ephrath ended on Mount Carmel. It was a new birth for a dying world. The precious pedals of the rakefes would longer be so bowed. Their full bloom of exaltation would have to wait.

The beauty of Rachel and Shoshana found its bloom in sacrifice. They were the Amaranth: the imaginary flower that never dies. Their fate had an all too un-imaginary similarity to the stunning Amaranth, which is the color of blood red. But their fate also had a palpability, unknown to the Amaranth. Rachel and Shoshana lived in the imagination of G-d. As such, absent their dainty fleshly residence, they had eternal life in the palm of G-d's hand. The Amaranth turned green with envy.

Heaven had been moved by a sacrifice that only heaven could fully comprehend: sacrificial love and obedience to G-d. The heavens seethed. The ground was scorched. Mount Carmel became an earthly crematorium for the condemned. The cremated flesh of the condemned released them to the judgment of G-d. The lost souls of the condemned found their home. There would be no rest, only torment. Eternal torment. And solace among the living in G-d's justice. In the natural, evisceration would have been proportion. But proportion according to human design succumbed to the prophetic architecture of heaven.

> *"He uncovers deep things out of darkness,*
> *And brings the shadow of death to light."*
> *Job 12:22*

Now, on the horizon there was a sign from heaven. Our season of anguish would give way to the eternal things of G-d. For the G-d of creation hated death. And we longed for Him to breathe life into us again.

Ethan's first cry was that of an anguished son. It stirred mansions in high places. History began in the garden. So did anguish.

David's mourning for Rachel turned into concern for his son. That changed on the plane ride to Tel Aviv. Ethan's eyes were affixed on a far horizon, well beyond the stoic and steady cut of a winged marvel of a machine. The wings were writing a narrative, he thought. Once and a while, the wing's tips would find a willing wisp of a cloud, and with just enough celestial ink, pause, and ever so gently move up, then down. All the stories, all the anticipation, all the hopes and dreams.

Somewhere along the line, there had a be a comma in all this. The wings obliged.

For the first time, Ethan smiled after all the screams. They were the screams of an infant that laid the foundation for the voice of a man. He knew that. Now the man softly took the hand of his father. It was the least he could do. David was father to the man. He kissed his father's hand, and held it to his cheek for a moment. It was a moment dedicated to a lifetime of moments. "I love you, father. Don't worry, her love saved her. Remember what you used to read to me: 'Whoever rejoices in the sufferings that come upon him in this life brings salvation to the world.' That was for this day, father. That was for this day." David sobbed in relief.

Ethan again took his father's hand. This time he led him from the burial of a woman who had ravished him as a student, but left him as a man. When they first met, David had maintained a steady and faithful gaze at the Word. She once told him, "The truth won't leap off those pages into your heart, David. Remember, truth and spirit. Truth and spirit." Yes, it was her holy buoyancy he would remember. His eyes would never leave the pages of the truth. But it was her holy buoyancy that gave his step toward G-d, just the right lilt. As they walked to the car, David stepped ponderously. His frailty was the residue of a heart splintered and splattered over a life well-lived in the sight of G-d. And G-d saw. And it was G-d's perfect hand that took every cell, every sinew, every odd smattering, and put David's heart back together again. Now, David would have the heart for G-d's truth again.

There is comfort in the perfect symmetries of G-d. Yes, until His Kingdom Come, the faithful in a fallen world would rejoice in the perfect symmetry of G-d. Faith is a gift but, in the natural, mercy is a necessity. His mercy. There was no living without Shoshana. There was only faithfully enduring. And His mercy saw me through an unimaginable day. Like holy pillars sent from heaven, my brother, Aaron, was on my left, and Shoshana's father, Rabbi Shlomo Levy, was on my right. Aaron gently placed his hand above my left elbow; as I gently placed my hand around Rabbi Levy's right shoulder. I was desperately worried about Shoshana's father. First his wife, now this. And none of us could for long take our eyes off Ethan. G-d certainly hadn't. Ethan pointed us to a truth. It was mercy.

Ethan kissed David, and told him and Aaron to wait for us back at my apartment. Ethan wanted Rabbi Levy and I to join him. It wouldn't be too long, he said. Daniel provided the car and driver. I don't know why, but it reminded me of Ashdod. But I left it there. I had to. It led to Shoshana. Rabbi Levy and I got into the back seat. Ethan was still outside saying his good byes to Daniel and Colonel Stern. Suddenly, Rabbi Levy and I were alone for the first time since Shoshana's death. Our training wouldn't allow us to count the driver. Shoshana's father leaned ever so imperceptibly in my direction. "Isaac," he said softly. I was a little startled. "Isaac," he said. He raised his voice just a bit. "Yes, Rabbi," I said. "No, Isaac, not Rabbi. Please, call me Shlomo. You loved my Shoshana beyond any father's dream for his daughter. I have much to learn from you, Isaac. So now, you can be my Rabbi. Besides, that's the way Rosie would want it." He laughed. He made me laugh. So, Shoshana told her father our secret, too. She knew I liked to solve puzzles. Now I could wonder who else knew about "my Rosie."

Ethan got into the car and said nothing to the driver. It didn't take long for me to figure out our destination. I turned to Rabbi Levy. "John," I whispered. He nodded expectantly. As the car pulled up in front of the monastery, Ethan quickly turned his head, and almost admonishingly, asked us to wait in the car. Then he said, "I won't be long." He could see the disappointment in our eyes. "Please, wait here. I promise I won't be long." I didn't understand, but we waited, nonetheless. As we waited for Ethan, Rabbi Levy and I were bantering back and forth. All I could think of is that Shoshana would be on the floor, laughing. I would say Rabbi Levy, then he would say, "No, Shlomo." He would teasingly say, Rabbi Singer, then I would say,

"No, Isaac." Back and forth. Back and forth. He began recalling the happy times in Morocco before his wife was killed. He spoke about his memories of Shoshana as a child, as if it were yesterday. I was in the presence of a man I never really knew. I looked at my watch. Almost a half an hour had passed. Rabbi Levy continue to regale me with story after story. I looked at my watch again. Suddenly, there wasn't a sound. I looked over at Rabbi Levy. He was looking passed me at the monastery gate.

What strode through the monastery gate was the perfect symmetry of a vision. It began in a hospital room, and whatever came against it would succumb to its holy obedience. It was a vision for the broken hearted. I asked the driver to lower my window. The arc of John's rainbow of a smile surely pushed away the shroud covering Mount Carmel. It was a sign. But I couldn't help but think, it was just a tad early. After all, I wanted any excuse to make sure that Father John Broderick clearly understood: if he was back, so I was.

At sundown, it was Passover. Passover: the day of the first Blood Moon in a tetrad that would be completed in the next eighteen months. "Don't you think it is a little early for miracles, John. The first Blood Moon won't appear until later tonight." His voice was a little weak, but it told me the bear of a man *was* back. "My apologies Isaac, my sense of timing is a little off. Besides, we won't be able to see this Blood Moon from Jerusalem." He managed a wink. Then he handed Ethan a piece of paper. One of the other Franciscans helped John get back to his room. He wasn't quite ready to walk on his own.

"We have one more stop to make," Ethan said. I didn't understand. Now he said something I had never heard before. "Don't worry, Uncle Isaac, we'll get home before sundown." Uncle Isaac, I thought. It was very American, but I liked it! I had no idea where we were going. But I didn't have to wait long. We stopped at the Mount of Olives. Ethan turned around. He handed me the piece of paper he got from John. "Uncle Isaac, this is the note I gave to Father John at the Western Wall. It is a part of my petition, my prayer, which I left for our Father in heaven. I thought you might want to read it here, looking at the Eastern Gate. My father told me you refused to go through the Eastern Gate during the `67 war. G-d will honor you for that, Uncle Isaac."

I was a little disoriented. But I did as Ethan asked. As I opened the note, I stood looking at the Eastern Gate. All it said was, "I pray we will not falter between two opinions any longer. If the Lord is G-d, let us follow Him." I closed the note, and bowed my head. I heard familiar female voices. "Isaac," they said, "History begins in the garden, it ends in the city."

THE END

BIBLIOGRAPHICAL ACKNOWLEDGEMENTS

1.) Chapter Four: Klein, Aaron J. (2005). Striking Back: The 1972 Munich Olympics Massacre and Israel's Deadly Response. New York: Random House, Inc.

2.) Chapter Four: Fox,Writer. YOM KIPPUR WAR 1973/MIDDLE EAST CONFLICT... http://writerfox.hubpages.com/hub/Yom-Kippur-War.

3.) Chapter Four: Zionism and Israel - Encyclopedic Dictionary, Yom Kippur War.

4.) Chapter Five: Goni, Uki. The Real Odessa: Smuggling the Nazis to Argentina... http://greyfalcon.us/The%20Real%20Odessa.htm.

5.) Chapter Five: ben David, Rabbi Dr. Hillel. A Time for Judgment.

6.) Chapter Five: Bernstein, Carl; Politi, Marco. (1997). His Holiness.

7.) Chapter Five: Dalin, David G. (2007). John Paul II and the Jews.

8.) Chapter Five: Gur, Haviv Rettig; Keinon, Herb. (2009). Jerusalem Post.

9.) Chapter Seven: Omer-man, Michael. (2011). This Week in History: The Jews of Basel are burnt. Jerusalem Post.

10.) Chapter Seven: Organization of Former SS Members. Jewish Virtual Library.

11.) Chapter Seven: McCarthy, Andrew. (2012). National Review.

12.) Chapter Seven: Aminoff, Gary. (2012). Islamic Fascism: the Nazi Connection. American Thinker.

13.) Chapter Eight: (2001). The Jerusalem Post Internet Edition.

14.) Chapter Eight: Brown, Mary Beth. (2005). Hand of Providence: The Strong and Quiet Faith of Ronald Reagan.

15.) Chapter Eight: Bell, Jeffrey. (2004). Hand of Providence: The Weekly Standard.

16.) Chapter Eight: Kennedy`s Secret Overture to the U.S.S.R. My, How He Hated Reagan... http://www.corson.org/other_articles/ted_kennedy.htm

17.) Chapter Nine: Ferreri, Enza. (2014). Nazism Paved the Way. American Thinker

18.) Chapter Nine: Hater, B. G. (2009). Hitler and the Secret Satanic Cult at the Heart of Nazi Germany.

23.) Chapter Nine: (2009). TEN YEARS ON; Saudi Arabia`s Textbooks Still Promote Religious Violence. Hudson Institute.

24.) Chapter Nine: (2011). Antisemitism Documentation Project. Special Dispatch No. 4345. MEMRI.

26.) Chapter Nine: Hunter, Timothy N.(1996). Appeasing the Saudis. Middle East Quarterly.

27.) Chapter Nine: Pipes, Daniel(2001). The Muslim Claim to Jerusalem. Middle East Quarterly.

29.) Chapter Nine: Shoebat, Walid; Shoebat, Theodore. The Obama`s Wahhabist Fundraising Empire.

SUGGESTIONS / CORRECTIONS

Our website is http://www.gleanersfieldpress.com. Please feel free to drop us a line with any suggestions and especially with corrections at http://www.gleanersfieldpress.com/contactus/.

If you would like to be on the mailing list for advanced notice of the next book in the series, please go to the website and sign up for the mailing list. *There may even be something special in it for you...*

"The LORD bless you, and keep you;
The LORD make His face shine on you,
And be gracious to you;
The LORD lift up His countenance on you,
And give you peace."
Numbers 6:24-26